SONS OF MY FATHERS

Michael A. Simpson

STORY MERCHANT BOOKS
LOS ANGELES
2016

Copyright © 2016 by Michael A. Simpson.
All rights reserved.

No part of this book may be reproduced or transmitted in any form or by any means, electronic or mechanical, including photocopying, recording, or by any information storage and retrieval system, without the express written permission of the author.

www.authormichaelasimpson.com

Cover Illustration by Stephen Gardner
Interior format by IndieDesignz.com

ISBN-13: 978-0-9909436-7-9

Story Merchant Books
400 S. Burnside Avenue #11B
Los Angeles, CA 90036
http://www.storymerchant.com/books.html

Acknowledgements

Someone once said that every story about the south is a ghost story. This one certainly is. It's inhabited by the spirits of my forefather Baylis Wilson Simpson, his wife Permelia, and their sons and daughters who lived in Cherokee County, Georgia, during the time of our nation's Civil War.

This book is also the story of my parents, Harold and Carlotta, my brother Ron, and our family's experiences during the Vietnam War. Forest Park, Georgia, where I grew up, is a major influence, as are the lives of my classmates and friends, especially those who died in Vietnam. You are not forgotten.

My expression of thanks begins with Chi-Li Wong, Kenneth Atchity and the Story Merchant team who patiently guided me in the development of this book. I thank friend and author Fred R. Willard, who wrote my favorite novel set in Atlanta, *Down On Ponce*, and provided thoughtful comments and invaluable input; Mike Mitchell, a relative of author Margaret Mitchell, who walked "The Dead Angle" with me and offered insight into the Battle of Kennesaw Mountain; Peter Weyrauch, for his knowledge of 60s and 70s-era muscle cars; Darryl Rhoades, whose friendship and creativity have inspired me since our school days; Jim Butler, for sharing the adventure as lifeguards and always taking the dare; my cousin James Kirk Burton, Lieutenant Colonel, United States Army (Retired), who clarified certain military information; and Butch Blasingame, Dwight Brown, Ralph Towler and Bill Wilson, for more than forty-five years of music and friendship that offers living proof that "rock is an attitude, not an age."

I also offer grateful acknowledgement to Nona Williams and Simpson Clan Genealogy Resources, who provided the history of my forefather Richard Simpson who emigrated from London, England to Talbot County, Maryland in 1668; Acey and Carol Burton, and their daughter Kharis Bramlett, who provided family information and photos; Kathleen Akin, who provided letters from Baylis and Permelia Simpson's daughter, Sarah Elizabeth, to her husband William A. Fowler, who served in the 52nd Georgia Infantry Regiment, CSA, and correspondence written by Sgt. Silas Milton Simpson, son of Baylis and Permelia, who served in the 28th Georgia Volunteer Infantry, Army of Northern Virginia, CSA; the Georgia State Archives, which provided a photo copy of the Baylis Simpson Family Bible; attorney Lee Williams for reviewing certain legal aspects of the story; and attorney Jonathan W. Hibbert for his kind assistance in securing records from the U.S. District Court, Northern District of Georgia.

I also acknowledge these special people who now live in memory– Coach Kenneth Avinger, who recommended me for my summer job as a lifeguard, which was the greatest experience a teenage boy could have in the late 60s; my Uncle James Virgil "J.V." Simpson, who instilled in me his love of motorcycles and guided the purchase of my first one; Bob Youmans, who was a brother to me, not by blood but by choice; author William Diehl, who mentored me as a writer; my two favorite radio deejays growing up that I had the pleasure of meeting, WQXI's "Skinny" Bobby Harper, and WLAC's legendary John R; friend and Capricorn Records co-founder Phil Walden, who encouraged me to write this book; and Jim Varney, the funniest person I've ever known. His love of history was infectious.

Finally and most importantly, I'm eternally indebted to my parents for their example of timeless love and devotion through more than sixty-five years of marriage, until my mother's death in 2013; my dear brother Ron, who lives in the hearts of those who knew and loved him, for his blessing and encouragement to tell our family saga; and to my wonderful wife Judy, who always believed in this story and in me. This book wouldn't have been possible without them.

*Dedicated to the memory
of my mother and brother*

*For
Harold, Alex, Caden and Bradley Simpson
and
the sons of our fathers yet unborn*

SONS
OF
MY FATHERS

Chapter 1

*"May the red rose live always,
To smile upon earth and sky,
Why should the beautiful ever weep?
Why should the beautiful die?"*

"May the Red Rose Live Always"
Stephen C. Foster

Spring 1864

GOD HAD GIVEN UP on Georgia. The winter in the mountainous part of the state that locals still called "Cherokee country" had been brutal—full of snow, bitter cold, and harsh winds. A wet spring followed. By early April, the rolling hills around Baylis Simpson's home remained boggy and impossible to plant.

Baylis had exhausted the better part of the day in the field trying to turn a row with his mule. He sunk the animal up to its harness in mud, and all he got for the effort was an earful of braying.

The harvest would be late. Food was already scarce, and Baylis knew that if the crop failed, his family would starve come winter. Not just his wife and their two children still at home, but the families of his married sons and daughters. With eight sons and sons-in-law off at war, he was counting on a bountiful yield to feed more than twenty mouths. *Just him and a damn mule.*

Fatigued beyond the weight of his fifty years, Baylis made his way out of the field as twilight gathered. In the distance, the gray-blue smoke curling from the stone chimney of his clapboard house meant his wife Permelia would soon have supper prepared.

Home seemed empty with so many of his offspring gone. He would have expected more grandchildren from his four married daughters had it not been for the war. His three older sons—Merdit, Silas Milton, and Pleasant Marion—were away fighting for the Confederacy, but he felt blessed to have Ulysses, their nineteen-year-old brother, home on furlough recuperating from a shoulder wound. Ulysses was especially close to Virgil, Baylis's youngest son. Spending time with Ulysses had lifted the ten-year-old's spirits.

As Baylis walked in the cool air, mud oozing over the tops of his worn brogans, he grimly considered that the worst of God's hardships on Georgia wasn't the cruel weather or the soggy soil. It was the devil named Sherman.

Baylis's cousin Leonard Simpson, a lawyer in Atlanta, had sent word that three Federal armies under the command of General Sherman were itching for drier days and the chance to finish the job they had started on the Confederate Army of Tennessee.

After the disaster of Missionary Ridge, the rebels had lost Chattanooga to the Union Army in late November. The Confederates spent the winter in the wet, cold fields and mountains surrounding the railroad at Dalton, nursing their wounds like a dog with a crippled leg until General Joseph Johnston assumed command and began to revive their spirits.

Leonard expected that when these two mighty armies renewed their bloodletting, the war would spread like warm butter over most of North Georgia. That day was coming soon. In his letter, Leonard urged his cousin to take precautions. Baylis's farm stood on a broad line between Chattanooga and Atlanta. As the Yankees pressed forward, everything would likely be laid to waste as part of Sherman's "hard war" to "make Georgia howl."

Despite the words of defiance in the local newspaper, Leonard only had to read the staggering casualty reports printed in the *Atlanta Intelligencer* to know how desperate the times were. Even in eight-point type, there had been days when the names of the Confederate dead covered an entire page.

Thousands of slaves had been pressed into service to build defensive fortifications around Atlanta, which was now under martial law. Movement about town by Negroes was limited, and strangers were no longer welcomed. Passes were required to enter the city or walk the streets after dark. Leonard felt that Atlanta's fate would be decided by summer.

Though Baylis served in the Georgia State Guards Infantry, he had no fondness for Yankees or slaveholders. He traced his family's roots in the "New World" to his ancestor Richard Simpson, who had emigrated from England to Maryland in 1668, and his love for his country ran deep. The thought of it being torn asunder with such bloody abandon filled him with quiet rage.

The bitter conflict had already cost the Simpson family dearly. Sarah, Baylis's oldest daughter, was still mourning the death of her husband who had been killed the previous year at Vicksburg. William Fowler's passing had taken the light from Sarah's soft blue eyes and left her alone, a widow at twenty-five, to raise two small children.

As part of a large, close-knit clan of farmers and tradesmen scattered across North Georgia, there was no way to avoid the war's grief. It had touched every family for miles around, in one sad way or another. Baylis had long since lost count of the friends and relations killed or wounded in the conflict. And he feared the worst was yet to come.

After a series of skirmishes, the two armies restarted their death dance on May 13. One hundred thousand Federal troops poured out of Snake Creek Gap west of the tiny village of Resaca to face General Johnston's 60,000 entrenched grays. Intense fighting occurred along the entire Confederate line. It lasted two days and left more than 8,000 corpses, turning the ground red and the creeks pink. The rebels, outflanked by the larger army in blue, were again forced to withdraw.

Pursuing Johnston's rebels like they were trying to tree a rabid coon, Sherman's army pierced deeper into Georgia over the following weeks along a path that stretched ten miles wide. Passing to the west of the Western & Atlantic Railroad, the Federal horde mercifully left untouched the Simpson farm, which was east of the line, nestled on a remote foothill of the Blue Ridge Mountains. Baylis, facing his fifty-first birthday in just a month, could think of no better gift.

Baylis beseeched God that the war would pass over his family without further loss, like the Angel of Death passing the doorposts marked with lamb's blood in Biblical times. He worked for days in the fields to the distant drumbeat of cannonading and rifle fire as Union soldiers battled entrenched rebels at New Hope Church, Dallas, and Pickett's Mill. As the fighting pushed farther south, it appeared Baylis's prayer had been answered.

Then the rains came again. For more than two weeks in June, Noah's flood poured from the skies, overflowing the Etowah and Oostanaula rivers and bogging down both armies in mud and muddle. It was as though God wanted to wash the whole horrible enterprise away. But the armies wallowed in the mire and fought on, determined to see it through to its bloody end.

Finally, the rains ceased. Under turbid skies, Baylis moved back into the fields with Virgil. Ulysses, feeling stronger as his wound healed, joined them. They carried muskets as a precaution. With Union Provost Marshal guards stretched thin trying to stop McCollum's raiders and other guerilla bands from sabotaging the railroad line to the west, Federal forces seldom ventured farther east. While the farm's remoteness kept it safe from bluecoats, the disintegration of civilian law made them easy prey for thieves with predatory instincts–the Union stragglers, Confederate deserters, and common outlaws who were plundering farms and causing terror in Sherman's wake.

Baylis spent his nights carving "Joe Brown Pikes" for the Georgia State Guards by candlelight. The pikes were named for the state's Governor, who believed the steel-tipped lances would be the miraculous salvation of the Confederacy. Baylis knew better. Men with pikes were no match for an invading army with repeater rifles.

With Ulysses's shoulder almost healed, Baylis knew his son would leave soon for the fighting. He was saddened but not surprised when Ulysses told him it was time.

"What about Ann? Do you plan to ask for her hand before you leave?"

Ulysses had been courting Ann Calley Tate, a young woman in the county who was fond of making him sorghum "candy pulls." He had known her for years, and his heart was set to marry her.

"I love Ann as Adam loved Eve." Ulysses stared into the bleak night. "But I'll not be making her a widow like my sister. Women in black are already thicker than hen lice in these parts. We have no need for another one."

June 24, 1864

Morning broke under clearing skies. It was to be Ulysses's last day home. Baylis and his sons moved into the field as first light dappled through the pines. "Roastin' ears," the first corn that could be cooked for eating, had tasseled and would soon be ready to harvest.

Baylis's youngest daughter, Terissa, spent the early morning with Melissa, his six-year-old granddaughter, washing their long hair. The Simpsons had a tradition that the females didn't cut their hair from baptism until marriage. It was a point of pride and a sign of chastity. Now fourteen, Terissa's raven hair was halfway down her back. She was a beautiful girl with sparkling blue eyes, and Baylis had no doubt that his daughter would have many suitors once the war ended and the young men in the county came home.

Melissa, the oldest child of Baylis's daughter Sarah, had been baptized for only a year, but her golden curls were already close to her shoulders. A humorous child full of mischievous spirit, Melissa held a special place in her grandfather's heart. Baylis likened her rambunctious play to "a blind dog in a meat house." She often came for visits and was a great source of comfort for Baylis with so many of his own children gone.

While the sun dried their hair, the girls went to pick huckleberries in the woods. Melissa's seventh birthday would be in a few days, and Permelia had promised to bake a pie for the occasion. Berry cobbler was

Melissa's favorite. She loved the way it stained her tongue blue and delighted in showing it to her grandfather.

Permelia, in a homespun cotton dress and palmetto hat, was scrubbing clothes against a washboard in the shade of an oak tree when she noticed the motley strangers approaching up the dirt road. Baylis had cautioned her to keep a watchful eye, and she was immediately suspicious.

The bandits spotted Permelia, and two of the younger ones started off in a run toward her. She sprang up and fled into the woods. Her first thought was for the safety of the girls. She frantically searched through the dense pines, afraid to call out loudly for fear that their response would lead the marauders to them.

The robbers quickly looted the bare wood home of its modest provisions. They found beets, onions, beef jerky, and flour—not a king's feast, but better than the hardtack they had been eating.

Unaware of the danger, Terissa and Melissa arrived at the cabin door with an apron full of berries, pleased with their morning's work and giggling the way young girls often do. Before they could react, the men seized them.

The largest, a ginger-haired deserter called Duff, decided Terissa was in need of a "proper education." It had been more than a year since he had known the company of a woman, and he intended to gratify his needs.

The older girl knew the horror that was coming. "Please," Terissa begged. "Don't let my niece see this."

Duff's answer was a backhand blow that sent her sprawling onto the hardwood floor. The Irishman with bowl-cut hair knelt beside Terissa, tearing her cotton housedress away to reveal her young flesh. She could smell his sweat and the stench of his rotted teeth. Struggling, she managed a deep scratch across Duff's face before he pistol-whipped her unconscious.

Duff raped Terissa as the other men held Melissa. A few watched. Most looked away ashamed. None were willing to move against Duff. He was too large and too mean.

With an animal grunt, Duff satisfied himself. He rolled off Terissa's limp body, pulled his trousers up, and slipped his pistol back into the waist. There was blood on his pants from the flower he had taken.

Melissa stood frozen in the center of the men, her small body rigid from shock. Her eyes were riveted on her young aunt.

After a moment, Terissa moaned as the pain of what had happened pulled her back to consciousness. She hurt so bad she couldn't move without her insides stinging like a hot poker.

Melissa rushed to her. Clinging to her aunt, she cried.

Duff looked at the child's golden hair falling softly across her aunt's breasts. "That'd be as pretty a sight as I've ever seen." He decided to cut a lock as a souvenir.

Duff grabbed Melissa and yanked her up. He reached for the bowie knife in his boot and, with a stroke of the blade, sliced off a handful of her hair. As he did, Melissa managed to bite his hand and draw blood. Duff impulsively thrust his knife into the girl's stomach. With a shudder, she collapsed onto the floor. Blood pooled around her young body.

"We need to be a gettin'," the younger, rangy-looking bandit said, his voice sanded with dread. "There may be men folk 'round here belongin' to these girls."

The thieves decided to hide the horror of what Duff had done by burning the house. They grabbed what they could carry, then set a fire, leaving the two girls inside to die. The robbers retreated down the road, thinking that was the end of it.

Having not found the girls and fearing the worst, Permelia hurriedly made her way back home. The house was already ablaze when she arrived. She heard weak coughing and rushed inside.

The eerie cry of a screech owl pulled Baylis's attention away from his work and to the smoke. It was too coarse and black to be from the chimney.

"Fire!" he screamed to his sons, and ran toward the house. Ulysses and Virgil grabbed the muskets and followed.

They arrived to find Permelia staggering out the door with Terissa. She collapsed on the ground with her daughter, overcome by smoke. Permelia's eyes told Baylis his granddaughter was still inside. He quickly soaked himself in the mule trough, ripped off his shirt to cover his mouth, and raced into the inferno.

Moments later, Baylis emerged with Melissa in his arms. Setting her down on the ground, he discovered the large gash in her stomach. The sight of so much blood on one so innocent stunned him. When Baylis looked to Terissa for an answer, he saw the humiliation and shame in her eyes. It was then that he realized Terissa's dress was ripped and crimson stained.

Ulysses moved to Terissa, took his uniform jacket and draped it over his sister's shoulders. Baylis held Melissa and gently pushed her soft curls from her eyes.

"He cut my hair, granddaddy," was all the child could manage. Then she trembled, a small, sad quake, and died.

As Baylis rocked Melissa's lifeless body in his arms, Permelia wept, sorrow-stricken beyond words or consolation. Virgil turned away and cried. Ulysses, hardened by war and not inclined to grief, stood protectively over Terissa and gazed into the distance.

"Sister, which way did they go?"

She motioned toward the road.

"How many?"

"Nine. Maybe ten . . ." Her voice broke. "I managed to mark the one who done this . . . on his face. He's got Melissa's bite on his hand."

Ulysses held his father with hard eyes. "What are we going to do, Pa?"

Baylis stared at his granddaughter, now quiet and still in his arms. He answered his son by dipping two fingers into the blood on Melissa's dress and etching lines across his forehead.

Ulysses understood. *The stain would remain until her death was avenged.*

Baylis carried Melissa's body to Permelia, placed her in his wife's arms and kissed the child's brow. He moved to Virgil, who was still looking away, eyes shut, unable to bear the sight of the dead girl. Baylis spun his youngest son around and held his chin.

"Look at Melissa," Baylis said. "Look and remember."

Virgil opened his eyes and forced himself to take in the gruesome sight. Then Baylis turned the boy to face him.

"Take the wagon and find Elon. Tell my brother what you've seen. Tell him I have need of him. Then come back here and protect your Ma and sister."

Virgil nodded. Baylis took his musket, checked the load, and placed it in his son's hands. He turned to Ulysses.

"We'll go south along the ravine. If they stay on the road, we'll overtake 'em soon enough."

Baylis put his short-handled axe into his belt, took a pike, and started off in a slow run. Ulysses grabbed his Enfield rifle-musket and Colt revolver and followed in his father's steps.

There wasn't a valley or hillside for miles around that Baylis didn't know. The narrow road the thieves were on slithered down the side of the mountain. Being little more than a winding gully through the wilderness, the killers wouldn't be able to make a fast pace. By cutting straight down the mountainside, it would be only a matter of time before Baylis and Ulysses found their way in front of the bandits.

Then there would come a reckoning.

Elon rode by horseback to aid Baylis. He was joined by Otis and Willis Cash, two cousins in the First Georgia Cavalry who had refused to retreat past their homes when the Confederate army withdrew farther south. Instead, the Cash brothers had joined McCollum's partisan band that was attacking Federal supply lines.

Like Baylis, Elon had spent most of his grown years in North Georgia. It was easy enough for him to figure out where his older brother would bushwhack the outlaw scum. By the time Elon and his cousins found Baylis and Ulysses, the Simpson men were already laying in wait on the side of the road in a thicket of shortleaf pine and honeysuckle.

The bandits soon came down the path, loud and full of themselves, eating the raw onions and beef jerky they had stolen. Baylis knew which man he wanted to kill; Duff had a nasty scratch on his face and fresh blood on his trousers.

With a crackling fuselage of musket fire, the Simpson kin took the robbers by surprise, killing five instantly. Ulysses wounded another two with his pistol. Baylis charged forward and speared one man with his pike, impaling him to a tree like a deer carcass waiting to be dressed.

Baylis faced Duff in the middle of the road. He was the last thief not dead or dying, and the Simpson kin knew to leave him alone. The savage who had killed Baylis's beloved grandchild and used his daughter like a harlot elm peeler belonged to him. Duff pulled out his knife and stared at Baylis oddly, not sure what to expect from the old man with blood streaked across his forehead.

Enraged by the red stain on Duff's blade, Baylis lifted the short-handled axe out of his waistband and came at the huge man. His first swing nearly severed Duff's knife hand. It hung by skin and tendons.

Duff stumbled to his knees, blood squirting out of the wound. Baylis waited until the man raised his eyes, then opened Duff up from his chest to his stomach with a chop of the axe. He finished the man off by separating his head from his shoulders with three well-aimed blows. The last thing Duff saw was the hate in Baylis's eyes.

When Baylis had finished, Ulysses took his pistol and put a round into the head of any bandit still groaning. After the killing was done, Elon, a Methodist preacher, bowed his head.

"Lord God Almighty, forgive us our sins this day," Elon shouted, as was his custom whenever he read the Holy Book or invoked his Savior in prayer or proclamation. "I know these men had fallen away from your righteous path, and we were only the instruments of thy justice. But we pray some day this killing will stop, 'cause we're mighty sick of it. Please accept these newly departed into your bosom." Elon stopped, thought for a moment. "All 'cept for this big headless one. I'm certain there's an especially hot corner of hell waiting for that sumbitch, and I ain't gonna waste your precious time trying to talk you out of it. Amen."

Long shadows lay across the dirt road like fallen timbers as Baylis turned to carry his heavy heart home. Ulysses followed him in silence, knowing it was best to leave his father alone with his grief.

Elon and the Cash brothers moved off on horseback. They barely crested the hill before shots rang out. A moment later, the men retreated at a furious gallop back toward Baylis and Ulysses. Otis, the oldest Cash brother, was slumped in his saddle, his arm dangling beside him like dead wood.

"Yankee cavalry!" Willis, the lumpish younger brother, yelled as he pulled up on his mount. "We're cut off!"

"They'll be here soon," Otis managed through the pain. His shirt was already red. He quickly tied a rag around his arm using his yellowed teeth.

Ulysses knew there was no way back to the farm. "How far to the Confederate line?"

"Last I heard tell it, Johnston was a making a stand at Kennesaw," Willis said.

"*Taint* gonna make a spit of difference. Bragg lost the war at Chattanooga," Otis said.

"Only a fool would try and skedaddle past Federal cavalry." Willis glanced to his wounded brother, then turned to Elon. "Me and Otis are going to meet up with McCollum's band. Ya'll do what you have to."

The brothers spurred their horses and moved off at a fierce pace. Elon pulled on his horse's reins and waited. "I don't relish taking on Yankee cavalry. And I am of no mind to join partisan guerillas. That's all I got to say 'bout it."

Ulysses's eyes found his father's gaze. "Which way?"

Baylis soaked up the question. "Kennesaw."

The men knew that they would be safe from the cavalry only as long as they stayed off the narrow rural roads and moved cross-country, through the heavily wooded hills laced with high-banked streams. Following the setting sun, the Simpson men treaded quietly across the piney terrain. Whenever gunshots swelled in the distance, they would divert their course to lessen the chance of being discovered by the Federals.

As twilight settled around them, they came upon a lathered, riderless horse in a barren field, its eyes full of the devil's panic. Baylis recognized the mount immediately: *it belonged to Willis Cash*. He eased forward and calmed the animal.

Ulysses ran his fingers across the saddle's drenched leather. "Blood's fresh."

Elon took a quick look and said what they all were thinking: "Hard to imagine any man bleeding that much and being among the living."

Baylis offered the horse's reins to Ulysses. The men moved cautiously through the field, forded a muddy brook, and eased down a densely wooded slope. As they approached the Western & Atlantic rail line in the clearing ahead of them, a breeze stirred the smell of blood and death.

They stood quietly at the edge of the trees, listening and watching. When they were satisfied that no Yankees were lying in wait, they stepped carefully into the open.

What they found silhouetted in the moonlight among the steel and timbers was as grisly a sight as any of them had ever beheld: Dozens of dead men—some bayoneted, others with faces or limbs blown away—discarded on the ground like broken scarecrows.

"Most of these boys ain't in uniform," Ulysses spoke softly.

"Must be some of McCollum's partisans," Elon whispered.

Ulysses bent down to examine one corpse. The back of the man's skull was blown away. "This fella's hands are tied behind him. He was shot up close."

"Poke 'round. See if you can find the Cash boys," Baylis said quietly.

As the men began their grim search among the litter of corpses, Baylis realized one thing clearly: *they would be lucky to be alive come sunrise.*

Chapter 2

*"I think I'm going back,
to the things I left somewhere in my youth,
I think I'm returning to
those days when I was young enough
to know the truth"*

"Going Back"
Bob Dylan

Five Generations Later
June 1962

OTHER THAN HIS MOTHER'S lullabies, the whistle of the Dixie Flyer was the earliest sound Michael Simpson could remember hearing.

Since the time of Baylis Simpson and the Confederacy, the locomotive's melancholy cry had announced its passage through Forest Park, a quiet Georgia town of hard work and modest dreams snuggled on Atlanta's southern doorstep. The rail line pierced through the heart of this blue-collar community, running parallel to Main for several blocks before bending south, just before the street emptied out onto Jonesboro Road in front of the Fort Gillem Army base. The road was the same one that Rhett Butler and Scarlet O'Hara used for their imaginary escape from Atlanta. The fictional Tara plantation was said to have been located just a short stride down its blacktop.

Every night of Michael's young life, the Flyer's whistle beckoned him, filling his imagination with a long-vanquished landscape of graceful mansions and stately plantations, of hoop-skirted ladies who thought about things tomorrow and men who frankly didn't give a damn.

During the Civil War, as the Union Army moved down from Kennesaw Mountain to lay siege to Atlanta, Yankees had destroyed the train line south of Forest Park to keep Confederate troops from being resupplied. Its rails had been torn up, heated in bonfires of creosote-soaked ties, then wrapped around the trunks of young oaks. A hundred years later, those scars of war could still be seen. Old folks called them "Sherman's neckties," though all but a few of the steel-girded oaks had long since toppled to the ground. Legend was that the area around these ancient trees was haunted by the souls of rebel soldiers killed defending the rail line.

Michael had often suspected that his older brother, Ron, a strikingly rebellious twelve-year-old, was sneaking out of the bedroom they shared for late-night rendezvous with the swift-moving locomotive. It was just the kind of thing Ron's best friend, Alex Granger, would talk him into.

Long before Ron was juiced with the adrenaline rush of adolescence, Alex had the ability to talk him into doing things he'd never do otherwise. And the things Alex loved doing most were always dangerous. His tastes ran to everything forbidden, and that made him, in Michael's eyes, cool beyond cool. As the years passed, Michael hardly saw Ron unless he was in the company of Alex, and the younger brother instinctively cultivated a curiosity about the kind of fun the older boys might be having without him.

Michael never asked Ron about his nocturnal voyages. Instead, he bided his time, waiting for the right moment to join them.

Michael prided himself on what he believed to be a talent for looking asleep when he wasn't, an indispensable skill for a ten-year-old boy to possess. Half the trick lay in keeping your face hidden, and in covering yourself with thick blankets—the kind that wouldn't give away the glow of a flashlight. He spent many a flashlit hour, when he was supposed to be slumbering, apprenticing himself to *Green Lantern*—*"In brightest day and blackest night, no evil shall escape my sight"*—and the *Justice League of America*, studying their exploits and looking forward to the day when he would be called upon to save the world. Or, if he didn't feel like ridding the Earth of some ultimate evil, he would slap on his 3D glasses and scare the bejeezus out of himself reading an old issue of *House of Terror*. For a kid with his wild imagination, it was a no-fail recipe for insomnia.

And so it happened that he was awake beneath his covers one night when Alex tapped the windowpane with a pebble to rouse Ron. The rustling of azalea branches outside the window was quickly followed by Alex's gruff whisper: "*Psst*. Ronnie. Time for the Flyer!"

Raising his blanket slightly, Michael glimpsed Ron across the room, flinging his covers back to hurry to the window. "*Shhh*. Not so loud. You'll wake up my brother."

Alex's face appeared at the window screen, his eyes bright with daring, an unlit cigarette tucked behind one ear. He was the same age as Ron, but while Ron's freckled face still revealed its soft, little-boy roundness in unguarded moments, Alex's was nothing but toughness and hard angles, the sort of look a boy gets when he loses his father too early. He was all boy, all the things every little kid secretly longed to be.

Ron glanced back furtively to make sure his brother was still asleep. On cue, Michael squeezed his eyes shut in a fake slumber that shouldn't have fooled anybody over the age of seven.

Ron hurried to the window. The small, gold cross dangling from a chain around his neck sparkled in the moonlight. "And quit calling me Ronnie," he added. "It's Ron now, you weenie."

Alex popped his switchblade and deftly levered out the bottom corners of the window screen. "If I'm a weenie, then bite me, *Ronnnnnnie*."

Michael snapped off the flashlight, stowed his masked mentors under his pillow, and prepared to catch his big brother in the act.

"Wanna see the hair on my chest?" Ron tugged up his tee shirt.

"You got *one* hair," Alex held up the screen for Ron to climb out, "which I'm gonna pull out if you don't hurry up."

"That's still one more than you, buttwipe." Ron threw a leg over the windowsill.

"Are we gonna go or stay here and talk about your puberty?"

Michael felt a giggle rising to the surface. Though he tried to fight it down, an avalanche of laughter burst through. The jig was up.

"Now see what you've done. You woke up the kid." Alex never called Michael by his name.

Michael bolted out of bed and quickly pulled his Levis on over his Hopalong Cassidy pajama bottoms.

Ron leaned his upper body back in through the window. "What do you think you're doin'?"

"Goin' with you to watch the train." Michael fumbled with his zipper, then slid his feet into the pair of Keds waiting at the foot of the bed. No time for lacing.

Outside the window, Alex groaned, "This ain't Howdy Dowdy Time. The squirt stays home."

Michael knew this would take some effort. First, he tried the old standby: the whine. "Come on," he droned in his best wheedling tone. Then, seeing that his whimpering was getting him nowhere, he hauled out the big guns: "If you don't let me go, I'll tell."

The dreaded words. Ron froze. Alex shot Michael a look.

"Jesus H. Frog." Alex ran a hand through his short-cropped hair, then gave Ron a glance. "All right, but Mickey Mouse is your problem."

Michael, beaming ear to ear, scrambled out the window after the older boys. As the last of him cleared the window frame, the heel of his Keds snagged on the bottom of the sill. Ron's arm quickly shot out to save his little brother from taking a header into the Burford hollies. Once on firm ground, Michael glanced up furtively to verify that Alex hadn't seen his slip-up. Ron steadied his little brother, then loped ahead to catch up with Alex.

The boys moved silently over the dew-wet grass of the perfect lawn that had absorbed the sweat of countless lawn-mowing Saturdays. In ritual solemnity, Ron and Alex paused, unzipped, and urinated at the foot of the young elm planted when Ron was born. Michael's little red oak stood to the side, unpeed-upon, still too small to survive such a steamy baptism.

While the older boys emptied their bladders, Michael stood splay-legged, face tipped skyward, staring in awe at the canvas of stars above him. Michael had never been outside this late.

For the rest of his life, Michael would look back on this night as his first great adventure, one of many for which Alex would serve as tour guide. It was also the last night he would see the world through eyes of total innocence.

Ron stage-whispered in Michael's ear, "You better pee."

"Let the runt find out the hard way."

Michael would have peed then—and should have—but as he glanced downward, he thought for a moment he was still seeing stars. Tiny lights crawled in erratic, jigging paths across the ground, filling the air around him with winking yellow beacons. Michael stretched out his fingers, trying to hold a firefly gently inside his fist.

Like the howl of a far-off, lonesome animal, the approaching Flyer's wail pealed through the night. The older boys hastily shook out and zipped up.

"Leave the lightnin' bugs alone. C'mon!" Ron grabbed a fistful of Michael's pajama top and began hauling him towards the street.

Ron and Alex knew the Flyer's ritual well. On clear, still nights, the whistle could first be heard when the train approached Mountain View, five miles northwest of Forest Park. From that moment, they knew they had ten minutes to get to the outskirts of town.

The boys pelted past four blocks of modest frame and brick houses, then turned onto Main Street. They moved down the deserted sidewalk, traveling west in the direction of the approaching train.

The town had long since put itself to bed. Forest Park was mostly a community of one-of-a-kind, family-run businesses. About six o'clock every evening, all the moms and pops closed up and went home to their suppers. By eight o'clock, even the Piggly Wiggly had shut its doors. By midnight, Forest Park might as well have been a ghost town.

Most of the stores the boys passed were familiar to them from the time they had observed the world from the seats of their strollers: Culp's Hardware (*"if it's in stock, we've got it"*), Saul's Shoe Barn, Tillman's Drug Store (where Michael regularly plunked down his weekly allowance quarter for six lemon-lime pixie sticks and a comic book), and the Witherington Brothers full-service Gulf Station (where the guy who pumped the gas would bang his head into the soda pop machine if you gave him a nickel).

Just off Main Street, Michael's eyes fell upon the familiar, tidy green door with *Simpson Typography & College Press* lettered in gold on its window. It was the printing shop his parents had run for years.

He was fascinated by how much the businesses had changed with the coming of night. Normally bright and bustling, they were all now silent and strangely eerie.

Passing the town's only movie theatre, Michael sniffed the scent of stale popcorn through the ticket window. He stopped to gaze into the shadowed lobby of Mr. Butler's "Little Show." The theatre was the town's unofficial babysitter on Saturday afternoons, a place where kids were dropped off to allow moms a few blissfully uninterrupted hours to do their shopping and cleaning. Michael had journeyed through many a double feature there in the company of Frankenstein, The Wolf Man, and The Mummy.

Ordering a "mixed drink" in Forest Park meant getting a combination of grape, cherry, orange, and cola from the soda fountain in the theater lobby. The town boasted half-a-dozen churches, but not one bar or liquor store.

The officially "dry" community was surrounded by not-so-dry neighbors. A ten-minute drive north on Jonesboro Road would put you in the parking lot of the Blair Village liquor store.

Growing up in Forest Park, you were taught three great religious truths:

1. *Jews do not recognize Jesus as the Messiah.*
2. *Protestants do not recognize the Pope as the leader of the Christian faith.*
3. *Baptists do not recognize each other at the liquor store in Blair Village.*

A few blocks farther down, the boys passed the First Baptist Church, the heart of the Simpson family's community life. The Flyer shrieked again, louder and closer. Alex and Ron knew that this second whistle meant the locomotive was halfway between Mountain View and Forest Park. They picked up their pace. Michael lagged behind, laboring over his flopping shoelaces.

"Tell the Mouse to keep up, or we ain't gonna make it," Alex hissed to Ron.

The boys reached the western edge of Main Street, the town's last intersection before the road curved away and the tracks peeled north through open meadows and pine forest. A rail crossing without gates, signals, or lights marked the spot.

With Alex in the lead, the boys moved off the sidewalk and onto the rails, quickly following the tracks that sliced through the woods, and then farther along through a large cornfield. As they scrambled down the tracks, the gravel and wood ties hummed beneath their feet. The sound of the fast-approaching mechanical beast grew louder.

Several hundred yards down the rails, Ron grabbed Michael's shoulder and pointed to a small gully eroded beneath the train tracks, just large enough for three boys to squeeze into side by side. Alex was already snaking his way into it. Ron motioned for Michael to follow, then crawled in behind Alex.

It was all happening too fast for Michael. He thought they were going to *see* the Dixie Flyer, *not crawl under the rail tracks and let the train run over them!*

Ron waved Michael in. Overcoming his fear, the younger boy cautiously squirmed on his back in the sulfur-smelling earth, with the tracks inches above them. As the behemoth chugged nearer, dirt shook loose from the gully walls and rained down onto their faces.

The loud, demonic churn of the approaching train unleashed an animal instinct in Michael. In uncontrollable panic, he wriggled free of the gully and bolted into the darkness of the corn. Ron started out for his brother, but Alex held him back.

"You'll miss the train!" Alex yelled over the roar.

The Flyer's blunt-nosed engine shoveled a mass of displaced air around the corn stalks as Michael sprinted through the field. It was followed by uncountable numbers of boxcars and flatbeds. Michael saw the tracks bend beneath the weight of the train, heard Ron and Alex scream with terrified delight.

As he pounded blindly through the corn, Michael became aware of the warm dampness spreading from the crotch of his pajama bottoms. His cheeks burned with humiliation, as if he wouldn't get enough of a ribbing already for running away. If Alex found out he'd peed himself, his adventures with the older boys would begin and end in a single night.

All at once, Michael found himself running. He dizzily fought his way through the corn, hoping against hope that his course through the towering stalks would let him out somewhere near the crossing. Behind him, faster than it came, the Flyer was gone, its clatter and roar fading into black shadows.

In the distance, Michael could hear Ron and Alex pour out of the gully, laughing. Ron started calling out for him, but then Alex groused, "Let the Mouse find his own way home." They were talking too loud, their ears still numb from the Flyer's passing.

"I can't," Michael heard Ron reply, "My dad'll paste me good if he wakes up and finds out Mike's not there."

"Sure, *yer* jarhead daddy will belt your ass. Which you'll deserve, 'cause I told you not to bring the squirt."

Their voices faded as Michael flailed his way through the corn and back out onto the gravel of the track bed. His trail had cut too shallow, and he emerged several yards from the place where the rails met the road. He could still hear the Flyer retreating as it made its way towards the unlit crossing, the throb of its engine deepening as it slowed for its pass through town.

The night seemed all too dark and enormous for Michael, with his big brother out of earshot. After the adrenaline had worn off, he thought about calling out for Ron, but he decided to press on to the crossing instead. Once in familiar surroundings, he could head for home by himself if he dared, or wait for Ron to come and get him.

A dull metallic gleam caught Michael's eye at the edge of the woods on the far side of the tracks. A twist of steel jutted from a deep rut around the trunk of an ancient white oak. Michael realized, with a prickling along his scalp, that he was looking at one of the last surviving oaks garroted almost a hundred years ago with a Sherman necktie.

Michael knew that the spirits of rebel soldiers haunted these steel-girded trees. He dared not look into the darkness just beyond the oak, afraid of what he might see. Yet at the same time, he fought a part of himself that wanted to look.

A sudden, deafening crash on the rails ahead jolted him, followed by the long, drawn-out squeal of metal on metal. Then a long hiss. Then silence.

The sultry voice of Patsy Cline called to Michael through the stillness: *"I fall to pieces, each time I see you . . ."*

Michael made no conscious decision to rush toward the sound, but he realized several seconds into his run that he was doing so. When he rounded the bend, the sight that met his eyes robbed him in an instant of the pleasure he'd gotten from ghastly fiction. Forever afterward, Hollywood's painted latex horrors and corn syrup blood would seem silly and vain by comparison. From the first moment he beheld the sight, he knew that he would never, ever completely escape the grisly image.

In a shallow ditch to one side of the railroad crossing lay what had been, moments ago, a '57 Chevy convertible. Its radio was still on.

"I fall to pieces, how can I be just your friend?"

The driver's side of the car had crumpled from the train's impact, the front end bowed nearly ninety degrees to its back end. Michael could see its headlights and its taillights at the same time. Its convertible top, one of the new vinyl kinds, hung stoved-in and ragged, like an umbrella turned inside out in a windstorm. The oily tang of gasoline hung in the air, testimony to the car's ruptured fuel tank.

"You want to forget; pretend we've never met . . ."

Michael saw the driver's silhouette inside the car. As his eyes adjusted to the smoky darkness, he realized it was a teenage boy slumped over the wheel. Michael felt his stomach leap inside him with the visceral knowledge that no living person could assume the teenager's posture. The boy's upper torso had folded itself around the steering column. But that was probably not what had killed him. Michael saw that the boy's neck hung open, from just below his ear to the place where his Adam's apple was supposed to be, neatly sliced by some bladelike edge created from the implosion of his car.

"And I've tried and I've tried, but I haven't yet . . ."

Michael couldn't stop from looking at the boy's face, which appeared only mildly surprised by what had happened to him. The only ghastly features were his eyes: the pupils seemed too wide and too dark, giving him the appearance of a child's stuffed animal that had become somehow demonically possessed.

A slight movement in the gravel drew Michael's eye. A teenage girl lay there, on her back, a few yards from the wreck. For half a moment, Michael wondered how she came to be lying there, so close to where the accident had just occurred. Then his frozen mind slowly understood that the fractured hole in the Chevy's windshield was from her body leaving the car.

The girl trembled all over, little violent tremors, as if a fever chilled her. Michael didn't know whether she was alive, or if this was what people did when they were newly dead. In horror movies and comics, corpses always moved some. They'd been known to unexpectedly sit up and point to their killers, or even chase them around.

Michael didn't know when it was that he stopped staring at the macabre scene, but he soon became dimly aware that he was stumbling around in the brushy stubble beside the tracks, sobbing uncontrollably. He didn't know he was in shock; he thought he was caught in a nightmare, an endless falling dream, in which he kept hurtling towards the ground with every shaky footstep.

Then all at once, Ron was beside him, his hand clasping him on the shoulder.

"Hey, whatsa matter?" Ron had raccoon eyes from the dirt that had fallen onto his face while under the train tracks.

Michael could do no more than blubber and point. "I saw . . . over there . . ."

A dirty-faced Alex appeared out of the corn, taking a drag from the cigarette he was smoking with almost post-coital satisfaction.

"Peanut probably saw one of them Johnny Rebs." Alex made a little ghost howl for effect.

Michael grabbed Ron's sleeve and tugged. He led his brother by the arm along the gravel track bed, Alex trailing behind, until they rounded the curve that opened upon the view of the wreck. Nothing had changed since Michael had last stared at the site, except that the puddle of gas had grown wider, and the girl on her back had ceased shaking.

The two older boys stared in stunned silence. Then Alex muttered, "Holy shit."

A faint movement seized their attention. The girl's eyes shot open wide as she slowly raised her arm, reaching out in a last act of desperation, to no one.

"She's not dead!" Ron lurched towards the girl, but Alex grabbed his arm.

"Wait! Ronnie, somebody's coming!"

Farther up the track, beams of flashlights sliced through the smoky darkness. The Dixie Flyer had halted down the tracks; its engineer and crew were trotting back to see what they had hit.

Alex tried to tug Ron away. "We ain't supposed to be here. We're in bad trouble if they see us. C'mon!"

Ron stared, bewildered, looking first to Alex, then to the girl. He jerked free and lurched into a staggering run toward the broken figure lying on the gravel. Alex leapt after him, cinching his arms in a hammerlock around his best friend's chest.

"Dammit, let go!" Ron grunted, trying to disentangle himself. "We need to help her!"

"No! We gotta leave now!" Alex yelped in a voice wild with fear, as he tried to drag Ron towards the corn.

As the two boys tussled on the gravel, Alex's cigarette dropped from his lips. A breeze booted it rapidly across the railroad crossing and toward the spreading gasoline. The boys stopped fighting just in time to watch its tiny orange glow coming to rest in the puddle of fuel. Alex locked eyes with the girl on the ground. An instant later, the world exploded in a torrent of red and black. The earth shook.

Michael felt his eardrums thump. A hot breath of wind seared the inside of his nose. He could still see the girl, even though flames whipped her from her scalp to her fingertips. Even as she died, the girl's eyes never left Alex's. She arched her back once, then lay still. At that exact moment, Alex staggered back, as if struck by some violent, unseen force. The color drained from his face.

Ron grabbed Michael by the collar of his pajamas, dragging him away from the blazing wreck. Michael began pumping his legs until Ron was no longer pulling him, but leading him. The three boys vanished into the corn only seconds before the Flyer's crew arrived.

The dark rows of corn folded in around the three boys. Alex stumbled along at the rear.

"I felt it." Alex was crying. "I felt it when she died."

"What are you sayin'?" Ron was breathless.

"Her spirit. It went clear through me," he whimpered wildly.

"That's crazy talk."

"I ain't crazy!" Alex was sobbing now. He clapped his temples between his hands and squeezed, tromping in blind circles through the corn. "I'm tellin' ya, she knew. She knew I could've helped her."

"Shut up! Just shut up!" Ron's own panic was rising as he followed Alex's erratic path.

"She knew I killed her. I lit her on fire . . ."

Ron grabbed his friend's shoulders and spun him around forcefully. "That's enough!"

"She's gonna make me pay. 'Cause of what I did, the Flyer's gonna take me one night. It'll bring my death, for sure."

Ron held on tight until Alex finally looked him in the eye. "Listen to me! It. Wasn't. Your. Fault."

Alex's knees betrayed him, forcing him down on the chunky red earth between the cornrows. He wrapped himself in a ball, rocked, and cried. Ron knelt beside him, keeping a firm arm around Alex's shoulder. Michael stood aside, burning with shame at seeing his hero fall apart. Alex hugged his knees, face buried, taking deep, shuddering breaths. Finally, he let out a deep sigh. In a broken, lost voice, he asked, "What are we gonna do?"

Ron thought about it for a long moment, then pulled himself up off the ground. "C'mon. Stand up."

Ron eased Alex and Michael into a huddle. His voice was hoarse. "Here's what we're gonna do." He looked into the eyes of his best friend and his little brother. At that moment, it almost seemed to Michael as if he were in his father's calming presence.

"Swear," Ron said, and solemnly spit into the palm of his hand. "We ain't never gonna say nothin' 'bout what we've seen here. Not to each other. Not to anyone. Not ever."

Alex looked at Ron, then down at his feet. Then he spit into his own palm. "Swear," he echoed.

Michael opened his small hand and spit into it. "Swear," he repeated.

The boys pressed their palms against Ron's, then against each other's. The vow was sealed. And with that, they turned and moved slowly into the darkness.

The oath stuck. Although that night would haunt them for the rest of their lives, the three boys never spoke of it again.

Chapter 3

April 1968

AFTER THAT NIGHT AT the train tracks, the three boys became nearly inseparable. Their pledge of silence had, in some strange way, brought them even closer.

It would be another six years before the treacherous railroad crossing would gain lights and a gate. The unmarked intersection of rail tracks and pavement remained a deathtrap for unsuspecting drivers who fell prey to the train that earned a reputation as "the Widowmaker." Those intervening years took all three boys out of childhood and over the rocky landscape of adolescence.

Ron, a natural athlete, soon shed his boyish awkwardness, and his polished good looks never failed to turn young women's heads. Michael, much to his horror, remained what girls called "cute" well into his late teens. Shy, observant, and passionately full of ideas, he had no idea just how appealing the opposite sex found him.

These teenage years affected Alex the most. A hell-raiser even as a child, his defiant mischief-making took on an intangible, almost desperate quality. After failing to rescue the injured girl, he believed he owed the universe a life. The guilt of that imagined debt weighed on him ceaselessly. Ron noticed how Alex suffered from this twisted, misplaced culpability, but out of respect for their oath, he never discussed it. Instead, he supported his friend with his loyalty. Hardly a day passed that didn't find Alex and Ron together.

~~~

At 5:00 a.m. Easter Sunday morning, Ron snapped awake from a heavy sleep to the thundering growl of a hot rod engine.

The night before had been another exhausting evening of nicotine and alcohol. Both Alex and Ron had recently broken up with their girlfriends, so it was a dateless Saturday, but somehow they'd managed to make the best of it.

They had street-raced Ron's '68 Mustang, surreptitiously acquired two six-packs in Blair Village with their winnings, then cruised the parking lot of Carroll's Hamburgers on Jonesboro Road before moving on to the Varsity Drive-In Restaurant in downtown Atlanta, all the while listening to the foggy bottom voice of DJ "Skinny Bobby" Harper as he spun the Top Forty on WQXI, "Quixie in Dixie." They had nursed unfiltered Camels, drunk Pabst Blue Ribbon, and eyed nubile females (or as Alex would say, "scoped babes"). In other words, they had risen to the height of misbehavior expected of high school seniors.

Long after midnight, Ron had crept home, flopped into bed, and fallen into a thick, dreamless sleep—which he would have continued to enjoy for another three or four hours if it weren't for a miserable lowlife named Chuck Leach.

On the eve of Michael's thirteenth birthday, Harold had moved the family to Tanglewood Lane so that the boys would each have their own bedroom. It was a nicer neighborhood, at least by Forest Park standards, with many families who were also members of the First Baptist Church.

The Leach family lived on the cul-de-sac behind the Simpsons. Chuck, their only son, worked a paper route, delivering the *Atlanta Constitution* with its ever-burgeoning headlines of the Vietnam "police action" and domestic unrest. Chuck's father, Earl, had demanded his son take the job to "build character" after he'd been caught drinking and driving. Chuck was intent on making everyone in the neighborhood pay dearly by sharing his punishment.

Chuck owned a souped-up, metallic blue '68 Chevy Chevelle Malibu SS 396, his second most beloved passion after football. He dumped every dime he made into the car, right down to the two noisy "glass pack" mufflers. Chuck would crank the engine at precisely 5:00 a.m. every morning, even on Sundays, loudly goosing the gas for a good ten minutes until he knew beyond all doubt that the engine was warmed and all his neighbors awakened. This was the way he announced to the world that he was beginning his daily run.

Then, in a blast of blue smoke, he would peel rubber, tires squealing all the way to the end of Stillwood Cove. He would take the curve onto North Avenue at suicide speed, then blow through the next three stop signs. You could hear him all the way out to the First Baptist Church, five blocks away.

All the neighborhood kids wanted to kill him. They had repeatedly petitioned their parents to say something to Chuck's folks. The parents had no great love for Chuck's predawn wake-up calls either, but his father owned a law firm and was well-to-do and powerful in a way few others in this blue-collar neighborhood could ever dream of becoming. Anybody who tried to deal with Chuck soon found out that the Leaches believed in revenge. Chuck acted like as much of an asshole as he wanted, because he thought nobody in Forest Park had the balls to stop him.

The jocks at Forest Park High particularly had it in for Chuck. He had left their football team their sophomore year to transfer to Woodard Academy, a private prep school that attracted college sports recruiters who seldom bothered with the less affluent schools. The "townies" had to bust their asses for a shot at the kind of opportunities that always seemed to land in Chuck's lap, simply because he was the right guy's son.

During their junior year, some of the guys on Forest Park's football team had tried to recruit Ron and Alex to help "blanket-party" Chuck. For months they whispered about their plan to jump him late at night, throw a quilt over his head, beat the crap out of him, and run like hell. As comforting as it was to ruminate over, somehow nobody ever got around to actually making it happen. Chuck, a mean-tempered brute with biceps the size of most guys' thighs, had blackened more than a few eyes at Forest Park High. Even the jocks were terrified of him.

From the beginning, Ron and Alex had both declined the invitation to Chuck's blanket party. Alex was certainly amenable to the *idea* of busting Chuck's face in, but as the school's reigning champion of obnoxious pranks, he felt the scheme lacked the essential ingredient of imagination. It was simply too mundane.

Ron's refusal ran deeper. He believed that you couldn't fight violence with violence—any more than you could put out a brush fire with a blowtorch. There had to be a better way to break this bronco. Chuck had it coming—no doubt about that. But Ron wasn't about to stoop to Chuck's level of violence. He hadn't worked out all the details yet, but he'd decided that Chuck's comeuppance should come from his own "assholery."

As Ron shuffled pillows, fruitlessly trying to chase down a few more Z's, he decided it was time to take the idea up with the master. That afternoon, he would see Alex at the church's covered dish supper, and—after a couple passes at the fried chicken, casseroles, and iced tea—he'd discuss the matter with him.

Ron lay sleeplessly in bed for a few more hours, letting his senses drink in the start of the day. Long about 7:00 a.m., he heard the familiar noises of his mother bundling into the kitchen, percolating the coffee, and humming softly as she marshaled mixing bowls and pans, flour, spices, and ingredients. By eight o'clock, the aroma of boiling potatoes and chopped pickles began to creep down the hall. Preparations were unmistakably underway for the church covered-dish social to be held after the morning worship service.

As was the custom, the Simpson men took their time washing up, shaving, and dressing, then eating breakfast and reading the Sunday paper, while Carlotta Simpson made fragrant miracles in the kitchen. At the top of the hour, the nine o'clock news crackled from the radio with the latest update on the Vietnam conflict. These days, not even the solemnity of a holy day could stem the flow of violent tidings out of 'Nam.

Harold Simpson listened to the report that the Marines at the remote firebase at Khe Sanh had finally been relieved. After ten weeks of fighting, the U.S. had lost 1,000 killed and 4,500 wounded. Harold, a former

Marine and veteran of two wars, had followed that bloody battle with particular concern since it involved his beloved Corps.

"Once a Marine, always a Marine," was Harold's simple explanation when asked about his intense interest. He was a man of few words, much like his own father Melvin, lovingly called "Papa Simp," who the family often visited in Cartersville north of Atlanta where he lived with Laura, his wife of 50 years. Michael had spent many afternoons with his grandfather roaming the hills surrounding the town searching for Civil War-era minié balls and Etowah Indian arrowheads, and learning the Simpson family's oral history. At Harold's insistence, Grandpa Melvin had signed to allow his son to join the Marines at 17 during World War II.

If you knew where to look, you could still make out Harold's faded tattoo of the United States Marine Corps motto showing through the right sleeve of his white Sunday shirt. An American eagle was perched on top of the world, holding a ribbon in its beak that read "Death Before Dishonor. *Semper Fidelis.*"

Semper Fidelis. Always faithful. Harold promised Carlotta when they married that he would never stray. After all, he had *Semper Fidelis* tattooed on his arm. To stray would mean not only breaking his oath to her, but also the one he made to the Corps. Harold was one of thirty teenage Marines who had gotten inked at Sailor Charlie's Tattoo Parlor in San Diego before shipping out to the South Pacific. Four came home. Like most things about World War II, it was something Harold seldom talked about.

Not long past nine thirty, Harold growled at his boys for not having their jackets on and their hair parted straight. By quarter to ten, after Carlotta took a quick spray from the inhaler she used to control her asthma, the Simpsons piled into their forest green Ford LTD. The church was only a ten-minute walk away, but driving was a point of pride on such occasions in this blue-collar town where no hard-won possession was taken for granted. Between the two boys rode a foil-covered tower of casserole dishes, still warm to the touch.

Ron and Michael were anchored quietly beside their father through the prayers and sermon. Harold Simpson sat solemnly at attention during the entire service, an unassailable mountain. You didn't dare step out of line on his watch.

Carlotta Simpson, her angelic voice ever in demand, sang a lilting duet with the minister of music. She possessed the sweetest alto voice in Clayton County. Certainly, no one would ever convince Harold or his sons otherwise.

Michael's deepest notions of comfort were wrapped up in the sounds of her singing. She buoyed him with that voice, nourished him, loved him. Even on Sundays, when she sang in the church choir, her youngest son could never quite escape the feeling that she was singing only to him.

During Reverend Fletcher's prayer, Ron made the mistake of glancing over at Alex, who began mouthing the words in an exaggerated posture of reverence. Whenever Ron looked over, Alex rolled his eyes and gestured to the heavens in a parody of the preacher's piety. Ron had to turn his head away from Alex and keep his eyes fixed on the far wall to get through the pastor's entreaty without busting a gut.

Alex was the only person Ron had ever known who had the balls to make fun of church. His irreverence never failed to put Ron into hysterics. To a kid who had been raised in abject fear of the Lord, there was absolutely nothing cooler.

Or sadder. Because Ron knew the real reason Alex thumbed his nose at the church. Alex had never made peace with the idea that a loving God would stick him with such a raw deal in life. If God were kind and just, how could He give a young man loads of talent, intelligence, and drive, but no way to do anything with it? Alex wasn't an atheist; he did give the Big Guy *some* credit, but only grudgingly, and only on his own terms.

With the services over, it was time for the food. The men busied themselves setting up folding chairs, while an endless parade of mothers formed a casserole brigade. Young girls in cotton dresses poured pitchers of frothy iced tea. Ron, Michael, Alex, and the other boys, being young Southern gentlemen, had nothing more to do than stand around pleasantly—and try to keep from getting food on their Sunday suits.

The din of friendly chatter slowly lost out to the muffled clink and clatter of eating. Bellies were filled, eyes slowly glazed over, and belts were discreetly loosened under the tables. Finally, the time came for neighbors to linger over coffee and gossip. It was Ron's cue to make an inconspicuous exit to sneak a smoke with Alex and Michael.

Since hardly anybody used the musty Sunday school room in the church's basement, it made the ideal spot for an illicit cigarette break. Without a word spoken between them, the three boys arrived at this familiar assignation within a minute of each other. Alex fished a pack of Marlboros out of his jacket pocket, tossed one to Ron, and lit them both with a single flip of his Zippo.

Alex had worked on Ron for years to get him smoking, and had finally succeeded. Michael had only smoked one cigarette ever, guiltily in the backyard at Ron's urging. The boys were too naïve then to realize that their father would smell it on them when he came home that night, and they'd both dealt with their father's belt.

Harold understood the perils of smoking. He had taken it up during his military service in World War II, permitting himself this one small pleasure because he'd been told it would help calm his nerves. And besides, he didn't expect to make it through combat alive. He came home from the war with a two-pack-a-day habit.

Years later, his doctor showed him a small dark blotch on an x-ray of one of his lungs and asked, "Do you love your boys?" Harold did; nobody ever doubted that, even though he wasn't always good at putting it into words.

"If you do, hand me that pack of cigarettes in your shirt pocket and never buy another one."

Without hesitation, Harold handed over his unfiltered Camels. The iron-willed Marine quit cold turkey that day.

Likewise, Michael would never again be tempted by tobacco. After administering the corporal punishment, Harold told the story of his own former habit while his youngest son still winced in pain.

"Kegerator," Alex said idly.

Ron and Michael shot each other a quizzical look.

Alex took a drag from his Marlboro. "Keg-er-a-tor," he repeated, expelling the word in four gouts of smoke. "It's my new invention. It's gonna get my ass invited to every party from here to Atlanta. And it's gonna make me rich." Alex described his plan to fix up an old refrigerator so that it was watertight, and fill it with beer. Then he'd stick a pour spout on the front. *Kegerator.*

"And you'd do exactly what with all your money, Alley Oop?" Ron was always amused by Alex's ideas for new inventions.

"I'd build us the world's fastest car. You'd be my driver. We'd beat all the NASCAR records. Fame and fortune, Ronnie boy. Babe-o-rama." Alex leaned against the church wall, propped a leg on a chair, and closed his eyes, obviously dreaming of the large-breasted women who would one day beg him for his autograph.

"What about me? What would I do?" Michael asked, not about to be left out.

"Somebody's gotta polish the chrome," Alex said dryly.

The older boys shared a good-natured laugh at Michael's expense.

Ron understood what motivated Alex's outrageous fame-and-fortune fantasies. They were his way of fighting against his bleak prospects.

Alex faced two overwhelming obstacles. One was the guilty fear that someday the universe would expect payment in full for the girl's death. The other was the fact that he was vastly overqualified for the simple blue-collar existence that lay before him.

Many young boys in Forest Park never bothered to worry about the future because they didn't believe they had one. A few dreamed of college and lucrative careers; the rest accepted the mundane lives and modest fates they saw stretched out before them.

But Alex never could. Unlike the other kids, he knew there was more to life than a house by Spivey Lake in Jonesboro. Alex was as intelligent as Ron (who was Mensa material), but his true gift was street smarts. Alex had strangely dead-on, accurate instincts, which he'd possessed from his earliest years. And what those instincts told him was that he had no future. So he gambled and raced and fought his way towards manhood, full of an ironic, doomed hipness.

That's what made him perfect for the task of bringing Chuck Leach down.

"We could rub Vaseline on a football and see how far we could shove it up his ass," Michael suggested.

Like Ron, Michael held a visceral dislike of Chuck. In a drunken stupor, the bully had once dropped a litter of newborn kittens into a bag, tied them to his car's tailpipe, and suffocated them in the exhaust. That unspeakably cruel act had repulsed Michael to his very core.

"Waste of a good football," Alex replied.

Alex, more than anyone else, possessed a special reason to hate Chuck. He loved football every bit as much as Chuck did, and was by far the better athlete. Alex displayed a natural grace on the football field that might very well have led him to a professional career.

Until recently, Alex had banked on a football scholarship to the University of Georgia as his ticket out of "Bluecollarville" as he called his home town. But he had the disadvantage of going to a lower-class high school, one the recruiters seldom bothered with. So, although the Leach family practically had enough money to *buy* a college, Chuck was the one who'd landed a coveted football scholarship to the University instead. He never passed up an opportunity to rub it in Alex's face.

"We could suffocate him with exhaust from his own car," Ron offered. He was only half-joking.

A crooked smear of a grin swept over Alex's face. "That's got some poetry to it."

"And you'd do what with the body?" Michael asked.

"I got some free weights and a couple yards of chain. Nobody'd find him at the bottom of Pinerock Lake." Alex had worked summers at Pinerock as head lifeguard. He had recently gotten Michael a job after his friend had turned sixteen.

"Yeah, but do you really wanna swim in all the pus and stuff that'll leak outta his dead body while he decomposes?" Michael asked.

Ron snorted in disgust. "Jeez, bro . . . good thing we already ate. You sure know how to ruin a guy's appetite."

Alex grabbed Michael in a hammerlock and administered a noogie on his head. "Beav, you really gotta stop reading those comic books." He turned Michael loose. "Let me think on this one. It's gotta be perfect. Now, let's go get dessert. Your mom make her banana pudding?"

Back at the tent, over a mason jar of sweet ice tea, Alex began hatching the details of the plot against Chuck.

"This is gonna be simple. Brilliant, but simple—like all my ideas. All we need is about a hundred foot of rope."

Ron turned to his little brother.

"Yeah, yeah. I'll find some."

Michael, as the cadet of the trio, always ended up with procurement and logistics duty. He had long ago become something of an expert at "liberating" biology lab frogs so that, with Alex's assistance, they could mysteriously find their way down gym shorts. He also knew the best sources and going rates of trade for firecrackers, stink bombs, and the special kind of trick chewing gum that blackened your teeth. Ron didn't feel the least bit of remorse foisting these unpleasant duties on Michael. After all, before his younger brother had joined their dynamic duo, all the dirty work had fallen to him.

Ron was helping himself to another mound of peach cobbler when something began to gently wiggle its way into his consciousness. The feeling was subtle, but the more he focused on the goings-on under the tents, the more he sensed it. Something in the tone of the conversations around him didn't sound the way it normally did. The usual cheerful buzz, typically punctuated by hearty male chuckles and the ladies' reserved chirrups, had changed somehow.

Ron tried to listen casually and picked up a few snatches of what was being said.

"Johnson should've seen Tet for the opportunity it is, and called up more troops. We damn near destroyed the VC. I say we finish the job."

"Have you heard? The sum'bitch Johnson announced he's retiring after that Eugene McCarthy fella nearly dusted him in the primary."

"Guess he figured it was a vote for peace."

"Hell, the way I hear it, folks voted against Johnson in New Hampshire 'cause they felt he wasn't being tough *enough*."

"I think ol' Johnson is rattled now that Bobby Kennedy joined the race."

"Whether Johnson's running or not, we still gotta give the military what it needs to get the job done."

To Ron, and to most of the kids he knew, Vietnam was just another item on the nightly news. It was something grown-ups talked about, and that made it, by definition, a subject he couldn't be bothered with. But Ron couldn't help but notice that most every conversation had something to do with Vietnam. Stranger still, the boastful confidence with which they usually spoke of the whole affair had been replaced with something different. Ron searched his mind for a word to describe it. Then it came to him: *dread*.

Out of the corner of his eye, Ron saw his mother talking to Alex's mom, Ginger Granger. Their heads bobbed close together, and every so often Carlotta would place a hand on Ginger's sleeve.

Since Ginger's husband had been killed by cancer, Carlotta had seen to it that her family practically adopted Ginger and Alex as their own. Indeed, Alex looked to Harold for the fathering he'd missed since his own dad's death.

Today, Ginger seemed especially in need of Carlotta's care.

"Okay, so tonight then," Alex was saying. "You with us, Ronnie?"

"Sure. I'm in," Ron mumbled distractedly.

Furtively watching Ginger and his mom, Ron became more certain that this was no light picnic chat. He saw Ginger turn to look at Alex with wistful, desperate eyes. Ron tried to act like he hadn't noticed, because she appeared to be fighting back tears. Not wanting to embarrass her, he looked over at his own mother instead . . . and instantly met her eyes.

Carlotta Simpson was gazing straight at him, with the same haunted, tearful look.

Chapter 4

April 1968

LATE THAT NIGHT, RON lay awake in his bed, thinking about the frightened look on his mother's face. He knew that she and Ginger had probably been talking about Vietnam. But the sense of dread on their faces was deeply personal. It wasn't just their apprehension about the war; it was their fear that their sons would become a part of it.

Ron had always assumed that, when he was old enough, he would join up. He felt it was his obligation to follow his father into the military—as his fathers before him had done. Family lore was that his kin had fought at the Battle of Trenton with General George Washington. Service to God and country was what he had been taught, what was expected. *When your country calls, you answer.* That was how his dad put it. But before, his service to his country had always been an abstraction. *Some day. Some time.* Now this was real.

Would Vietnam be his war, like World War II and Korea had been his father's? He knew so little about Vietnam. Why was his country fighting there? He wasn't even sure he could pick the place out on a map.

Ron slipped out of bed and went over to the globe on his desk. He quietly spun the painted metal orb in the moonlight that seeped through the curtains. He saw Asia, then eased his fingers across the smooth surface until he found Vietnam. He moved back to his bed and slipped under the covers. What a small, faraway country, he thought. *What could such a tiny place have done to incur the wrath of America?*

Midnight came and went. Nearly two hours had ticked by since he'd heard any noise at all from his parents' bedroom, except for their nocturnal breathing. He expected at any moment to hear the muffled footfalls of his little brother making his way down the hall.

Michael had earned a room of his own when he'd turned thirteen, but he still spent a fair chunk of his time hanging out in his brother's room. Now, Michael padded softly down the hall, noiselessly turned the knob, and let himself into the room.

Ron raised his head from the pillow. "You ready?" he whispered.

"Ready," Michael replied, holding up the thick coil of rope he'd swiped from the maintenance shed at church.

The two brothers slipped out of the house without a single sound. It was amazing what years of practice could accomplish. Michael and Ron made out the dim orange glow of Alex's cigarette among the shadows of the hedge.

"Time to camo up," Alex muttered, tossing a small can at Ron. As the boys' eyes became accustomed to the darkness, they could see thick, blotchy stripes across Alex's face. Ron opened the can of brown shoe polish and smeared a few streaks of the pungent stuff across his cheekbones. Michael followed suit. Then the three commandos melted into the shadows, making for the street outside Chuck's house.

There it sat, the metallic blue Malibu Super Sport, parked at the curb, ready for the next morning's assault on the senses. Alex whapped Michael on the arm and whispered, "You go tie it off."

Michael protested, "Why me?"

"Gotta pay your dues, *Beav*. Besides, you're the smallest. You're harder to see."

Michael scouted the street in either direction, and carefully examined the Leach household for any signs of life. He bent low and quickly crept to the curb. He dropped to the pavement and scooted under the Malibu's rear axle. He looped one end of the rope around it and tied it off, making double sure the knot would hold. Then, feeding slack from the coil of rope on his arm, he scuttled out and dashed back to the shadows, where Ron and Alex waited.

"Good work, squirt," Alex said.

"Okay, now somebody's gotta do the other end."

The older boys didn't dignify Michael's statement with a response.

"Aw, come on!" Michael whispered in protest.

"You're *still* the smallest," Alex whispered back.

"And you *still* gotta pay your dues," Ron added *sotto voce*.

Alex led the way through a gap in the Leaches's hedge. A light went on in a back room inside the Leach house. Ron felt Alex touch his shoulder. All three boys dropped onto the grass.

Slow minutes ticked by as a second light went on in the kitchen. The boys heard the clink of a glass and the running of the kitchen tap. A few seconds later, the kitchen light went out, followed by the light in the back room. Alex pressed a hand on each of their shoulders, indicating for them to hold. After what seemed like an hour later, Alex rose and made his way to the Leaches's front screen porch. Ron clambered to his feet and placed himself where he could watch both the house and the street. Every successful mission needs a lookout.

Alex popped his switchblade and zipped open a neat, square hole at the bottom edge of the screen. He held his hand out for Michael to give him the end of the rope, which he fed through the hole. He pulled a lumpy foil packet full of Crisco from his pocket and rubbed a glob onto the screen door's two hinges. Then slowly, painstakingly, he opened the screen door without a sound, motioning for Michael to enter.

Michael sank to his knees and crawled inside the screen porch toward a long aluminum glider. Ron saw him pull gently on the rope as Alex fed him slack through the hole. Michael crept to the bench, slipped the rope around one of its legs, and tied it off before passing it through the other leg. Michael belly-crawled to the hat stand by the front door and fastened a quick knot around its base. He did the same with the wrought-iron table and four chairs on the far end of the porch, and slipped the last few feet of rope around a wicker plant stand for good measure.

The hours crept by. When the sky to the east had just begun to pale, the boys heard the door to the Leaches's house open and close. They watched Chuck open the Malibu's door and plunk his considerable weight into the driver's seat. They heard the familiar scrape of the hemi engine turning over, then the deafening roar as all eight cylinders caught. The boys held their breath. The suspense was unbearable.

Chuck gunned the engine for what seemed like forever. Then he popped the clutch. The Malibu's tires screamed, and the slack popped out of the rope. The glider, table, chairs, hat rack, and plant stand went airborne, surrounded by the screen from the porch. The whole mess cleared the hedge and hit the ground in the middle of the street. With an unbelievable screech and clatter, the porch furniture chased Chuck down the street. By the time Chuck realized he was being followed, the commotion had brought out half the neighborhood.

Alex eased into the light just long enough to catch Chuck's eyes. He wanted to make sure the cat killer knew whom he could thank for his humiliation. Alex offered his best "eat-shit" smile. Then he, Ron, and Michael quietly melted into the shadows, savoring their victory.

Chapter 5

June 24, 1864

Permelia sat on a wood bench, cradling Melissa in her arms. Long after her granddaughter's body had cooled to the touch, she swayed the child back and forth. Terissa sat unmoving beside her, soaked in shock and grief.

The sun drifted down to the treetops, and the world fell silent. The stillness was broken only by the dusky call of a brown thrasher and Permelia's hushed tones as she sang a lullaby she had learned as the child of a sharecropper.

Hush-a-bye, don't you cry.
Go to sleep little baby.
When you wake, you shall have
All the pretty horses.

A yellow-winged butterfly dipped and circled around her, then fluttered away.

Blacks and bays, dapples and grays,
Go to sleep little baby.

Permelia was empty of everything she had ever known or felt. Her husband and sons were gone, her grandchild dead, and her daughter violated. Her home was little more than smoldering ruins, the only home she and Baylis had ever known. She had birthed their children there, nursed them through sickness, and taught them to read by firelight from the family Bible. From the door she had waved good-bye to her sons when they left to join the Confederates in Virginia.

Most everything was gone now except those memories. The fierce fire had burned her home like so much kindling until its sheltering roof caved in. Her refuge was taken from her, the one place she had always found strength. Whenever life's disappointments had knocked her back, she would pick up a familiar heirloom, wipe it clean, and put it back where it belonged. She'd repeat the process until the whole world was back in order. Life was so twisted now that nothing had a place.

She pulled back from the dark well of her heavy heart, prayed for strength, and gathered herself.

What to do? Where to begin?

She stared at Melissa's favorite blanket. The child had brought it outside to sit on. Permelia took it and laid it on the wood table outside, under the ancient oak where the family ate during warm weather. She placed Melissa on it with care, like laying a sleeping child to bed, and pulled the blanket over her, covering her face with the modesty allowed the dead. She sat beside Terissa, her arm around her shoulder, stroking her hair, comforting herself as much as her daughter.

"Darlin', I'd love to sit here holdin' you all night, but even if we ain't hungry, we need to eat."

Terissa nodded.

"We need to gather the berries you picked. Would you do that?"

She could feel Terissa relax the tiniest bit. Permelia's arm slid off her shoulder with a reassuring caress.

Terissa's voice broke as she spoke. "Mama, why did God let this happen?"

It was a question Permelia didn't want to hear. She felt incapable of answering.

"I wish I knew, child. Sometimes God's reasons are mighty hard to see." She thought in silence. "You know what Jesus said on the cross:

'Why hast thou forsaken Me?' Some say it was 'cause He knew His life was the fulfillment of prophecy. But your Uncle Elon, who knows his Bible, he says it was 'cause in His heart Jesus felt the pain of us poor humans. To me, that sounds about right."

Terissa considered it with a faraway stare, then rose and silently started plucking the berries off the ground.

Permelia looked around the side of the house and was relieved to see her big wooden tub. It was blackened a bit on one side, but it was still sound. She dragged it to the hand pump that capped the well and began filling it with water, when an odd sound startled her. Two dogs were running across the field closest to the house, playing. No threat, just nature's comedians at work.

As they ran, they threw something back and forth, dropped it, and picked it up again before running some more.

Neighbors had left the dogs when they abandoned their farm to flee the Yankees. The animals now fended for themselves. They came up to the house often, looking for morsels of food. Baylis, who liked dogs, would always find them something, even when there wasn't a lot. They were friendly, and, as Baylis said, it wasn't their fault they'd been cast off. He gave them names and used them for hunting.

The animals saw Permelia and came running to her, wagging their tails. One, an English setter that Baylis had named Ramble, dropped their plaything at her feet. He smiled at her and panted.

She looked at the ground. Lord Almighty, she thought. *It was a human hand.* She looked closer and saw it bore the bite mark Melissa had given her killer.

The severed hand was nasty, but she picked it up and threw it as far as she could. She was afraid the dogs would think she was playing and retrieve it, but they were busy doing their best to cheer up Terissa.

"What was it, Ma?"

"Just something crazy," Permelia said. "You know how dogs are."

It was crazy, all right. Everything had gone crazy. She may not understand what God was doing, but it was pretty clear what Baylis had been up to.

～

The laundry had been finished late the day before, and with the prospect of clear weather, Permelia had hung it on the clothesline. She usually didn't like to leave clothes out like that, because she never could tell what might happen in the night. But now she was glad because it meant not everything had been lost in the fire.

Permelia took stock of what was at hand, and pulled a towel, washrag, and Melissa's Sunday dress and drawers from the line. Close by, she found a long butcher knife, which the girls had left by a stump on top of the family Bible. She wondered if things would have been any different if Terissa had remembered the knife earlier. She might have drawn blood from an outlaw or two, but they would have killed her and done what they wanted anyway. The girls had brought the Bible out of the house because Melissa wanted to look at the pictures and study some words while her birthday pie was baking, but they hadn't said anything about the knife.

Terissa gathered the blackberries in a large scarf, but she was reluctant to put them on the table now that Melissa's body lay there wrapped in the blanket.

Permelia saw her dilemma. "You can put that on the bench and come over here, darlin'. We need to clean you off."

Terissa laid the scarf down and walked to the tub without conviction, like she was far away in a dream. Permelia helped slip off her bloody dress, brogans and drawers.

"If you can squat in the tub, baby, it would be good. I know it's cold, but it will just be a little while."

Terissa stepped in the tub, crouched, and splashed herself with water. She quickly began shivering and shaking.

"That's enough, child. Let me warm you."

Terissa stood, and Permelia wrapped the towel around her. She took the washrag and gently cleaned the delicate spot that Terissa was ashamed to touch, carefully removing the dried blood. The woman made comforting noises, something between speech and song. Terissa cried quietly.

Permelia draped the blanket around her daughter and held her tenderly. "What that man did . . . he was the devil dressed like a man, but you had no part in it. You're just as pure as the day God blessed me with you."

Terissa cried harder as she spoke. "I'm not, Mama. I'm not pure. Not no more."

"It was done to you, darlin'. You couldn't have done no different. He was too big and too strong."

"Ain't no man going to want me. Not after what he did."

"It won't be like that, sweetie. This war has changed everybody. One way or the other, the devil has put his hand on all of us. And ain't none of us ever going to be the same for it. Any man worth his salt will understand that."

Permelia dried her daughter's tears. "You're safe now. That man who did this is dead. Your daddy killed him."

"How would you know such a thing?"

"I seen a sign."

"God sent you a sign?"

"Yes," Permelia said, "but it was Ramble who delivered it."

"Daddy's dog?"

"He brought me a severed hand. I know it belonged to the outlaw. I could see the mark where Melissa bit him."

Terissa's eyes and nose dipped down. "I reckon he won't be botherin' no one no more."

~~~

The stiffening would start soon. Permelia knew that preparing Melissa for burial would be more difficult then. She dreaded doing it, but there was no choice. It had to be done.

She had a great uncle who had died in an awkward position and stiffened before they found him. Carrying him back to the house had been a labor. They had to use a wheelbarrow. They had forced him down in his coffin, but in the middle of the funeral, he popped back up like a hand-cranked Johnny-jump-up. The young women started screaming, and the preacher said this was not the resurrection of the dead. Her great uncle had been a good man, but he left an ornery corpse.

She would rather not repeat this with Melissa. What with all Terissa had been through, it wouldn't help her a bit.

Permelia pulled the blanket back. Except for the blood, the little angel looked like she was peacefully asleep. She lifted Melissa's arm. It was still limp and pliable. She took the sharp knife and cut her dress off and pulled off her drawers. She worked fast and tried not to think how pitiable the poor child looked or how her worn heart was being torn by grief. This was the last service she could do for her grandbaby, and she would find her way through it with God's help.

She got a wet washrag and a towel, pulled up a leg, and cleaned the mess that had been released when she died. She thought it was just like changing a baby's diaper, something she had done often enough.

Permelia cleaned around the awful wound. It was a mess, but the blood washed off. She cut a length of rag and placed it on the gash, a patch to catch any that might leak out. She slipped a pair of drawers onto her, then sat her up and tried to slip her dress on. She needed three hands for the limp body and the dress.

Terissa found her focus and joined her. As Permelia held Melissa, Terissa pulled the dress over the child's head and worked her arms through. Then as Permelia lifted her higher, she pulled the dress to its full length. They laid her back down, and Permelia folded her grandchild's arms across her chest. Lovingly, she combed her hair.

Now there wouldn't be any sitting up as they read words over her tomorrow.

～

Permelia had given much thought to their quarters for the night. There were only two choices: in the barn or outside in the woods under the stars. It was now near dark. They needed to get settled. The woods might be the safer course, she thought, as it was less likely that they would alert deserters, thieves, or other kinds of the devil's mischief that might be lurking about.

Permelia heard the sounds of hooves and a creaking wagon coming up the dusty road. She took the big knife and led Terissa in the direction of the woods. The poor child was shaking.

"Don't you worry, darlin'. I suspect that's Virgil a'coming home. But we need to be right cautious."

Terissa nodded. She understood, but was still trembling.

If anyone came their way, Permelia knew they'd just find a burnt home, a little dead girl, and a Bible. As sad and otherworldly as that might be, Permelia imagined there was ruined damnation all over the hills around them. The Yankees were like a mechanical beast with sharp steel jaws, grinding up Georgia without tears or pity. The tears all came from those unlucky enough to be in their path. She tried not to hate the Yankees. But that was more than she could manage. For now, God would have to forgive them. She could not.

Permelia peered hard through the creeping twilight and finally saw the familiar wagon, moving slow and deliberate. "Thank our blessed Lord. It's Virgil."

She and Terissa walked toward him, waving so he could see them in the closing darkness. He rolled to them and stopped.

"Sorry I took so long," he said. "Elon gave us all he had 'fore he left to help Pa, so I had to load it on my own. Then with these roving Federals, I made my way real quiet-like, so we wouldn't be relieved of our bounty."

"We will hide what we can in the woods come the morn'." Permelia said.

"Elon gave me this." Virgil held up his uncle's double-barreled shotgun.

An unusual and expensive weapon for farmers in the area, a well-off traveling man had offered it to Elon for some spiritual service. The man figured eternal salvation was worth more than any gun and had given it to the preacher with pleasure. Most local farmers just used shot in their muzzleloaders. Even the big ones at .75 caliber were dwarfed by the shotgun's gaping bore.

Permelia was amused to see Virgil holding it. "Son, you shoot that thing, it's likely to knock you like a mule kick."

"Yes, ma'am" he said. "But it will surely clear the crowd in front of me."

She smiled. Not grown yet, Virgil was already the model of his father.

Permelia rummaged through the wagon. "Well, my goodness. It looks to be a horn of plenty."

There was most of a cooked ham, roasted ears of corn, canned vegetables and peaches, some sweet cabbage relish, and pickled okra. There were also wool blankets, a canvas tarp, planks and hand tools, lamps, lamp oil, men's clothes, straight chairs, a rocking chair, and a mirror.

"Looks like an Atlanta drummer's wagon," Permelia said, "You must have cleaned your uncle out."

"Close to it," Virgil said. "Elon said to take everything. If he needed anything, the Lord would provide."

~

They ate a supper late, even coaxing Terissa to have some. Then Virgil took the wagon to the barn and put the horses up. He used some of the oil and matches to start a fire and brew coffee. They would need it if they were going to sit up with Melissa. It had been a long, horrible day, and he was exhausted.

As the night wore on, Terissa made a pallet on the ground. Permelia put her elbows on the table and began nodding off.

"Some say you need to sit up with the dead to keep the devil from coming and stealing their souls," Virgil said. "You believe that, Ma?"

"Don't reckon I do," she said. "Melissa was sweet and innocent. I see no sin in her. Anyways, I figure the devil got his share of souls from 'round these parts today with all those dead thieves."

"You can go to sleep if you want. I couldn't if I had to."

His mother didn't answer, but he soon heard her slow and steady breathing. She was already asleep. He was glad she could lay her burden down for a spell, especially because tomorrow promised to be almost as bad as today. They had burying to do, and they had to figure out how to survive after that.

Once his father and Ulysses had killed the marauders, they would have come home to help. But since they hadn't, Virgil knew that the federal cavalry probably had cut them off—or worse, taken them prisoner or killed them. He could tell his mother didn't want to talk about that. Neither did he. So the thought was held in silence.

There were likely patrols all over the area looking for McCollum's raiders. If they came, the Federals would likely relieve them of their vittles, but they probably wouldn't mess with them like the looters had.

The Federals might be chasing the thieving killers, too. Hard to say. Or maybe it was part of Sherman's plan to destroy the state. Turn outlaws loose on the women as revenge for fighting the war in the first place. If Confederates knew their daughters were being raped, they might desert.

It sure was lot to think about, but from where he sat, there was no way to know anything for sure. He stared into the night and found no answers there, only more darkness.

Chapter 6

THE STENCH OF HUMAN death curdled the cool night air around Baylis. Hunger and loss kept him on edge. At least he was still alive, he thought, though living was scarce solace for the sorrows of the day.

Anticipating the worst never prepares one for it. He knew that. He had lived in fear that the war would take his family since the conflict started. And now, again, it had.

When his daughter Sarah had lost her husband, Baylis had accepted it. After all, William was a soldier, and soldiers die. It is, plain and simple, the way of war. But why take his beautiful granddaughter, a loving child so young? God's way often made little sense to Baylis, and he had long since given up on asking the Almighty to explain Himself.

He thought of Permelia and longed for her tender eyes and gentle touch. He knew if he allowed himself to dwell on his worries, they would drive him mad. With great effort, he tried to settle his mind.

Baylis nibbled on the kernels of hard corn he found on the ground, dropped by the bluecoat cavalry feeding their horses. A summer storm rolled and rumbled in the distance, punctuated by cannonading and the angry crackle of rifle fire. At times it was hard for Baylis to distinguish between the heavenly and man-made thunder.

The three men had taken cover from the threat of bad weather beneath an abandoned flatbed freight wagon turned on its side. It offered a hope of comfort that would surely prove false if the rain came. Baylis had agreed to take the first watch and give Elon and Ulysses a chance to rest. But judging from the way his son was shifting on the ground, Baylis was certain Ulysses had found no comfort in sleep.

Elon was another matter. He was so serene he could have been one of the dead. Baylis wasn't surprised. Elon was never a man to carry his troubles to his slumber, no matter how grave. He simply offered his burdens up in prayer, leaving his life in God's hands. Elon's heavenly entrustment had been especially long that night, ending with a recitation of the twenty-third Psalm. But once finished, he slipped into unconsciousness with ease.

Early in life, Baylis realized that God had a use for his younger brother after Elon started praying over dead squirrels and birds found around the family farm in South Carolina. By the time he had reached the age of six, Elon had already professed his faith and begun preaching, standing on a tree stump back behind the house with crows, coon dogs, and an occasional rabbit for his congregation.

Baylis slipped out a canteen that he had taken from one of the dead soldiers and quietly drank. He grimly stared at the blood on his hands.

He felt the paper in his coat pocket and pulled it out. It was a letter his daughter Sarah had written to her husband just before he was killed. It was yellowed, dirty and torn. It didn't matter that clouds blotted the moonlight. Baylis had studied the words so many times he could recite them by heart. It read:

My dear and loving husband,

William, you don't know how lonesome I am. One week seems as long as a month. I want to see you so bad I can't sleep at night. I want you to come home if there is any chance of it, though I know it's a bad one. I wish you could get a pass from your Captain. I pray to Our Heavenly Father that the time is not far off that you will be here to stay.

I hope peace will be made shortly and the Lord will spare your life, that you will be permitted to return to your family. There is no thought more dear and precious in this world.

I wrote a letter to your Captain to request that they send you home if you were to die, that it is my wish if it is yours. I want you beside me in this life if it is our Heavenly Father's will to spare your life. If it is not His will, then it is my prayer that we shall someday meet at His throne, where we may sing praises to Him forever.

Your loving wife,
Sarah

Ulysses cracked his eyes open. His careworn face was chiseled with fatigue. "What's that?"

"A letter Sarah wrote to William before he was killed," Baylis said quietly.

"What are you doing with something like that?"

"Your sister asked me to send it by post. I never had a chance to before we got word of William's death, and I never had the heart to tell her. I've carried it with me for months, not sure what to do with it."

"Unless we find a way to get out of this mess, I figure you can hand the letter to William up in heaven yourself."

Baylis carefully slipped the paper back into his coat pocket. "Didn't know you were awake."

"Half sleep," Ulysses said. "Learnt it in the fighting."

"You learn anything there that would help us make a plan?"

Baylis waited for Ulysses to speak. Though his son was young in years, he knew the war.

As Ulysses considered what to do, the woods began to glow with the cool light of dawn. It lit their faces with a faint, rosy glow. The birds' morning songs broke the stillness in the dense pines. Elon stirred awake to the sound. He pulled himself up, yawned, and scratched the nap of his neck.

Ulysses pointed south. "From the sounds of it, I'd say we got the Yankee army before us. Somewhere's around a hundred thousand men. Behind us and to our sides, we got Yankee cavalry. They're probably protecting their flanks, scouting our lines."

"Don't sound like we're likely to survive a skedaddle in either direction," Baylis said.

"As the cavalry sweeps back toward Sherman's line, we're in danger of being discovered if we stay here."

"I reckon there's no good answer, then."

"No sir, not one," Ulysses said. "There's no way to pick up a turd by the clean end."

Elon listened to this and thought for a moment. He announced to no one in particular, "It's best to be about the Lord's work." He stood, stretched. "Help me with this wagon."

Baylis and Ulysses rose, and the three men righted the flatbed. Elon moved over to the bodies of Otis and Willis, still lying stiffly where they'd been found in the darkness the night before. Elon turned to his brother. "Ulysses and I will place our cousins and the other recently departed on the wagon bed. Why don't you hook up the horses? Look for two that are lame and feeble."

"Why on earth would you want lame horses?" Baylis asked.

Elon's only answer was a grim smile. He began dragging Willis's body toward the wagon. Ulysses scooped up Otis by his shoulder and followed his uncle.

Baylis struggled with the harness, which showed signs of being chewed by starving horses. Evidently the Yank supply lines were as thin as the newspaper stories claimed. There couldn't be a bushel of forage between here and Chattanooga. He set two horses to pull the wagon and tied another to the back. Ulysses and Elon finished piling the wagon with dead Confederate partisans.

Elon paused to rest, looked skyward, mumbled a few words, and then picked up a discarded musket. He stared at it like it was a venomous snake. "In my name, shall they cast out devils!" Elon exclaimed, quoting from the Good Book. Suddenly, he struck the weapon against the ground in a violent frenzy.

"Tain't gonna do no good, uncle. Those things are tough. You can't pound 'em into a ploughshare."

"Best to let him have a go of it," Baylis said. "Even with God for counsel, this here's more than any man can bear."

After repeated blows, Elon leaned against the wagon, having spent himself into exhaustion.

Ulysses looked to his uncle and spoke in a hushed voice. "Don't rightly see how tending to these poor souls is going to help our present situation."

Baylis turned to Elon. "What do you have in mind, brother?"

"Joining the dead," he replied.

Chapter 7

May 1968

IT WAS A SATURDAY night late in May. Alex pulled his '65 Plymouth Fury up to the curb, and Michael scrambled into the back seat as Ron climbed into the front. Michael had no complaint about his rear guard position tonight. Being invited on this very special mission was honor enough. All high school guys aspired to this night, a time-honored rite of passage. Next Monday would kick off Senior Week, and the time was ripe for the requisite senior prank.

Anybody who knew the veteran pranksters expected big things of them. Ron and Alex had to be in their finest form tonight. This one would live on in legend for future generations of Forest Park seniors.

While Ron had inherited his father's towering height, Alex never made it past five foot eight. Like a lot of shorter guys, Alex possessed certain traits that made him big for his size. He made up in rowdiness for what he lacked in height. Ron, on the other hand, disliked the idea of coming across as intimidating when he didn't need to be.

Alex was always getting the two of them into trouble, and Ron was always trying to get them out of it. Alex loved picking fights, while Ron, though larger and stronger, was forever trying to talk his way out of them. All in all, they balanced each other out.

The three boys had been talking about this night for weeks, trying to brainstorm a plan worthy of Alex and Ron's reputation. But nothing had come to them yet. They drove around Forest Park for a while, listening to Skinny Bobby Harper spinning vinyl on the radio. Then they drove past the high school. Fifteen minutes to midnight, and still the muse hadn't hit.

"The Clevengers are movin' out." Michael pointed to a shiny new "For Sale" sign on a tidy lawn. "Too bad. Carl's a good ball player. Cool guy."

"The cool people always move away. It's the assholes that stick around forever," Alex said.

"We could swipe the sign and stick it in Chuck's yard," Ron half-joked.

"Stick it in Chuck's yard; get rid of *one* asshole. Stick it in front of the school. . ." Alex trailed off. He continued cruising down the block. Then when he reached the corner, he suddenly pulled to a stop at the curb and cut the headlights.

He turned to Ron. "Get behind the wheel, and be ready."

"Ready for what?"

Alex was already gone. Less than a minute later, he came lumbering back to the car with the Clevengers's For Sale sign slung over his back. He flung it to Michael in the back seat, hopped in the passenger's side, and hollered, "Go! Go!"

Ron gunned it. By the time they got to the other end of town, Michael was riding on a pile of clattering metal signs, and Alex had a couple more parked under his own derriere.

"Ok, now what?" Ron quizzed.

"Not enough yet. Drive to Jonesboro."

Twenty-two pieces of real estate went off the market in Jonesboro over the next two hours before Alex added the last sign to a pile on the passenger seat. He clambered on top of the pile and turned to Ron and Michael with his impish grin. "*Now*, back to the school!"

The car slipped down McDonough Street, past hundreds of unknown soldiers' graves in the town's Confederate cemetery. Michael silently studied the unmarked headstones laid out in the shape of the Confederate

Battle Flag. The ghosts of the Civil War were always within easy view in Clayton County.

Pulling to a stop at the traffic light in front of the town's granite-slab train depot, Ron watched as a cop car pulled up behind him.

"Damn!" Ron abruptly cursed, like a sneeze during pollen season.

"Don't worry 'bout it," Alex counseled. "Just drive normal-like."

The light turned green. Ron nervously dropped Alex's Plymouth into first gear. Then he gunned the engine. And stalled it. The Fury rolled to a halt in the middle of the intersection.

By the time Ron got the car started again, the officer behind them was flashing his lights. Ron pulled to the curb. Michael stretched out across the mound of signs to make them as invisible as he could, doing his best to look nonchalant.

"What's the problem here, boys?" the jowly officer asked, leaning in.

Ron shot Alex a look: *you do the talking*. But Alex was preoccupied. He was trying hard not to squirm, but it became pretty obvious to Ron that one of the sign's leg spikes was poking him someplace he'd rather not be poked.

"Nothing, sir . . ." Ron began.

Alex tried again to move the sign that was causing him distress without rustling the others. But with a sharp, metallic clank, the pile shifted.

"What's that noise, son?"

Ron glanced over at the hangdog look on Alex's face.

"I'm gonna need you boys to step out of *yer* vehicle."

As soon as Alex stood up, the pile of signs underneath him started to slip. He tried to steady the pile, but instead started an avalanche. A half-dozen real estate signs in every size and color spilled out onto the pavement with a clatter fit to wake General Lee from the dead.

The officer shot them a humorless look. "Lock up your car, boys. Let's go."

Ron glanced at Michael, then said, "My kid brother, he wasn't in on any of this. We just brought him along for the ride. Do you think you could, you know . . . let him slide?"

The cop's pink face lowered into a frightful scowl. He studied Michael a long moment. "*Awright*. Toss them signs in the trunk of my cruiser. Then he can go."

A complicated wave of relief and shame washed over Michael. If he were made of the same stuff as Alex, he thought to himself, he'd stick with them, even if it meant being arrested. Instead, he accepted the keys Ron tossed him and climbed behind the Plymouth's wheel.

As he turned the corner, Michael glanced in the rear-view mirror. His older brother was watching him as he drove out of sight. An inscrutable expression lingered on his face.

∽

Neither Alex nor Ron had seen the inside of a police station before. They sat across the desk from the tight-lipped Jonesboro Night Duty Sergeant while they were fingerprinted and processed. Alex seemed to find the whole thing amusing.

"Either you boys ever been arrested before?" the sergeant asked.

"No sir," Ron mumbled, dropping his eyes.

"No sir," Alex barked crisply, as if answering a drill sergeant. He looked the officer steadily in the eye.

The sergeant gave Alex the stink eye, let out a sigh, and flapped their newly created police files against the top of his desk. "I'm gonna give you fellas a break this time. Gimme your phone numbers, and I'll have your fathers come get you."

"My dad'll get both of us, sir," Ron said quickly. Out of the corner of his eye, he saw Alex look away. Ron hoped he wouldn't need to explain that Alex had been without a dad since the age of six, and that this was just one more fatherly task Harold Simpson would perform for Tom Granger in his absence.

The officer dialed the Simpson's home number. He held a terse conversation of one- and two-word sentences, punctuated by a number of "yes sirs" then placed the receiver back in its cradle. "Looks like you boys got a little time to kill," the sergeant told them. "Mr. Simpson says he'll come for you in the morning."

The Duty Sergeant rose from his desk and led the boys down the hall to a holding cell. He held the door open for them, then locked it behind them.

"Hope this lesson sticks like flypaper," he said, not unkindly. "I'd hate to see you make a reg'lar habit of spendin' your Saturday nights in the hole." Then he turned and was gone.

"What's that god-awful smell?" Alex whispered.

"I think it's Night Train. *Used* Night Train," Ron whispered back. As his eyes adjusted to the musty light, he could make out two enormous figures slumped against the far wall. They were breathing heavily.

"Ah, for *Chrissake*!" Alex cried indignantly. He rattled the cell door loudly. "Hey, Barney Fife! You stuck us in the goddamn drunk tank!"

"Will you shut up already?" Ron shushed.

Their cellmates stirred and sat up. The first man was a mountain who could have topped three hundred pounds. He wore a black silk bandana around his head and a heavy, jeweled ring in the shape of a cobra on the knuckle of his left middle finger. Malodorous vomit caked his beard.

The second man, though not as large, worried Ron considerably more. He studied the two boys with a rapacious stare. Ron squirmed. He had seen some men, bad men, look at women that way, as though they were fixing to devour them.

"Who the fuck's makin' all that racket?" the man with the bandana slurred, clapping a hand to his skull.

"Uh, sorry," Ron said lamely.

"You sure as hell are," said the drunk, rising from the cement floor.

"We didn't mean to wake you," said Ron, stifling the urge to back away.

"Yeah, you obviously need your beauty sleep," Alex interjected. Alex's balls had more brass than Herb Alpert's Tijuana band.

Ron shot his best friend a look. No matter how hard Ron tried to diffuse a combustible situation, with one comment, Alex could stoke the flames.

The man with the predatory eyes rose to his feet. "Well, well, I was hoping my prom date would show tonight," he said in an empty tone. "And damn, I forgot your corsage."

"We don't want any trouble," Ron said, in a voice as firm as he could muster.

The vomit-stained drunk eyed Alex. "Then your little boyfriend better shut his fuckin' hayseed mouth 'fore I fill it with something."

"Yeah, with what?" Alex snapped back.

Ron cringed inwardly. "Now, let's just all stay cool. No one wants—"

The drunk giant charged forward and slammed Ron against the wall, cutting him off mid-sentence. Ron's head snapped back hard against the bricks.

As Ron winced in pain, the giant moved his face into Alex's. "I'm gonna fill your faggot little mouth with my cock. I bet you'd like that."

"I got a better idea." Alex looked at him with crazy eyes. "One you'll like much better."

The giant and the predator exchanged looks. Maybe this was going to turn into a *real* party.

"Yeah? What is it, faggot boy?" the giant asked with a crooked grin.

"Why don't you fill your mouth with this?" Alex's fist rocketed out to hammer the big man squarely on the jaw, sending him spinning against the wall. Alex was lucky the man was still so drunk. Sober, he would have been impossible to knock off-balance.

Ron moved to back up Alex. There was no getting out of it now. Ron reached down and quickly undid his belt, recalling a Marine fighting technique his father had once showed him. He slid the belt out of its loops and wrapped it around his fist, leaving the edge of the buckle exposed. Then he turned his back to Alex. Now that they were a double-fronted fighting unit, it would be harder for the two goons to take them down.

The man with animal eyes lunged at Ron. He went straight for Ron's throat with fingers that looked like they could easily choke the life out of him. His eyes told Ron in no uncertain terms that was exactly what he intended to do.

Ron threw an uppercut to the man's face with the dangling belt buckle, opening up a J-shaped flap of skin just below his eye. The man howled with rage. He kicked Ron in the chest, slamming him hard against the steel bars. Before Ron could move, the man was on him again. Ron swung wildly with the fist that gripped the belt, barely managing to stay on his feet.

Out of the corner of one eye, he could see Alex exchanging punches with the huge man, getting in two or three for every one that the enormous drunk managed to land. The boys were holding their own, but they couldn't fend off these brutes forever.

The Duty Sergeant stormed down the hall. "That's enough! Knock it off now, or I'll get the hose!"

The two drunks took their time in backing away. It gave Alex one last opening, and he took it. He kicked the beast hard in the balls with enough force to send a football through the goals at thirty yards. The big guy doubled over and howled in pain.

"Who's the faggot now?" Alex screamed.

"*Gawddammit*, I said that's enough!" The desk sergeant bellowed. "Next man who throws a punch will answer to my nightstick."

Alex's left eye was swelling closed, and the right side of his neck sported a lobster-red welt, no doubt caused by the giant man's cobra ring. Ron felt his own face. His forehead and cheeks were hot and tender; his nose leaked a trickle of blood.

The sergeant cuffed the drunks to a bare steel cot in the corner. Then he turned a baleful eye to the boys, both of whom were still breathing heavily and dabbing at their battle wounds with the backs of their hands.

"I gotta cuff you boys, too? Or are you gonna behave?"

"No problem here, sir," Ron managed through his pain.

For once, Alex was quiet.

Ron had never known that a single, sleepless night could take so long to pass. Harold signed them out the next morning and led them to the car without uttering a word. As Ron and Alex climbed into the back seat, Harold casually appraised their bruises.

"Desk Sergeant says you got yourselves into a sticky spot last night."

"We gave as good as we got," Ron answered curtly.

"Better," was Alex's one-word amendment.

Harold slid into the driver's seat, cranked the ignition, and said with finality, "Yessiree, I bet you boys did."

Chapter 8

July 1968

MICHAEL STEPPED OUT THE door of his family home, stopping to let the warm sunlit air, thick as flannel, caress his cheeks. He inhaled the fragrance of azaleas in full bloom and the grassy Saturday smell of freshly cut lawns. Over the years, he had learned to sort these subtler aromas out from the odor of fuel wafting down from jets landing at Hartsfield. Atlanta's airport had grown like a cancer and now endangered the health and vitality of Forest Park.

Michael pushed his 650cc Triumph Bonneville motorcycle off the carport so that it, too, could enjoy the warm spring sunshine. He tightened the bolt on the throttle that was forever working its way loose, and rubbed at a smashed june bug on the front chrome fender with the corner of his beach towel.

Michael had recently made a down payment on the machine, his first big purchase, with savings from his summer job at Pinerock Lake. Most sixteen-year-old males couldn't wait to buy their first car, but not him. He had wanted a motorcycle ever since watching Steve McQueen in *The Great Escape*. Michael had persuaded Mr. Butler at the Little Show to give him a movie poster of McQueen's squinty-eyed loner, Virgil Hilts, straddling a vintage World War II–era motorbike. He had reverently tacked the cinematic treasure up on his bedroom wall. (Michael would eagerly note to visitors that Virgil's bike was actually a 1962 Triumph TR6 "Trophy Bird" redesigned to look like a German Military BMW.) The poster of McQueen still hung there five years later, Michael's constant alpha-wolf companion.

Michael's Triumph wasn't exactly on a par with Ron's Mustang, but it was *his*. He hadn't been so proud of a possession since the transistor radio he'd gotten for his tenth birthday. He lovingly unchained the machine from a concrete carport pillar and tucked the chain into his army-surplus backpack.

As Michael loaded his pack and towel onto the back of the Triumph, he spotted his father in the front yard, shirtless beside a wheelbarrow full of gardening tools, kneeling at the foot of the elm tree. Harold Simpson carefully peeled a section of the elm's bark away, and held it up close for examination, his brows knitting into a frown of concern.

Michael ambled over. "What's up, Pops?"

When he saw his son approach, Harold quickly reached for his tee shirt. He never liked for his sons to see the jagged network of silver-blue scars that laced his back, and his two boys had never dared to ask how he got the ancient wounds.

"The tree's diseased," Harold explained, holding up the sliver of bark for Michael to see. "Elms grow too fast. Makes the wood soft."

Michael took the spiny tree skin in his hands and examined its silky red-brown underside. In between the fibers, a cottony, mildew-like substance grew.

Harold wiped the sweat from his face with the back of his hand. "Hate to lose the tree."

"The oak's a lot smaller." Michael nodded at the red oak lifting up its velvety ochre leaves to the sunshine. "Oaks grow slow, but the wood's strong. That tree could outlive all of us."

The thunder of a passenger plane far overhead drowned out Harold's voice. With a mechanical motion born of years of practice, father and son tipped their heads back to follow the airliner's path across the cloudless turquoise sky.

"Airport is killing this town," Harold grumbled after it passed. "When we moved here years ago, I never figured I'd have to smell jet fuel in my yard on a Saturday mornin'."

~

When Michael turned his Triumph off Riverdale Road and into Pinerock Lake's gravel parking lot, he could hear the Young Rascal's "Good Lovin'" booming over the PA system.

As he rode beneath the pines, Michael smiled with the knowledge that Alex was already warming up the place with his wild energy. Alex was fond of cranking the volume until the speakers thumped. Mr. Andrews, the lake's hard-drinking owner, always complained that the sheer force of the sound waves rocketing through the surrounding woods must have knocked the owls from their nests.

Michael pulled up in the parking lot and stood for a moment, savoring the view. No body of water formed by nature would recognize Pinerock Lake as its kin.

Mr. Andrews had bought fourteen acres of raw pine forest dirt cheap. He then bulldozed it, dammed the stream, and filled up the lake himself before trucking in its wide beach of thick sugar-white sand. Every summer, Mr. Andrews dumped enough chlorine into his homemade water resort to keep the private lake an otherworldly Kodachrome blue. No fish lived in Pinerock Lake, but every summer, hundreds of local families paid membership dues for the privilege of dipping their sunburned hides into its perfect, azure waters.

Michael entered the lifeguard's lounge to a motley chorus of greetings. Kenny Jones, perhaps his closest buddy besides Alex and Ron, snuck up from behind and tried to pour a Dr. Pepper down the back of Michael's swim shorts. Alex was in the corner, taking wagers on who would spot the first bikini of the day.

Michael discreetly scanned the lounge for Diane. He caught sight of her just as she entered, the sunlight momentarily forming a fuzzy jade corona around her as she came through the door. Michael had to make a conscious effort to keep from staring.

Alex, as head guard, had decreed that no guy under his command would date Pinerock's first female to wear the distinctive Red Cross patch. "I don't watch soap operas," was Alex's succinct explanation for the ban.

Diane had been hired to keep an eye on the "kiddy area" in the lake's shallow end because none of the male guards liked that duty. Alex instinctively knew that no good would come of fraternizing with her. When he announced his no-dating edict, just before she arrived the first day, he had looked straight at Michael.

Michael had been trying to figure a way around Alex's policy all summer. He spent hours working through every possible scenario, but none of them ever made sense. And even if he could figure a way to ask Diane out without *really* asking her, he doubted he'd ever have the nerve.

Diane had no idea what magic her coltish, gawky figure, a tall girl's tangle of shins and elbows, had on Michael. In an oversized tee shirt and tennis shoes, her strawberry blonde hair in constant uncombed rebellion, she would dunk and rough-house with him like a rowdy sister. The sensations that coursed through Michael often left him feeling vaguely incestuous.

A sharp jab to the ribs brought Michael out of his daze. Alex was beside him, smiling in a way that let Michael know immediately that he was on to his fantasies.

"Listen up, you pie-holes. I got an important announcement."

The room quieted. For a moment, Michael feared Alex was about to share his secret with the entire room.

"Did you hear?" Kenny interjected. "The Beaver died in Vietnam last week."

"No kiddin'? Jerry Mathers bought the farm?" Michael was astonished. It just didn't seem possible. Not the Beaver.

"Yeah, that pork sausage Shelley Winters said so on Carson last night."

"I saw it," Wanker chimed in, "Shelley cried on the couch. Even Johnny got a tear." Warren had been caught jerking off in his tent by his Scout Master on a camping trip when he was thirteen. Kenny had anointed him with the nickname "Wanker," and after a few years, no one even bothered to call him anything else.

"Don't believe all the shit you hear on the idiot box," Alex cut in. "Now enough with the current events. We're expectin' a good crowd today. Ol' man Andrews wants the beach looking especially sharp."

Mr. Andrews was forever carping about the way the beach looked. "Aesthetics, boys," he'd grouse. "We gotta look a cut above the city pool, else folks won't bother to spend their money here."

Alex glanced at his clipboard. "Also, the lake's pH has shot up, so we'll be doing a dose of chlorine after closing tonight."

Alex shot a look at Michael, as though mulling something over.

"We're running behind this morning. *Mikey* will head up the rake brigade while I tractor the beach. Let's hustle."

"Mikey" was about as close as Alex ever came to using Michael's real name. Michael was thankful that at least his friend didn't call him "squirt" or "beav" or "mouse" in front of Diane and the other guards.

As everyone dispersed, Alex turned to Michael. "Once the lake's open, meet me over where we're clearing land for the new picnic area."

With that, Alex moved away.

Michael greeted Diane perfunctorily as she passed by. He suddenly felt shy around the girl, even though he'd been working with her all summer. He grabbed a soft-toothed rake and followed her out the door.

The lifeguards formed a line in the water with Michael in front, nearest the shore. Rakes at the ready, they listened for their cue.

"You catch Star Trek last night?" Wanker asked, to no one's surprise. Wanker, the newest lifeguard, was also the shortest. He was in the water almost to his waist at the back of the rake line.

"Shut up with that Trek shit," Kenny grumbled, "before I boldly go and put my rake up your ass."

"It was just a rerun, anyway," Michael said.

"Last night was the one where these aliens have the power to move stuff just by concentrating. They captured Kirk and Uhura," Wanker continued, undaunted, "and made 'em kiss."

"Uhura?" Diane asked.

"The colored chick in the short mini," Kenny said.

"Yeah, I've seen it." Michael tried to sound bored whenever Star Trek came up. In fact, he had never missed an episode, not even the reruns, but that hardly needed to become public knowledge.

Wanker, on the other hand, had blown a week's salary on a pair of custom-fitted rubber Spock ears, which he sometimes wore even to the beach. It was the best he could do, since his parents had turned down his request to have his ears surgically pointed.

"The TV Guide said the aliens forced the crew to 'inflict *indignities* on themselves,'" Wanker continued. "Kirk got to smooch this hot fox. What kinda indignity is that?"

"They meant because she's *colored*," Kenny pointed out. "That was the indignity, you dweeb."

"No chance that kiss'll ever happen at this lake," Diane said.

"It's not like they don't have their own places to swim," Kenny replied, a little defensively.

Michael shifted uncomfortably at the water's edge. He hadn't realized that "private lake" actually meant "whites only" until after he joined the staff. Working at the lake just seemed like a fun job. He had always been a strong swimmer and had easily passed the Red Cross life-saving course taught by Coach Avinger. When Alex offered him an opportunity to be a lifeguard, he jumped at the chance.

But Michael was increasingly troubled by the policy. Though he knew it was legal, it just didn't *feel* right. His folks didn't tolerate racism and wouldn't allow the use of what his mother delicately referred to as the "n-word."

The country was still teetering unsteadily from the violent upheavals that had followed the April assassination of Martin Luther King, Jr., in Memphis, Tennessee. Riots had occurred in more than a hundred American cities following King's murder, with 50,000 federal and state troops called out to quell the violence in what had been the largest domestic military emergency since the Civil War.

Robert Kennedy's words about that great tragedy still rang in Michael's ears: *"In this difficult time . . . it is perhaps well to ask what kind of a nation we are and what direction we want to move in . . ."*

Despite his misgivings, Michael had convinced himself to keep the job, figuring the policy wasn't really hurting anyone. It was, after all, a great job for any young guy.

"Let's go," Wanker shivered. "The water's cold."

Michael shook his head, "We start with the beginning of the next song. It's the rule." Nobody could say how the tradition had started, but the lake had opened this way for as long as any of the lifeguards could remember.

"And quit jumpin' around, Wanks," Kenny added. "You look like you're jerking off back there."

Over the lake PA system, Van Morrison was lustfully crooning his last "*la te da*" for the "Brown Eyed Girl." A phonograph needle could be heard screeching across the grooves of the record. Then, with the rhythmic soul shout of "*One, two . . . one, two, three, four,*" James Brown and "his band of renown" eased into the opening horn groove of "Cold Sweat."

On the beat, as one, the lifeguards began raking the lake's sandy bottom, scratching off the light crust of algae and pushing it out into deep water. Michael had to work hard not to stare at Diane. He glanced at her for half a second, then quickly tended to his rake.

With the algae safely herded into deeper waters, the guards turned to policing the horseshoe-shaped beach for trash while Alex finished "fluffing up" the sand with Woodstock, the lake's ancient tractor.

After old man Andrews dumped so much cash into purchasing the lake's pristine white beach sand, he hadn't felt particularly inclined to spring for a decent tractor. The Frankenstein machine, all peeling orange paint and rust holes in the floor plates, had been raised from the dead at Hal's Auto Salvage. With the exception of Alex, Pinerock lifeguards universally feared the clunky old machine.

Two summers ago, it had sent Mr. Andrews to the emergency room for stitches after one of the many bits of baling wire that held it together came untwisted. Less than a month later, Woodstock had thrown a head guard from the driver's seat and broken his collarbone, elevating Alex to the top dog position. Just last summer, the rogue machine had caused two small brush fires and stunk up the lakeside with the odor of faulty wiring. And such disasters happened only when it bothered to run at all. These days only Alex drove the tractor, and he did so with the pride and bravado of a truly gifted mechanic.

At eleven o'clock sharp, the lake opened, and families began pouring noisily onto the tractor-fluffed sand. Michael made his way over to the broad meadow west of the beach. Alex pulled up on Woodstock moments later and cut the engine.

"Look," Alex started unceremoniously. "This is my last season."

Michael was startled by the unexpected news. He knew Alex liked the job, and many guards worked at Pinerock Lake through their college years. He figured Alex would have stayed for two or three more seasons.

"Why's that?"

Alex pulled at his jaw. "I just don't see myself here, that's all. It's time for me to move on."

Michael looked away, at a loss for words. Working with Alex at the lake was one of the few things they had ever done without Ron. The job had been a great experience.

"You'll be up for head guard next year," Alex continued.

"You really think I got a shot?" Michael had never even considered the possibility of being promoted.

"That's why we're standin' here jabberin'." Then came the kicker: "It's an extra *twenty-five cents* an hour. Do the math. That's *ten dollars* extra a week. Enough for a second date."

Michael's eyes went wide. "That's serious dating."

"I got a feeling that might be important to you soon." Alex let the thought sink in for a moment before adding, "If you learn to use the tractor, you'll have an in with ol' man Andrews."

Suddenly, it dawned on Michael. Alex intended for him to drive Woodstock.

Michael eyed the beast warily. The extra cash and the prestige of being head guard did sound tempting. Besides, what better way to learn how to tame the beast than from the master? Michael figured Alex would help him learn all its finer points, carefully guiding him until the day he was ready to drive it alone.

"So you wanna try it?" Alex started the engine, reached down and offered his hand. Michael hopped cautiously aboard the rusted behemoth, then nearly tumbled backward as the tractor lurched forward.

Michael clutched the bucking machine's rear fender with white knuckles. Every story he had ever heard of people being thrown off and crushed by their tractors flashed through his mind.

"This is the left brake, this is the right brake," Alex shouted over the engine's roar. "Use them to help turn the tractor. This is the throttle, this is the clutch, this is the gearshift. Got that?"

"I'm not sure . . ." Michael shouted over the din. He risked a glance over his shoulder towards the beach, where he thought he saw Kenny and Wanker laughing and pointing in his direction. He could find a way to bear it if they witnessed him looking clumsy and scared. But if Diane saw it, he knew he would spontaneously combust with shame.

Michael turned back around to Alex, only to find himself staring at an empty seat. He looked around frantically and spotted Alex standing a few yards behind, grinning broadly. Alex had jumped off the moving tractor.

Michael scrambled into the seat and mashed his feet against the brakes. Nothing happened. A thick stand of pines loomed directly ahead. Michael yanked the tractor's huge steering wheel to one side, but the berserk metal beast continued its kamikaze course toward the trees. At the last possible second, Woodstock lurched to the left, clipping a few saplings. Michael risked a brief glance at Alex, whose head was tipped back in a fit of mirth.

Now the tractor was hell-bent towards a stack of steel trashcans. Michael wrenched the heavy wheel around, remembering at the last minute to add some left brake. He stomped down hard on the brake, and Woodstock suddenly fishtailed, sending trashcans careening. Alex was now doubled over with laughter.

The tractor's nose headed this time for the water. But by now, Michael's confidence had bloomed. He lifted his backside off the metal seat, slowly wrenched the wheel to the left, and shifted his weight onto the left brake. Woodstock obediently sashayed to the left in a handsome arc, then made a beeline straight for Alex.

Being Alex, he didn't flinch, but stood his ground and looked straight into Michael's eyes. Michael waited as long as he dared, then throttled back, leapt into the air, and landed with all his weight on both brake pedals. At the last possible moment, Woodstock squealed to a halt.

The persnickety old engine sputtered into silence. Michael sat blinking in the tractor's seat, waiting for his hearing to come back.

Alex leaned forward, patted the tractor's nose, and chuckled. "I guess you got the hang of it."

Chapter 9

June 25, 1864

ELON'S PLAN MADE SENSE, or as much sense as crawling under a pile of corpses could make. But when Baylis wedged his body into the wagon among the dead and pulled a cadaver on top of himself, he wasn't sure he could last the day there. The smell was enough to make a boar hog vomit.

The young man next to Baylis had blue eyes, fixed on the distance, maybe the place where his dead dreams lay. The soldier couldn't have been much older than sixteen. The grief around Baylis didn't make his own anguish feel any smaller.

Baylis prayed for God's protection for his family, and that when his death came, it would be merciful. There wasn't much left to hope for, just that he wouldn't have his legs blown off and die screaming.

Elon had made a little crevasse through the bodies so Baylis and Ulysses could have fresh air. Mostly Baylis could see stands of oaks and hickories, some shattered by artillery fire as they came closer to the sound of guns.

"Well, I'll be damned." It was Ulysses shifting his weight in the wagon bed beside him. His son was breathing shallow.

"I don't know if I can do this, Pa," his son whispered. "My leg's all stoved up and cramped. And I got blood drippin' on my face."

"We're coming up on Big Shanty," Elon said as he gave the reigns a jiggle. "I see Yankee cavalry yonder down the road, heading this way. You boys best be quiet, or we'll all be shot for spies."

Minutes later, Baylis heard a jangling and clanking that sounded like a band of tinkers. The cavalry's unsecured swords, cups, and pans were beating against each other. Good thing they weren't trying to sneak up on anybody.

"Halt. Get the Lieutenant up here," a voice boomed.

"Whoa, there," Elon called, and the wagon stopped.

"What the hell you think you're doing?" It was the booming voice again.

"I am a minister of the Gospel, and I'll thank you to watch your speech with me, sir."

"Very well, Reverend, where are you're going?"

"I'm taking these children of God home for a Christian burial."

"The dead don't need those horses, but Sherman's cavalry do."

"Does that uniform make you a horse thief?" Elon asked.

"Be careful what you say, sir."

Baylis heard the sound of a horse being reined to a stop as the lieutenant cantered up to the front of the column. Through a slit between the wagon's sideboards, Baylis could see the man was sweating more than the weather warranted. His gaunt face was strained from the rigors of combat, and his eyes held the look of a man who had seen too much killing.

"What's the problem here?" he asked the sergeant.

"I'm taking these horses."

The lieutenant looked toward Elon. "That's a god-awful stench." He inched his horse closer to the wagon and grimaced at the sight. "Don't you think we have enough dead here? The air is thick with their putrid smell. Where in *tarnation* are you taking these bodies?"

"I'm a man of God taking these fallen soldiers home. These here are all local sons and fathers. I would ask your understanding and mercy, sir."

"We need the horses," the sergeant protested.

"These lame horses are too feeble to be of use for war, sir."

The lieutenant glanced at Elon's horses, then turned a jaundiced eye to the sergeant. "Give the preacher a white flag and a pass through the lines, and let him be on his way." He gave Elon a salute. "Good luck to you sir, and may God have mercy upon us all."

Elon eased the wagon forward with a jostle of the reins. He set off toward Big Kennesaw Mountain, which rose in the distance 800 feet above the rich clay piedmont. It was an imposing sight.

As the wagon passed the railway at Big Shanty, Baylis was amazed at what he saw through his air hole: hundreds of oak barrels, tins of rations, cases of guns, and powder—more goods than he imagined could be in one place. And soldiers, thousands of them. He's never seen so many men in one place in his life. They looked beat to hell, but well-fed and ready for more fighting.

The Confederate guns on Kennesaw Mountain fired. With each volley, the locomotive at the station answered with a toot of its steam whistle. The shells fell just short of the Yankee lines.

Baylis knew their wagon would make an attractive target for the Confederate gunners as it moved forward. Elon would have to wave the white flag with all his strength.

Chapter 10

August 1968

AFTER THEIR OVERNIGHT STINT behind bars that spring, Alex and Ron had kept themselves somewhat in check. Even after graduation, they still misbehaved as much as possible; after all, they had a hard-earned reputation to keep up. But Ron in particular had had all the prison experience he hoped to get, and he made sure that their exploits never again carried them onto the wrong side of the law.

But legitimate fun was often hard to come by in Forest Park. If you were unlucky enough to be stuck in town on the weekend, you had your choice of shooting pool at the bowling alley, skating at the roller rink, or having a steamy-windowed evening with your date at the Thunderbird Drive-In.

You *could* take a date out for a "sit-down" dinner at Harbin's, but then you ran the risk of bumping into your friends' parents and having to carry on polite conversation. And how could you hope to score points with a girl talking to somebody's folks? Besides, what sort of girl wanted to go a restaurant that her parents went to?

It was no small wonder, then, that on weekends, the town experienced a mass exodus of teenagers. The moment kids were old enough to beg, borrow, or buy a set of wheels, they headed for Atlanta, which loomed due north like the Emerald City.

On this humid, heady August Saturday evening, Alex, Ron, and Michael, all sporting golden summer tans, got themselves on the yellow brick road as quickly as they could. They knew that nights like these would soon become a thing of the past.

The three boys were finishing what they instinctively knew would be their last summer together. Alex and Michael had worked as lifeguards at Pinerock Lake, while Ron helped out at his parents' print shop. Now, at summer's end, Michael would return to high school soon, a senior at last. Ron and Alex were staring their futures in the face. It wasn't a pretty sight.

The summer had not been without its good times, but an intangible tension haunted every hangout, drag race, and party. More and more often, the boys would notice a gap in the crowd, a friend of a friend who suddenly wasn't around anymore. They didn't have to be told that this hometown kid was now courting death in a foreign country, thousands of miles away from the nearest moon pie and magnolia tree.

Ron's Mustang sped past the familiar road sign: *Atlanta, 25 miles*. Beneath it, some racist yahoo had scrawled, "Home of Martin Luther *Coon*." Underneath the weathered epithet, someone had added an equally repugnant retort in fresh letters: "*Not any more.*"

The twilight turned soft and blue outside the car's windows. On the radio, Little Richard was hawking Royal Crown Hair Jelly. Then came the familiar gravelly drawl: "This is John R., way down in Dixie. WLAC Nashville, Tennessee, fifteen ten on the A.M. dial. I'm talkin' 'bout the late, great Otis Redding now. Come on in Otis, and let yourself go." Otis Redding's "Hard to Handle" spilled into the night from the 50,000-watt clear-channel station.

"Baby, here I am, a man on the scene. I can give you what you want, but you gotta go home with me . . ."

Soon after they entered the city, Ron turned onto North Avenue and cruised into the Varsity Drive-In, the world's largest fast food palace. The odor of fried grease wafted across a vast, brightly lit parking lot shimmering with Mustangs, Barracudas, GTOs, Chevelles, Corvettes, and all other manner of muscle cars.

Ron passed curb service—for guys with dates, *not* guys looking for them—then slid the Mustang into a space in the parking deck.

Drifting through the back entrance into the stainless steel and glass interior, the boys waded into a large mass of teenagers from two-dozen Atlanta-area high schools, all standing, sitting and waiting in line. This gigantic, greasy, cacophonous stew of exploding sexuality, illusory invincibility, and doomed innocence was heaven on Earth—or at least it seemed that way to the crowd of hormonally challenged teens.

Alex, Ron, and Michael queued up in the fast-moving service line and waited their turn at a counter that seemed longer than a football field.

"What'll ya have, what'll ya have?" came the famous chant from Erbie, the black man who was taking orders with the speed of an auctioneer. The service was so fast and the number of customers so large that a conveyor belt was used to crank out the miles of hotdogs and hamburgers sent from the kitchen to the service counter.

Like most loyal customers of the "V," the boys prided themselves in knowing "Varisty-eze," the specialized lingo the employees used. Along with serving fried culinary delights, the staff provided a nonstop floorshow, yodeling out the orders in this rapid-fire, fast food slang—"Joe-Ree and a Bag-of-Rags," "walk a dog through the garden," "Yankee Dog and a V Orange."

The boys ordered "glorified steaks sideways with strings" (burgers with everything, onions on the side, fries), fried peach pies and Coca-Colas. All in all, it seemed like a King's feast.

As the boys waded through their food, Alex's eyes wandered the cavernous restaurant until they came to rest on Mona Woody, a ripe-busted bleached-blonde from Forest Park's cheerleading squad. Alex knew she would be here with her girlfriends, and he had made no secret of his plan to land her. But, smooth as he was, he didn't mind taking his time. For him, the chase was half the fun.

Michael watched discreetly as Alex advanced across the restaurant to Mona's table, and produced a single pink carnation from inside his jacket. He placed the flower in front of the delighted girl.

Alex smiled. "Have a nice day."

Then he turned, as if to go back to his own table. Suddenly, he pivoted on his heel, turned back to Mona, and said, "Oh, and while you're at it . . ." He pulled a beautiful red rose from his inside jacket pocket and placed it in her hands, ". . . have a nice week."

Alex moved back to his table without a single backward glance.

"You're not gonna talk to her?" Michael asked.

"That's all the attention she needs for now," Alex replied, "You leave a girl wanting more, before you know it, she'll be chasin' *you*."

Michael risked a glance over at Mona. Sure enough, she had picked up the rose, blushing from the attention. For the rest of the evening, Mona kept cutting her eyes at Alex, who never gave her a second look.

They would be going steady within the week.

After the excitement died down, a discomforting pall fell over the boys' conversation. These days, uneasiness set in, suddenly and unexpectedly, at almost any time. Mostly, they found a way to laugh it off. But lately, it hadn't been easy.

"So, what's next?" Ron asked, snatching the bull by the horns.

"Johnny Reb's Restaurant for a couple Jack Daniels and Cokes. Then a blowjob from their beautiful redheaded waitress. After that, I'm open." Alex flipped his Zippo and lit another cigarette on the heels of the previous one.

"You know what I mean. Pinerock closes for the season in, what, two weeks?"

"I take it you don't think my NASCAR career's takin' off any time soon."

"Working at Hal's Auto Salvage isn't exactly on the road to NASCAR," Ron said pointedly. "Which is where you'll be come fall."

"It's in the auto *bid-ness*, ain't it?"

"Seriously, man. What are we gonna to do? Are we just gonna sit around with our thumbs up our asses, makin' shit for money, until we get shipped off to 'Nam?"

"It's not like you gotta worry. Your draft number's so high it's in the nosebleed section. No way you're going." Alex flicked an ash and grinned at Michael. "And you . . . hell, the war'll be over by the time you're outta diapers."

"Why don't you go to the University?" Michael asked.

"College is a *helluva* draft deferment," Ron added.

"Then you go. You got the grades. Your folks have enough money to help you out. You could work part-time." There was a trace of bitterness around the edges of Alex's voice.

Ron's refusal to go to college was a source of friction with his parents, and Alex knew it. The truth was Ron had no good reason for not going, not one he was willing to admit out loud. But deep down inside, he knew why he hadn't. It would have meant abandoning Alex at the precise moment when he would face the draft. His friend already had been dealt so many bad hands over the course of his life. Ron wasn't about to shuffle the deck and toss him another.

"Why didn't you apply for a scholarship?" Michael asked. "You might've got one. Then you'd have a deferment."

"Maybe I don't want a deferment," Alex said quietly.

"Say again?" Ron asked.

Alex made a pretense of studying the parade of muscle cars passing outside the window. "I'm saying maybe what I wanna do . . . is enlist."

"Why would you wanna do that?" Michael asked.

"For the adventure, little buddy. Like they say, travel to exotic places, meet interestin' people—and *kill* 'em."

"Yeah, or be killed," Ron countered firmly.

The boys sat in silence, picking at the remnants of their food. Ron felt Alex had been looking for a way to break this news for a while. He could see the pattern. Once, back in their senior year, Alex had brought to school a glossy, full-color Green Beret brochure he'd gotten at the local Army Recruitment Center by pretending he was eighteen. He had wielded the brochure like a talisman, waving it in front of girls and other lesser mortals to work his magic.

All at once, Ron understood that Alex's announcement was no rash, last-minute decision. The brochure had been far more than a way to impress girls. It represented the one sure route of escape Alex had from his dead-end "townie" existence.

Ron realized that when Alex studied the brochure's action photos of steel-eyed commandos out on ops, he was picturing himself as John Wayne—not the Hollywood blueblood, but the manly screen persona he'd worshipped from boyhood.

Despite the Duke's waning hipness, his name had become synonymous with gung-ho young men who plunged themselves wholeheartedly into military service. Doing something stupidly macho in combat was referred to as "pulling a John Wayne."

And this, Ron feared, was exactly what Alex was doing. When Alex held the Green Beret brochure in his hands, his mind's eye saw the Duke, uniformed and heroic, as he appeared in *Back To Bataan* or *Sands of Iwo Jima*. Now, he had a chance to be his own John Wayne, and the backdrop for his adventures would be yet another exotic locale across the Pacific—in a place called Vietnam.

Alex had been a king all through high school. Now, with his last season at Pinerock Lake ending, he faced the inevitable reality of being dethroned. He had nothing more than a pauper-sized future. But the Green Beret brochure had changed all that. It promised him a glorious reign over all his tomorrows, laying it all out like a fortune-teller tracing his palm.

"If I enlist, I get my pick of which branch of service I want. If I wait 'til my draft number comes up, I get tossed to wherever warm bodies are needed that week. And after I come home from my tour, I got college in the bag, paid for courtesy of Uncle Sam."

Ron was blunt. "You do this, you're gonna get yourself killed."

Alex still wouldn't look his best friend in the eye, but returned to his focused study out the window.

"Don't worry 'bout me, Ronnie boy. You know nothing's gonna punch my ticket outta here, 'cept the Dixie Flyer."

It was as close as Alex ever came to speaking of that night at the train.

Chapter 11

December 1968

THE CROWD AT THE Fox Theatre in downtown Atlanta was emptying out. The Simpson family stepped out of the theatre's opulent Peachtree Street entrance and strolled in the cool night air down the sidewalk.

With its lavish, cast stone facade and grandiose Arabic-themed interior, the "Fabulous Fox" was one of the country's most ornate movie palaces. The 4,600 seat auditorium, one of the largest movie halls ever built, evoked a Middle Eastern courtyard, replete with artificial sparkling stars and floating clouds.

Harold Simpson had watched Tim Holt and Bob Steele westerns at the movie palace as a teenager, after leaving home in Cartersville at fourteen and hitchhiking to Atlanta in search of work during the Great Depression. When he had time off from his grocery store job, he spent his Saturdays handing out the theater's advertising flyers in exchange for admission.

Harold had first introduced Carlotta to the Fox when they began dating in their late teens. She enjoyed the pre-movie "Sing Along" with the "Mighty Mo" Möller organ, the largest of its kind in the world. Carlotta even occasionally cajoled Harold into joining in with his gruff bass voice as the lyrics were projected on the screen.

Michael always insisted that they arrive early on family outings to the Fox so he would have time to study the palace's gilded onion domes and slender towers. Exploring the theater's many mosque-like alcoves, he could easily imagine himself on an expedition in Egypt, in search of some ancient lost pyramid.

Ron knew that the stars winking in the auditorium's night sky were nothing more than tiny light bulbs embedded in the arched, indigo-painted ceiling, and that the drifting clouds were produced by a special projector. He also knew the quickest way to maneuver a young female horizontal was to start with a romantic evening under the balcony's huge Bedouin canopy.

It wasn't often that the Simpson family went to the movies together anymore. There were few films Harold enjoyed since westerns had lost their popularity. These days, he preferred his evening newspaper to the silver screen. Carlotta refused to allow her sons to choose movies after they took her to see *The Blob*, citing sharp differences in aesthetic tastes.

But tonight was an exception. The family had driven into Atlanta together to see the new John Wayne movie, *The Green Berets*, as a Christmas present for Harold.

No one had the slightest doubt who Harold's favorite star was. In the family den, a faded *Flying Leathernecks* movie still, featuring John Wayne in military pilot's gear, was framed on the wall. Beside it was a photo of an eighteen-year-old Harold Simpson as a World War II Marine Corps aerial gunner in a SBD3 Dauntless Dive Bomber.

"When John Wayne hits 'em, they stay hit," Harold noted, holding open the LTD's passenger door for his wife. "Not like Rowdy Yates in those spaghetti movies."

Harold was talking about Clint Eastwood, who had played a character named Rowdy in *Rawhide* before moving on to Italian "spaghetti" westerns. Harold insisted on calling him Rowdy, which was his way of letting everyone know that he considered Eastwood little more than a television actor.

"Wayne never did TV," Harold would say proudly. "He was always too big for the little screen."

Michael knew it wouldn't be productive to mention that the Duke had guested on "I Love Lucy." In the episode, Lucy discovered that the cement slab with John Wayne's footprints in front of Grauman's Chinese Theater had come loose, and she and Ethel decide to heist it.

The relative merits of these two cinematic bastions of masculinity—Wayne and Eastwood—were slowly driving yet another wedge into the widening generation gap. To many teenagers, the Duke seemed dated. Clint's "Man With No Name" persona was now the rage for young males looking for a jolt of testosterone.

The Duke's latest movie, which glorified the military action in Vietnam, weighed heavy on Ron's mind as they drove home.

"Dad? Can I ask you something?" Ron began, hesitantly.

"'Course."

"Why are we at war with Vietnam?"

"It's not a war; it's a *police action*," Michael interjected, proud to show that he kept up in social studies class.

"But we're the most powerful country in the world, and Vietnam is this small, little country. How come we're not winnin' this war?" Ron pressed.

"*Police action*," Michael corrected.

"If the politicians would let the military do what it needs to do, we could win the war," Harold said with certainty.

"So it *is* a war, then?"

Carlotta shot a worried glance at Ron. She generally stayed out of these types of conversations, but she had a keen sense for recognizing when the yellow flags were going up during one of their father–son talks.

"It don't matter what it's called," Harold responded, a sharper edge in his voice. "If the military gets sent someplace, you can rest assured there's a good reason."

"But how do they decide if it's a good enough reason?"

"We put people in office because they're supposed to make those decisions so we can get on with our lives. President Johnson's the man that made that decision. Come January, a new man will have that job."

"Did you *want* Johnson to send all those troops to Vietnam?"

"Can't say as I did. But even if I don't see eye to eye with the president on everything, it's still our country, and it's our duty to support the war."

"Even if no one can explain *why* we're fighting?"

Ron knew from the tightening of Harold's jaw that his father was troubled by his questions. Ron looked away, unwilling to pursue the discussion further. Something dark and solemn had entered into an otherwise pleasant family evening.

Harold drove the rest of the way home in silence. Ron knew his father wanted to ask him why he had become so interested in the war, although he wasn't sure his dad was ready to hear the answer.

A few nights later, Harold got the answer to his unspoken question anyway.

When the weather turned cooler, and late autumn nights called for long sleeves and coats, Carlotta Simpson was fond of cooking beef stew from scratch. She'd cut up a chuck roast and drop it into a deep boiler with the last of the summer's carrots, pole beans, and Vidalia onions.

The Simpson family seated themselves at the table and joined hands in prayer. Then everybody dove into the meal. Normally beef stew's biggest fan, Ron picked and poked listlessly at his food.

"You're awfully quiet tonight, sweetheart. Is anything the matter?" Carlotta asked.

"M'fine," Ron half-answered. He helped himself to another bite of stew, in the hope that a mouthful of food might discourage further questions.

"When's Alex reporting for his induction, son?" Harold inquired.

"Day after tomorrow."

"Oh, poor Ginger. It's so close to the holidays," Carlotta sighed in a half-whisper.

Ron glanced at his mother and father. "And I'm gonna be right behind him."

Blood drained from Carlotta's cheeks. Michael studied his plate. Harold put down his fork, and cleared his throat.

"Son, I don't know if that'd be the smartest idea."

"Why not? You served your country. Now it's my turn."

The rest of the family sat in a frozen tableau, waiting for Harold's response.

"Why don't we talk outside?" He rose from the table and strode out the sliding glass door in the den without a backward glance. Ron joined him a moment later.

Harold settled himself at the picnic table as Ron sat uneasily on the edge of the wooden bench. The restless, cool air had swept out the lingering tang of jet fuel that the summer heat sometimes trapped in the backyard. But it also brought the low rumble of jets on final approach to Atlanta into sharper focus. Year 'round, it now seemed you were either smelling the airport or hearing it.

Harold inhaled the Georgia night the way he'd once inhaled his after-dinner cigarettes. Ron knew his father never spoke hastily. His teaspoon of words always held a tubful of thought.

"Son, you're smart as a whip, and you're fair-minded," Harold began in measured tones. "Any kind of injustice or mean-spiritedness rides you clean off your rails." Harold glanced at his son for a moment, then looked away. "You also think too much and know too little. I'm not sure if that mix adds up to a military man."

Ron understood that whenever his father pictured his elder son striding forth to meet his future, it was in an academic's cap and gown, never a soldier's helmet and fatigues.

"What kind of Simpson would I be if I didn't serve my country? You were a patriot in two wars. Heck, the family's been fighting one conflict or another all the way back to . . ."

An unspoken word hung between them, weighing them both down. *Kennesaw.* Ron knew that the family's Civil War scars proved William Faulkner's dictum that *"In the south, the past isn't dead . . . it isn't even the past."*

"I know in my heart it's right for me," Ron started again evenly.

"We Southerners got it bred into us that it's our job to fight for our country. I'll grant you that," Harold said, then looked straight at his son. "But I'm just not sure you're cut out for the military."

"Jesus, Dad, is that all the faith you have in me?"

"Faith's got nothing to do with it, son. Combat changes a man in a thousand different ways, none of 'em good. You have no idea . . ." Harold's voice died.

Ron let his father's words breathe for a moment. "There are no good wars. Isn't that what you always say?"

There was a long silence between them. Then Harold spoke quietly, "I thought you didn't understand this war or why we're fighting it, anyway."

"I'm not sure that I do, but I love my country—and that's what matters. You always say that when your country calls, you answer."

"Yes, I taught you that, same as my father taught me, and his father taught him. But son, you haven't been called. You got a high draft number. There's no chance of being drafted."

"You didn't wait to be drafted. Why should I? If the President says it's the right war, shouldn't that be good enough for me? He's the Commander-in-Chief."

Harold's words were being thrown at him. His discomfort showed.

"I was hoping you'd get your education and have more of an opportunity . . ." His words stopped short.

Than I did.

Ron could hear the rest of the sentence as plainly as if his father had spoken it. The man had left home at fourteen during the Great Depression to keep his brothers and sisters from starving, enlisted in the Marine Corps at seventeen, and was overseas fighting for his country by eighteen. He wanted something more for his sons.

Ron knew that no matter how much he argued for his own decision, his father would feel the guilt, as if he'd snatched the college diploma out of his son's hands and given him a military assault rifle.

"The Army recruiter gave me a flight aptitude test. He said I should be able to qualify for Rotary Wing Aviator School. After training, I'll be a warrant officer. The pay's good, and when I come out, I'll be able to get my commercial pilot's license."

Carlotta appeared at the screen door, teary eyed and tremulous. "You two want coffee or pie?"

"No thank you, mama."

Carlotta closed the screen door. Harold fixed his boy with a grim, sad look.

"I can't tell you what to do. You're too old for that. But I want you to know that you don't have to die in Vietnam to be my son." Harold's somber words fell hard between them. "I hope you'll think about that before you make your decision."

Ron spoke into the cool darkness, "It's done already. I signed the papers this morning. My induction date's next month."

Chapter 12

June 25, 1864

BEFORE DAWN, VIRGIL GATHERED his tools, took Elon's shotgun, and walked to the small family graveyard. It was a plot on a rise at the edge of a pasture, so it had been turned and cleared for years. It would dig easy.

Of course, easy still meant he had a hard morning's work. Then he needed to build a small coffin with the pine planks he had brought from Elon's farm.

It would be a simple pine box. His people never made a fuss over things like caskets. It made no sense to bury the dead in a fancy wood box when they were being returned to the earth and their soul was with Jesus in heaven.

He busted the soil with a long-handled mattock and shoveled it out, repeating the process over and over. As he fell into the rhythm of it, he concentrated on his work and tried to forget the troubles of his family and the whole world as he knew it.

The sun came up and warmed his shoulders, and he was content. He liked work. That was how he had first earned the respect of his father, whose esteem he treasured above all else.

His mama joked that if he wasn't careful, he'd be a grown man in a few years. He thought to himself that it would only be true if the war didn't get him. He knew war made boys into men real fast. He could already feel the years he had aged these last days.

※

Permelia stirred with first light, but waited awhile before rousing Terissa. She didn't want the girl to wake up alone, but there were chores to do. Finally, she figured it was time.

"Terissa, darlin'." Permelia spoke softly, hoping to ease her daughter awake, but she woke with a start.

It took only a moment for Terissa's troubles to return.

"I need to check on the chickens. You want to come with me?"

"Yes, ma'am." She shook off the sleep, stretched, stood up, and smoothed out her stained dress.

It made Permelia feel old to see how quickly her daughter recovered from a night's sleep on a pallet on the ground.

They walked to the ruins of the house. Coals still gave off heat, but mostly everything that could burn had burned.

Permelia didn't want to think about all she had lost. She would have been devastated even if Melissa hadn't also been taken from her, but her bereavement for the child made everything else seem trivial. Still, she knew it would take a long time before they could live in comfort.

The chickens had gone back to the henhouse and were patiently waiting to be fed. They probably had spent the night roosting in the trees, but hunger or habit brought them home. She counted a dozen. They were all there.

She found one egg deposited in the box beneath their perch. She thought they might be put off from laying for awhile because of the all of the excitement, but was surprised to find three more eggs in the yard. She gave the four to Terissa.

"You might look around, see if you can find any more. I'm going to see what I can find of use in the house." Her home wasn't much more than a pile of cinders, but she thought she might be able to salvage a few things.

She picked up a beanpole from a pile next to the clothesline. The line was stretched between two small oaks, but when it was heavy with wet clothes, she would use a pole with a small notch in the end to hold it up in the middle so the clothes wouldn't touch the ground.

She stepped into the ruins, pushing hot embers out of the way with the pole, and made her way to where the kitchen had been. The iron stove had fallen through the floor and was covered with debris from the collapsed roof, sheets of scorched tin, a few lengths of roof beams. She pushed them aside.

The stove appeared to be whole. Maybe it was warped and would leak smoke, but she imagined Baylis could fix that. He could fix most anything.

She prodded with the beanpole and hit something solid, then pushed the cinders and ash aside. *Well, look at this,* she thought.

"Terissa, I found our iron pots and fry pans, that big serving spoon, and the cleaver, too. It will need a new handle."

"I found us another egg," Terissa said, stepping carefully into the debris and cinders. She stopped and stared at the spot where she had been raped. It was now little more than black soot. She turned away quietly.

Virgil smelled ham and eggs cooking on his mother's open fire. He was hungry, but didn't have any time to lose. He would eat after the burial.

It wasn't yet noon, but the sun had climbed in the sky when Virgil finished digging. The grave still had to be deep enough that no animal could dig it up. He added a bit to the ends so he would have room to stand in the hole and have use of the tools. They couldn't lower the coffin with ropes either, with only two people. Terissa might be unable to help, since she seemed to be drifting in and out of a great stupor.

He didn't want to think about that. Instead, he threw the mattock and shovel up over the grave's edge, then scampered out and walked back to the house. Permelia saw him and waved.

"Going to the barn to make a coffin," Virgil shouted. It seemed odd to be yelling something like that. Talk of death was usually conducted in muted tones. But Permelia was far off and couldn't have heard a hushed voice. The past couple days had caused a lot of confusion, he thought.

Virgil wasn't a sophisticated carpenter, but he built simple and practical things well. With a saw, a hammer and nails, and the pine lumber from his uncle's farm, he built a tight and sturdy box-shaped coffin. It would last awhile, something short of eternity, but as long as Melissa needed to shelter her little body.

It made no sense to carry the casket, so he put the mule's tack on and hitched it to the wagon. He put the coffin in the flatbed and gave Betty a "giddy-yap." She pulled the wagon at a walk to the table under the oak tree where Melissa's body lay.

Permelia and Terissa had gathered flowers, wild herbs, and rabbit tobacco to decorate the coffin and stifle the smell of death. Melissa had lain without cooling in the summer heat, so it was time for her to be buried.

He noticed that his sister had changed out of her blood-stained dress and was now wearing a collared shirt and buttoned trousers, some of the clothes that Elon had provided. It seemed a might peculiar, but not more so than anything else these days. He wondered what his father would think.

Virgil retrieved the coffin from the wagon and placed it on the bench next to the table. Permelia peeled back the blanket that covered Melissa. Their faces tightened. The girl who had once looked lost in an innocent sleep now had dark, sunken eye sockets and parchment skin.

Permelia delicately rubbed Melissa's skin with a damp cloth.

"You want to make a pallet with the blanket in the coffin, Ma?" Virgil asked.

"It was the child's favorite. I reckon it should go with her to the hereafter."

"I'll pick her up, and you can pull out the blanket." Virgil lifted Melissa and held her close. "She's so light," he said to no one in particular.

Permelia folded the blanket in the coffin to make a pallet and to hold Melissa in place so she wouldn't roll around. Virgil laid her down, and then he and Permelia lifted the coffin and placed it on the table.

Permelia arranged the flowers and plants, then took a deep breath to settle her thoughts. Terissa watched her mother with a dull-eyed gaze.

"Melissa was the sweetest little girl I ever saw since my Terissa. And I know Jesus loves His little children. And God is smart. Just look around at all the things He made. So He knows what a precious child she was. That's why I know Melissa is up in heaven. And I know she's looking down on us and wondering why we are so sad, her being in a better place and all. I know she wants us to be happy for her."

Together they recited the Lord's Prayer. Then Permelia read passages from the family Bible that Baylis had Elon mark years ago for such occasions. She had heard them read so many times of late that she knew them all by heart.

Then she prayed, "Lord, please take care of my grandbaby Melissa up there in heaven and have mercy on those of us who are left down here in our veil of tears. We will miss her smile as long as we gather breath. We are in a hard time, so please grant our enemies compassion and mercy and us wisdom and courage to do what we must. Amen."

Virgil responded, "Amen."

Terissa stepped forward, took the sharp knife, and silently began cutting her own hair, laying the trimmings into the casket beside Melissa's head. Permelia and Virgil understood: *Simpson women never cut their hair from puberty until they were no longer maidens.*

Permelia's eyes pooled with tears. "Oh, sweetie," was all she could manage. She dabbed at the moisture with a cloth.

"Please don't do that, sister," Virgil said.

Terissa ignored him and continued. When there wasn't any long hair left to shorten, Terissa gave a subdued nod.

Virgil reverently hammered the top onto the coffin. When he finished, he and Permelia carried it to the wagon and slid it solemnly onto the back.

"Y'all want to ride or walk?" he asked.

"We will follow on behind as is custom," Permelia answered.

Terissa slumped, the weight of loss heavy on her face. The burden seemed too much.

Her mother pulled her daughter close. "Lean on me, sweetie. We are just going to walk our baby girl home."

Virgil got the mule to step slowly toward the burying ground, and the women followed.

As a cushion to their sorrow, God had offered a beautiful day to see Melissa off. Virgil silently gave thanks for the kindness and then began to hum "Bonnie Blue Flag" to himself. It wasn't much of a funeral song. It was just what came to mind.

Chapter 13

January 1969

UNTIL THE COLD, DAMP January morning Ron stepped onto a commercial jet at Atlanta's Hartsfield Airport for transport to Louisiana to begin basic training, he had never been in an airplane or traveled west of the Mississippi. His idea of military aviation came mostly from building model airplanes, watching war movies, and his father's own guarded reminiscences of combat as a Marine aerial gunner during the Second World War.

"*Welcome, soldier, to the United States Army. Stand proud!*"

Ron read the exhortation that greeted the recruits and draftees as they stepped off the bus in front of Fort Polk's Reception Station. The dark green oval billboard with bright orange letters, perfectly centered on a latticed, white wood fence, seemed upbeat, even cheerful in its own surreal way.

Squinting at the sign as he stood shivering in the cold rain, Ron suspected this was probably the most pleasant experience he would have for the foreseeable future.

The fort was named in honor of Leonidas Polk, the Episcopal clergyman who had picked up a sword to become the Confederate general known as the "Fighting Bishop." Ron thought it ironic that a U.S. military base was named for a rebel general killed during Sherman's Georgia campaign. He was sure Baylis Simpson would have seen the humor in it.

"Fort *Puke, Lousy-anna*," as it was known to the young men who stepped through its gates, was the principal U.S. Army infantry training facility for the Vietnam conflict. Signs—"fight, win" and "engage, destroy"—were everywhere to remind the men of their purpose. It was also where potential helicopter pilots like Ron were sent for basic training.

Even for Ron, a young man of nineteen in good shape, physical training, or "PT" as the drill sergeant called it, proved the most grueling experience imaginable. Under constant harassment from the instructors, he endured an endless series of forced marches, obstacle courses, and field maneuvers. Calisthenics routinely started at 5 a.m. in the field in front of the mess hall, where recruits would do a mile run before breakfast. Sit-ups and push-ups tallied into the hundreds each day. The only time the company wasn't marching was when they were running.

Ron knew the instructors' unrelenting insults were meant to weed out recruits who couldn't handle the intimidation and stress. A man unable to cope with a sergeant howling like a banshee a mere inch from his nose would never stay focused amid the chaos of combat.

To remain unrattled during the daily verbal assaults, Ron resorted to a mental trick his father had taught him from his own basic training on Parris Island, South Carolina, during World War II. "Just imagine the instructor standing in front of you yapping like a poodle is naked, and he's got the smallest dick you've ever seen, about the size of a Vienna sausage."

The mental image worked like magic. Ron never broke.

More nerve wracking for Ron were the close-formation drills. Novice recruits, many of whom had never held a weapon in their hands before, lined up one behind the other and marched with bayonets on their assault rifles.

"See that individual in front of you?" the drill instructor liked to shout. "If you lose control of your weapon, that individual is going to have a *significant* emotional experience!"

Ron felt more at ease on the rifle range. He had spent many winter Saturdays during his teen years hunting bobwhite quail in millet fields with his dad and his prized pointers Sport and Ramus, and he was used to the feel of a weapon in his hands. He was, like his father, a good marksman. Ron's scores were among the best in the platoon.

Not long after Ron's arrival at the base, his company was verbally assaulted in the mess hall by an ugly, large primate named Coogan, a misfit cook who had failed to make a rank higher than corporal after ten years in the army. Banging on a table with his meaty fist, the sweaty Neanderthal challenged any new trainee "straight leg" present to a fight. There were no takers, although Ron knew that Alex would have gotten in the man's face had he been there.

A few weeks later, Coogan was court-martialed for having "unlawful sexual intercourse" with a dead chicken he was preparing for the company's evening meal. (Was there a *lawful* type of intercourse with a chicken, Ron wondered?) For the offense, Coogan was busted back down to private, but, much to the chagrin of the recruits, he was *not* relieved of his kitchen duties.

Despite this grossly unappetizing situation, Ron soon discovered that most any food tasted good, no matter how questionably prepared, if you were hungry enough. And after hours of unrelenting physical demands each day, he was always ravenous.

During meals, recruits were required to sit at attention at their table, take a bite of food together on command, and chew it the exact number of times the sergeant instructed them. Missing a bite or having an eating utensil improperly placed resulted in demerits and kitchen duty.

The time spent in boot camp seemed more like months than weeks, but soon Ron was in the best physical condition of his life. His once sinewy and boyish body was now muscular and rock solid.

The first time Ron realized just how much strength he had gained was during a close-combat drill with "pugil sticks," three-foot-long padded poles. As his platoon stood in a loose circle in the white sand, Ron and an opponent squared off in the center, each wearing a helmet with face guard, thick gloves, and a crotch protector on the outside of their khaki pants. Wielding the pugil sticks with two hands like a rifle, the gladiators stood back to back and took five paces. Turning at the sound of the instructor's whistle, they began sparring, each man trying to deliver "death blows" for points.

Ron had parried several thrusts by his larger adversary when he found an opening and lunged his pugil stick forcefully into the man's chest, knocking his opponent down hard onto the ground. The blow left the trainee dazed and writhing in pain. As the sergeant blew his whistle and roared his approval, Ron felt only regret for the misery he had caused.

One night, about five weeks into boot camp, Ron was able to put his strength to better use. His company was tasked with a live-fire infiltration course, followed by a forced ten-mile march with sixty-pound backpacks deep into Fort Polk's 198,000 acres. Whenever the drill instructor thought that the recruits weren't trying hard enough, he would order them to raise their assault rifles above their heads as they "double-timed." The sustained effort was crippling to men already exhausted.

A sandy-haired recruit named Jack, running beside Ron, began to falter and teeter. Seeing that Jack had reached his breaking point, Ron reached out and grabbed the young man's arm to steady him and offer support.

"You don't want those guys in back of us to run over you!" Ron said between labored breaths, indicating another platoon just yards behind them. Ron held the man up for the last mile of the run. When the company reached bivouac, Ron released the soldier's arm and Jack collapsed onto the ground. The exhausted man weakly nodded his thanks.

Drenched in stinking sweat and caked with dirt, Ron could barely stand to be in the same tent with himself. But he had never felt more proud. The experience had crystallized his thoughts: *he was now certain what he wanted to do in the military. He wanted to serve his country, not by killing, but by helping his fellow soldiers.*

Ron Simpson wanted to be a medical evacuation pilot.

Chapter 14

Summoning Lazarus
June 25, 1864

AFTER SLIPPING THROUGH THE Yankee lines, it didn't make sense to get shot by the Confederate Army of Tennessee, so the plan was to give the right flank of Joe Johnston's rebel line a wide birth. With a little luck, the Simpson men could work their way around the graycoats entrenched along the crest of Kennesaw Mountain and off to the south.

Once Elon was sure they were out of the reach of Sherman's cavalry pickets, he stopped the wagon by a small creek swollen with the heavy spring rains.

"Lazarus, come forth!" he yelled.

"'Bout damn time." A muffled shout came from beneath the corpses. It was Baylis.

Climbing down from the wagon, Elon rolled the bodies aside until he freed Baylis and Ulysses. "Just remember this time in hell as a reason to be one with the Lord," he said.

"This war has provided more lessons in the disadvantages of hell than I require," Ulysses lamented.

"'Bout all I can say for your plan, brother, is that it worked," Baylis added sourly. "But I reckon it's better to lay with corpses than to be one."

The men knew that to be true. They also knew they could join the ranks of the heavenly army most any time. That went without saying.

"I suspect there is plenty of burying being done behind the Confederate lines in Marietta. We should go there and tend to these dead, then you can join the lines," Elon said.

"I'm 'bout played out," Baylis said. "It would be nice to stretch my legs and wash this stench off."

"We should move on," Ulysses protested. "I'm due back to my regiment."

Baylis knew Ulysses was determined to join the fight as soon as possible. "I suspect the fightin' can wait the afternoon."

"I never knew fightin' that couldn't," Elon affirmed.

The men removed the horses from the wagon and let them drink from the creek and rest. Baylis and his son tried to wash off the charnel odor with little success, while Elon scavenged watercress from along the creek's muddy bank.

At the water's edge, Baylis caught his reflection in the stream. The streaks of Melissa's blood were still etched across his forehead. He hoped the soul of his granddaughter was in a better place, though in truth the retribution had brought only justice, not consolation. He splashed water on his face and solemnly washed the red stains away.

The creek bank was strewn with items that had been discarded by refugees fleeing the fighting. Iron pots, knapsacks filled with personal belongings, even an upright piano dotted the muddy clay soil, keepsakes of broken lives now forever lost.

One family treasure held Baylis's eye, a child's battledore "reading book." Baylis picked up the thin, rectangle cardboard that was folded in thirds. The battledore reminded him of one that he had made as a present for Melissa's birthday. The thought brought a heavy sadness to his already troubled heart.

"I thought you might have need of this." Ulysses was holding a Griswold & Gunnison .36 caliber pistol and ammunition. "It's right nice. I found it along the creek bed."

Baylis nodded and accepted the pistol, slipping it into the waist of his trousers.

Hitching the horses once more, Elon eased the wagon forward with a shake of the reins, with Baylis and Ulysses now sitting beside him. After the passage through the bleeding edge of the fighting, the countryside behind Kennesaw seemed oddly serene. Smoke poured from the cook fires of some farmhouses; other homes appeared deserted.

A column of Southern cavalry trotted toward them on the road, their gear secured and muffled. They seemed quiet compared to the jangling Yankee horsemen. Too many days of fighting and too little food and shelter showed on their faces. They looked like drowned rats, but tough as the head of an axe.

Elon waved his white flag at the approaching riders. As the soldiers identified the wagon's dreadful cargo, first by smell, then by sight, their faces turned somber.

A captain in dusty butternut on a light-colored mount pulled beside them, and Elon stopped the rig. With a smooth complexion and ruddy cheeks, the captain looked too young to shave. From the way the man was scratching his scalp, Elon thought he must have head lice.

"What in heaven's name!" the captain said loudly.

"I'm a minister of the Gospel, bringing our dead home," Elon shouted, as was his custom whenever he mentioned the Holy Book.

"Lord have mercy, Reverend, I would know you're telling the truth by the smell that blows before you." The captain winced at the stench.

"These two live ones," Elon continued, nodding to this brother and nephew, "are intent on joining the fight."

The captain stopped scratching. "You men must have wanted to get in the fight pretty bad to ride with a cart full of the dead."

"It was the only ride that presented itself as a way through the Yankee lines," Baylis said.

The men laughed at the thought of it.

"Where are you men coming from?"

"We crossed the railroad north of Big Shanty," Baylis said.

"How did you get past the bluecoats?"

"My boy and I hid beneath the bodies. My brother, being a man of God, drove the rig."

"We got stopped by the doodles just north of Big Shanty," Elon announced proudly.

"And the Yanks let you pass?" The captain seemed puzzled by the thought.

"They had plenty of dead already. Didn't seem to mind if we took some," Elon said.

"At Big Shanty, what did you see?"

"More men, food, and powder than I ever thought could exist. It's like they moved the whole north there," Baylis said.

"Damnation, we heard the Yankees was starving." The officer shook his head in amazement.

"Maybe starving for home, but they ain't starving for food. Least not anymore," Elon said.

"I reckon once Sherman's boys got out of the mountains and reconnected with the railroad, supplying the Yanks got a mite easier," Ulysses said.

"Maybe they'll lose their belly to fight on a full stomach," the captain said. "Where you boys headed?"

"To see to the dead, then my boy and I are headed to Kennesaw," Baylis said.

"Head on up this road about five miles, and you'll see The Georgia Military Institute. There's a sign at the gate, a big building, and a dozen barracks. The cemetery is two hundred yards north. You can walk to the square. There are wagons heading to the lines from there."

Elon got the team shuffling with a snap of the reins. The wagon creaked as it built momentum.

The officer spurred his horse to a strong gait and led his men forward. Elon waved to the men as the troops passed the wagon.

"God bless you all. See you boys at the pearly gates."

"What we saw at Big Shanty, that really isn't good news," Ulysses said after the cavalry had disappeared behind them.

"'Bout all we can do is fight for our homes and pray someone gets sick of the killing and comes to their senses."

"Hasn't happened yet," Elon said. "And it seems like there are a lot of Yankees. We could trade 'em dead for dead, and they'd come out the winner."

They had traveled for an hour, and as homesteads became more frequent, they began expecting the military school.

Ahead they saw an older woman with wispy white hair and a prim appearance standing in the open gate of the untidy rail fence that lined the road. She waved a handkerchief in their direction.

"Any news of the fighting?" she yelled. She caught the odor of their cargo and turned away, her body convulsing in a gag.

Baylis had become accustomed to the intolerable smell. He knew it must be unbearable for her. She recovered and looked back towards them, forcing cheer.

"I have some cornbread for passing soldiers. You must be hungry."

"Don't trouble yourself ma'am. You needn't come any closer. This ain't a pleasant load we're carrying." Baylis said.

She walked toward them briskly, covering her nose with her handkerchief.

"I know they are our dead. One of them could be my son. I appreciate you doing this."

"A Christian burial is the least we can do, madam," Elon proclaimed in his booming, Pentecostal voice.

She handed them a large square of aromatic cornbread. Elon took it, quickly blessed it "to the nourishment of our bodies, amen," and broke it into three pieces. The men were too hungry to be polite. They ate like starving dogs.

"This here's delicious," Ulysses said through a mouthful. "Thank you for your kindness."

"Are we close to the Military Institute?" Baylis asked.

"It's a half-mile yonder up the road. But you won't be finding no one there. Governor Brown done sent all those children off to fight the Yankees." She stifled a sigh. "It's a dreadful thing. Some of those boys couldn't have been more than fourteen."

So children were now fighting the war? It made Baylis think of his own young son. He could still see the frightened look in Virgil's eyes when he had placed the musket in the boy's hands. It was a gloomy thought, one more that Baylis did not need.

Chapter 15

February 1969

BY THE TIME RON begin flight training at Fort Wolters in Mineral Wells, Texas, more than 20,000 students had already completed the five-month program. To meet the needs of the military in Vietnam, the U.S. Army Primary Helicopter School was graduating rotary-wing aviators at the rate of five hundred a month. By 1969, Fort Wolters had become the largest flight training facility in the history of aviation, and Vietnam had become "America's helicopter war."

North Texas was unlike anything Warrant Officer Candidate Ron Simpson had imagined from reading Zane Grey novels in high school. For one thing, it was damn cold, regularly dropping below freezing at night during the winter months. Even snow wasn't uncommon.

Then there was the countryside around the massive base. Instead of the arid, flat plains and scrub brush Ron had expected, he found the hilly landscape beyond the camp dotted with clumps of blackjack oak, box elder and sumac. The view was spectacular when the raw light of morning leaned against the Palo Pinto Mountains, nestled like inverted snow cones in the distance beyond the Brazos River.

Leaving behind the constant misery of basic training, Ron arrived at Fort Wolters full of excitement at the prospect of beginning his flight instruction. Although it was common knowledge that only a portion of those who began flight school would end up with aviator wings, Ron was convinced beyond any doubt he would be one of them.

Immediately upon arrival at Fort Wolters, Ron and his fellow "WOCs" found a new species of monkey on their backs, the Training And Counseling Officer. A TAC officer addressed a warrant officer candidate simply as "candidate," although it seemed to Ron that it always came out sounding like "*candy*-date."

Training officers understood the grim reality that these aspiring rotary pilots would soon face "in country" and wanted to make sure that every aviator was properly trained and "good to go." That meant, among other things, disabusing all candidates of the notion of being a "*he . . . row,*" as the TACs derisively slurred the word. Army aviation was about teamwork, they stressed repeatedly, not hotshot flyboys.

Ron's first weeks at Fort Wolters were filled studying navigation, the theory of flight, and the principles of rotary-wing aircraft under the demanding tutelage of the TAC officers.

"Brace the wall, *candy*-date Simpson," a training officer would bellow at the slightest mistake or infraction of rules. Ron would spring to the wall, chin tucked in, shoulders back. "All parts of your body better be against that wall, *candy*-date."

One of the most common infractions was not having a shoelace tied or tucked away in the proper military fashion. "Do I see a fuse in your boot, *candy*-date?" the officer would roar, looking at the dangling lace. Demerits would follow, and then the humiliation of being issued "technical equipment," usually a rake, shovel, or broom, to work off the infraction.

After four weeks of preflight "ground school," Ron moved up to "the hill," the base area where students began flying rotorcraft under the close supervision of an instructor pilot. Ron loved the experience. There was nothing like the exhilaration he felt the first time he lifted off in a helicopter. Nothing had ever felt that good in his life, not even sex with Cindy Kockenlocker in the tenth grade.

Ron trained primarily in the OH-13 "Sioux," the same aircraft he and Michael has seen featured in *Whirly Bird*. The helicopter had two seats, one for the instructor pilot and one for the trainee. His instructor was a crusty, middle-aged pilot named Brice, a staunch Goldwater conservative. Brice liked to boast that he prayed nightly for God to miraculously anoint as U.S. President General Curtis LeMay, the legendary "Mad Bomber" lampooned as the insane General Jack D. Ripper in *Dr. Strangelove*.

Brice, who had served in Korea as a helicopter pilot, had two fingers missing from the middle of his left hand, a souvenir of his combat experience. He was often grumpy and mean-spirited, but his skill and knowledge gave him impeccable training credentials.

Ron quickly discovered that while helicopters were incredibly versatile craft, they were also very unforgiving. Just hovering the beast was like balancing on a large ball while simultaneously juggling bananas and drinking a beer. Ron learned the meaning of the word "coordination" as he struggled with the right and left pedals, the collective stick in his left hand and cyclic stick in his right.

The learning curve for the student pilots was steep, endless, and at times, deadly. A few weeks into training, there was a midair collision between two helicopters over the Holiday Inn in downtown Mineral Wells, killing two instructors and two trainees. Parts of the aircraft plummeted into the hotel's pool, which was fortunately empty of guests at the time owing to the cold weather.

In the weeks that followed, there were other collisions. Student aviators made so many hard landings that the Dempsey Heliport maintenance hanger worked three shifts around the clock to keep the training craft operational. Fort Wolters Hospital and its medevac helicopters did fire-sale business.

The first great test that a student pilot must pass during training was the solo flight—the first time flying without his instructor pilot in the cockpit.

The May morning broke clear and sunny for Ron's first solo venture, with light wind, no clouds, and visibility stretching for forty miles. All good omens, he thought, as he arrived at the Main Heliport, helmet and gear in hand. He was so nervous he felt like he had just finished off a bottle of the "Laxative Water" from the nearby town of Mineral Wells.

Walking out to the helipad, Ron couldn't recall a single thing Brice had taught him. The butterflies in his stomach had scrubbed his mind clean. Not a sentence or even a word remained. But at that exact moment, there was one thing and only one thing Ron knew with absolute certainty: he wanted to *fly*.

After a thorough preflight inspection, Ron filled out his logbook, then climbed into the aircraft cockpit with Brice and flew out to Stagefield Two, code-named "Sundance."

Brice stepped out and fixed Ron with a hard look. "If you goddamn crash, don't come whining to me. Call your mama and tell her about it." He shut the cockpit door. That was about as pleasant as it ever got with Brice.

On that cheerful note, Candidate Simpson taxied out, took off, and single-handedly slipped the surly bonds of Fort Wolters. He flew downwind, crosswind, and landed, then repeated the sequence twice more. In twenty minutes, it was all over. He had conquered gravity and cheated death. His face hurt from grinning.

Brice and another instructor pilot stormed from the tower like they were spring-loaded and headed toward the helicopter.

"Get the hell outta my aircraft, *candy*-date Simpson," Brice barked. There was a tough glint in his eyes.

Ron immediately unstrapped and climbed out, wondering what the hell he had done wrong. His mind flipped through the hundreds of rules and regulations that had been hammered into him. *Which one had he violated?*

Brice and the other instructor pilot jerked Ron up by his flight suit, carried him to a muddy water hole, and unceremoniously dumped him into it.

"Not bad for a dumb shit," Brice said. It was the only time Ron could remember the old bulldog actually smiling.

Ron pulled himself out. Brice shook his hand and presented him with his pair of solo wings. Then his instructor scribbled into Ron's logbook the prettiest sentence he would ever read: *"Candidate Ron Simpson did this day perform solo and unaided flight in the OH-13."*

Chapter 16

May 1969

DRIVING DOWN RIVERDALE ROAD on the opening Saturday at Pinerock Lake, it seemed to Michael as though only weeks had passed since they opened the lake for last season, with Alex at the helm as head lifeguard. Yet so much had changed.

The news had been full of chaos all year. Despite Nixon's election, unrest over the war and other social upheavals continued. In March, James Earl Ray had pleaded guilty to the murder of Martin Luther King, Jr., and a month later, Abbie Hoffman and the rest of "The Chicago Eight" were arraigned after the mayhem of the Democratic Convention.

Nothing seemed immune to bedlam and change. His brother and best friend had been hundreds of miles away for the last six months. While Michael fretted over algebra exams and edited the school paper with his friend Kathy Perkowski, Ron was breathing in rotor wash and copter fuel, and praying he'd win his cherished wings. The family had only seen Ron twice during that time.

Michael had seen little of Alex either during those months, but he was certain that his friend was raising his own inimitable brand of hell in the Army Ranger School at Fort Benning in Columbus, Georgia.

When Alex did come home, he was still Alex, energized by a million volts of cynical charm, with a drop-dead squint straight from the Fuck You School of Hard Knocks. No one did cool better than Alex Granger.

Michael marveled at the speed with which the year had charged by. Like the Dixie Flyer, his senior year had signaled its approach long in advance, seemed to take forever to arrive, then suddenly roared past all at once and was gone, leaving him stunned and breathless.

Grandpa Melvin Simpson had warned him that the older you get, the quicker each year would pass. At this rate, Michael expected to find himself celebrating his eightieth birthday sometime next month.

Most of last year's lifeguards would be back: himself, his pals Kenny and Wanker from Forest Park High, and, of course, Diane. But one thing would set this summer in a whole different league from last year: *Alex wouldn't be there to lead them.*

Mr. Andrews would name the new head guard for the season before opening this morning, and Michael certainly hoped that it would be him. But driving his motorcycle toward the lake, Michael knew the rustling in the pit of his stomach wasn't caused by ol' man Andrews's impending decision. It came from imagining how a year's worth of maturing might have changed Diane.

It didn't take Michael long to learn what a difference the year had made. As he pulled up into the gravel lot, he could see Diane sitting on top of a picnic table under the trees, reading a paperback. Her once-rebellious hair was now swept back neatly along round shoulders. Her long limbs had willowed, and her body had taken on a series of voluptuous curves that left Michael mesmerized.

He cut his engine off and kicked down the stand. He wanted to say something to her, anything, but her beauty left him tongue-tied. All he could manage was a wave.

Mr. Andrews was nowhere in sight. After a few moments of goofing off with Kenny and Wanker, Michael took the initiative to organize a brigade to rake the algae off the lake's sandy bottom near the water's edge.

As the guards trundled across the grass toward the beach, rakes in hand, Diane paused to remove her cotton tee. Michael glanced back in time to see her pull the shirt over her head, revealing a new form-fitting one-piece swimsuit, through which Michael fancied he could just make out the silhouettes of her nipples. It brought to mind the Roxanne Swimsuit ad he had seen: *"Some girls have developed a lot more than just their minds."* Michael was so enthralled he almost stumbled over his own feet, and it took him a moment to realize Kenny was talking to him.

"Graduation's in four weeks," Kenny was saying, "I was thinkin' after the season ends here, we oughta go to Daytona Beach, get jobs as lifeguards down there."

Diane caught up to the boys. The crew lined up at the water's edge, waiting for the next song to boom out on the jukebox.

"I can't," Michael replied. "I got a letter from the University of Georgia yesterday. I was accepted."

Kenny's eyes went wide. "No way! That's too cool, man!"

"Way to go, Simpson!" Wanker chimed in.

"You're going to college?" Diane asked.

"Is that hard to believe or somethin'?" Michael's nervousness around Diane made him feel defensive. She went to Hilltop Academy, a private school. It was an established fact that Hilltop girls didn't date guys from Forest Park, whom they considered their social and educational inferiors.

"No, not at all," Diane said flatly, sounding slightly stung. "It's just I'm going to UGA this fall, too."

"Really?" Michael tried to hide his delight. "That's great."

On the lake's PA system, the opening organ riff of "Do Wah Diddy Diddy" kicked in, followed quickly by Manfred Mann's acrid wailing, *"There she was, just walking down the street . . ."*

In unison, the guards began to rake the algae and sweep it gently toward deeper water.

Wanker, overexcited as usual, was babbling. "So, I wonder who'll be head guard this year, now that Alex's gone?"

"I bet Shaky will give it to you." Kenny flicked an eyebrow towards Michael. "Shaky" was the nickname Kenny had given Mr. Andrews because of tremors the old man got when he wasn't drinking.

"Why Michael?" Diane's tone was brittle. "I've been here almost as long he has."

"Yeah, guarding the kiddie pool. That don't count," Michael said.

"*Doesn't*. Doesn't count," Diane interjected sharply. "Didn't they teach you anything at Forest Park?"

"Not all of us can afford to go to some rich school," Michael replied testily, embarrassed to be corrected by her.

"Hilltop's not a rich school," Diane protested, her annoyance rising. "It's a private school—"

"—that rich people send their kids to," Michael insisted.

"I'm out here working with you dweebs. Does this look like my folks are rich?"

He watched her eyes light up. Somehow, she was even prettier when she was a little pissed.

"Like your dad can't afford college. That's a load." Now, all at once, he saw angry tears welling in her baby blues.

"Maybe he doesn't wanna pay for me to go, okay?"

Michael knew he'd hit a nerve. His own awkwardness had made him say something stupid, but it was too late to take it back.

Kenny moved in to smooth things over. "Hey, hey. It's our first day. You guys know the rule. No arguments until Day Two. Anyway, I got a better idea. Why don't I be head guard?"

Michael shot Kenny a glance that could burn asbestos.

Thirty minutes later, having finished with the algae, the guards turned to cleaning up the winter's leaves and debris off the beach. The conversation had cooled as the rhythm of work picked up.

"Heads up," Wanker groaned, breaking the silence. "Here comes Shaky."

"That's *Mister* Shaky to you, numb nuts," Kenny laughed.

Michael looked up to see the resort owner trudging unsteadily across the sand. He had seen Mr. Andrews walk this way before, gingerly, as though the slightest misstep would cause his head to explode. He couldn't read the ol' man's eyes through his dark sunglasses, but the unshaven stubble on his chin was clear evidence of another bender.

"I want the sand on the beach fluffed up this morning before we open," Mr. Andrews said, stopping in front of them. He glanced at Michael. "Do you remember how to use the tractor?"

"Yes, sir," Michael replied, silently hoping he did.

"Good." He gave the guards a brief inspection. The set of his mouth revealed his displeasure. "You two," he said with a scowl, wagging a forefinger at Kenny and Wanker. "You both need haircuts. We won't be having hippie guards at this lake." Their hair was barely over the tops of their ears.

"Yes, sir," they both replied in unison.

Then Mr. Andrews's eyes fell back on Michael. "You're the new head guard," he said with a matter-of-factness that suggested his reservations. "I'll tell you one damn thing, you got some pretty big shoes to fill."

With that, he turned and began his mincing eggshell-walk back toward the concession stand.

As Wanker and Kenny laughed and gave their congratulations, Michael felt a pleasant warmth spreading through him, not unlike the happy heat from a slug of beer. His elation was tempered by the disappointed look in Diane's eyes. She offered only a faint, brittle smile before turning back to cleaning the beach.

Despite Diane's cool response, by the time Michael got back to the lifeguard's lounge, he was grinning from ear to ear. He stood in front of the polished metal mirror outside the men's showers and reveled in a sweet moment of vanity. *Head guard.* It made him feel just a tiny bit sexy. He admired the way his chrome lifeguard's whistle, tied around his neck with a new white shoelace, glinted in the piney light. Then he stepped outside to survey his realm.

The lake had just opened but was already happily abuzz with mothers and their young children. A few teenagers had begun to trickle in; the rest would arrive later in the afternoon as they got off work or completed their chores. Of course, the scarcity of post-pubescent females hadn't stopped Kenny from "scoping" for bikinis. It just made the task more challenging.

Michael loped up to Kenny and tossed him a bottle of suntan lotion. "Get your mind out of your shorts, and put this on."

Kenny methodically smeared the lotion on himself. "It's not even noon, and I'm already sweatin' like a coke bottle at a Sunday picnic."

"You'll get used to it."

Kenny nodded to a gangly teenage girl in a lime-green bikini unfolding her towel near the water. He checked his watch. "Alright!"

"What?"

"I win the 'First Bikini of the Day' Contest. I guessed the arrival time."

"It don't . . ." Michael started, then caught himself. "It *doesn't* count if she's jailbait." Michael pointed a thumb at the girl. "That's definitely jailbait."

"No way, bubba," Kenny insisted. "She's at *least* sixteen."

Michael gestured to a middle-aged woman on a purple beach towel, her nose buried in a paperback romance novel, and a small dark-haired girl playing in the sand nearby. "Listen, you gotta keep a special eye on Mrs. Lacey's daughter over there. Little Julie's epileptic. She has seizures."

Due to the deafening roar of rushing hormones in his ears, Kenny didn't respond. Michael whapped him on the shoulder.

"Doofus, pay attention. This is important."

"Yeah, yeah. The girl's a spaz. I got it."

Michael sauntered on, glowing with confidence. He'd savored his first taste of authority and found it sweet.

Michael's gaze trailed down the beach to where Diane was retrieving a paper boat out of shallow water for a distraught child. He couldn't explain, even to himself, the wave of sadness that washed over him.

In his mind, he'd already lost Diane. She was achingly pretty, but she belonged to a social world where he would never be welcomed. All last summer, she had been close because she was just another pal. In one year, she'd become something unapproachable. She had never shown the slightest indication that she thought him beneath her, but Michael knew, with a sinking sensation, that he would never have the courage to test those waters.

As he watched Diane, he let out an involuntary sigh.

"You like her, don't you?"

Michael turned toward the voice. His eyes fell upon a woman he couldn't recall seeing at the lake before. She appeared to be in her late twenties or early thirties, with dark eyes, olive skin and a thick, raven-black sweep of hair that rode the warm breeze. He couldn't help but notice that her revealing red bikini was the smallest he had ever seen, exposing her delicious curves.

"Well . . ." he stammered, mortified.

"Come on, I know you do," the woman teased.

"I haven't even asked her out yet," Michael finally managed.

"I wouldn't wait if I were you. She won't be free for long."

The woman was trying to spike a beach umbrella into the sand. A gust of wind wafted off the water, sending the umbrella twirling out of place.

"Here, let me get that for you, ma'am," Michael said. He hoisted the umbrella and plunged it deep into the sand.

"*Ma'am*! Listen to you! Like I'm some blue hair." She tapped him playfully on his shoulder. "Call me Loraine."

"I'm Michael. Michael Simpson."

Loraine looked him over appreciatively, from head to toe. Michael felt himself flush under her gaze.

"So, Michael Simpson, what do you do when you're not assisting damsels in distress?"

He wasn't sure what to make of her question. "Well, I'm starting at UGA in the fall."

"Oh, a college man," she said, a smile flickering around the edges of her mouth.

No one had *ever* referred to him as a man before. It made him feel powerfully masculine.

"A little advice." Loraine glanced down the beach at Diane, then leaned in close to him. "A young girl like her won't make the first move. Trust me on this." She playfully brushed her long-nailed fingertips across Michael's shoulder. He felt a wave of tingles wash all the way down his spine and into his groin. "Fortune favors the bold."

With that, she whipped open her beach towel, and bending over to adjust it, she exposed a cheeky view of her sinuous buttocks. She settled under the umbrella.

"Have a good day," she said with a warm smile and slipped on her sunglasses.

With a sheepish nod, Michael turned and moved down the beach. He was green, but he recognized that Loraine had come on to him. A small voice told him something wasn't right about an older woman flirting with a teenage boy. For all he knew, she was somebody's mother, or at least somebody's wife. Michael finally decided Loraine was just teasing him and eased her from his mind.

∞

At last, the jagged shadows of the pines stretched across the beach, and chilly mothers began folding their umbrellas, rewrapping half-eaten peanut butter sandwiches, and bundling their wet and sandy offspring towards their station wagons. Teens flapped chlorinated water out of their ears, headed for their muscle cars, and peeled out of the parking lot with radios blaring. By six o'clock, closing time, the last of them were gone, and the white beach lay empty once more.

At the end of what had seemed like an endless day, Michael finally left his lifeguard post and headed for the lounge, his head swimming with thought. Loraine's flirtation had boosted his confidence, and he had spent the remainder of the day thinking about Diane. After all, he was head guard now, and Alex's rules about guards dating other guards no longer applied. But no matter how he tried, he couldn't imagine himself in front of her, suave and confident, saying those all-important words.

All at once, he spotted Diane. She had just come from the lounge and appeared to be making her way towards the parking lot. But when she spotted Michael, she made a pretense of straightening up a stack of umbrellas.

Michael thought about passing her by and walking straight to the men's showers. It would have been the easier thing to do. But Loraine's words were still humming in his ears, and he wanted desperately to summon up the courage to speak to her. Before he could make up his mind, Diane spoke first.

"Hey," she said hesitantly, fussing over an unruly umbrella tie.

"Hey," he echoed back. The daunting task of putting together a sentence loomed.

"Since you're head guard, I want to ask about working extra hours this summer." She wouldn't look at him. "I'm on a partial scholarship this fall and could use the money."

No wonder she had been so testy that morning, Michael realized bleakly. Her family wasn't giving her any help, and she was trying to do it all on her own. Michael stood frozen in place, feeling lower than whale shit for his callous words earlier.

"Just let me know what days you want to work." A handful of words bubbled up from inside him. "Look, I'm sorry about what I said earlier. I was being a jerk."

She smiled at him. "Forget it. You're the better guard, anyway. You deserve the job."

Her smile gave him renewed confidence. Finally, just as he was ready to ask her out, Diane glanced past Michael into the parking lot and stiffened. "I gotta go," she murmured. "See you." She brushed quickly past him.

When Michael turned to the gravel lot to see what had whisked her away from him, he felt as though he'd been punched in the gut.

Chuck Leach stood there, leaning rakishly on the hood of his Malibu Super Sport, leering at Diane as she hurried toward him. To Michael's horror, Chuck slipped a sinewy arm around her waist and tipped her chin back possessively. What Diane clearly wished to be a simple peck in greeting, Chuck turned into a production number. Diane squirmed against him in vain, but it was several seconds before Chuck pulled his tongue off her tonsils and released her.

He likes to mark his territory. That's what Alex had said once about Chuck and his girlfriends. Michael wondered sourly if this kind of public display was what Alex meant.

Diane folded her arms across her chest, a dark shadow settling on her adorable features. Chuck smugly glanced at Michael as Diane climbed into the Super Sport, leaving Michael to nurse a queasy stomach.

Kenny ambled out of the lounge in time to see Chuck's Malibu stampeding out of the gravel lot. He scoffed at Michael's shocked expression. "What, you didn't know? Diane's been dating Captain *Douchebag* for a couple months now." Kenny clapped his pal on the back and headed for the parking lot.

Michael eventually got control of his stomach, but the shock remained. *Pretty Diane was Chuck Leach's girlfriend.*

Chapter 17

June 25, 1864

THE WAGON CARRYING THE dead creaked its way up the muddy road etched with ribbons of water. Ahead the Simpson men saw a strange-looking man, scarecrow thin with curly red hair and bulging eyes, pacing and babbling to himself. He was wearing a threadbare frock coat and a tie loosely looped in a bow. Across the field from where he walked stood a large brick building, clusters of clapboard barracks, a cookhouse, and out buildings.

"There be the Georgia Military Institute," Elon said.

"There be a mad man, too," Baylis nodded.

"I say. I say," the odd man yelled and began running toward them.

"There be an Englishman," Ulysses said.

"They all act like that?" Elon asked.

"I met two in the army. They sound funny like that, but they acted regular," Ulysses said.

"Hello there, travelers!"

"Greetings, sir." Baylis nodded to the man.

"I was a professor at the Institute, but they have closed, and now I am without employment." He looked in a bad way.

"Very sorry to hear that," Baylis said.

"They took the stores with them, so I'm afraid I'm a bit hungry."

"We need to look for food, too," Baylis said.

"I'll walk with you," the man said. "Show you the way to the graveyard, so you can lay your comrades to rest."

"That's a kindness," Elon said.

The man took the lead horse by its bridle harness and led the team up the road, then turned it onto a well-worn track. He looked back to Elon.

"My names is Milton, by the by."

"First or last?" Elon asked, encouraging the horses forward.

"Both."

"Milton Milton?"

"Yes."

"I'm Elon. And this is Ulysses and Baylis."

Ulysses acknowledged Milton with a languid toss of his hand. "Your parents must have greatly liked that name to bestow it on you twice."

"They were admirers of the renowned poet. There is a legend that he was of our family."

"Must get confusing," Elon said.

"My name? It is difficult to tell if one is being formal or overly friendly." Milton self-consciously brushed the dust from his shoulder. "I say, by the by, you wouldn't know anyone that wishes to hire a professor, would you?"

"No, I couldn't say that I do. What do you teach?"

"Mensuration."

Elon's eyes sparked. "Why in blazes would you teach menstruation at an institute of young men?"

"Menstruation?" Milton looked at him quizzically.

"Yes. I think it more odd than a squirrel wearing a king's crown."

"I can't imagine why one would. Why on earth do you ask such a thing?"

"The miseries born of the curse of Eve are not a proper subject for children's ears. Delicate matters of the sexes should never be taught in school."

"I agree wholeheartedly, kind sir."

"Then why do you teach menstruation?"

"I do not."

"Sir, you just said you taught menstruation."

"No. I did not say that, sir."

Ulysses interrupted. "I think my uncle is unfamiliar with your accent. What did you say?"

Milton spoke slowly. "Men-su-ra-tion."

"And what might that be?" Ulysses asked.

"The science of measuring things."

"You can take the measure of a man?"

"If a man be a thing. If you can give me his height, his width, and his depth, then, sir, I can tell you his volume."

"Seems like a useful enough skill, but I ain't sure what work it may lead a man to," Baylis said.

"I also teach evidences of Christianity," Milton said.

"Then there is your work!" Elon proclaimed as though he was warming up for a sermon. "Go forth and preach the Gospel of our Lord."

"Become a missionary?" Milton asked. "There is a living in that to be found here?"

"An educated man like yourself who can preach with the fire of the Pentecost can always find a warm meal and a bed to sleep in. Maybe, even his own church," Elon offered.

"Then that is it, sir. I shall go forth and preach the good news of the Gospel, for who needs more evidence of Christianity than God's great creation?"

Milton swept his arm out toward the horizon as the wagon broke from the high scrub, drawing Baylis's eyes toward a cemetery a short distance away.

In a grotesque way, the burial ground with its rows of hummocks reminded Baylis of the Yankee depot at Big Shanty. But instead of being piled with the preparations and provisions of war, this depot contained war's harsh effects collected for final disposition. There must be two thousand graves, he thought. Many more were being dug as he watched. The dead were lined and stacked like cordwood, some in pine burial boxes, but most simply lying stiff and discarded on the ground.

"If you're going to be a preacher, you better look to where you point before you declare it God's work," Baylis said.

"Sorry," Milton said. "Living so close, I have become accustomed to the carnage. It is, indeed, the sad and pathetic work of man, but surely, God is here."

"Surely, He is," Elon agreed.

Baylis wasn't so sure. These days it seemed like the devil was loose in Georgia. Soon, the whole state would be dented by craters filled with shattered trees and pieces of the dead.

They pulled the wagon to the point where the bodies were being unloaded. Six black men climbed on the wagon and began gently removing the bodies. As the slaves placed an older man with an officer's uniform on the ground, Milton cried out.

"My goodness. I believe I know that man." He looked closer. "Yes, I do. It is Captain Grayson, the father of one of my students, young Master Richard. Oh, dear. I must find the poor lad and tell him about the cruel fate that has befallen his beloved father."

"You know where he is?" Baylis asked.

"With the army somewhere on Kennesaw," Milton said.

"We are traveling there to join the fighting. You can travel with us. Someone may know his whereabouts."

"Thank you, sir," Milton said.

Baylis had taken Milton for a fool. But, of course, there was no reason a fool couldn't also be thoroughly decent. He found himself warming to the man.

"I'm going to stay here and help with the burying," Elon said. "Then I must prepare my soul for the Pentecost tomorrow. Y'all can take the wagon to Marietta."

"I've had about enough of the wagon," Baylis said.

"It's not a long walk," Milton said. "I can show you the way."

Baylis turned to his brother. "We may never meet again in this world, but I hope to see you in the next."

"You are a righteous man, and I know we shall meet there, as God has promised," Elon said.

Elon turned to Ulysses. "May God bless you, and protect you and make His Face to shine upon you."

"Amen," his nephew said.

"I don't much expect the three of us will be standing above ground when this is over," Baylis said. "Anyone who makes it through this must swear to look out for the family."

"I swear," Elon said.

"As do I," Ulysses said.

"In the end, it's family. That's all that matters. The rest is just whatnot," Baylis said quietly. He knew it wasn't much of a goodbye, but they had said what needed saying.

Elon bear-hugged his brother, then slapped his nephew on the back. "If there's killin' to be done, make sure you're the one doin' it, and not the other way 'round."

Elon turned and stepped into the field of corpses.

Baylis and Ulysses followed Milton back down the road to the Institute. As they walked, Baylis turned to catch a glimpse of his brother. Something in his heart told him that it would be the last time he would see him. At least in this life.

Chapter 18

July 1969

THE DAY HAD TURNED drizzling with a rumble of dark grey clouds, but nothing could dampen Ron's spirits. He was going home on leave after graduating from Primary Helicopter School at Fort Wolters.

As the Greyhound bus crossed the Alabama state line and pushed up the highway toward Columbus, Georgia, Ron smiled as he recalled a recent letter from Alex. His friend had been transferred to Fort Benning, a base he called the "Benning School for Boys," after completing advanced infantry training in the simulated jungles of North Fort Polk's "Tigerland."

True to form, Alex had been cited for numerous personal conduct infractions during his stay at Fort Polk. To work off his demerits, he had been assigned to company supply. There, he paid for his sins under the constant ire of a beef-headed master sergeant named Willard, who had a limp from stepping on a steel-barbed "ankle biter" booby-trap on his second tour of 'Nam.

Not being a man to accept punishment lightly, Alex had discreetly "liberated" a case of ten thousand condoms heading for Vietnam out of supply. That night, he stealthily made his way to the "General's Cannon," a 105mm howitzer which was fired every day at the raising or lowering of the flag. Under cover of darkness, he loaded the entire case down the gun's muzzle.

At first light the next morning, the color guard marched to the flagpole with great ceremony, dutifully attached the stars and stripes to the halyard, and began to raise it. At that precise moment, the captain of the gun ordered the cannon fired. A confetti blizzard of condoms burst into the crisp dawn air, raining down onto the gravel.

The base commander ordered that if the perpetrator were caught, he would receive a summary disciplinary Article 15 and confinement in the stockade. Although the military police even dusted the cannon for fingerprints, the condom prankster remained unknown. No one was ever able to pin the mischief on Alex.

Despite a river-wide streak of rebellion, Alex had excelled at Advanced Infantry Training before moving on to complete Basic Airborne Training and the U.S. Army Ranger School at Fort Benning. Ron was impressed that his friend had earned the black-and-gold shoulder insignia and black beret of one of America's most elite fighting forces.

When Ron knew he was going to be home, he phoned Alex, who requested and received a weekend pass. With both friends in Forest Park at the same time, they intended to make the most of it.

~~~

The summer evening was turning fuzzy and golden as the two soldiers turned into Pinerock Lake's gravel parking lot in Ron's Mustang to pick up Michael. They found him standing sullenly outside the lifeguard's lounge.

Alex followed Michael's withering gaze to Chuck's metallic blue Super Sport at the far end of the parking lot. Michael's scowl darkened as Diane exited the lounge, hurried toward the Malibu and climbed in.

"Don't even think what you're thinkin'," Alex warned when Michael slumped into the Mustang's rear seat. "It's like a pickle and peanut butter sandwich. Bad fuckin' idea." He let Michael simmer in the thought for a moment, then added, "You'll just make trouble for Diane and yourself. Chuck don't like his women even looking at another guy."

"*Doesn't. Doesn't* like," Michael corrected impulsively.

"I read he's gonna be red-shirted for UGA next season," Alex said bitterly, spitting the words out like poison. He still maintained that Chuck was going to college on *his* scholarship. It was rare for a sophomore football player to be red-shirted or sent up to the varsity team, a sure sign that the coaches saw major potential in him.

"You *read*. That's a joke." Ron teased, trying to lighten his friend's mood.

"Hey, I fuckin' read."

"Okay, the sports section, maybe. That and interviews with Playboy centerfolds."

Alex finally cracked a crooked grin. "My favorite is when 'she likes *loooooong* rides.'"

Michael remained lost in thought, staring at the Malibu's taillights. He became aware of Alex's eyes on him, and quickly tried to cover his obsession.

"Malibu Super Sport. Nice wheels," Michael said with a jerk of his chin towards Chuck's car. "I hear it's great for draggin' lawn furniture."

"That baby has four-hundred-and-twenty-six cubic inches. Probably a four-barrel on a high rise tricked with a hemi," Alex recited from memory. "It's king of the street, 'cept for Ron's 'stang, of course."

They lost Chuck's Malibu SS on Riverdale Road when Chuck turned into a car dealership and the boys took the turn toward the liquor store in Blair Village.

"What's the drinkin' age in our blessed Peach State?" Alex asked. Ron and Michael both groaned.

"Twenty-one," Ron sighed, "Same as the last time you asked. And the time before that." Ron could remember the first time Alex asked the question. It was on his friend's fifteenth birthday.

The moment they were out of the liquor store parking lot, Alex popped the tops on some beers and passed them around. Like most teenagers, Alex worried about DUIs about as much as he did the recently passed seat belt laws, which was to say, not at all.

On their way out of Forest Park, the boys approached the railroad crossing where the Dixie Flyer and the '57 Chevy had tangled eight years earlier. Less than two years ago, the city had finally put up warning lights and a gate on either side of the intersection. Since then, the Flyer had claimed no more lives, at least not on that spot, but Alex was still superstitious.

"Pull over. Rent's due on the Blue Ribbon," Alex said predictably.

In the Mustang's rear-view mirror, Michael and Ron bounced a glance at each other. Since that fateful night, Alex had refused to ride across the intersection for fear of getting hit by the train. He wasn't willing to tempt fate, crossing gate or not.

"I'll pull over when you say why you *really* want me to stop," Ron replied.

"I really wanna take a piss, Hoss. Now who's pulling the car over, you or me?"

Ron stopped the Mustang a few yards short of the crossing. Alex hopped out, unzipped, and watered the honeysuckle bushes by the side of the road. Then, with a guilty glance both ways, he stepped gingerly over the tracks. Ron, accustomed to this long-familiar ritual, dutifully drove the Mustang over the crossing and waited while Alex climbed back in.

Alex never talked about his loathing of the crossing, and his two friends knew better than to push the issue. No male under the age of twenty-five completely believes in the possibility of dying, but Alex always had a keener sense of his own end than most anyone his age. And if he thought the Flyer would someday bring his death, then, by God, no one was going to convince him otherwise.

Chapter 19

July 1969

ALEX AND THE SIMPSON brothers decided to check out the Red Charpeg, a teen club on Jonesboro Road with the look of a Forties roadhouse bar. The club was located in a wood plank building nestled between a used tire shop and a mobile home junkyard.

Michael felt a faint wave of discomfort wash through him as he, Ron, and Alex walked through the club's entrance. It struck Michael that Ron and Alex appeared considerably older than the other teens and college students gyrating and gesturing on the dance floor. They hadn't seemed any different only a handful of months ago. Now, standing beside them felt altogether too much like standing next to *grownups*.

Alex and Ron pushed through the dense cluster of bodies at the entrance like rock stars amid adoring fans, exchanging handshakes and backslaps with several friends. As Michael trailed in their wake, he decided that the age gulf was mostly an illusion, courtesy of Alex and Ron's military dress. Their uniforms commanded attention, particularly *female* attention, almost everywhere they went. Standing beside Ron and Alex had always left Michael feeling translucent; tonight he felt near invisible.

Michael scanned the room. On the stage, The Celestial Voluptuous Banana was kicking through "You're Gonna Miss Me" by The 13th Floor

Elevators as an ever-shifting menagerie of dancers flailed to the music. The "banana band" was Michael's favorite local group, and Darryl Rhoades, their sharp-witted drummer, was widely considered to be one of the top percussionists in the Atlanta music scene.

A smattering of club-goers huddled in the dark-paneled concession area where overpriced colas and potato chips were being hustled. On the sidelines around the dance floor, clusters of young people engaged in the ear-cupping, incomprehensible bellowing that passed for meaningful conversation in a loud club.

Alex and Ron, already several beers into the night, were both feeling loose amid the club's frenzy.

"What are those stains on your uniform, ranger?" Ron asked Alex, mocking a booming officer's voice.

Alex snapped an exaggerated salute. "Sir, those aren't stains, sir. They're medals, see?" He placed an index finger on each of the awards. "Sharpshooter, Good Conduct . . ."

"Good Conduct? Must've stolen that one. Or did the Army finally beat your ass into submission?"

"*Sua sponte*," Alex replied with a lopsided grin. "That means 'of one's own accord' for you uneducated types."

"Ah, yes, the Ranger motto," Ron laughed.

Alex turned to Michael, a sudden look of mischief bolted onto his face. In one deft pounce, Alex pinned him in a playful hammerlock. "Who's your uncle? C'mon, Hoss, say it!"

"Uncle Sam!" Michael yelped, flailing helplessly under Alex's grip. Alex released him and tussled his hair good-naturedly, as he had since Michael was in fourth grade.

As Alex and Ron moved on to greet more friends, Michael looked around. All at once, he locked eyes with Diane. She was standing by herself. Chuck was nowhere in sight. She seemed lost in the middle of all the chaos, robbed of any party spirit. She was gazing steadily in his direction, but Michael couldn't trust his instincts. Maybe she wanted him to come over and talk to her. Or maybe she was looking near him by sheer coincidence.

Michael stood frozen, trying to sort through the possibilities. He decided he'd never know whether she wanted to talk to him unless he went over and actually *talked*. Summoning his nerve, he started towards her.

Before Michael had taken three steps, Chuck appeared out of the crowd and wrapped a meaty paw about her waist. Startled, she dropped her gaze at once. Michael stopped in his tracks as Chuck fondled her possessively.

Chuck's two jock buddies, Marty and Ira, sauntered over with a pair of liquor bottles in brown paper bags just as Darryl Rhoades announced a "pause for the cause" and the Celestial Voluptuous Banana shuffled off the stage.

"C'mon," Ira slurred loudly, dangling his brown bag under Chuck's nose. "Forget your wood for a minute. Let's go outside and freshen your cup."

Chuck turned to follow his pals, but Diane tugged on the sleeve of his football jacket. Michael couldn't make out what she said, but Chuck shook his head, roughly yanked his arm from her grip, and lurched toward the exit. Diane was alone again, looking gloomier than ever.

Deejay Tony "the Tiger" Taylor mounted the stage, plunked a 45 onto a turntable, and cranked Tommy James and the Shondells's "Crimson and Clover" over the band's sound system. The floor coupled up quickly.

All at once, Michael was on his way to Diane. When he was standing before her, he found he knew what to say.

"What the heck's a 'Charpeg,' anyway?"

Her soft blue eyes crinkled with laughter. "I heard it was a combination of the first names of the couple who own the place. Like Charlie and Peggy, or something like that."

She glanced around at the couples dancing, then her eyes came to rest on him again. "Guess Chuck's not too interested in dancing tonight."

"Don't . . ." Michael started, before catching himself with a sheepish grin. "*Doesn't* look like he's gonna stay on his feet long, anyway."

She smiled gently, but only for a moment.

"He doesn't even care that's it's our song. The only things he's ever interested in are drinking and . . ." Diane's voice trailed off, and her eyes turned stormy. She studied the exit warily. "Look, this is such a great song. Do you want to . . .?"

"Sure." Michael placed his arm quickly around her waist.

For a few awkward moments, Michael couldn't figure out how anybody made dancing appear so effortless. But then Diane placed a hand on his shoulder and smiled at him. After that, the last thing on his mind was whether his dancing was up to form.

Michael savored the exquisite sensation of having her face so close to his. Suddenly, her warm gaze turned to horror. Michael felt a heavy hand clamp down on his shoulder as he was forcefully spun around to face Chuck.

"Hey, dipshit. What do you think you're doing?"

Michael felt his thoughts clouding over. His blood pounded in his ears as his mind scrambled.

Diane quickly put herself between Chuck and Michael. "Chuck, he's just a friend."

"Stay out of this!" Chuck growled, pushing her back roughly.

Diane spun on her heels and stormed off through the gathering crowd, hoping Chuck would follow her. But Chuck wasn't interested in calming his date. He wanted a brawl.

Chuck turned his rage back to Michael. "Now look what you've done, upsetting Diane that way. You gotta be a real chickenshit to hide behind a girl's skirt."

Michael felt outside of his own body. He numbly saw himself stand up straighter. He'd seen Alex play out this scenario dozens of times. But he couldn't recall what came next. Was he supposed to throw a punch at Chuck? No part of the massive football player looked particularly vulnerable to his fists.

Somewhere in his peripheral vision, Michael thought he saw Ron and Alex watching. But he wasn't going to take his eyes off Chuck. The guy was known for throwing sucker punches. If Michael was going down, he wanted to do it looking the asshole in the eye.

Chuck's sidekick Marty drunkenly sneered, "Don't you know you should leave women alone until you're dry behind the ears?"

"I am dry behind my ears." Michael's own voice surprised him. It had grown deep and quiet.

Chuck's lips curled into a thin, cruel smile as he slowly poured his drink over Michael's head. "No, you're not."

On cue, Ira and Marty laughed like trained orangutans. Michael felt the bourbon sting his scalp and his ears. Some dripped down his left eye, but he refused to give Chuck the pleasure of seeing him wipe it away.

Then Ron was there, clenching Chuck's forearm in a steely grip, firmly pulling it downward. Michael had not realized how strong his brother had become. No one had ever laid a hand on Chuck before.

"Why'd you wanna waste a good drink?" Ron said evenly, trying to back things down a couple notches. "You should have more respect for whiskey than that." He released Chuck's arm, but never took his eyes off the brute.

"Well, if it isn't Mary, Irene, and Chuckles." The cigarette dangling in Alex's mouth bounced up and down like a baton as he spoke.

"Oh, crap, more townie trash," Ira scoffed with a contemptuous belch.

Alex stabbed a finger into Ira's chest, hard enough to send him back on his heels. "Want to repeat that, ass munch?"

Ron clasped Alex's shoulder, trying to edge him back. "Let it go. You creamed these mooks enough on the football field."

Chuck, Marty, and Ira howled with condescending laughter.

"While you guys are still reliving A-wipe's little high school glories," Marty taunted Alex, "we're playing *college* ball."

With that, Alex shifted, balancing his weight to assume a fighting stance. Ron knew what was coming next, but before he could try to defuse it, Ira made the mistake of giving Alex's military uniform a derisive glance and saying, "What are you playing, weenie boy, G.I. Joe?"

Alex's eyes locked on Ira, who had no more idea the line he had just crossed than a deer knows when he's in a gun sight.

"I'm been studying palm reading," Alex announced with a calmness that seemed almost supernatural. "*Lemmesee* your hand. I'll tell your fortune."

Alex wore the same demented smile that the Simpson brothers had seen thousands of times. But there was something new in his eyes: *a bone-cracking hardness.*

"Do what?" Ira was totally thrown by the request.

"I'm speaking English, Tonto. Watch my lips move. Let. Me. See. Your. Palm."

Not wanting to look like a complete wuss, Ira inched his hand forward. Still staring at him, Alex reached out and grabbed Ira's hand in a vise grip, turning the palm up, and bending two of his fingers back almost to the breaking point.

"What the—!" Ira winced in pain.

Alex cut him off with another jerk back on the fingers. With no trace of emotion, Alex pulled the cigarette out of his mouth, flicked the ashes off, and blew on the burning tip.

"Now pay attention. This is your fortune. I predict that you will never again disrespect the uniform of a United States Army Ranger."

With that Alex abruptly stubbed his cigarette into Ira's palm. Ira went white with pain, his knees almost buckling. He toothed his lip, biting back tears of pain.

Marty moved to help his friend. Before he had taken the second step, Alex had him by the balls, squeezing them like a ripe Georgia peach. Marty cried out. Alex released the jock's gonads, and Marty dropped to the floor, writhing in pain.

As Chuck moved to intervene, Ron leaned in to him. "I'm saying this as a favor. I wouldn't interrupt Alex if I were you. It'll only get worse."

Alex was still staring at Ira. The soldier had never blinked.

"So you wanna know what I've been playing, *Irene*? I've been playing Ranger. You know why? 'Cause Rangers lead the way." Alex came in close. "What you're now feeling in your palm isn't pain. It's just—" he stopped to emphasis his words, "a temporary inconvenience that can be healed with a little salve and your mama's wet kisses. So, suck it up, buttercup."

Alex studied Ira like a tiger eyeing its next meal. "Now *Irene,* are you in the mood to feel *real* pain?" Alex's eyes had heated into tight black coals.

Staring into those crazy eyes, Ira knew without a doubt that he didn't want any more of what this guy was serving up.

"No," Irene whimpered.

"Then you will *gawddam* respect the uniform of a United States Army

Ranger, or I will lead the way down your throat, rip out your larynx, and show it to you."

Alex's voice was so stone cold it even sent a chill up Chuck's spine. There was no doubt he meant every word of what he said.

"Alex, let him go," Ron said quietly. "He's just a stupid asshole."

After a long moment, Alex released Ira. Ira cupped his hand, and pushed off through the crowd. Marty staggered up, then slunk back, averting Alex's gaze. He quickly retreated after Ira.

Alex turned and stared at Chuck. "Anybody else wanna dance with me?"

Chuck considered Alex briefly. A thin smile etched across his face.

"I've got a more civilized way to handle this, Bojangles." Rummaging in his pockets, he pulled out his car keys and dangled them in Ron's face. "How 'bout a run to Blue Lights?"

Alex let out a hissing laugh, lighting another cigarette. "Save your gas, blowhole. Nobody's ever beat Ron at Blue Lights."

Chuck read the hesitation in Ron's eyes and smirked, "Well, of course, if little Ronnie here's not up to it anymore . . ."

Michael glanced at his older brother. He knew Ron would defuse a fight if he could. But he would never walk away from a direct challenge to race. For Ron there was only one answer.

"See you on the blacktop."

All the way to Blue Lights, Michael's bloodstream chugged with adrenaline. His heart pounded so fiercely that he could barely hear. He'd been watching street races at Blue Lights since he'd entered high school, but tonight was special. Chuck was the only guy in the county, besides Ron, who had never lost a race there. The two reigning champs had never competed against each other before; the victory could easily go either way.

Ron pulled his Mustang onto the deserted street that was the starting point for the race. The latticework of roads around them had, not long ago, been the community of Mountain View, a small hardscrabble enclave of modest family dwellings and mobile home trailers that dated back to the Civil War, when it was little more than a railroad stop called Rough & Ready.

When Atlanta's Hartsfield airport began to suffer growing pains, the airport authority had bought up every house in the area, using the crowbar of Eminent Domain to leverage out the most stubborn holdouts. Then they bulldozed the entire neighborhood—every house, every picket fence, every hickory, azalea, and oak.

People who once gossiped over back fences, played their televisions too loud, yelled at their kids too much, and depended on each other more than they knew, had melted away into the surrounding suburbs and beyond. Mountain View simply ceased to exist. What had outlived Sherman could not survive the airport.

For years these acres had sat empty, waiting for the wheels of progress to turn. Michael always felt an odd creeping in his scalp when he looked at the ruined landscape. It looked especially eerie by moonlight: block after block of perfectly paved roads and sidewalks, flanking the weedy overgrown cancers of former lawns, still opening here and there onto concrete driveways that led to . . . *nothing.*

The races took place along a mile stretch of abandoned street that had once been the main thoroughfare. At the end of the mile, the street took an abrupt ninety-degree dogleg to the left to avoid a thick curtain of oaks and pines. Then the racecourse continued for a few more blocks before ending in a cul-de-sac that overlooked the airport. After rounding the elbow in the road, which the local teens called "Dead Man's Curve" in honor of the Jan & Dean song, you had a full view of the twinkling blue taxiway lights guiding jets to the runways.

The trick to winning the race to Blue Lights lay in handling that dogleg curve. If you took the turn too fast, you risked flying off the course and slamming into the trees. A number of kids had done just that over the years and been seriously injured. But if you took the turn too slowly, a worse fate awaited you: you'd be branded a "pussy boy" for chickening out early, and you'd inevitably lose the race. Whoever slowed down first cleared the way for the other vehicle to take the turn on the inside and gain a car-length's lead, more than enough to reach the finish line.

Ron possessed a few key advantages. His '67 Ford Shelby Mustang was one of the faster street-legal cars of its day, with a four-barrel, 289 cubic-inch engine. With a top speed of 120 mph, the car could do zero to sixty in a tick over six seconds and a quarter mile in fifteen.

Another advantage was having Alex Granger as his mechanic. He was the best wrench monkey under twenty-one years of age in the county. Alex loved everything about the "'stang," as he called it—how the engine smelled and sounded, and how it responded to his fine-tuning. The many modifications Alex had made to the steed included beefier shocks and springs, a Holley carburetor, and fifteen-inch wheels to better hold the road. He had also connected the muffler using a hose and post clamps, so it could be easily removed during street races.

Over the years, Ron had also perfected a technique that allowed him to take the crucial curve at higher speeds than anyone else dared. Michael had seen him in action, but only at a distance. He had no idea how Ron managed the feat, and his brother refused to tell.

Since the day Ron's Mustang came on the scene, nobody had ever made it to the turn before him, much less been willing to wait as long as he did before braking. Those challengers, and there had been dozens over the years, inevitably arrived at the cul-de-sac at the race's end to find Ron grinning victoriously and Alex's hand outstretched waiting to be paid. The two friends had funded many a night's adventure from race receipts earned at Blue Lights.

Ron pulled the Mustang up to a crude, hand-painted line on the pavement and let the engine idle. From his perch in the rear jumpseat, Michael watched for Chuck and his buddies to arrive, while Alex worked under the hood, adjusting the idle up.

Closing the car's hood, Alex scanned the area for patrol cruisers. Local cops often made sweeps at Blue Lights in a futile attempt to stop the lead foots who courted sudden death there. The police also liked to roust cars parked overlooking the runway, which was known throughout the county as *the* place for "necking and drinking."

Satisfied that they were safe from patrols, Alex slipped back into the car. On the Mustang's radio, DJ John R. introduced "Cool Jerk," by the Capitols. One of the great truths of being a teenager was that some magic summer nights came with their own soundtracks.

"You knew I was tired of doing this race shit," Ron muttered out of the corner of his mouth. "I can't believe I let you get me sucked into it again."

"Come on, Ronnie boy. It's an adventure."

Ron shot Alex a sharp look.

"Look, if you're gonna go out, you wanna go in blaze of glory, Hoss," Alex insisted. "Right?"

"I'm not interested in going out in a blaze of *anything*," Ron said wearily.

"Lighten up, will ya?" Alex cocked his head over his shoulder, glancing to Michael. "Jesus, I think the Army's turned Ronnie into a mama's boy."

Michael didn't answer. He was too busy staring at the pair of approaching headlights.

Ron's jaw dropped. Gone was the Malibu Super Sport, a formidable street racer in its own right. Chuck and his jackass pals were now hanging out of the windows of a gleaming, black, spanking-new 1969 Dodge Charger RT.

"Wow, look at those wheels," Michael murmured, even though Ron and Alex were already doing just that. "Guess that's why Chuck stopped at the dealership today."

"Only a douchebag would race a brand-new car without breaking in the engine first," Alex said.

"Is that the 440?" Ron asked.

"426. It's faster."

"*Faster?*"

"That puppy has dual four-barrel Holley carbs, a high lift cam, modified exhaust manifolds, and hi-flow, closed chambered heads. *Hot Rod* road-tested it for their last issue. It did a hundred and eight per in the quarter mile." Alex gave a crooked smile. "See, I told you I read."

"What's the time on the quarter?"

"Thirteen-point-four-four. It's tricked with solid lifters and a cowl induct system that opens in response to engine demand."

Streaks of blue-white moonlight played across the Charger's powerful contours and gleaming grill. From the thundering growl of its engine, even Michael could tell Chuck had made special modifications to his baby.

"We're fucked," was all Ron could manage.

Michael felt icy fingers tickle his stomach. What would it feel like to watch Ron *lose* his last run to Blue Lights?

When Chuck and his acolytes pulled up to the line with a flourish, Ron opened the Mustang's door, and motioned for Michael to bail out and wait for them, as he had on many such occasions. Michael didn't budge.

"Out, bro," Ron commanded. "This is dangerous."

"Come on, man. I'm old enough to handle this," Michael protested. "I start college in the fall, for chrissakes."

Alex turned to Michael. "How much do you weigh?"

"Let's see, 'bout a hundred and sixty I think."

"Man, you're a skinny fuck." Alex threw a glance to Ron. "If he's staying, we'll need to lighten the trunk."

Ron shot a look to his brother and slowly nodded. *Michael was staying.*

Alex bolted out of the car, hustled to the trunk, and began pulling out cinder blocks.

Cinder blocks? Michael watched quizzically.

"The front end's heavy 'cause of the big engine. The blocks help balance the 'stang and get rid of the understeer."

Alex hopped back in and wiped his hands on his pants. "Let's do it."

With seconds to go before the start of the race, Chuck and Ron revved their engines to crescendos of fury, the decibels testifying to the chomping horsepower beneath the cars' polished hoods.

When Michael was convinced that the revving couldn't get any louder, Alex popped a beer, took one last, long swig, and hopped up from the passenger seat and perched in the window frame.

With every inch of lungpower, Alex shouted over the deafening roar of the engines: "Three . . . Two . . . One . . ."

Before Alex hollered, "*Go!*" Chuck floored the Charger's accelerator and burned away in a cloud of smoke.

"That little shit!" Alex screamed, pounding on the Mustang's roof, "Go! Go!"

Michael felt his stomach slosh against his ribcage as the Mustang leaped from the starting line. The sheer force of the acceleration knocked him back in his seat.

The cars raced full gallop down the deserted street. In seconds, the Mustang was neck and neck with the Dodge. Ron shouted something at Michael from the driver's seat.

"What?" Michael bellowed.

"Alex's belt! Hold onto it!" Ron hollered again.

Michael hooked his fingers through Alex's belt just in time to keep him from tumbling out onto the pavement. Alex hiked himself as far out of the Mustang's window as he possibly could. Ron swerved toward the Dodge slightly, and Alex let loose with his nearly full can of beer. The beer made a satisfying *splat* against the Charger's windshield, white foam billowing in all directions.

"You cheatin' asshole!" Alex roared.

Just when Michael thought he couldn't hold on any longer, Alex popped back in from the window. Michael let go of his belt and looked ahead. The trees beyond the dogleg curve loomed large in the Mustang's windshield.

"Get ready," Ron warned loudly over the thunder of the engine.

They were heading toward the turn, and Ron showed no signs of slowing down. Michael saw Ron glance quickly over at Chuck, who was just off the Mustang's passenger side, pacing him. Now they were almost at the turn, Michael could see a maniacal fear spread across Chuck's porky features. Chuck's car abruptly lost speed and popped into Ron's rearview. Chuck was braking.

As Ron's car pulled slightly ahead, Michael suddenly felt a cartwheeling sensation, not unlike a Tilt-A-Whirl. He heard rubber grinding against asphalt, and realized that the front of the Mustang was pivoting. The blurry image of Chuck's Dodge skidded just behind them, in the throes of the turn, weaving to regain control.

Before the sidewise motion ceased, Ron stomped the accelerator. The Mustang now pointed straight for the end of the racecourse. Behind the boys, the Charger went wide, bumping and bouncing over the curb and eating through the wild grass and weeds before slamming hard back onto the blacktop with a zig and a zag.

Moments later, the Mustang pulled to a halt at the end of the cul-de-sac. Ron and Alex were already whooping in victory. Alex leaned across and honked the horn wildly. The three boys tumbled out of the car.

Seconds behind them, the brand-new Dodge Charger limped in, bedraggled and dented, with shredded leaves and twigs protruding from its grill. Without a word to the champions, Chuck's ailing Dodge turned and shambled off into the night.

The three friends piled back into the Mustang and drove to the top of the small crest overlooking the gutted neighborhood and the twinkling blue taxiways beyond. Several other cars had already arrived, and a few cheers of congratulations greeted Ron as he pulled in.

On the radio, Jerry Butler soulfully testified about how "Only the Strong Survive" as the guys spilled out of the Mustang and stretched. Alex fished a fresh trio of beers out of the cooler in the trunk and popped the tops.

"Looks like you haven't lost your touch, Ronnie boy." Alex chortled, handing Ron a beer, then Michael.

"I don't understand. How'd you make the turn that fast?"

"Didn't you see me yank the emergency brake? Alex has it rigged to lock the back wheel on the driver's side to help you do a sharp turn slide."

"You come in hot, jerk up the e-brake, and turn the wheel to the left," Alex piped in, gripping an imaginary steering wheel for emphasis. "At ninety degrees, you let off the e-brake, stand on the gas, and turn into the skid, depending on how much your ass is hangin' out. The real trick's knowin' when to pull the e-brake up, and when to release it and accelerate out of the turn.

"That kind of turn is called a bootleg," Ron added. "It was used by bootleggers trying to outrun the law. You do one right, you can take a hairpin turn at incredibly high speeds."

"But doesn't that kinda mess up your emergency brake?"

Ron thumped Alex on the back. "That's why I always bring my ace mechanic along."

"Few dollars and a couple hours' work, and I'll have a new brake put in. But a whole truckload of new brakes'd be worth it, just to see the look on Chuck's motherfuckin' face!"

Alex and Ron clicked beer cans and took a deep drink.

A light went on in a corner of Michael's brain. "So, it's not just who's the *fastest*—"

"It's who's the *smartest*, little bro," Ron finished. "Don't ever forget that."

Michael sat quietly, beaming with beery admiration.

Evening settled around them. The summer moon had risen up high and small, letting the light of the stars push through. Not a breath of wind moved the grass. The boys could hear muffled radios playing softly in nearby cars.

"Toss me more piss water," Alex said. Ron passed him one of the last beers from the cooler that had been growing warm in the Mustang's trunk all evening.

Alex raised his beer. "A toast! To those old enough to kill for their country, but can't vote or buy a beer for doin' it. *Saluda*." He tipped the can up and drained it.

"Can you believe graduation was just last year?" Ron sighed.

Alex took a long drag from his cigarette. "Sometimes it feels like it's only been a couple weeks. Sometimes, it seems so long ago it might as well've happened to somebody else."

"It feels like only a month ago that Mitchell Youmans got busted for runnin' his boxer shorts up the flag pole during Senior Week."

"And Matt Riddling sneaked into the Principal Kirkland's Office after the morning pledge and played 'Dixie' over the school PA instead of the 'Star Spangled Banner.'"

"Remember the night Roy Orbison played that concert in the gym?"

"That was the year Joey Griffeth took a dump on Coach Avinger's desk and I got blamed for it."

"Honest mistake," Ron laughed, "Sounds like something you'd do."

"I remember I fell out laughing in the hall, with Coach Avinger hanging onto me, 'cause Joey said it couldn't have been him because his was a lot darker than that."

"Remember Jimmy Butler driving his 'ol man's '48 Plymouth across the school's front lawn? That was fuckin' legendary. Ol' man Kirkland dropped a brick."

"Young people, young people," Alex said, mimicking the formal, stoic tones of their high school principal. "This is no way for young people to act."

From the back seat, Michael listened quietly, content to let Ron and Alex have this moment to themselves.

"I hear Dave Meaders drew number thirty-four in the draft lottery and joined the Navy," Alex said quietly. "He's in intelligence."

"No shit? Mom says Walter Sheppard started a gospel quartet. He always had a helluva voice."

"Remember the first time we saw Fireball Roberts in the Daytona 500?" Alex asked.

"We were sophomores. That's when I decided I was gonna be a race car driver and you'd be my mechanic."

The night had already begun to slip away from them. Alex leaned back on the hood and studied the fuzzy pinpricks of light in the night sky.

"Wonder what the stars look like in 'Nam." Alex took a deep sip of beer.

There was nothing Ron or Michael could add to that. So they sat in silence, watching the planes take off and land.

"Say, squirt. You being head guard now. Must be hard livin' up to a legend like me."

Ron guffawed. "Legend in your own mind, maybe."

"I didn't think I'd make head guard this quick," Michael admitted.

"What's Shaky Andrews gonna do? Nothin' but snot noses left with the real men gone." Alex fished in the pocket of his jeans and came up with a bright chrome whistle on a chain. He tossed it to Michael, who caught it and held it up like some sacred totem.

"Your whistle?" Michael asked.

"I want you to have it."

"Man, thanks. I don't know what to say."

"You're gonna do okay." Alex drained his beer and crumpled the can in one wiry move. "You just gotta remember, Michael, you wanna crush the cans, you gotta buy the beer. You want people's respect out there, you gotta earn it. You understand?"

Michael nodded. In more than ten years of friendship, it was the only time he could remember Alex ever calling him by his real name. *Beav. Squirt. Mouse. Mikey.* Never Michael.

John R.'s mellow voice drifted in from over the clear 50,000 watts of Nashville's WLAC, into the fast-waning night. Michael felt at last like an equal member of the trio, for the first and final time.

Chapter 20

June 25, 1864

Baylis, Ulysses, and Milton stepped onto the grounds of the Georgia Military Institute and moved to a large cistern close to a building, shaded by a large oak tree.

"The food stores are gone, but there is fresh water and some clean clothing," Milton said.

"A bath and clothing would be most welcomed," Ulysses said. "I know we smell worse than skunks."

Baylis drew buckets from the cistern, and they washed naked, outdoors, with soap. The water was cold, but after several latherings, the soap removed the last of the death stench, and they felt blessedly clean, like a baptism had removed their sins.

Milton returned with towels and neatly folded butternut pants, hickory cotton blouses, and sack coats. The men dried themselves and dressed.

"I got officer's uniforms," Milton said. "Given the current calamity, no one will begrudge you. I found you some blankets and haversacks too."

"Thank you for the kindness," Baylis said.

"I shall make my own ablutions." Milton knelt to wash his hands and face. "They say cleanliness is next to godliness, yet I must confess that I've found no such words in the good book."

Ulysses rubbed the gold braid on the uniform that denoted the officer's rank. "Look at the chicken guts, Pa. We was promoted."

Baylis took his knife and unstitched the braids and removed them from the uniforms. The men dressed, then slipped their pistols into the waists of their trousers.

"You both look quite presentable now," Milton said, placing the officer's braids in his haversack. "It's a short walk to the square."

"Looks like your students left in a hurry," Baylis said, as the men started back across the grounds. The Institute looked half put away.

"Governor Brown resisted right to the last not to send them, but Jeff Davis up in Richmond insisted. One of the cadets Joe Brown sent was his own young son." Milton said. He then added with a sigh, "It's a sad thing. These lads are our future."

"When we destroy our young boys, it's like we're grinding the seed corn," Ulysses said.

"Some hoped that the boys would become teachers to counteract the abolitionist educators streaming in from the North. Our Good King William abolished slavery thirty years ago, and I believe we are happier for it."

"Slavery puts no gravy in my bowl. I barely got the money to own myself," Baylis said. "I'm not in that fight."

Milton laughed.

"Then we are in the same situation, but you are much closer to home. You could walk, but I doubt, sir, that I could swim," Milton said.

Close to home, Baylis thought, but no way to get there.

Chapter 21

July 1969

RON ENTERED THE CHURCH alongside his parents and brother, feeling conspicuous in his Army uniform. The only other military uniform in the congregation belonged to Alex, who looked smartly turned out, if slightly hung over, standing patiently beside his mother, Ginger, and Mona, who had joined the church when she started dating his friend.

Ron knew that Mona's zest for good times had earned her an unfair reputation in the town. Many of the older folks in the congregation shunned her, refusing even to welcome her in the Lord's house on a Sunday morning.

As Ron moved down the aisle, he spotted Bobbie Mae Turner, the church's resident gossip. She had made a point of stopping to speak with Ginger, obviously pretending that Mona wasn't even standing there. From the look on his face, Alex was more than a bit annoyed. He couldn't care less what people thought of him, but acting that way toward Mona rubbed a raw nerve.

Mona, an only child whose divorced parents were not members of the church, didn't seem to mind Bobbie Mae's behavior. She was always the last to see malice in anyone. It was clear from the way she held onto Alex's arm that all she cared about was being with him.

Ron and Michael scooted into a pew beside Alex and Mona, while Carlotta and Ginger took their places in the choir and Harold settled down in front with the other deacons. After the opening hymn, Reverend Fletcher moved to the pulpit for opening announcements.

"Today we're honored to have two of our sons with us who are currently in military service, Alex Granger and Ronald Simpson. You boys stand up and let everyone get a look."

Ron and Alex exchanged sheepish glances. *Ambushed.* With forced grins they rose to applause, and sank back into their seats as soon as propriety allowed.

Reverend Fletcher fixed his gaze on the congregation. "These young men continue the South's proud tradition of service to our nation. In every American conflict since the Revolutionary War, the South has had the most volunteers and the most casualties."

"We've also had the most homicides and chili cook-offs," Alex whispered.

"We've also produced the most Medal of Honor winners and awards for valor," Reverend Fletcher continued.

"Guess that means we won the War Olympics," Ron muttered.

The pastor paused, letting his words sink in. "With that in mind, I'm proud to announce that our deacons have voted to join with others of our faith to support the war by attending the Affirmation Vietnam Rally at Atlanta Stadium. The event's planned for August. I pray that the spirit moves you to attend and support our young men in uniform."

Ron felt a ripple of dissent pass through the congregation. The mood in the community, like the country itself, had grown testy. The war was now a matter of contention even in this proudly patriotic town and conservative church. If you voiced an opinion, either for or against, you'd be expected to argue your position.

Ron observed, from the corners of his eyes, a few silent, unconscious expressions of protest in Reverend Fletcher's flock. Arms were crossed, throats were cleared, and eyes dropped hastily. Those parishioners dared not voice their opinions openly during worship, but they were already working out reasons why they couldn't attend the rally.

During Fletcher's sermon, Ron glanced at Michael and discovered, with amusement, that he was gazing across the aisle at Diane, who was visiting the church with her parents.

Little bro's first love. Ron grinned. Young men always thought their wild pangs of *amour* were invisible to everybody else. Michael wasn't fooling anyone, least of all his older brother.

Curiously, Diane didn't have Chuck in tow. The chump was probably too humiliated from the night before to show his face, Ron thought.

Ron caught a meddlesome pair of eyes glancing Michael's way. He turned, almost imperceptibly, to see Bobbie Mae taking a nosey interest in Michael's display of puppy love. Ron looked straight at Bobbie Mae, his eyes boring into her, until she became aware and quickly turned back to the preacher.

The sermon dragged past noon with a languid, drowsy pace. The crowded chapel was stuffy even with the stained glass windows open, and the warm sun's glint and the drone of the preacher both conspired to drop Ron's chin onto his chest in slumber. Just as he thought he couldn't possibly keep his eyes open any longer, Reverend Fletcher called for the invitational hymn.

"*Softly and tenderly Jesus is calling,*" the choir declared as one voice, "*calling for you and for me . . .*" The richness of their harmonies filled the church. Ron quietly mouthed the words as he tipped his head back to catch the honey-soft tones of his mother's alto voice sweetening the mix.

After three verses, as Alex later noted, "There were only busy signals, so the Lord ended His call."

With the service over, Alex walked Mona to her car, and then he and Ron pushed across the parking lot toward Ron's Mustang. At the car, Alex glanced up, a hint of mischief just below his smile. Ron had seen that look a thousand times. It always meant trouble.

"I got a present for you," Alex said, switching on his shambling charm. He pulled an eight-track tape from his jacket and held it up for Ron to see. It was the Byrd's new release, *Ballad of Easy Rider.*

Alex reached through the passenger window, popped the tape into Ron's player, and cranked the volume. The first strains of "Jesus Is Just All Right" belted forth loud enough to vibrate the car chassis.

Ron glanced at the startled faces of the church elders who were fanning across the asphalt towards their cars and Sunday dinners. "Maybe we'd better turn that down until we get outta here."

Alex cranked the volume as loud as it would go and yelled over it, "Why? IT'S A SONG ABOUT *GEE-SUS!*"

"*I don't care what they may know, I don't care where they may go,*" the Byrds chirped noisily. "*I don't care what they may know . . .*"

Shaking his ass, Alex began singing off key at the top of his lungs. "JESUS IS JUST ALRIGHT, OH YEAH! JESUS IS JUST ALRIGHT!"

Alex was just being Alex. There was little Ron could do other than let him have his fun. Alex's lark was clearly intended as a message to all the church elders who disliked rock 'n' roll and had treated Mona so poorly that morning. And, after all, what adult would ask a soldier serving his country to turn down his music—even rock music—especially when the Lord's name was being praised?

But apparently, praising Jesus at one hundred decibels was too much for eighty-seven-year-old Chester Fleagle. Chester had a sixty-six-year record of church attendance, and he was fond of reminding the "youngsters" (being anyone under the age of fifty) that he was born before the Model T and had little use for cars, music, short skirts, or dancing.

Chester, whose cheap toupee sat on his head like a dead squirrel, bobbled across the parking lot, waving his cane and proclaiming loudly, "Jesus is more than *jest* all right, boy! He's *yer* Lord and Savior!"

Alex sized up the whey-faced geezer, reached in the car, and dropped the volume down. He then threw his arms into the air and hollered, "Praise *Geeee-sus!*"

Chester responded with an equally enthusiastic, "Amen!"

Alex proceeded to shower the unsuspecting old man with a rhythmic, syncopated chant of spiritual praise, punctuated by "hallelujahs" and "amens," like some fevered Pentecostal preacher firing up the radio airwaves with the "*thunda* of the *Lowd.*"

Suddenly, Ron realized: *that was exactly what Alex was doing.* He was mimicking Reverend Ike, the flamboyant black minister they sometimes listened to on the radio. Over the years, he and Alex had skipped church on Sunday nights as often as they could to spend the time drinking Pabst. For entertainment, Alex would tune in the "close your eyes and see green" revivalist who sounded like Little Richard on speed as he preached the blessings of prosperity. *"Money up to your armpits, a roomful of money and there you are, just tossing around in it like a swimming pool."*

Alex knew that neither this old man nor any other white adult in Forest Park had likely heard Reverend Ike. He had the preacher's act down to an art, and easily fell into the rhythm of Ike's delivery.

"Forget about your pie in the sky in the sweet by and by . . ." Alex was rhyme-talking so fast Ron was certain that the hard of hearing old man didn't understand most of the nonsense his friend was saying (*"this is a do-it-yourself church, don't be left in the lurch . . . my garage runneth over"*), but he was whipping Chester into a religious frenzy. All Ron could do is lean against the car and try desperately not to laugh.

Alex built to a crescendo, then turned to his friend. "Won't you offer us up a prayer, brother Ronald?"

Ron was speechless, literally biting his tongue to hold back the guffaws. Tears were running down his cheeks as he struggled not to give Alex away.

Chester Fleagle looked at Ron, misinterpreting the clinched emotions of his contorted face. "I can see the Lord is moving us all!" he cried out, arms heavenward, his cane stirring the air.

By this time, other church elders had heard the praising and praying and trotted over to join the spontaneous revival taking place in the parking lot.

Alex duly led the group in a fervent laying-on of hands. "Now, let's feel the anointing *pie-wore* of the *Lowd*." Alex, the master of timing, popped in the Byrd's tape, once more at full volume, and encouraged everyone to join in the "praise singing."

And they did.

"Gee-sus is jest aw-right wit me, Gee-sus is jest aw-right, oh yeah . . ."

It was the funniest Alex "kiss-off" Ron had ever witnessed.

Chapter 22

Marietta, Georgia
June 25, 1864

WAR HAD COME TO Marietta, and the cupreous clay streets of the once peaceful village were choked with panic and confusion. Canvas-covered wagons loaded with wounded and dying rebels snaked through an ocean of refugees desperately fleeing the invading army, which was now just a few miles away.

Baylis had never seen such chaos. It reminded him of an anthill that had been stepped on, although the noise was closer to pigs squealing on their way to slaughter.

Milton stared wide-eyed as they waded through the pandemonium. "*Was ever such a tohubohu of people as there assembles?*" Milton asked over the tumult.

Ulysses looked at the teacher strangely.

"I quote William Thackeray. Are you familiar with his satirical writings, kind sir?"

"You have me at a disadvantage," Ulysses said. "You are a man of book learning. I am not."

"His volume *The Luck of Barry Lyndon* is a favorite of mine. I used to read it to my wife and daughters."

Baylis thought it odd that the man would quote books at such a time, although he knew his brother quoted scripture on most any occasion.

"You are married, then?" Baylis asked.

"Yes. They are in London. I had hoped to bring my family to your great state before the war began."

A mangy brown puppy appeared, nipping and yapping at Baylis's heels, another lost soul trapped in skin and bones. The town seemed full of them. The old man tried to shoo it away, but the flea-bitten animal was having none of it. When Baylis realized a cavalry horse was on course to trample the small canine, he quickly scooped it up.

"Now, now," Baylis said, calming the puppy with a scratch behind its floppy ears. "I'll find you something to eat."

Ulysses shook his head and laughed, shouting over the commotion around them, "How you going to feed that thing, Pa? We can't even feed ourselves."

"Mister! Mister!" a freckle-faced boy with bowl-cut hair shouted, running toward the men. "That's my dog."

"And I believe he's missing you," Baylis handed the puppy to him. The boy turned and disappeared into the crowded street.

Some of the clapboard and brick houses the men passed were as high as three stories. Many of the stately residences with grand verandas and balconies draped in honeysuckle stood eerily vacant, their manicured shrubbery left unattended.

Other homes had been turned into hospitals for the sick and injured that were pouring in from the front lines. Convalescing rebels were everywhere, filling porches and yards and propped under trees. The tormented screams of wounded men having their arms and legs amputated created a devil's serenade that pierced the sweltering afternoon air.

Baylis had never liked towns, and this hell did nothing to alter his opinion. Village life seemed an altogether unpleasant way to live, even under the best of conditions. He could never understand the purpose of putting houses so close together that your neighbors knew everything about you. The beautiful gardens and orchards that dotted the wide street seemed scarce compensation for such a loss of privacy.

The sound of cannonading grew louder, rumbling over the clamor and commotion as the men jostled through the crowded street toward the village center. Soldiers stood on rooftops, watching the artillery shells explode over Kennesaw Mountain a short distance to the northwest.

The bedlam was worse in the middle of the town. In past visits, Marietta Square had been piled with cotton bales waiting to be shipped north by train. Today the large park overflowed with refugees and wounded rebels awaiting transport south to Atlanta.

Most all the women were dressed in black, having lost a family member to the Confederate cause. Baylis knew there must be a god-awful lot of women all over the south wearing the same mournful costume these days.

The war had taken much from people like him, too, but there was no designation for his lot. What do you call a man who'd had a daughter raped and a grandchild murdered? There ought to be a name, Baylis thought, and some insignia so strangers would know what not to say, what distances to keep.

Ulysses stopped a young man in a private's uniform and shouted over the clamor, "Where's the provost?"

"Over yonder," he yelled back. The soldier pointed toward a uniformed man up the street, standing behind an overturned crate being used as a standing desk.

With Milton trailing them, Baylis and Ulysses pushed through rivulets of townspeople, mostly men too old or infirm to fight.

"This wound in my leg always throbs before the shooting starts," a corporal with a long beard was saying as Baylis passed.

"That means it don't want to get shot no more," a one-legged soldier with a crutch replied, his grin full of stained teeth.

The provost was a small man with large sergeant stripes. Stuffing his corncob pipe with tobacco, he eyed Baylis, Ulysses, and Milton suspiciously from behind the crate desk.

"I've come here to report," Ulysses said over the din.

"Report what?" Provost Sergeant Chumley said.

"I was on recuperative furlough. I want to rejoin my boys at the lines."

"You got your permit for leave?"

"It got burnt up in a fire, but here's proof I got wounded." Ulysses pulled his shirt over his head, revealing the wound from the musket ball that dug through his arm and shoulder. It was mostly healed, but the scar was still sharp and red.

"That'd be a nasty-looking thing," the provost said.

"Yes, sir, it still hurts like the mischief." Ulysses pulled his shirt back down.

"I hope you killed him who done it to you."

"Can't say as I did. I never saw him."

"I'll be durned if that ain't how war is these days. You don't have to look a man in the eye to shoot him," Chumley paused to light his pipe. "You feeling well enough to fight?"

"Well enough to fight a Yankee."

"I'm his Pa," Baylis said. "In the State Guards Infantry."

"Weren't you boys and your light artillery folded into the Army of Tennessee before Missionary Ridge? How come you ain't with them?"

"I had agricultural leave to raise provisions. But I've decided to join the fight."

"And I'm supposing your permit was burnt up, too?"

"Yes, sir, same fire. I didn't think to bring you an ear of corn as witness to my labors."

Chumley squinted through a puff of smoke. "The calluses on your hands are witness enough." He then focused on the Englishman. "And you?"

"Professor Milton of the Georgia Military Institute. I'm seeking one of my young students to tell him of his father's passing."

"Well now," Chumley returned his stare to the Simpson men, "you'uns can't be deserters. All of them are running in the other direction. But we can't be too careful. We've had spies and raiders in these parts."

Chumley motioned down the street. "Our line is up along that mountain," he said, pointing toward Big Kennesaw. "As you get closer, someone can help you find your regiments."

Baylis heard a cultivated Southern voice behind them.

"Milton, is that you?"

Baylis turned to see a tall man in a worn but clean officer's uniform, a patch over his left eye. The man's left arm was amputated below his shoulder, the uniform sleeve neatly folded and pinned.

"I say, Captain Jeffers, you are looking so much the better. A picture of health," Milton said, then turned to the Simpsons. "The good Captain is the father of Timothy Jeffers, one of my young gentleman from the Institute."

Jeffers walked toward Milton, his arm outstretched in greeting.

"What goes, my friend?" Captain Jeffers asked.

"Traveling on charity," Milton said.

"But what of your wages?"

"The Institute left rather quickly for the war. They said I would be paid, but then there was no one to do it."

"How terrible. You can't be left so far from home and penniless."

"My friends here have a brother who is a man of God, currently tending to the burial of your dead. He suggests I might become a missionary of sorts."

"A splendid idea," Jeffers said. "You revealed yourself as a true Christian with all the hours you spent entertaining me as I recovered. You were a savior."

"You are kind to say so, but it was a pleasure to spend time with a man of cultivation and accomplishment."

"Let me advance your wages. I can collect them from the state later."

"I would not impose," Milton said.

"Nonsense. You know I have many more Confederate dollars than arms or living friends."

Milton hesitated. "I would have to think it over, kind sir."

Captain Jeffers signed the orders the sergeant gave him.

"We're on half rations. You can draw them at the quartermaster's tent," Chumley said to the Simpson men.

"I believe I can do better than that," Captain Jeffers said. "Let me provide the three of you with a first-rate dinner."

Milton seemed heartened that the invitation had been extended to Baylis and Ulysses. "That's very kind of you," the professor said. "I shall seek your forgiveness in advance for eating like a starving man. But that's precisely what I am."

Baylis didn't see much point in refusing the meal and eating Confederate Army fritters and fat meat.

"Thank you," Baylis said. "My boy and I have been running so hard we haven't had regular food."

"They came through the Union lines under the guise of carrying the dead. Went right through Big Shanty, they did. I met them at the graveyard, and we resolved to travel together."

"That must have been quite a journey. I'd like to hear your story."

Not far off, Baylis heard a man screaming loudly, and others taunting him.

"That sounds like someone's making a corner of hell," Baylis said.

"Probably, the Home Guard found another deserter," the captain said, looking about to locate the sound. "They cut their Achilles tendon and make them crawl before they kill them."

"The men they catch are generally of a higher character than the guards," Sergeant Chumley added. "A step below chicken thieves, they are."

Another scream was heard. Captain Jeffers and the provost sergeant walked briskly toward the clamor. Baylis, Ulysses, and Milton flowed behind.

Up ahead, a man was crawling upon the ground, begging for his life. He tried to push his shoulders up with his hands so he could look his tormentors in the eye, but his arms shuddered and gave way.

"Please, mister. I got a family. Have mercy," he pleaded as six soldiers hooted and kicked him.

"Here's your mercy," a man with a ruddy nose said. He pointed his rifle at the man's head and pulled the trigger. Fire exploded from the muzzle, and his brains flew out the back of his skull.

"What the blazes is going on here?" Jeffers demanded.

"We executed a deserter," the man who had fired the rifle said. He rolled the body over with his foot. "See how ugly he was."

The man's face bore a horrible wound that had healed to a prominent scar. Baylis imagined the poor soul had suffered in the fighting until he reached his breaking point and ran. *Who was to say it couldn't happen to any man? That after exhibiting limitless bravery, one could finally reach his limit?*

"Wasn't much of a firing squad," Jeffers said.

"That's the way I do 'em."

"And who are you to decide how justice is dispensed?"

"I am Captain Loomis of the Home Guard."

"Ah, the Home Guard. A bit removed from your area of command aren't you? Are you on a looting expedition?"

"Who be you to ask such a thing?" Loomis said.

"I am Captain Jeffers, Army of Tennessee. I command the Provost Guard in Marietta."

"Well, Captain, your Army of Tennessee would appear a bit outnumbered. There are six of us with rifles, and all you got is one eye, one arm, and one pistol."

Ulysses caught his father's eye. Baylis knew his son was prepared to back Jeffers if it came to that. Ulysses opened his uniform jacket slowly, showing the Home Guard the revolver in the waist of his pants. Baylis put a hand inside his coat, found the butt of his .36 caliber pistol, and drew it slowly along his covered side and held it out of sight, at his leg.

Captain Jeffers stared at Loomis. "No sir, I have you at the disadvantage." He pulled his Colt revolver and pointed the six-shooter at Loomis's head.

Baylis and Ulysses leveled their pistols at the guards.

Milton, unarmed, fumbled with his jacket, awkward and uncertain what to do. He obviously wasn't used to confrontations involving loaded weapons. Sergeant Chumley was unarmed, too, but made such a ferocious face he didn't appear to need a weapon.

"You see, all of you are cowards, and I am not," Jeffers said to the guards. There was a frightening smile on the one-eyed captain's face, as if he had already decided he would die in this war. Perhaps he even considered death his friend.

"Well, yes, sir. Sorry for the misunderstanding," Loomis said.

"Take that body with you to the graveyard. You don't want my men to find it. He could have been their comrade."

"Yes sir, we'll do that."

The guards grabbed the body by its legs and dragged it off.

Jeffers looked at the sergeant and cocked his head toward the departing men. Chumley gave a quick nod of understanding and trailed after them.

"Let's make fast for the square," Jeffers said. "I don't want them to find their courage once they are out of pistol range."

"Those soldiers are no better than bummers thieving for the Yankees," Baylis said as the men moved quickly across the square.

"I feel uneasy about them wandering these environs," Milton said.

"Don't worry. Sergeant Chumley will send cavalry after them. Before the night is over, they'll taste the saber. And our chicken coops and widows will be safer tomorrow."

"When you are in the lines, you know who the enemy is," Ulysses said. "Life in the ditches is much simpler."

The captain led them across the street to the Fletcher House Hotel. The four-story brick edifice, the tallest in town, was nestled on a corner next to the railroad track that cut through the village.

The sudden quiet as they stepped through the doors was a startling contrast to the wild commotion outside. As Baylis's eyes adjusted to the dimness, he soon understood why.

In the hotel lobby, there were only dead men and ghosts.

Chapter 23

July 1969

MICHAEL SIMPSON HAD BEGUN to feel more comfortable in his own skin. Maybe it was Alex's whistle, which hung from a large white shoestring around his neck. As Michael stood at the base of the main lifeguard tower, surveying the swimmers in the water, the whistle imbued him with an aura of confidence, as though some of Alex's ballsy essence was channeled into him through it.

Or maybe it was because Michael could no longer rely on his brother and best friend for advice. Now he was making his own decisions without their guidance for the first time in his life. To his surprise, he felt at ease doing it.

Even Kenny had calmed down since landing his first successful summer date a few weekends earlier. Today he was working up his lexicon of boob taxonomy.

"*Pooters*," Kenny declared from atop the guard tower, gesturing with a nod to a nubby-chested girl on a beach towel a few yards away. "Joanne Lee definitely has pooters."

Michael observed her for a brief moment. "If she has pooters, what do you call what her older sister's has?" The girl of nineteen summers who lay on her back next to Joanne had ripe, conical breasts that poked sharply upward in defiance of gravity.

"Those?" Kenny grinned, "Those're *poons*."

"Poons?" Michael laughed.

"Yeah, but I also saw a pair of Nortons a couple a minutes ago. Nortons are the best." Kenny eagerly scanned the beach. "There." He nodded in the direction of Loraine, who was planted under an umbrella on a large beach towel, reading a magazine.

Michael casually glanced Loraine's way. She looked up, caught his eye, and gave him a smile. He smiled back, then his gaze settled back on the lake.

As the summer ripened, Michael had indulged more and more in the guilty pleasure of Loraine's flirtations. It was difficult for him to refuse, because she sought him out nearly every day. She would park her beach towel within easy view of the main lifeguard station, and always found excuses to talk to him. It flattered him silly that this beautiful woman had singled him out.

"Look who's here," Kenny said edgily.

Michael followed Kenny's gaze over to where the beach met the carefully tended grass. Chuck Leach was parading onto the white, fluffy sand with some curvaceous blonde in a lime-colored bikini. She clung to his beefy arm like her hands were glued. Michael had never seen her before.

"What's that about?" Michael asked.

Kenny nodded toward Diane, who sat, suddenly rigid, at her guard station on the north beach. "My guess is Chuck's here to rub his new squeeze in Diane's face since she broke up with the jerk."

Michael felt his stomach lurch. "Diane broke up with Chuck?" he tried to ask casually. He had barely spoken to her since the night at the Red Charpeg. She had been in a sullen, withdrawn mood for days. Now he understood why.

"Jeez, Simpson, do you live in a cave or somethin'? She dumped the Chuckster right after that night your bro handed his balls to him. I think she finally got tired of the guy's bullshit."

Michael's mind was spinning its wheels. He had tried to push Diane out of his mind after that Saturday night. He had decided that if she was Chuck's girl, there was no place for him in her life. But now Diane was free. Diane was *available*.

"Don't know why the two of 'em ever dated anyway," Kenny was saying. "Chuck don't have much use for any girl who won't put out for him. I bet he was probably keeping that new slice on the side." Chuck shepherded his latest trophy to a spot on the beach where he was sure Diane could see. He spread out a large beach towel, then stripped off his tee. He handed her a bottle of Coppertone, which she dutifully began rubbing on his brawny shoulders and back.

"Looks like Diane's about to pop a vein," Kenny said.

Michael glanced back to Diane. Her features were set like granite. He excused himself from Kenny and drifted down the beach to her guard stand. When he climbed to the top of the platform, he found her staring straight ahead, her face pale with fury.

"You okay?" Michael asked quietly.

"Sure," Diane replied tersely. "Why shouldn't I be?"

"You want a break?"

"You think I need a break 'cause I'm a girl?" Diane exploded. "Afraid I might fall apart and ruin my zinc oxide? You guys are all the same."

"Hey, whoa. Take it down a notch, alright?"

"It's just . . ." Diane started, then blew out a sharp breath. She sat in silence for a moment, trying to calm herself. "It's been a long day, that's all." She offered him a thin, half-hearted smile. "Look, I'm okay, really. I'll take a break when it's my turn."

Michael nodded. With an unspoken truce, he descended the ladder and started back across the beach. He glanced at the swimmers in the lake and tried to deal with the emotional stew churning through him. Sexual longing was only one part of the combustible mix of sensations he felt—the spark that ignited the whole mess, setting a blaze that engulfed him completely. The fire's aftermath left his stomach queasy and his palms damp.

A sultry voice interrupted his obsession. "Hey, college man." It was Loraine beckoning him with her siren song from under an umbrella on the sand.

Michael wandered over to her.

"What's with the deep looks?" She glanced over to Diane. "That little blonde still got you twisting in the wind?"

"Sort of," Michael said numbly. "She broke up with her boyfriend."

"That's good news, isn't it? Now you've got your chance."

"But she won't hardly talk to me . . ." Michael's voice trailed off in misery.

"She's probably just touchy from her breakup," Loraine explained. "What you wanna do is offer her a *chance* to go out with you. Let her take it or leave it. And don't attach yourself to the outcome too much."

Michael let out an involuntary guffaw.

"I'm serious!" Loraine laughed. "Girls hate it when guys sound like they're begging." She adopted a nasal, wheedling tone, "Diane, would you go out with me Saturday night? Please, please, pretty *pleeeease*?"

Michael laughed.

"If you were asking her out, where would you take her?"

"I guess a movie or something."

"No, no. That'll never do, sweetie," Loraine shook her head, sending a tiny rivulet of shimmering black hair cascading over one shoulder. "She's probably had loads of guys take her to a movie for a first date. You wanna take her someplace different. Distinguish yourself."

"I don't know anyplace she wouldn't have been a million times."

"Well, then, maybe a special event. A concert, or at least a ball game."

"There's Freshman Orientation up at college . . ."

"Perfect! That's something you two have in common."

"Doesn't sound like a real romantic occasion."

"That's the point. If she thinks you're romancing her, she'll probably run scared. Start off doing something together that you have a mutual interest in. When she sees she can just relax with you, she might open up."

Michael glanced at Diane sitting, hunched and rigid, at her station. She didn't look like she was opening up to anybody any time soon.

"Trust me, I'm giving you the woman's perspective, beefcakes. Most guys your age never get this kind of inside scoop." The breeze lifted the light scent of perfume from her skin and blew it, like a kiss, toward his face.

"I guess you're right."

"Sweetie, I'm never wrong," she smiled. "Now go on, before some other guy beats you to the punch."

Michael grinned and strode purposefully down the beach toward Diane's lifeguard station. He meant to march right up to her and invite her to orientation. He started out burning with confidence from Loraine's sensual shot in the arm. But the closer he got, the less certain he became. When he was near enough to read her mood, he saw that her brows remained knitted and her face shadowed.

"It's time for your break," was all Michael could manage when he arrived at the white wooden stand. *Chicken*, he thought to himself.

Diane stood, climbed down, and stretched.

"Hey, are you still going to UGA in the fall?" Michael asked, mentally flagellating himself for his cowardice and the stupidity of his question.

She gave him a curious look. "Sure, why?"

"Oh. Good. I mean, that'll be a good thing for you, to start college in the fall."

"Yeah."

With that, the conversation died an agonizing death.

"I'll be back in fifteen minutes," she said, turning away.

Michael almost let her go. At the last possible second, he said, "Freshman Orientation's next Saturday up in Athens. You wanna go together? I mean, you could ride up there with me."

Diane glanced across the beach toward Chuck, apprehension crossing her lovely face. Michael could read that look: *it was fear.*

She turned back, but wouldn't look him in the eye. Michael felt his stomach fall into his bowels. She was going to say no, and he would have to spend the rest of the season living with the stinging reminder of her rejection.

"Understand, this isn't a date," she said hesitantly.

Michael felt his nervous defensiveness rising, just as it had opening day of the season. "I'm just askin' if you wanna share a ride."

Diane glanced at Chuck again, bit her lip, and said, "As long as we split the cost of gas."

"Sure, sure. That's fine." Michael did his best to sound nonchalant.

"Okay," Diane said, and turned away.

Michael could barely hold himself together until Diane was out of earshot. Then he congratulated himself: "Touchdown! Yesss!"

Michael was smiling as he climbed the lifeguard stand, but he missed the look on Chuck's face. If Michael had seen it, he would have understood clearly why there was fear in Diane's eyes.

Chapter 24

July 1969

THE INTENSE FOUR MONTHS of Advanced Flight Training Ron faced at the U.S. Army Aviation Center at Fort Rucker stood in sharp contrast to the easy thrill of jockeying OH-13 trainers. Now, Ron spent his days wrangling a heavy Bell UH-1 Iroquois "Huey" through some of the most harrowing maneuvers a pilot could hope to walk away from.

Fort Rucker sprawled across over 60,000 acres in southeastern Alabama, in an area of rolling woods the locals call the "Wiregrass Region." Early Spanish settlers had grazed their cattle herds along the riverbanks on the tall, bunched wild grass with peculiar wire-like blades and spikes. Though the grass gradually became scarce, its name stuck to the area.

During the Civil War, rebel soldiers trained in the center of the camp, which was later named for Edmund W. Rucker, a one-armed Confederate general. Ron recognized the irony of training at yet another place that was as shackled to its southern past as he was.

At Fort Rucker, WOCs had more freedom and something of a social life, as long as they didn't pick up too many demerits. They were taught how to be officers in the Army, learning the protocol and the code of conduct. Warrant officers had their own set of values, and in most cases they were not very tactful when dealing with what they called "R-L-

Os"—Real Live Officers. They held a special distaste for "butter bars," Second Lieutenants.

Although Fort Rucker's WOCs enjoyed a certain brassy liberty, Ron knew from day one that the rules had changed and that the Army's grip on his future had tightened.

"Every candidate who expects to learn rotary aviation the *right* way at Fort Rucker, step forward," Senior Tactical Officer Williams bellowed. The WOCs of Company B, 5th Battalion, 1st Brigade braced at attention on the camp's parade field that first day.

The heat from the scorching morning sun was working its way under Ron's uniform, tickling the skin of his neck and needling down into his collar. He struggled against the overwhelming urge to scratch himself.

Ron had heard a thing or two about STO Williams from his bunkmates. The man carried a reputation for being a hard-ass, but he was well respected. He had two tours of duty in 'Nam under his belt, a chit on his resume that immediately elicited esteem from those under his command.

Williams stood a towering six foot four and possessed the steely muscles, hardened daily by his work. Yet the officer had a soft baby-face, with round cheeks and puckish jawline, a middle-aged man's crinkles starting around the corners of the eyes. Only in the eyes themselves, fiercely focused as they were, could Ron see the face of a career officer. Williams seemed to know the disadvantages of his soft features. He tended to gaze at his officers from under a single heavy brow, losing much of his face's boyish sweetness to foreshortening.

Ron had been a hair's-breadth away from having a man like this for a father. Harold Simpson had seriously considered becoming a "Marine lifer," and had nearly done so, twice. He left active duty after World War II to marry Carlotta. When he was called up for service as an instructor during the Korean War, they approached him again with the tantalizing option. Carlotta, with two tiny boys tugging her skirts, had used a southern woman's quiet resolve to persuade him that the Marine Corps was no place for raising small children. Harold reluctantly passed. Instead of mastering raw young recruits on Parris Island, he would master typefaces in his print shop. Ron and Michael narrowly escaped a boyhood of transience and impermanence, an existence slavishly dependent on—and utterly devoured by—the Corps.

Several candidates had stepped forward smartly with STO Williams's booming query. But it sounded like a trick question to Ron—"*In the military, you never volunteer for anything*," Harold Simpson had told him—so he kept his place in the row.

"You're not here at Fort Rucker to learn the *right* way or the *wrong* way of rotary aviation," the STO growled. "Here you will learn the *Army* way."

Ron held a mental smile. It wasn't the first time his father had been right.

Chapter 25

July 1969

ON SATURDAY MORNING, MICHAEL spent a full quarter hour in front of the bathroom mirror, wrestling with the same rebellious thatch of hair that had given him trouble since sixth grade. He even resorted to borrowing a squirt of his mother's hairspray to force the unruly lock into submission.

Michael gunned the Mustang's powerful engine along the perimeter loop, winning back the precious minutes he'd squandered in tending his coiffure. He made a mental note to thank Ron again for letting him use the Mustang while he was away at Fort Rucker.

Michael pulled onto an unfamiliar street and made his way through a well-to-do neighborhood. His spirits sank as the houses grew larger and more extravagant. The perfect lawns he now passed were not tended by sunburned dads, but by professional gardeners. He was sure the mothers who called these grand residences home had never cleaned a toilet. Michael Simpson, a printer's son, felt obscenely out of place.

Michael found the address that matched the number Diane had given him. The house was a two-story, all-brick colonial with dove-gray trim. Michael approached the house with trepidation and pressed the doorbell. He heard chimes sound deep inside the house. He waited. And waited.

After what seemed like an eternity, the massive oak door swung open to reveal a man in a steel gray cardigan and black slacks. He held a martini in his hand and a practiced scowl across his features. The man might as well have been wearing a sign around his neck that read, "Barry Goldwater Republican." He didn't open the outer glass door, but instead sized Michael up with an unfriendly eye.

"Well, what is it?" the man grumbled.

"I'm Michael Simpson, sir."

"So?"

"I'm, um, here to take your daughter to Freshman Orientation at UGA."

The man sipped his martini and slowly, deliberately sloshed it around in his mouth, while appraising Michael from head to toe. After a long moment he said, "So?"

Diane appeared behind the somber battleship of a man, and gave Michael a reassuring smile. "Daddy, this is Michael. Michael, this is my father."

"I don't like him, dear."

Diane squeezed past him and opened the screen door. "Don't mind Daddy," she said with a laugh.

The man shot a disapproving glance at Diane's tight bell-bottomed jeans and peasant blouse. "I hope you don't plan to go to a place of higher education dressed like that."

Diane sighed with the petulance of a teenage girl. "Yes, Daddy, I do. And yes, I'll be home by eleven. And yes, I'll behave. And yes, I love you and Mom." She turned, stretched on her tiptoes, and gave him a peck on his cheek. "Now quit acting like such a bear. You're going to scare Michael away."

"That's the idea," he rumbled. But as they turned to walk to the car, Michael thought he saw the tiniest twinkle of goodwill in the man's stony eyes. He wouldn't have bet on it, though.

"Don't worry about him," Diane said as they climbed into the Mustang and pulled away. "He's just overly protective sometimes. Especially with somebody new."

Michael sneaked a look at Diane as she settled into her seat. She looked younger somehow, covered in soft, flowing cottons instead of a form-fitting swimsuit. Her strawberry blonde hair, usually swept back, and often soggy at the lake, had been brushed smooth, and formed a perfect frame for her slim Nordic features.

"I think he's still mad at me for breaking up with Chuck because his family has so much money," she explained. "And dad's crazy about UGA football. He was hoping for season tickets."

"You don't look like your dad at all," Michael said, giving himself an excuse to stare. "You must take after your mother."

"No, it's because he's my stepfather."

"Wow, I've never known anybody whose parents got divorced."

"They didn't," Diane said, shaking her head, "I never met my real dad. He died before I was born. In Korea."

"I'm sorry."

"It's not so bad, really. It's not like I ever got to know him."

After weeks of furtive practice, Michael had become adept at reading Diane's face. He saw at once the sadness in her eyes that betrayed her words.

As they traveled the sun-drenched county highway, Diane fiddled with the radio until The Who's "Magic Bus" filled the car. Michael breathed a sigh and felt himself gradually relaxing. They talked about the lake, college, Ron's flight training in Alabama. For the moment, at least, she was the old Diane he'd known last year. A friend. A comrade in adolescence.

UGA campus was abuzz with activity. After driving down East Broad Street, they parked across from the university arch. A wave of pedestrians swept around them. Michael gawked openly at the sea of flowing hair—on *males* and females—and all the bright costumes and swinging beads.

"Where'd all these people come from?" Diane asked nervously.

"They must be in summer school."

"No wonder they're in summer school," Diane said, eyeing the impromptu clusters of laughing, chanting students. "Wasting time when they should be studying."

A young guy with a stack of pamphlets cradled in his arm and Shakespearean sonnets written in purple ink all over his blue jeans approached the Mustang and slipped a sheet through the open window.

"Peace, my brother," he shouted, "Peace, sister." He offered a pamphlet to Diane. She glanced at it with distaste and pitched it back out the window.

Michael examined his copy. *Stop The War NOW,* it read. *Bring Our Troops Home.* He pocketed the flyer.

~

Michael couldn't recall a single day in his life that passed as quickly as this one. He had expected hours of sweaty palms and nervous small talk. Instead, Diane seemed happier and more relaxed than he had ever seen her. They sat side by side for freshman orientation, then bought sandwiches at the Bulldog Room café and ate them on the lawn in front of Milledge dorm. Afterwards they toured north campus, eyeing the stately old buildings, and sipped colas while sitting on the cement wall in front of Memorial Hall. If this was his future for the next four years, Michael could live with it just fine.

At the end of a day that had not held one sour note, Michael and Diane made their way back to the Mustang. Diane was babbling excitedly. "What a groovy day! I really love this place. I wanna check out the university bookstore before we start back."

"I'll get the car, pick you up in front," Michael offered.

With a smile, Diane disappeared inside the red brick building.

Michael pushed up Lumpkin Street past several fraternities, then turned back onto Broad Street and moved past a row of shops toward the Mustang.

Michael sensed something was wrong when he heard the sound of metal hammering against metal, and the fractious tinkle of broken glass crunching on pavement. His curiosity turned to alarm once he realized where the sound was coming from.

Michael came upon the Mustang just as Chuck Leach shattered the last headlight with a tire iron. His buddies, Marty and Ira, leaned on Chuck's Dodge, laughing at his handiwork. The Mustang, to which Ron had lovingly dedicated many summers' worth of paychecks, was in ruins. Not a panel remained undented, not a window unshattered, not one of its formerly perfect surfaces remained unmarred. Chuck had destroyed the car.

Michael stormed up to Chuck in a blind fury. Chuck turned and casually leaned against the broken Mustang.

"How do you like the customizing? Figured you needed a secondhand car for that secondhand snatch you're driving around."

"You asshole!" As Michael's fist shot toward Chuck's jaw, he caught a momentary glimpse of a bar of metal swinging at his gut. Then, as if a flash bulb had been fired, his vision exploded in pain. The tire iron connected with his two lower ribs, and Michael crumpled to the ground, clutching his side in agony.

Michael couldn't get his lungs to draw breath. He lay gasping on the sidewalk like fresh-caught tuna, praying that Diane wouldn't come looking for him.

Chuck leaned in close, almost pressing his lips to Michael's ear. "Now go home to your mama where you belong. And leave Diane the fuck alone. If you don't, the pain you're feeling will only get worse, you little faggot."

Chuck and his pals climbed into the Dodge and drove off, leaving Michael lying in a heap on the cement walk in front of the ruined Mustang.

After several agonizing seconds, Michael found that he could breathe again, although with great pain. A minute passed before he dared to ease himself to his knees. When he tried to stand, the pain that shot through his left side caused him to vomit violently onto the pavement. He collapsed across the Mustang's hood, gasping and crying out in fury.

Then he thought of Diane. She would have to see him this way. She would feel responsible. Worst of all, she would *pity* him.

Michael had no idea how much time had passed before he finally managed to ease himself behind the Mustang's wheel and drive the battered car up to the bookstore.

Diane was waiting at the curb, scanning the street, worry darkening her face. When she saw Michael and the Mustang, she put a hand to her mouth. "My god, what happened? Are you okay?"

"Just get in," Michael grimaced.

"I'm not going anywhere 'til you tell me what happened. Who did this to you?" She was clearly afraid that she already knew the answer.

"I don't wanna talk about it," Michael groaned, holding his ribs. "Please, just get in the car."

Diane's eyes filled with tears. She climbed in.

With searing pain in his side and rage in his heart, Michael drove slowly home.

Chapter 26

August 1969

THE NEXT MONDAY WAS the hottest day of the season, and the beach was packed, a wall-to-wall carpet of sweaty, tan bodies. It was the largest crowd Michael had ever seen at the lake.

Late that afternoon, Michael was on the main guard stand, his sunglasses and tee shirt hiding the bruises. The air had gone out of him.

Across the sand, Michael could see Diane approaching. With extra guards working, he had managed to avoid conversation with her all day. Except for a mumbled hello, they hadn't really spoken since they had returned from Athens.

She stood beside the guard stand and traced the sand with her toes. "I know Chuck messed up the car," Diane said quietly.

"You must be Nancy Drew." Michael glanced at her, then went back to scanning the swimmers in the water.

She looked up at him. "I'm sorry . . . you're in the middle of something."

"Between you and Chuckles? Yeah, I figured that part out."

"Chuck's having a hard time accepting that we broke up."

"No kiddin'." Michael's sarcasm was dripping from his lips along with the sweat.

Diane struggled with what to say next. "Are you going to the Affirmation Vietnam Rally next weekend?"

"Dunno. Why?"

"Just thought we could ride together if you were."

That was the last thing he had expected to hear. Michael studied her for a second, not really sure what to make of the invitation. "This is some kind of pity party, right?"

"Maybe we shouldn't go out again . . ."

"We didn't go out, remember? Just shared a ride and gas."

"Forget it." Diane abruptly spun in the sand and started away.

"Diane, wait!" Michael called after her. He climbed down off the watch stand. "You're right. We shouldn't go out again . . ." he said, moving close to her, "not unless it's a date. Not some share-a-ride, split-the-gas thing cause we're friends. But a I-pick-you-up-I-pay *real* date."

Diane's eyes held his for a moment. "I'd like that."

Michael's smile broke free for the first time that day.

Michael picked Diane up on his motorcycle just as a tomato-red summer moon was chasing the last of the sunset from the sky. Having her arms wrapped around his waist as they moved up the highway toward Atlanta was as close to heaven he could imagine.

Sitting in the Atlanta Stadium under a full moon, Michael could still feel where Diane had held on to him. The scent of her Wind Song perfume lingered on his leather jacket. It was a perfect night.

Michael always enjoyed going to the stadium, known as "the house that Hank built" after Aaron hit his 500th home run there the year before. It held more than 50,000 people, and it sounded like every one of them began singing along when Staff Sergeant Barry Sadler, down on the field, started to croon "Ballad of the Green Berets" with its dramatic military cadence.

In the upper level, Diane nestled closer to Michael and held his arm tightly. Her touch was electrifying.

"Sounds like half the world's singing," she said.

"I think somebody's off-key," Michael joked, hoping to hide his real feelings. The war was increasingly unpopular, and he wasn't sure if he'd even have come to the rally if Diane hadn't asked him. But he didn't have the heart to tell her. Besides, he was with her on a real honest-to-God date and that was all that mattered.

"You have such a beautiful voice. You should be singing along," Diane said.

"Who me?"

"I hear you singing with the jukebox in the mornings when we're getting ready to open."

Michael tried to hide his embarrassment. "I don't wanna sing along with Sergeant Barry. I'd rather look at you."

She smiled at him, then looked away. He could see her baby blues begin to glisten.

"Well, if you're that disappointed . . ." He cleared his throat loudly as though he was about to sing.

"Oh, silly goose." She wiped a tear, and was silent for a moment. "That song . . . I always think of my daddy. Sometimes I wonder what my life would've been like had he . . ." She couldn't bring herself to finish.

Michael put his arm around her and wondered how many more children now being born would say those words someday.

Diane slipped her hand into his as they strolled through the parking lot to his motorcycle. As he helped her with her helmet, she stared up at the sky.

"What a gorgeous moon!" Her mood had brightened. "Wouldn't it be cool if we could go for a walk around the lake?"

Michael jangled his keychain and pointed to a shiny brass padlock key.

"What's that?"

"One of the perks of being head guard. The gate key."

Diane snuggled close as he pursued the full moon south out of the Atlanta and turned off onto Riverdale Road. He stopped and unlocked the gate before driving into the gravel lot.

They kicked off their shoes and dropped them at the edge of the beach. The sugar-white sand whisked like cool silk between their toes. The light from the full moon was so intense they could almost feel its rays on their backs.

When they reached the far end of the horseshoe beach, Diane dipped a toe in the moon-spangled water, then turned with a playful glint in her eye, and said, "Race ya."

Michael blinked, not sure what she meant. "Race? Where?"

"To the dock and back." She indicated the glossy lake with a jerk of her head.

"I don't have a suit." Michael felt his words stumble out.

Diane grinned. "You gonna let that stop you?"

She lifted her shirt up over her head and flung it onto the sand. Her jeans followed. She was now down to bra and panties. Michael stood watching numbly, his brain spinning its wheels.

"Don't look like a train hit you. I've got bathing suits that cover less than this."

She was already splashing her way out to deeper water before he recovered enough to pull off his own tee shirt and jeans. He then found himself gliding through the cool, silvery water with Diane's luscious body only inches away.

After they had touched the dock and swam back to the lake's far side, they flopped down on the sand in their underwear. The warm moonlit air caressing their damp skin made them reluctant to put on their clothes.

Michael tried to find a way to compose himself sitting next to a half-naked Diane.

"I wouldn't have blamed you if you didn't wanna see me after what Chuck did to your brother's car." She rested her head on his shoulder, as though her dark thoughts about Chuck were so heavy that she needed support. "But I'm glad you did." She looked at him and smiled.

"I never understood what you saw in him," Michael said. He reached for her hand and held it warmly.

Diane shrugged. "I dunno either, really."

She looked away and pushed her heels through the white sand. "I guess I was thinking more about what everybody else expected of me, and not about what I wanted. Then he started pressuring me to . . . *you know.*"

Michael nodded.

"After a while, I realized if I didn't put a stop to it, he'd find a way to get what he wanted."

"So you and he never . . .?" Michael fumbled.

"If you're asking if you're the first, you are."

It took Michael a moment to catch the implication. "I am?" he stammered.

Diane nuzzled his ear softly and whispered, "If you want to be."

She touched his face. Their eyes pulled toward each other like worlds colliding. Michael kissed her tentatively, then again, deeper.

Diane responded with a hungry urgency Michael had never known from any girl. She tugged him up from the sand and led him back into the lake. With the soft water lapping all around their bodies, she slipped out of her bra and panties and changed his world forever.

Chapter 27

August 1969

THE SEVERAL MISHAPS THAT occurred during Advanced Rotary Wing Training at Fort Rucker underscored a central fact Ron had never considered before entering service: *rotary wing pilots do not carry parachutes.*

If a rotary wing aircraft was too disabled to make a forced landing, the reasoning went, it was too disabled to parachute out of. As a result, much time in flight school was spent practicing forced landings, or "autorotations" as they were called.

Approaching Fort Rucker's Hanchey Army Heliport from a relatively high altitude into the wind, the training helicopter engine would be cut off, disengaging it from the rotor. The aircraft would now be in a state of non-powered flight similar to a fixed wing glider. The student pilot would control the attitude of the helicopter and the collective pitch of the rotor blades to control its forward speed and descent. When it neared the ground, he would raise the aircraft's nose and pitch to slow airspeed and increase lift for a soft landing.

If these actions were properly done, the aircraft could be brought to a velvety-soft landing. However, if the airspeed was reduced too quickly, or if the lift remaining in the rotors was spent too soon, the bird would land with significant impact, often resulting in damage to the aircraft and injury to the student pilot and training officer.

Officer Williams impressed upon Ron in no uncertain terms that in the midst of a loss-of-power emergency, there would be no time to think about what to do. Ron would have to respond automatically if he was to save himself and the aircraft's passengers. There would be no time for a "three-finger fuck-around," as Williams called it.

While Ron's first few attempts at "power off" landings were harrowing, he soon got used to them. He practiced the intricate maneuver so often that it became second nature. After a while, Ron believed he could perform an auto-rotation in his sleep.

~

Just when Ron was certain he had survived the worst of it, his nightmares began. His hellish dream was always the same. His helicopter was spinning helplessly out of control, spiraling down through a thick tomb of black sky. The gauges in front of him made no sense. The markings were written in a language he had never seen. Nothing made sense.

Ron shuddered awake in his bunk, his sweaty sheets clinging to him like the skin of a moist fruit. He grabbed for the edges of his cot and gripped them until he could convince himself that the world was *not* spinning.

For the past two weeks, Ron had been flying helicopter instrument trainers under the "hood," an opaque visor that masked the view through the windscreen and forced student pilots to fly solely by their aircraft's gauges. The hood was the only part of advanced flight training that terrified Ron. Although he understood the need for the skill—bad weather could always creep in unannounced—it seemed insane to voluntarily rob himself of a perfectly clear view of his flight path.

The mere idea of blindly propelling several tons of machinery forward at 120 knots— "beating the air into submission" is what pilots called it— sent chills through his belly. The instant Ron slipped the hood on, isolating his vision to the tiny horizon of mute gauges, he felt awash and alone.

Every night since he'd been given that infernal set of blinders, the same nightmare had spun him out of his sleep. One minute, he would be flying straight and level under the hood; the next, he'd glance up to find chaos cascading across the instrument panel. Needles swept their gauges, the altimeter spinning as half a dozen indicators crept toward the red line.

Ron worked the pedals and stick, but only pulled the machine into a tighter spin. He whipped off the hood just in time to see a field of yellow wiregrass coming up fast. The gyrating copter plummeted into hot Alabama earth at over ninety knots. The world went black, and Ron felt the tingling sensation of life leaving his body.

Then his eyes would fly open in the dark of his barracks. He'd bolt upright in his cot, gripping its rails, waiting for the spinning in his head to subside. It would take a long while, blinking in the darkness, for Ron to believe that he wasn't dead.

Chapter 28

August 1969

SUMMER HAD BEGUN TO shed its magic. As the season wound down, Pinerock Lake saw fewer bathers. This morning, already oppressively hot and sticky despite a dull canopy of clouds, only the die-hard regulars had bothered to show.

"The pH level's all messed up." Michael was at the water's edge with Kenny, eyeing the lake's dark green color. He scooped up a swampy handful of water. "Algae's growing." As the summer progressed, the lake water had rotted from Kodachrome blue to a sickly olive as the algae rallied against the chemical assault.

Michael glanced over at Mrs. Lacey, who was nodding drowsily over her stack of romance novels while her epileptic daughter played nearby. Michael could barely see Julie's lower torso below the lake's cloudy surface as she waded out waist-deep in the water.

Kenny climbed the main stand to relieve Michael for a break just as the heat was getting fierce. Because of the sparse crowd, they were the only two guards on duty.

Diane was on vacation with her parents, and Michael missed her. They had grown close since their first night of lovemaking. He smiled every time he passed the spot on the beach where they sat in their underwear that night.

She had called him twice from Destin, Florida, where her family was staying. Hearing her voice had only made him miss her more.

Michael swam out to the diving dock in the center of the lake. After a summer of simmering in the Georgia sun, the lake water didn't even feel all that cool—more like forsaken bathwater.

Michael dove deep, down to where the sunlight couldn't penetrate, until his fingers brushed the feathers of algae reaching up from the lake bottom. He swam that way for as long as he could stand, then surfaced, gasping a lungful of steaming air.

He was hauling himself onto the dock when he realized that he was missing something: *Alex's whistle had slipped from around his neck.*

The shock of its absence stunned him. He dove back under, opening his eyes to the sting of the chlorinated water, even though the lake's haze clouded everything from his sight. He pawed the algae until his lungs ached, then he resurfaced.

The moment his head broke the surface, Michael heard a whistle blowing. For half a second, his mind spun its gears—*he'd just been looking for a whistle.* Then he remembered the only reason he, and all the other lifeguards, carried one.

Michael scrambled onto the dock in time to see Kenny blowing his whistle again while dashing toward the water like a madman. Every head was turned toward the water, where the body of Julie, Mrs. Lacey's daughter, bobbed face down.

By the time Michael swam to nearest shore and raced the length of the beach, Kenny had pulled Julie onto the sand. Her face was chalk white, her lips a purplish blue. Now that he'd gotten her out of the water, Kenny didn't seem to know what to do.

"She's dead!" he sobbed, "Oh, Jesus, she's dead!"

As the crowd circled them, Michael shoved Kenny out of the way, knelt beside the motionless girl, put an ear close to her nostrils, and pressed his fingers into her neck. No pulse. No breathing. He pressed hard on her stomach. A stream of slimy green bubbles leaked from her mouth.

Mrs. Lacey parted the crowd. At the sight of her child ghostly still on the sand, she began to shriek.

Michael quickly hoisted Julie into his arms and jerked his cupped hands against the young girl's abdomen. With each movement, foamy water and vomit sprayed from her mouth. When he had emptied her, Michael lay her back down on the sand and began giving her CPR. The training came back to him effortlessly. But something deep within him knew that Julie was already beyond his aid.

"Kenny, call an ambulance!" Michael yelled as he pumped.

"She's dead!" Kenny warbled hysterically, collapsing in the sand beside Michael. "What are we gonna do?" He sobbed hysterically.

Michael impulsively reared back and slapped Kenny's face hard, the way he'd seen people do in the movies when somebody went on a jag. It worked. The whining stopped.

Michael went back to giving Julie CPR. As Kenny drew sharp, heaving breaths, Michael spoke calmly but forcefully: "Call the ambulance. Go to the parking lot. Wait for it. Tell them we need oxygen, and direct them here. Understand?"

Kenny blubbered weakly.

"You understand?"

Kenny nodded.

"Then do it. Now!" Michael roared.

Kenny finally shook himself out of his emotional tailspin and pounded up the beach.

As Michael continued working on the girl, he saw a stubble-faced Mr. Andrews starting across the sand from the concession stand in a wobbly run. Shaky had grabbed a whistle and was carrying a small plastic first aid kit, the kind you pull out when a kid needs a Band-Aid and a kiss on the knee. It seemed odd, Michael thought, almost surreal.

As he continued to count and pump on the girl's chest, Michael realized he was in shock, the same way he had felt on the night of the train. Only now Ron and Alex weren't here to tell him what to do. Nobody was there to help, except a silly old man with a hangover and a plastic first aid kit.

Michael continued to press his palms rhythmically against the girl's motionless chest. He was still pressing and counting, his arms aching from the effort, when the ambulance arrived.

Michael had never ridden in a medical transport before. The rural highway toward the county hospital passed in a haze of motion and sirens. Michael numbly watched the paunchy, balding paramedic give Julie oxygen and continue the futile search for a pulse.

Michael had never been in a hospital before, either. The hallway had a strange odor, he thought. *Disinfectant maybe?* He padded down the linoleum floor behind the gurney in his bare feet. He shivered and realized that he didn't have anything on but his damp swimsuit.

Then he was in the emergency room. The lights were harsh, as bright as the noon sun on the beach. He was standing quietly against a wall. Waiting. Hoping. Time seemed to be slowing down. The nurses' words sounded strangely distorted.

Michael noticed a large clock mounted on the wall. It reminded him of the ones in high school that taunted him as some boring class dragged on. Watching the black second hand sweep around its white face, Michael wondered why a timepiece was needed in an emergency room.

A young doctor was hovering over Julie, shaking his head. "I'm calling it." He glanced up to the wall. "Time of death—12:34 p.m."

So that's why you need a clock, Michael numbly realized.

As a nurse pulled a white sheet over the body of young Julie Lacey, Michael slid down the wall onto the coolness of the linoleum floor.

Mr. Andrews entered the hospital to find Michael sitting alone in the hallway on a wooden bench. Michael had no idea how he had ended up there or how long he had been sitting alone in a wash of sterile walls and strange odors. *Minutes? Days?*

The old man was carrying a tee shirt and a beach towel. He draped the towel over Michael's slumping shoulders, then sat in silence beside him. Michael could smell the alcohol on Shaky's breath. After awhile, Mr. Andrews placed a hand on the young man's arm and silently urged him up.

The ride back to the beach seemed to take forever. Michael rolled down the window of Shaky's battered truck and tried to clear his nostrils of the smell of alcohol and disinfectant. The warm breeze felt good against his face.

He watched the countryside pass and thought about how much his life had changed that awful afternoon. A young girl had died, someone he was responsible for. The burden of that thought was overwhelming.

Mr. Andrews peered at him at the corner of his sunglasses.

"Julie's mother said you did everything you could," Shaky said quietly. "She doesn't blame you. Nobody does."

"I blame me," was all Michael could manage. He felt broken inside.

The private resort was deserted by the time Mr. Andrews pulled his truck into the gravel parking lot. Hastily closed for the day, its stunned members had long since dispersed in hushed and sobbing clusters, leaving the algae-tainted lake to its bleak misery.

Michael stood alone at the edge of the shore and stared across the dark green water, then walked down the beach past the overturned umbrellas and trash.

In a spot close to where Julie had been pulled from the water, Michael found the young girl's pink Barbie beach towel lying crumpled in the sand next to her pink Barbie purse. He picked up the towel, then took her shiny plastic purse and gently cleaned the sand off it.

Staring at the child's belongings, his eyes were wet as a horrible certainty settled over him: *this would never have happened on Alex's watch.*

Chapter 29

June 25, 1864

WHEN BAYLIS SIMPSON STEPPED into the dimly lit lobby of the Fletcher House Hotel, he found a makeshift morgue, filled with rebel corpses waiting to be buried. Bodies were placed on every conceivable flat space, propped in chairs and leaning against walls. Seen in the flickering candlelight, it was an eerie sight. If it had not been for the odor, Baylis would have mistaken the cadavers for specters.

Milton stopped to gaze at the body of one young soldier in a tattered blouse stretched out on a counter.

"That's the Wofford boy," he said quietly. "One of our best students at the Institute."

"He died this morning from wounds sustained at Resaca," Jeffers said. "With so many dead, we lay them where we can until they can be given a proper burial." The captain turned to the Simpsons. "I hope this sight does not put you off your appetite."

"Sadly, sir, it does not. I confess I have seen worse, and in recent times," Baylis replied.

Captain Jeffers motioned for the men to follow, and they passed through velvet curtains into a dining room in the rear. A dozen older men wearing finely cut clothes were gathered around tables covered with linen tablecloths and fine china. The room was lit by large candelabras.

"These are our town fathers. Shopkeepers and land owners," the captain said of the men around him. "We've gathered to share a last meal before our fair town falls into the hands of the enemy and is destroyed."

The patrons glanced their way, nodded politely, and went back to their meals. Baylis remembered that he and Ulysses were wearing the clothes of officers and were likely taken as men of wealth who had returned from the field of battle.

The four men settled at a vacant table. A stooped man with white hair and dark skin served them.

"Ham and yams," Milton said, savoring the aroma. "What a delight." He began eating with great enthusiasm.

Captain Jeffers turned to Baylis. "So, sir, tell me of your adventure."

Since they were eating, Baylis spared the unappetizing details. "It was much as the professor described, sir. We posed as a burial party and came down through Big Shanty."

"We discovered something most grim as we crossed the railroad," Ulysses said after he had relished several bites. "It appeared that partisans were caught removing a rail. Some of their dead had their hands tied and were shot in the back of the head at close range."

"Oh, dear. You mean they were executed?" Milton asked.

Baylis nodded. "One prisoner had been tied to a tree and bayoneted to death."

The captain's face showed no surprise.

"General Sherman calls the partisans 'wild beasts' and has told his officers to treat them as such."

"How dreadful," Milton said.

"Sherman ordered that anyone harboring guerrillas in Union-occupied areas is to be arrested—men, women, even our children. Folks have been taken from their homes, summarily tried, then executed. Others have been sent by train out of state to Union prisons," Jeffers said.

"There is no law left in North Georgia, save for Sherman's whims," Ulysses said, his voice betraying the bitterness in his heart. "The bluecoats control the towns and secure the railroad. Those in the countryside are left to the bummers, deserters, and worse."

"Sherman intends to bring Georgia to her knees through whatever means necessary," Jeffers said. "The hardships endured by the innocent are of small concern to that devil."

"It is a shameful thing," Milton agreed. "If war is not fought between gentlemen, as gentlemen, it descends into barbarism. Yet the victor writes the history, and their brutal acts are cleansed from the record. The slaughter of the innocents is all but forgotten in the memory of time."

Jeffers savored a bite of ham and washed it down with whiskey. "A few days ago, McCollum's raiders derailed a Yankee train using a land torpedo placed under the tracks."

Baylis and Ulysses exchanged a look. They knew the Cash brothers had been riding with McCollum's band.

"The Yankees responded by taking civilian hostages. There were other reprisals against the locals. I heard rumors of torture."

"Now, Captain," came a voice from behind Jeffers. The men turned their attention to a distinguished, well-dressed man with dark hair and eyes who had stopped at the table. "We should not spread talk of things that we cannot confirm."

The captain stood. "Gentlemen, may I introduce Henry Cole. His family owns the Fletcher Hotel."

Cole appeared to be an unctuous man in his late forties, with the look of someone who does well flitting around the edges of disaster. Baylis could tell by the guarded tone in Jeffers's voice that the captain was not fond of him.

"The hotel is owned by my father-in-law," Cole said after the men exchanged greetings. "I own the inn next to railroad depot."

"We thank your family for the hospitality and the meal," Baylis said. "This is truly a feast. Ham is as scarce as hen's teeth in these parts."

"It was the last pig in the county. I butchered it myself," Cole said with satisfaction. "Enjoy yourselves."

After Cole had moved to another table, the captain seated himself.

"The gentleman's accent. It sounds Northern," Milton said.

"Mr. Cole's accent betrays his loyalties," Jeffers replied discreetly. "He is from New York and a unionist. Some think him a spy." Jeffers let the thought hang in the air. "James Andrews and his raiders stayed here at the hotel the night before their theft of the steam locomotive The General at Big Shanty."

"If he's a spy, maybe someone should settle him," Ulysses said.

"If they did, they would have much public grief and private gratitude. They would also be shot. His family has much power and influence. No one dares touch him without proof certain."

"It's the same the world over," Milton said. "Some of the worst scoundrels are from the best families."

"It remains my fondest hope that he may yet spend time in a Confederate prison," Jeffers added, sipping his whiskey.

The conversation ebbed for a time, the men too intent on eating to speak.

"I'm very interested in your passage through Big Shanty, Mr. Simpson. Tell me, what did you see?" Jeffers asked.

"A lot of supplies and soldiers," Baylis said.

"Our batteries were firing from the mountain, but the stockpiles were just out of range," Ulysses added.

"I'm afraid the North will win this war, not through the fighting, but with their never-ending flood of provisions and immigrants. More people arrive on their shores every day than are lost in the war. They can afford shot and shell when we must ration food and cannot replace our fallen sons."

"You don't think the French might intervene on the Southern side? There was much talk of it at the institute," Milton said.

"Only a country of fools would involve itself in a civil war so far from its shores," Ulysses said.

"I fear you are right, sir," Jeffers agreed. "There was hope the British would intervene, then the French. But I think they are both content to let us bleed each other dry while they watch from across the ocean."

After dinner and thanking their hosts for the excellent meal, Captain Jeffers bid his companions to follow him up the stairs to the building's flat roof.

"It is the most extraordinary view you could ever have of our current predicament," he said. "A sad sight, but one you may be lucky enough to describe to your grandchildren in better days to come."

To the northwest, the men could see flashes of light and hear rumbles of explosions against the night sky. The war never completely slept, and neither did the soldiers fighting it. The harassing fire was just to keep the enemy on edge, and since both sides were the enemy, no one could own a comfortable night's sleep.

"Billy Sherman is coming," Ulysses said. "He's coming for sure."

"From what I have heard of our defenses, there will be many Northern mothers and wives crying from grief," Jeffers said.

"A grief we should all share," Baylis said.

Jeffers dropped his head for a moment, then turned to Milton. "I choose not to mention it during dinner, but I'm afraid our brave lads from the institute suffered gravely at Resaca. There were serious losses." The captain looked stricken.

"Oh dear. Your son?" Milton asked.

"I have heard no news about Timothy, and I pray that is good news. Finally, saner and kinder heads have prevailed, and many of the younger boys have now been scattered in the rear serving picket duties."

"It is too unbearable," Milton said, "to raise and nurture these young men only to see them fall like so many autumn leaves."

"War is an altogether nasty enterprise," Baylis said. "Lives are spent like someone else's money."

For a time the four men stood silently, watching the panorama of human misery that stretched as far as the eye could see.

Staring into the dark, Baylis felt his five decades and more under the weight of his grief. He was worn out from his long journey from the fields of his farm to this town beside a mountain.

He wondered if Permelia thought him dead. No way to assure her otherwise. And it would mostly likely be true come the morrow. He thought of his wife's dark Irish eyes, her kind smile and lilting voice. She had been his constant companion for years beyond number, and now he was alone, without her warmth. His memories of her were as much comfort as he would find that night.

Baylis, Ulysses and Milton made their way through the streets until they found some cotton bales away from the gathering point for the wounded. Although they could still hear the tormented cries of the injured and dying carry across the square, it seemed as good a place as any to try for some sleep.

Baylis was so exhausted he felt he could fall asleep with a hatchet pounding against his head. He made his bed on a bale, then closed his eyes and slipped into a deep sleep, like the sleep of the grave.

Chapter 30

August 1969

THE LAST DAYS OF the season at Pinerock Lake were a lost cause. After the drowning, attendance dropped sharply. Even the sun was hiding. Michael was grateful for only one thing: Diane had been spared the trauma of Julie's death. Now with the crowds so thin, Diane had quit to prepare for college.

With Kenny on the main guard tower, Michael spent the overcast morning restlessly pacing the nearly empty beach. Only a few people were scattered about, and most were content to listen to their transistor radios or read. Most every magazine cover he saw had something about the war. It seemed to be the only thing anyone could think about.

Close to noon, he spotted a female visitor sitting by herself near the main lifeguard stand. It took Michael several moments to register that it was Loraine. Instead of luxuriating as she normally did, Loraine sat on her towel, legs drawn up, her chin on her knees.

When Michael approached, she gave a sad wave.

"We're all upset, too." Michael said gently, plopping down beside her.

Loraine looked at him quizzically.

"About Julie Lacey," Michael cued.

"Who?"

"The girl who drowned here. It's pretty much killed business."

"Oh, I'm sorry. I hadn't heard."

"What's got *you* unhappy, then—if you don't mind my asking?"

Loraine looked for a moment as though she had something to confess. But then she averted her eyes and said softly, "Nothing really. Just one of my moods."

Something in her melancholy eyes told Michael that this was more than just a mood swing. He sat beside her in silence. He had never seen this side of her. She was usually so outgoing and flirtatious. What could possibly have made her so depressed?

She could see the question in his eyes. "I'm sorry. It's just not something I can talk about right now." She smiled sadly. "Maybe another time."

He tried to think of something to lighten her mood, but failed. Nothing in his life provoked much laughter these days.

"I hope you feel better soon," he said simply.

"Thanks, sweetie." Her eyes held his for a moment. "You're such a doll. I hope your girlfriend understands what a lucky girl she is." She patted his hand gently. "Very lucky."

Her compliments left him feeling awkward and self-conscious. He stood up and dusted the sand off his legs. "In case I don't see you again, this may be goodbye, at least until next summer."

"Good luck in college," she said.

"Thanks. It all seems pretty intimidating at the moment."

"I'm sure you'll do well. You're a very bright young man."

He smiled and began to walk away.

"Maybe I'll call you sometime," she said.

He turned back to her, unsure what to make of her offer.

"Who knows, maybe you can help cheer me up." Her eyes told him she was looking for something more than a simple reply. He was at a loss for words.

Michael felt that something had changed, some line had been crossed. This seemed like more than just innocent flirtation. Or maybe not? It was confusing.

"Sure," he managed. "I better get back to work now."

Michael started down the beach feeling the warm sand under his feet. He spotted ol' man Andrews clomping toward him, walkie-talkie to his ear. He looked pissed. *What now?*

Shaky waved him on quickly. "Come with me. We have a problem at the gate."

Before Michael could ask anything, Andrews spun around and marched off the beach and across the lawn toward the parking lot. Michael hustled after him.

"What's going on?" Michael asked once he caught up.

"Just keep your mouth shut, and let me handle things," he huffed.

As they approached the wooden entrance booth at the front gate, Michael saw Bobby, the skinny, freckled-faced attendant, looking sourly at a young white mother in her early thirties. She was with a robust-looking black woman, holding what Michael assumed to be the mother's baby, as well as several bags. The mother's hands were noticeably empty.

"May I help you?" Shaky asked the white woman.

"Yes, I'm Mrs. Franklin. This young man," she said stabbing a finger at Bobby, "says I can't come in because I'm not a member."

"That's correct, ma'am. This is a private lake."

"But I've come here before, and I've never had a problem." Her eyes tangled with Andrews. "Is it because I brought my maid?"

Shaky didn't blink. "I'm sorry. We don't have the proper facilities."

"This woman's son is over in Vietnam right now fighting for our country. Is this how we thank him? By treating his mother like this?"

The woman's words hit Michael like a brick. He was filled with shame. In that instant, Michael made a decision. He stepped around Mr. Andrews and turned to the black woman.

"Ma'am, may I help you take this stuff down to the beach?"

Michael started to take the woman's bags. Surprise staggered across Shaky's face. He looked at Michael like the young man had lost his mind. And perhaps he had.

"What the hell do you think you're doing?"

"What's right, sir."

The black woman searched Michael's eyes and gently smiled. She stopped him from taking the bags, then turned back to the mother.

"If it's all the same Mrs. Franklin, let's just go. One war is enough. I don't wanna start another one."

With a final, hard look at Mr. Andrews, Mrs. Franklin and the woman moved back toward their car.

Michael had already pivoted and was moving toward his motorcycle in the parking lot under the shade of a pine tree. Now it was Shaky's turn to hustle to catch up.

"Where are you going, boy?"

"Home. I quit."

"This weekend is Labor Day. I'm already short of guards. You can't quit."

"I just did." Michael pulled his helmet off his bike and slipped the key out from under the seat where he kept it.

"Come on, son, did you just wake up and realize this lake is members only?"

"No. I just never had to deal with it before. And now that I have, I'm ashamed. That woman has a son in Vietnam."

"Why should you care if some nigger woman's buck is in the war?"

"Don't use that word in front of me. I wasn't raised like that." Michael climbed onto his motorcycle and slipped the key into the ignition.

"It's my lake and I can use any word I like."

"Yes sir, I guess you can. And I can work anywhere I like."

"Even a dimwit knows it's better to send her buck to Vietnam than good boys like Alex Granger and your brother."

Michael could feel his anger welling up inside him. "They're all good boys. Can't you understand that?"

"If you think Alex Granger or your own blood is no better than some nigger, then get off my property before I have you arrested for trespassing."

With that, Michael started his bike and drove away. He never looked back.

Chapter 31

August 1969

THE MULTIPURPOSE UH-1 had been produced in greater numbers and flown by more countries than any other helicopter in the western world. Extremely versatile, the Huey could be adapted for air assaults and attack transport, armed support, antisubmarine warfare, search and rescue, or "medevac"—medical casualty evacuation.

The distinctive short-nose fuselage had a "chin" plexiglass bubble for look-down visibility. Although Huey pilots sat in armored seats, many were killed or wounded by ground fire coming up through the plexiglass. The cockpit was open to the main cabin, which had large rearward sliding doors on both sides. These doors were manned by gunners when adapted for air assaults. The main cabin could carry up to fourteen troops in jump seats. The medevac version, which Ron hoped to pilot, could carry six stretchers in fold-down racks for wounded and one medical attendant. But by the time WOC Simpson entered his last phase of training, most aspiring pilots coveted the newest model, the UH-1D combat gunship.

The UH-1D Huey had a top speed of 127 mph with a ceiling of 12,700 ft., and a standard operational range of 306 miles. It could be armed with M60 door guns, pintle-mounted quad M60s, a 20mm cannon, 2.75 inch rocket launchers, a 40mm grenade launcher in the helicopter chin-turret, and up to six antitank missiles using a guided missile launcher.

While those stats, which had been hammered into Ron until he could repeat them on command, were enough to make his eyes gloss over, he understood their meaning all too well. The Huey gunship was designed for maximum lethal firepower. One instructor sublimely called the UH-1D "God's own killing machine" and "the instrument of His wrath."

Unlike Ron, none of his fellow WOCs in the top of his class were interested in flying UH-1V medevacs. They all wanted to jockey gunships. Ron soon learned why.

Medevac Hueys, known by their "dustoff" call sign because of the amount of dust they kicked up landing and taking off, often flew single-ship missions with no gunship support. In Vietnam, where there were no clear "front lines," medevac helicopters often had to fly into intense battles to retrieve the wounded and carry them great distances to medical help.

Even though they were unarmed and had large red crosses inside white circles painted on their sides and noses, they were not immune from enemy fire. The Viet Cong and the North Vietnamese Army considered the red crosses little more than a target. After all, if you shot down a Huey full of wounded soldiers, it meant that the Americans would have to send more choppers to pick them up.

With so many medevacs being shot down in Vietnam, dustoff pilots had three times the fatality rate of other chopper jocks. Ron's instructors often referred to them as "the walking dead."

Still, Ron preferred piloting a medevac to a gunship. At least, his conscience did.

During the last phase of training at the Department of Tactics, Ron flew Hueys exclusively. Operating out of Fort Rucker's Lowe Army Air Field, the four weeks of "tac" training provided Ron and the others with an experience designed to closely replicate being "in country" in Vietnam.

Like all instructors assigned to "gun school" tac training, Ron's jumpsuit-clad Instructor Pilot, Chief Warrant Officer 4 Thomas Gudgell, was a Vietnam combat veteran. Gudgell, called "Grudge" by the WOCs (never to his face), had just returned from a second in-country tour flying with the 187th Assault Helicopter Company, the famed Crusaders. Revered among WOCs, Grudge had been shot down twice in Vietnam—*on the same day*—and, upon returning to base, had volunteered for a *third* mission. One of the Crusaders's finest pilots, he held a company record for air combat assault time and a third-degree burn scar on his left cheek and neck to remind everyone of the price he had paid for the honor.

Even the Crusaders's ceremonies were the stuff of legends. The company was said to hold symbolic rituals that featured a sword first used during the eleventh-century Christian Crusades. That irony was not lost on Ron.

Onward, Christian soldiers. What was it about war and religion? Ron wondered. The two seemed inseparable, like living and breathing. The thought troubled him deeply.

How could anyone kill in the name of God? The more Ron observed the devastating killing power of the Huey gunship, the more he believed that God would not, could not, condone any taking of human life. At least not the God he knew and loved.

Chapter 32

Pentecost Sunday
June 26, 1864

BAYLIS'S DREAM BEGAN WITH the rape of his daughter, Terissa, with details that he wished he was not forced to see, then the death of little Melissa, her body slashed and her eyes open as she kept saying, "He cut my hair, Granddaddy" over and over. Then he was fighting the ugly, headless bandit, who wouldn't stop coming, no matter what limb the old man severed from the brute's body.

Baylis found himself in a wagon full of corpses being driven by an old slave. The wagon stopped in front of a Northern general with the legs of a goat and horns on his head. He held a scythe, like the harvester of the dead.

"General Sherman. It be all right if I load these dead men off this wagon?" the slave asked.

"No, old bones, you keep them men on there forever. They don't get off. Not even for the Judgment Day. These will be sent to fry in the brimstone fires of Hell."

Suddenly it smelled like his flesh was burning.

Baylis woke abruptly to the sharp tang of bacon grease.

"Here's your vittles, Pa." Ulysses nudged his father on the shoulder. "Got us a ration of skillygalee."

The old man slowly shook away the horrific images and took the wooden bowl his son offered. The hardtack had been softened in water, then fried. He could see crispy dead weevils floating in the grease.

"Yes sir, I reckon the high life is over," Baylis said, his voice ragged from his restless slumber.

Ulysses sat on the cotton bale and hurriedly began to eat.

"Milton found us a ride up to the front. I got us regular uniforms and some muskets from the quartermaster. We can give these officer's clothes back to the professor."

After eating and changing clothes, Baylis followed his son to a wagon stacked high with powder kegs. Milton was already sitting on top, eating a raw onion with great relish.

"This onion is most sweet. Captain Jeffers purchased them for us from a sutler." Milton held out two onions for Baylis and Ulysses and accepted the folded uniforms. "I'll return these to their owners," Milton assured them, placing the borrowed clothes into his knapsack.

"You'uns climb aboard," the teamster said cheerfully through a mouth full of chewing tobacco. "This here's some of the finest gunpowder ever made. Comes from Augusta."

Baylis and Ulysses cautiously stepped aboard the wagon and sat on the kegs.

"To ride in this wagon, it's best we make our peace with the Lord," Ulysses said.

"You boys got nothin' to worry about," the wagoneer said. "The Yankees hit us with a round, you'll be flying up to heaven before you know what happened."

With that, the teamster carefully urged the mules forward. The animals strained to get the wagon moving. It was so overloaded Baylis thought they might die in harness.

Creaking up the road, they were overtaken by a fine open carriage with a matched team of horses. In it were three young ladies dressed in black and a dandy in the sort of clothes you might wear to go courting.

As the carriage drew close behind them, Milton recognized the man's face. "I say, isn't that Henry Cole in that open coach?"

Ulysses squinted at the approaching rig. "Where's he taking those war widows?"

"To see the front, I would reckon," the teamster said. "Widows come up here from Atlanta. They want to see the Yankees that done killed their menfolk."

Milton waved, and Cole nodded as they slipped past.

"You s'posing he would use those poor women as an excuse to gather information?" Ulysses's voice was full of scorn.

"He certainly gets to ride in greater comfort," Baylis said.

"And with prettier company," the teamster added.

The mules pulled them through rolling country as Big Kennesaw Mountain slowly grew in the horizon. They made a sharp turn onto Dallas Road and were moving around a small rise when a teenage voice cried, "Halt, who goes there? Stop and be recognized."

The wagon groaned with the weight of the powder kegs as the teamster eased it to a halt.

A boy no older than fourteen stood before them wearing a tattered cadet uniform and holding a smoothbore musket. It was too long for him and front heavy. He could barely keep it pointed at the wagon.

"*Got tam* it to hell, son, this here's a Confederate powder wagon," the teamster said. "You shoot that fool musket, and we'll all be blown to perdition."

"I say, Thomas!" Milton cried.

The boy lowered the musket and yelled, "Professor Milton is here!"

A cheer of young voices went up, and a half-dozen cadets rose from their ambush on the rise.

Milton slid clumsily from the wagon, and the young boys gathered around him.

"I am looking for Master Richard Grayson. I bring news most sad for him."

"If it be news about the dead, I reckon he already knows. He got sent to glory by a Yankee at Resaca. A lot of our corps did," Thomas said.

"Then he is together with his father," Milton said.

"I figure we all will be together very soon. None of us are living through this war. The Yankees just come at you and kill you."

"You say we lost many?"

"Yes, sir. The names would fill a book."

"Oh dear. It is as Captain Jeffers believed."

"Timothy was one of the lost."

"Captain Jeffers's son?" Milton appeared as distracted as when the Simpsons had first seen him. "Such sad news. It was his only son."

"We *tain't* 'fraid neither, no *sirree bob*. We'll have our revenge by killin' as many of them bluecoats as we can. We're all prepared to die—*tain't* that right, boys?"

The young cadets gave a brave, defiant cheer. A sad smile etched Milton's face as he listened to their thunder.

"Young sirs," Milton said when their yells had sputtered out, "the best revenge you can take on these Yankees is to survive."

Milton pulled his haversack and knapsack from the wagon. "You boys shall help me make a list of the boys lost. Their parents must know."

The professor turned to Baylis and Ulysses. "There is nothing to carry me farther north. I must stay here and make a careful accounting. I wish you the best of luck, kind sirs."

"God be with you," Baylis said.

"And with you also."

∾

After several miles of plodding travel, the wagon pulled to a stop at a fork in the road. The teamster turned to Ulysses.

"This is as close as I go to where you'uns are heading. If you're a-lookin' to rejoin your regiment, your boys are out on an elbow in the line just south of that hill yonder called Little Kennesaw."

Baylis and Ulysses stepped off the wagon and gathered their muskets, haversacks, and wool blanket rolls.

"I'll walk with you," Baylis said, "then get directions to my own regiment from there."

The teamster dug a fresh wedge of tobacco out of his haversack and stuffed it in his cheek.

"The camp canard is that Billy Goat ain't got the stomach for a real fight, and he'll just try to flank us again. But I think you boys will be in the thick of it if he does attack. That elbow is so far out in front that the Blue Boys will kick it like a mule. There'll be a bloody go-to, sure as spit. I wager Mister Sherman will insist on it."

"What's a Yankee general care if soldiers are shot down? None of 'em care a good damn," Ulysses said. "Generals never do."

"I pray you are wrong about that," Baylis said.

Ulysses and Baylis thanked the man for the ride and started off toward the mountain.

Chapter 33

October 1969

THE WEEKS UNDER GRUDGE'S tutelage passed quickly for Ron. He learned how to do sling loads, how to land in "hot" landing zones while under enemy fire, and how to fly so low that he ripped leaves off the tops of the trees. Grudge also gave Ron something not found in any textbook—what veteran combat pilots called "air sense," the ability to think calmly under harrowing circumstances, when the "pucker factor" was off the gauge.

And then one day, the training was over. It was time to graduate.

The rows of folding chairs were hauled out and set up on Fort Rucker's parade field, and soon the families of the new-made aviators began filing in. With Ron's Advanced Rotary Wing Training now complete, the 197th Aviation Company, 10th Group, had one last flight. It was the graduation "flyover" of the whole class. As his company flew across the parade grounds in formation, the thought of those crackerjack new pilots sharing the same airspace set Ron on edge. But it went off without a bump.

Ron and the other Warrant Officer Candidates in his company had received their rank the day before. At today's ceremony, they would be awarded their wings.

Scanning the parade grounds, Ron spotted his parents in one of the first few rows. His father cut a trim figure in his dark suit, and his mother, in a pale blue dress, dabbed her eyes with a handkerchief. Ron's father may have appeared an unemotional rock, but his mother wore her large heart on her sleeve.

When his name was called, Ron rose stiffly and walked to the podium. He shook hands with the CO, received his silver Army Aviator Wings, then snapped a salute. Ron and the other Warrant Officers in his company were now classified "153-Alpha," ready for Vietnam.

After the ceremony, Carlotta, beaming with pride, pinned the wings on her son as his father snapped a photograph with his trusty Brownie Starmatic. Ron took the yellow envelope he had been handed, and gingerly fumbled open the clasp. Inside was his first assignment.

The first part he expected: He was being transferred to Fort Benning to await orders for Vietnam. Then Ron felt his stomach drop. He tasted something pungent in the back of his throat. He stared again at the document in bitter disappointment.

Warrant Officer 1 Ronald H. Simpson had been assigned to pilot a Huey gunship.

Chapter 34

November 1969

ALEX WAS LATE. THE Greyhound bus was already beginning its slow, slogging approach toward Fort Benning's main gate, and his friend was nowhere in sight. Ron's eyes flicked through the pack of scrubbed young soldiers waiting with him in the drizzling rain. Alex stood out in any crowd; it wouldn't be difficult to see him. They had gotten passes together and planned a big blowout in Forest Park. And now Alex was a no-show.

The bus groaned to a halt and opened its doors. Several dozen wet, jostling, high-spirited young soldiers climbed aboard. Ron trailed them and made his way to a seat. He lowered the passenger window with a loud clack and stuck his head out for one last look. *No Alex.*

The doors closed, and the bus began rolling away. Ron let out a sigh of frustration. *Alex had missed the goddam bus. Perhaps this was another one of his infamous pranks.*

Suddenly, a figure lunged from the curb and darted in front of the moving bus. The driver cursed loudly and stomped on the brake. Inches from the bus's grill, unflinching, Alex flashed a wily grin, and tossed the exasperated driver a salutary wave. The doors opened, and Alex swung himself aboard.

All the way to Forest Park, the two friends laughed, caught up, and shot the shit. Beneath the buzz cut and the ranger's uniform, Alex was the same backslapping, ass-kicking maverick. Nothing had changed. At least, nothing important at the moment.

As the Greyhound headed down the highway turnoff towards Forest Park, Alex fished through his duffel bag, pulled out an airline ticket, and wagged it at Ron.

"TWA to Indian Country. Got it yesterday."

It suddenly made sense. Alex had gotten leave because he was heading to Vietnam.

"I ain't sayin' I told you so," Ron said casually. "But you had to be a dumb prick to sign up to be a grunt." His military training came in handy when he wanted to keep his emotions hidden.

"A *grunt*? Rangers lead the way, you flyboy rat-fuck," Alex laughed, then punched his arm. "We can't all be medevac asswipes, you know."

"How many times I gotta tell you? I was assigned a Huey gunship."

"Don't wanna hear that shit. I get an ass full of shrapnel, I wanna look up and see you in a whirlybird on my six to evac me. I'm countin' on you," Alex grabbed Ron in a headlock. "Promise me, bro."

"Okay, okay. I'm gonna get reassigned to medevac. I've got my request in. Now quit horsin' around before I kick your ass."

Alex raised his hands in mock surrender, and then that trademark playful grin came creeping back onto his face. In a lightning-fast gesture, Alex bopped Ron's cap off. The resulting tussle didn't quiet until they'd received loud complaints from the other passengers.

By the time the bus pulled up at Forest Park's station, the storm clouds had emptied themselves and hung limp and deflated in a soft November evening sky. Ron stepped out into the light drizzle and inhaled deeply. He'd always remember the smell of clean Georgia air after a hard rain.

Michael, home for the weekend from the University of Georgia, had Ron's Mustang parked at the curb with the motor running, the windshield wipers thumping in rhythm to the Doors' "Light My Fire" drifting from the radio. The two soldiers tossed their duffels into the trunk. Michael stepped out of the car to let Ron take the driver's seat.

"Hiya squirt," Alex said, boxing Michael's shoulder playfully, "Who let you out of nursery school?"

Moments later, the three best friends were off and cranking the tunes as they made their way to the nearest burger joint. The good times were back, for a few days, at least.

Ron pulled into the parking lot at Carroll's Hamburgers, Clayton County's own answer to the Golden Arches. It was a tiny fast food franchise, just a handful of outlets doing their best to raise local cholesterol levels. For the time being, it was a countywide teen magnet, dragging in hungry pubescent hordes by the carload.

Alex snapped to attention when he saw Mona exiting the restaurant with a group of friends.

"Does Mona know you're being sent?" Ron asked.

"No. She ain't even expectin' me home."

Ron settled into a parking space and the guys stepped out of the car. Mona shrieked in surprise.

"Alex!" she squealed, launching herself at him. He scooped her up and held her while she smothered his face with wet kisses.

"Hiya, baby," Alex said under the deluge, "Miss me?"

Mona rubbed her ample breasts against Alex's chest. "What does it feel like, sugarbear?"

Alex set her down with one arm and fetched his duffel out of the Mustang. "I'll bail out here. Check you later, guys." Then he and Mona vanished into the crowd.

Michael and Ron climbed back in the Mustang and plowed back onto the street. A home-cooked meal was calling them.

∽

Ron stood for a moment in the doorway, drinking in the sounds and smells of home. A rerun of *Branded* flickered from the television in the Maplewood-paneled den. The theme song filled the room: *"Branded, scorned as the one who ran? What do you do when you're branded, and you know you're a man?"*

Ron could see his father out in the backyard feeding his prized pointers, Sport and Ramus. His mother hummed softly in the kitchen over a steaming pot of corn on the cob amid the crackle of grease from a skillet of frying chicken.

Carlotta gave her son a warm hug and a motherly kiss on the cheek. Then, so as not to overwhelm him, she turned back to the dough she was rolling for biscuits. Ron knew that his mother wanted to smother him with affection, but she possessed a Southern woman's graceful sensitivity. She understood, although she didn't like it, that a mother's true job was to make herself obsolete. Ron belonged to the larger world now, and that was as it should be.

The Simpson family lingered over fresh vegetables, fried chicken, and sweet iced tea. The little clock over the oven ticked audibly over the muffled sounds of chewing. No one felt in a hurry to start up a conversation. It was enough, for the moment, for the family to be gathered together in their warm kitchen of copper and wood, with second helpings going around and the aroma of warm banana pudding and coffee in the air.

When Ginger called to chat with Carlotta, Michael took the cue to go warm up the television in time for *Star Trek*. Tonight was the episode where Kirk restores the "balance of power" on a planet with two endlessly warring sides. Michael had seen it twice already, but there was always the chance he'd missed something.

Carlotta finished her phone call and began clearing dishes.

"Ginger sure is happy to have Alex home."

Ron remembered Alex's plane ticket, his face darkening with the thought. His mother's eyes told him she saw his look. He'd have to break the news.

"Alex's being sent to 'Nam."

Carlotta's hand flew to her chest. "Oh, good glory. Ginger doesn't know."

"Don't go gettin' in the middle of it," Harold said, "You let Alex and Ginger sort through that."

"I'm just thankful my boys are both home," Carlotta sighed, her voice breaking, "I know that's gonna change soon."

Harold reached across the table, took his wife's hand, and patted it gently.

Ron sank himself deep into the sofa between his father and brother and propped his feet up. While Michael explored a far-off galaxy with Captain Kirk, Harold and Ron parsed the newspaper, anticipating the dessert Carlotta was just pulling from the kitchen oven.

At the top of the hour, the *CBS Evening News* began its fanfare, and Walter Cronkite faced the nation with startling news: The U.S. Army's Inspector General had filed formal charges, included six counts of premeditated murder, against Lt. William Calley, a central figure in the alleged My Lai massacre.

A film clip showed Representative Morris Udall, who had aggressively pushed for an investigation of the "war crime" since it first came to light in March. Udall was now calling for a "full accounting."

Two black-and-white photos flickered on the television. One showed a dirt road littered with dozens of dead Vietnamese civilians. The second was a close-up of the lifeless bodies of a mother and her small baby, sprawled like marionettes in the dirt, both shot in the back of the head, execution-style.

Ron, Michael, and Harold sat up in disbelief. Like most every family in the country, they had become inoculated, by repeated exposure, against the grisly horrors broadcast from Vietnam's battlefields. But these images of raped and murdered innocents cast an especially dark shadow across the Simpson living room. It was as though the ghost of Baylis had appeared beside them.

Ron was filled with an unspeakable rage and shame. The soldiers responsible for that carnage were part of the same Army as him.

It was the first time Warrant Officer Ron Simpson ever felt uncomfortable in his military uniform.

Chapter 35

November 1969

RON SLEPT LATE THE next morning. When he couldn't stand to lie under the covers a moment more, he tumbled out of bed, showered quickly, and hurried over to Alex's. He doubted anyone would want to discuss the My Lai massacre at home. The parallels with their own family history were too hauntingly painful. But he didn't think he could bear sitting in silence.

Alex was already in the garage, taking the wheels off his Plymouth Fury and setting it up on blocks to weather his impending absence. Unlike Ron's family, Alex had no difficulty talking about distressing subjects.

"When it comes to countin' bodies, my Ranger captain says anything that's dead and ain't white is VC," Alex noted wryly from a mechanic's creeper between the Fury's front wheels. "I think they should bury the gooks and move on."

After all this time, Alex could still throw Ron a curve ball. "Jesus, Alex. You're talkin' about innocent civilians, even babies."

"Shit happens in a war." Alex stuck his head out from under the car. "War's gonna have casualties, bro." He ducked back under to tighten a bolt on the car's oil pan.

"This wasn't some friendly fire accident in the heat of combat." Ron's bitterness was rising. "Those killings went on for hours. *Hours.*"

"I heard the unit—what was it, Charlie Company—had taken casualties a couple of days before," Alex said from beneath the car, then popped his head out again. "Calley's men thought the gooks were helping the VC. Maybe some of 'em were angry, and things got a little outta hand."

"A *little?*" Ron stared at his friend, stunned by his casually callous tone.

Alex pushed himself out from under the car and wiped his hands. "I'm just sayin' it's hard to judge 'em, man. You weren't in those guys' boots."

"I don't wanna be in their boots," Ron said firmly. "I didn't sign up for that."

"For what? Killin' people? Sure you did, Hoss."

Ron loosened the nuts holding the last tire. Alex's hard-headedness was legendary, but his opinions seldom ranged this far afield of Ron's own. Maybe his months in the Army had done something to him.

"Don't go soft on me. I don't need that shit, not now." Alex pointed his wrench at Ron. "We volunteered, remember?"

Alex's unblinking eyes told Ron just how hard it was to have pity for anyone else when you had orders to Vietnam in your shirt pocket. At once, Ron understood clearly: it wasn't that Alex didn't want to care. *He couldn't.* Alex was shutting himself down emotionally, steeling himself for what he knew lay ahead in a few short weeks.

"I volunteered 'cause I wanted to help," Ron offered quietly, after a moment. "But I don't wanna kill. That's why I requested to fly medevac."

"One way or another, it'll still come down to killing. Either you'll be doing it, or you'll be helping some other sumbitch do it."

Ron turned back to loosen the last stubborn nut on the Plymouth's left rear wheel. Alex's stinging words hung in the air, but Ron chose not to respond further. The weekend had already drained him, emotionally and spiritually. Better to lay low until the danger of an argument had passed.

A rift had suddenly widened between them. The last few years had united them as comrades-in-misbehavior, as they drag raced and raised hell into an uncertain tomorrow. Now that future was upon them, pulling them both down different paths.

Ron began to wonder if the brittle silence was hurting them worse than any words could. He flipped on a tiny grease-streaked transistor radio. Janis Joplin immediately came to their rescue. From over the airwaves, her drugged and lonely voice grizzled forth: *"Bye bye, baby, bye bye. Guess you're on your own..."*

"Turn that up," Alex barked sullenly.

Janis was saying what neither of them could.

Chapter 36

November 1969

ALEX'S MONTH OF LEAVE before his deployment to Vietnam passed quickly. Accounts were settled, boxes packed, and addresses exchanged. Whenever Ron could get a weekend pass, the two friends' normally rowdy behavior had escalated into epic episodes of boozing, providing feverish bookends to Alex's more somber pursuits in between. But despite Alex's best efforts to appear relaxed, his eyes reflected the melancholy of it all. The future he had rushed towards his whole life had now arrived, and he wished he were somewhere, anywhere else.

Alex's sharp words about My Lai still bothered Ron, but he chose not to bring it up again. Alex already had enough on his shoulders, and Ron didn't want to add to his friend's burden by needlessly arguing with him.

Ron was able to get a pass for the Thanksgiving holiday. That weekend would be Alex's last before he was due to fly to San Diego, and from there to Vietnam.

On Sunday morning, as Ron showered and dressed for church, a heaviness settled into his chest. He still had a full day of leave, a lunch in Alex's honor, and one more night on starched sheets in his own bedroom. But he couldn't shake the feeling that the good times with Alex already lay behind them.

More than once during the morning service, Ron saw Alex slyly peek at Mona, who was sitting alone on an otherwise empty back pew. They had recently broken up. Although Alex had said that it was "no biggie," Ron knew his false bravado hid a painful truth.

Alex and Mona had been "going steady" for more than a year. She was salty and sweet, wild and lusty enough to go toe-to-toe with Alex, yet still completely in love with him. But Alex feared leaving Mona a widow, like his mom had been all these years, and gave her up precisely because he loved her so much. Better to leave her a free woman and take the chance she would still be there when he returned.

The morning sermon was unusually long. At last, with many a mother discreetly checking her watch, afraid her pot roast was burning, the service finally ended, and the parishioners spilled out into the sunny November afternoon.

While their mothers chatted, Ron and Alex stood patiently at attention, with fixed smiles that became painful as they accepted the greetings of their many well-wishers. Neither of them could wait to get the hell out of there, peel off their starched dress uniforms, and get some home cooking in their stomachs.

Just as the boys had finally waded though the last of the admiring flock, Mona made a hurried beeline for Alex. She took both of his hands in hers.

"I couldn't let you leave without one last hug," she said in a breathy voice.

Alex opened his arms to embrace her, and she melted into him. Alex's eyes went moist. He discreetly tried to wipe them so Mona wouldn't see.

Ron turned away to give them a bit of privacy.

"Now, now," Alex said gently after a long moment. "Just pretend I'm on a long vacation someplace or other. I'll be back before you know it."

"Watch yourself over there, sugarbear," Mona whispered, nuzzling Alex's ear. "And look me up when you get home."

When she let go, her mascara was flowing onto her cheeks. She squeezed his shoulder and smiled, her bottom lip quivering. Then she turned quickly and walked away. The two friends drifted in silence toward Ron's car in the parking lot, Alex's face full of bittersweet sadness.

Carlotta had outdone herself for Alex's farewell. The importance of an event in the Simpson household could be gauged by the amount of food that was prepared, and on this day, there were mountains of it.

After eating, Ron and Alex lolled in chaise lounges, soaking up the fall sun. Neither could bring himself to mention Alex's departure the next day. Instead, they talked, as they always did, about everything and nothing. The topic of the moment was Ron's interest in reincarnation.

"Don't tell me you really believe that crap," Alex was saying. He had his elbows on the armrest and an ever-present Marlboro dangling out of the corner of his mouth.

"What I'm saying is I've been reading about this Edgar Cayce guy, and I realized you can believe in reincarnation and still be a Christian."

"Whoa—right there, Hoss. Our name ain't the First Buddhist Church." Alex crushed out the stump of his cigarette on the aluminum edge of the chaise, and lit another one on its heels.

Out of the corner of his eye, Ron caught a glimpse of his mother waving to get his attention. He excused himself from Alex with an affable pop to the shoulder and ambled over.

"Honey, would you go get my medicine? I've got all this cobbler to serve up."

Ron retrieved his mother's inhaler from the bathroom and was on his way out the back sliding glass door when he heard someone weeping. Through the door, he could see his mother had moved over to the back step with Ginger. Alex's mom was taking deep, shuddering breaths into a dishtowel, trying to stave off more sobs as Carlotta consoled her with a gentle pat on her back.

"I didn't know how I'd get over losing Tom to cancer," Ginger said, after a deep sigh. "Now I've got to watch my only child go off to war. My heart's just about to break."

"I don't know how you've stayed strong this long, Ginger."

Ginger raised her eyes to the yard and smiled. Michael and Alex were horsing around. Michael had plucked Alex's cigarette from his mouth and wouldn't give it back.

"It's good to see the boys together again. Seems like the old times." Ginger's voice quavered again.

Carlotta hugged her tight. "You know you're like family. If you ever need a thing, our door is always open."

Ron stepped back noiselessly, then tiptoed back through the kitchen and out the front door. Stepping around through the side yard, Ron stood in the late afternoon sun streaking through the trees, watching Alex and Michael toss a football. He thought about the hundreds of times the three of them had played ball together, gotten in trouble together, shared the measles, poison ivy, double dates, warm beer, summer camping trips, and winter colds. In short, grown up together.

Now, with Michael in college and 'Nam just up the road for Alex and him, those years were already receding into memory. Only God knew what lay before the three of them, but Ron understood their lives would never, ever be the same.

Ron drove Alex to Hartsfield Airport the next morning. Later that afternoon, Ron would board a bus heading to Fort Benning. By evening, he would be in his barracks, but Private First Class Alex Granger's travels would have barely begun.

Alex had said all his goodbyes at home. He arranged it so that Ron would be the only one to see him off. Harold, one of the last to say his good-byes, took Alex aside Sunday evening and spoke to him, alone, man to man, for more than an hour. Ron had no idea what his father had said, but afterwards, his friend seemed more at peace.

As they made their way down the airport concourse, Alex fidgeted with a cigarette.

"Remember, no fuckin' huggin'. That's why I said *adios* to my mom at home."

"Get over it. I agreed to drive your ass here, not be told how to say goodbye."

Alex seemed engrossed in thought. "Remember our first trip to Daytona?"

"Sure, for the race." Ron smiled. "What's got you thinkin' about that again?"

"'Cause deep down, even then, watching the Daytona 500, I knew being some big NASCAR mechanic would never happen. Not to me. I was either gonna end up workin' at Hal's Auto Salvage or tossing baggage here at the airport."

They arrived at Alex's gate, and paused before it awkwardly.

"What I'm trying to say, Hoss, is this is what I wanted. Understand?"

"Yeah, I get it," Ron muttered in a low voice.

Alex extended his hand. Ron shook it hesitantly, then reached out and enveloped his best friend in a self-conscious, manly hug.

"Okay, fuck you," Alex slapped him on the back. "*Hasta la vista, amigo.* See you in the tall grass."

Alex shouldered his duffel, punched Ron's arm, then turned and ambled through his gate. Ron waited until Alex was lost from sight.

Chapter 37

January 1970

RON WAS HAUNTED BY images of My Lai. During the day, when he was busy, he managed to keep the visions away. But in the creeping stillness of night, stretched out on his bunk, he could see their dead faces: Vietnamese babies and toddlers lying deflated in the blood-smeared grass, blank stares, obscene jelly leaking from the backs of their heads. Their young mothers lay in crumpled heaps nearby, fingers outstretched to their butchered children.

The story had a macabre power over him. Whenever someone mentioned the massacre, he listened hungrily. Somewhere among the grisly details, there had to be a kernel of sanity that would permit him to make sense of it all. Despite his efforts, he could find none.

In the evenings, when the rotary aircraft had been put to bed for the night, Ron often kicked back in Fort Benning's Warrant Officer Day Room. The room offered a row of battered couches, a stack of ragged magazines, and a long-suffering black-and-white TV that only seemed to pick up *Bonanza* reruns.

While these attractions held little interest for Ron, he did enjoy hanging out with Moses Washington Formwalt, a black Warrant Officer with piercing eyes who was about to be shipped to Vietnam. Raised by his "clairvoyant" mother in the Florida panhandle after his schizophrenic father was institutionalized, Moses traced his ancestors back to slaves. For reasons unclear to Ron, "Mose" had taken a liking to him, although he insisted on calling him "Lassie."

Everything about Mose was intense. A dropout from Duke University where he had been studying world history and philosophy, Mose played acoustic guitar and discussed the Buddha's Eightfold Path with equal passion. His thoughts ran deep, and his opinions, though often radical, proved tough to argue with. Ron came to view these evening bull sessions as his lifeline.

As the two men played cards, Mose spoke out on everything from the war ("Marcellus had it right," Mose would say, using Muhammad Ali's middle birth name. "This war is white men sending black men off to kill yellow men") to the history of rock music, which Mose thought was "nothing but a juiced up version of field hollers."

Mose introduced Ron to what he called the "real holy trinity"—John Lee Hooker, Muddy Waters, and Howlin' Wolf—who had torqued up the blues to lay the foundation for rock. He explained that the term "blues" didn't come from the feeling of being sad, which is what most "white breads" thought, but from the way the singers and guitar pickers bent their notes. "Blue notes" were tonally in between two standard notes, blurring major and minor scales and opening up new avenues of musical expression.

Besides their mutual enjoyment of music, both Mose and Ron were drawn to discussions of religion like a pair of magnets to iron.

"So tell me, *Lassie*, how does a bunch of saltine-eating, grape-juice-drinking white boys claim exclusive rights to the God of all creation?" Mose asked one night, knowing that salvo would get Ron's attention.

"'Cause of Jesus' sacrifice," Ron replied, his rote answer sounding so by-the-book that it even rang hollow to his own ears. "Bible says you got to repent of your sins and accept Jesus' offer of salvation to get to Heaven."

"What about the ones that have never even heard the name Jesus? God's just gonna throw all those *po'* folks away like your mama's leftover tater salad?"

As Ron considered this, Jim Morrison yelped his way into Willie

Dixon's "Backdoor Man," rattling the speaker of the geriatric Army issue phonograph.

"The Gospel says nobody comes to the Father 'cept through the Son," Ron replied.

"So, you're tellin' me, all those yellow, brown, and red skins who have other religions gonna burn in the eternal hell fire just 'cause they happen to have a different belief?" Mose snorted a laugh. "You call that a *just* God? Shit, my DI at boot camp was more lovin' than that."

"I admit that part never made a load of sense to me either."

Ron thought of another verse from the Gospel, one that was seldom discussed in Bible class or read aloud in the congregation. *I have other sheep in my flock*, Jesus had said, *sheep that you don't yet recognize.*

Ron wondered silently whether Jesus could have been talking about the billions of good, non-Christian souls who lived quiet lives of devotion to the highest truths they knew. Could they somehow intuitively understand Christ and follow him, even though they'd never heard his name? Or maybe the "other sheep" were beings on other planets in far-off galaxies? Who could truly know?

"My God's better than your God, *nanna, nanna, nanna,*" Mose sing-songed before hammering away again, "That's the kind of holier-than-thou shit that allows a thing like My Lai to happen."

As always, the hairs on the back of Ron's neck prickled at the mention of the massacre.

"American soldiers splattered a hundred civilians all over the ground at My Lai, 'cause they suspected they might be VC sympathizers," Mose continued, on a roll. "And even if they were, so fuckin' what? What's wrong with sympathizing with some rice-eating *mofo* runnin' around in black jammies who just wants our ass outta his backyard and to leave him the fuck alone? Tell me what's worse: sympathizing with the VC or sympathizing with *us*?"

Mose paused to roll another cigarette and light it. He puffed a fragrant wreath of tobacco smoke, which encircled the two men, enveloping them in their own dome of silence.

"I mean, look at the people we're supporting: South Vietnam's one of the most brutal police states the world's ever known. And we helped them become that way. Hell, we gave 'em the guns and ammo. Who taught 'em to administer electric shocks to their prisoners' genitals? American CIA agents. They force people to drink soapy water, then they stomp on their stomachs. Where'd they learn to do that? Bingo. Americans, again. And we think God's on our side?"

Mose took a long drag on his cigarette. "The Bible says 'Thou shalt not kill,' yet everybody thinks they got a special exemption 'cause God is on their side. But when it comes down to it, no God of love would condone torture and genocide. If God was at My Lai, He was on the side of the innocent Buddhists that got slaughtered there."

Mose's sharp criticisms ought to have soured Ron's faith or make him feel defensive. Yet Ron always felt as though he were coming to know God better. It had also helped Ron to understand his own beliefs. His faith had matured from just being an echo of his parents' views to something more distinctly and uniquely his own.

If nothing else, Mose had helped him catch hold of one unassailable fact: *If there was a God of ultimate justice and fairness, He must be a lot bigger than most Christians knew.*

"If God meant it when He said we're not supposed to kill, what the hell are we doin' in the Army?" The question was the crystallization of fears that had been welling up inside of Ron for months.

"Me? Hell, I'm here 'cause of two things—Toadstool and sixteen."

"Toadstool and sixteen?"

"This dickhead Norris Thomas. He was a professor. I called him Toadstool 'cause he sat perched on this stool while he taught. He flunked me in Chem at Duke. I got put on scholastic probation, dropped out of school, then got drafted. My draft number was sixteen. So I figured if there's killing to be done, I'd rather do it from the air than on the ground."

Mose blew a lazy smoke ring. "Besides, the shitty rat's ass truth is a *brotha* has a better chance of survivin' a year in 'Nam than a year on most city streets in America."

He picked a piece of tobacco from the corner of his mouth. "And you? Feelin' what you feel, believin' what you believe, why are you here in this man's *muthafuckin'* army?"

Lately, that was a question Ron was having a hard time answering.

~~~

The next morning as Ron passed the mailroom, a clerk recognized him and raised a forefinger in salute. The private produced a thin airmail envelope.

"Letter for you, sir," he nodded, handing the envelope to Ron.

Ron turned the featherweight envelope over in his hands, saw the familiar, blocky handwriting on the front, and smiled.

Ron carefully carried Alex's first letter from 'Nam into the day room and searched for a quiet corner. In the middle of the room, the TV set spewed *"The Andersonville Trial,"* a military courtroom drama set in the Civil War era.

Ron turned the letter over in his hands, then sniffed it to see if any exotic aroma lingered on it. Did the air smell different in Vietnam? Finally, he slid a finger into the top flap and worked the letter open. He read:

January 2, 1970

Hoss—

Happy New Year and greetings from the sunny Mekong Valley. Wish you were here.

Not really.

Actually, I wish I was still back there, cruising the Varsity for chickpeas. The beer here tastes like carbonated piss, with a splash of bug spray. And most of the boom-boom girls I saw in Saigon have itsy-bitsy tits. Sure makes me miss Mona's ripe ta-tas.

Mostly all I've done so far is sit around in a firebase and get tangled up in wait-a-minute veins.

Out here, you get the feeling shit's going down all around you. Everybody's on a hair trigger, ready to jump if something happens. But nothing really has yet. Sometimes I wish something would happen, just so I don't go out of my fuckin' mind from the tension. Shit, I'd rather be out in the bush where at least I can do something. It's the waiting that really drives me off my nut.

I hear a lot of weird shit. I see stuff out the corners of my eyes that I just decide I didn't see. I can't explain it, but you'll see what I mean when you get here.

Let's just get this fuckin' job done, then come home and chase sorority chicks on Uncle Sam's nickel.

Alex

Ron read and reread the letter, hearing his best friend's voice in his ears. For several moments, his own troubles were forgotten. He wanted to tell himself that Alex was fine. But there was something Alex wasn't saying, a second letter traced, ever so faintly, between the lines of this one, with a message grimmer than Alex had the heart to express.

But, Ron decided, folding the letter and tucking it in the pocket of his uniform slacks, it was proof that Alex was alive and well. And that was proof sorely needed.

Chapter 38

The Kennesaw Line
Pentecost Sunday
June 26, 1864

UNDER THE OPPRESSIVE HEAT of a cloudless sky, Baylis and Ulysses trudged up a rocky hill toward the trenches, swatting at the insects darting and flitting around them. The cannonading and musketry had eased from the day before, and the bite of flies and mosquitoes had temporarily replaced the deadly sting of Yankee Minié balls. All along the defensive line that stretched for miles across hills and mountains, and the gorges that separated them, the Army of Tennessee was getting ready for more killing and dying.

In a clearing just behind the line of fortifications Baylis and Ulysses passed a cluster of soldiers attending a religious service. The chaplain, a stovepipe-thin man with a tangled salt-and-pepper beard and fiery eyes, was describing the coming of the Holy Spirit in the form of flames to the Apostles on Pentecost. The worn and somber rebels huddled around the preacher as he spoke, some holding Bibles, others clutching small crucifixes, all looking for assurances of life everlasting in the world beyond even as they prepared to sacrifice their lives in this one.

Baylis stopped to rest. He took out a cloth from his pocket, wiped the sweat from his forehead and listened. The chaplain had now moved to the Book of Samuel. He was talking about the civil war among the tribes of Israel in the time of David, and how reconciliation between the two armies came when David triumphed because "the Lord, the God of hosts, was with him." Waving his Bible, the preacher assured the men that, like David, their great cause would also triumph because "God is on our side."

In the war destroying his country, Baylis knew there were many men of faith in both armies that were certain God was on their side. One side or the other must be wrong, he thought. Or maybe they both were. Maybe God didn't take sides in war.

Maybe war was the devil's work, and men were blind to Lucifer's craven deceit.

~

When the Simpson men walked into Ulysses's company area at the end of a stony ridge, dozens of soldiers were busy rebuilding the headlogs and strengthening the "tangle foot" of chopped vines and saplings in front of the breastworks. The defenses on the salient were flimsy compared to what the men had seen elsewhere on their walk. It was apparent why: there were few large trees in the area to use for the fortifications.

Huzzahs and hollering greeted the appearance of the Simpsons as the soldiers gathered around them. Baylis could see that Ulysses was well liked by the men in his company.

"Welcome back to the ditches," a sergeant named Tedford said to Ulysses. "We got our reinforcements; now we can drive the Yankees back to Chattanooga." The sergeant slapped Ulysses on the back, "You smell sweet like a gent. You ain't gonna be able to stand my stink."

A young private named Colquitt said, "No wonder the sergeant reeks so—he's had the Georgia quick step for a week. We all have."

"I could have guessed as much by the flavor of the air about you," Ulysses said.

The men all laughed.

"We been washing when we can in rain water. That'd be all there is," a young private with red hair said.

"This here's my pa," Ulysses said.

"I'm Sanders, the camp's dog robber. I cooks for da boys," the private said with a gummy whistle caused by his missing front teeth.

"You up here to enjoy the view, old timer?" Tedford asked with a smile.

"No, sir. I'm with the Georgia State Infantry, looking to find my regiment."

"You a fresh fish? Done any fightin'?"

"Some. It was of a personal nature."

"We got in a bad go-to with bandits a few days ago," Ulysses explained. "My pa cut one of their heads off. I reckon that son of a bitch is down in hell right now looking for it."

"That's plenty good enough," Tedford said to Baylis. "You've seen the elephant for certain."

"You look too old to have been called up with the draft," Colquitt said.

"I volunteered. Then I received agriculture leave from Governor Joe."

"We got Georgia infantry are all up and down the line," Tedford said. "A bushel of 'em have been folded in with the 63rd Georgia. Those goober grabbers are a walk up that way." He pointed up the ridge toward Little Kennesaw. "The 1st Battalion Georgia Sharpshooters are down yonder way toward the road."

"I got a cousin in 1st Georgia," Ulysses noted. "Reckon we got Simpson kin all over this mountain."

"If it's all the same, I'll stop here for the night, then find my company in the morning," Baylis said.

"You're welcome to stay. We could use another good man."

Baylis and Ulysses set their muskets and provisions down and began to help strengthen the breastworks.

"We've been doing this for damn near a week with little to work with," Colquitt explained. "Every day the Yankees flatten it with artillery, and every night we reinforce it again. Since it looks like the Yanks took the day off for praying and sermons, we thought we'd get a start on it so's maybe we could get us a night's sleep."

Baylis noticed one soldier polishing a Cash & Wesson revolver with the tattered end of his blouse. Something in the man's glassy eyes made Baylis uneasy.

Colquitt caught his look. "Don't pay Nicholson no never mind," the private said. "He's agitated by soldier's heart. His nerves are fevered. He don't sleep or eat much. He just keeps a-polishin' that revolver."

Soldier's heart. Baylis had heard of men who, having known the horrors of war, developed that dark malady. It was said that they were prone to the hysteria of emotion and rash action.

Colquitt touched Nicholson on the shoulder. "Ulysses is back. This here's Baylis, his pa."

Nicholson looked up at Baylis briefly with a hazy stare then went back to his polishing without speaking.

"How long has he been like that?"

"Since Resaca," Colquitt answered.

"I tried to place him in Company Q to get him off the line," Sergeant Tedford said. "My request was denied on account there was no ailment that the doctor could place on him."

"You'd think that revolver would be as clean as a church maid by now," Colquitt said. "It's never left his hands since he took it off a bluecoat he killed. He takes it apart, cleans it then puts it back together again. Over and over. He's done it so many durn times I've lost the count."

"Nothing like a task to settle the mind," Baylis said. He then leaned into the work of building the defenses on the line, work that was certain to be destroyed by Union guns on the morrow. For a time, his mind and body were working as one, concentrating on the job at hand. For a few blessed hours, he forgot that everything he knew and loved was dying by flame and sword.

Chapter 39

February 1970

STATIONED AT FORT BENNING while waiting for deployment for Vietnam, Ron's life felt like a runaway train. For months, he had convinced himself that if he could fly medevac, it would allow him to maintain a delicate balance between obligation to God and country. Now that equilibrium had been destroyed. His orders were to fly a gunship.

Twice he had requested to be reassigned to fly medevac, and twice he had been denied. Expecting any day to be sent to Vietnam, he was out of options.

With the purest of intentions, he had sworn allegiance to two masters. He had vowed to serve God by submission to the authority of Christ, and he had promised to serve his country by submission to the authority of the United States Army. He believed both his God and his country to be benevolent, powerful, and wise, both worthy of his fealty. He had assumed, out of the innocence of a trusting heart, that his duties to each would not conflict with one another.

But now they did.

His commanding officers offered him no solace. When Ron first approached his CO at Benning and requested to be reassigned, the officer brusquely replied that a soldier is sent where he is ordered and does what he's told.

One point had become clear in Ron's mind: *he would not take a human life.* The Bible said don't kill, and it said so without equivocation. Where generations of Christians saw a comma, Ron Simpson saw a period. Nothing would override the one commandment he considered unbreachable.

More than anything else, Ron feared shipping out to Vietnam as a gunship pilot because he knew, as generations of soldiers had warned, that there were no pacifists in foxholes. When you're being shot at, when you see your own buddies blown to pieces before your eyes, you *will* become a killer.

Ron fought hard against a sense of hopelessness that crashed upon him like a flood tide. But after the arrival of a second letter from Alex, something deep within him began, slowly, imperceptibly, to give up.

February 3, 1970

Ron,

I don't know what to tell you. Nothing could prepare you for what you see and do here. I'm always looking over my shoulder. Always afraid. My paranoia is unbelievable.

Yesterday our squad was caught in a rice paddy when Charlie Victor started pounding us with 120s. Three guys died. One was blown up right in front of me. I wiped pieces of his intestines off my face.

I haven't written the ol' lady 'cause I don't know what to say. I can't tell Mom the truth.

Out in the bush, I live from moment to moment, praying only that if someone's gonna die, the fucking Grim Reaper will take the next guy humping the tall grass and leave me the hell alone.

It's never quiet, except when it rains and the insects are drowned out. No one seems to know what we are trying to do here. No one in command will tell the truth—this war is lost.

I just pray to God I make it home. All I gotta say about it is this—fuck you, John Wayne.

Alex

Ron Simpson sat on a bar stool in the officer's club with Alex's letter before him. He chased a shot of tequila with lukewarm Budweiser. He had been there a while. He despised himself for what he was doing. Until tonight, drinking was a thing he did for fun, with friends, on a Saturday night. Never before in his life had he used booze as an anesthetic. It did not make him feel proud.

Some time after draining his fourth shot glass, Ron became dimly aware of an officer seated a few stools down, devouring a raw, messy burger. Ron studied the man blearily. He could not have been more than three or four years Ron's senior. But something about him seemed obscenely weathered and aged.

It was the eyes, Ron decided. He remembered seeing a Lottie Moon missionary film in Sunday School years ago featuring the ravages of poverty in India. He recalled the helpless, hopeless people, too weak to stand, their brown hides stretched over protruding bone, elderly at the age of thirty. They had eyes like this man's. All joy at being alive had been extinguished. His were the eyes of the last lonesome drunk slumped upon the bar at closing time. It was a mockery of all goodness for those eyes to belong to such a young man.

No, those eyes should only belong to a dead man.

The officer seemed to sense Ron's gaze. He looked up from his burger and mumbled, through a mouthful of lettuce and onions, "Pass the baby shit."

Ron handed him the mustard and went back to nursing his beer. But he couldn't help sneaking another look. The man felt Ron's eyes on him once more and turned. He rubbed his greasy fingers on a napkin and offered his hand.

"Sal Rozamond."

"Ron Simpson," he said, shaking his hand. He stared at the double row of ribbons decorating the man's chest.

Rozamond followed Ron's look with a cheerless guffaw. "You think this fruit salad counts for something? It don't mean jack."

"Why's that?"

"They're gonna kick me with bad paper."

"A dishonorable discharge?"

"All because of the *Mere Gook Rule*," he said, wiping his mouth before throwing back a shot of tequila.

"The what?"

Rozamond studied Ron for a moment, then went back to eating. "You ain't been in country. I can see it in your eyes." The words escaped out of the side of Rozamond's mouth between bites. "No cherry turd could understand the *Mere Gook Rule*."

"I'm pretty intelligent. Why don't you try to explain it?"

"Intelligence ain't got nothin' to do with it." He put down the carcass of his burger and stirred a French fry through the ketchup at the corner of his plate. Then he leaned in close, as though sharing a secret. "A crime's not a crime if it's committed against a mere gook. The *Mere Gook Rule*. It's the first thing you learn in country." He plopped the fry in this mouth.

"You've had too much to drink."

"You think I'm fuckin' with you? Over there, even babies are the enemy."

"I don't think babies are anyone's enemy."

Rozamond took a drink, wiped the back of his hand across his mouth, and fixed Ron with a baleful stare.

"We've been in 'Nam for what? Ten years?"

"Something like that, yeah."

"All them little baby bastards born the first year we went in are old enough to handle AK's now. I've had friends killed by eleven, twelve-year-olds. So those babies you leave alive today ain't gonna return the favor if they meet your ass in a fuckin' rice paddy some day. Trust me on that."

Ron recoiled in disgust, and pulled himself to his feet. He pocketed Alex's letter, fumbled for his cash and threw it on the bar.

"Hey, keep your seat. I'm through anyway." Rozamond stood, paid his check, then fixed Ron with hard eyes. "Some free advice. Fuck their age. Fuck their sex. If you can't look any gook in the eye and kill 'em, you don't belong in combat. You'll just get good men killed."

With those lacerating words, Rozamond moved away.

Later that night, Ron was treading silently past the Main Post Cantonment with its red terra cotta roof and stucco walls when he spotted Fort Benning's interfaith chapel. The elegant 100-foot-tall steeple drew him like a homing beacon.

Stepping inside, the colonial-style chapel held the lingering aroma of carnations. Probably the last vestige of another funeral, Ron thought. No other soldier felt the need of God's house that night, but he had nowhere else to turn.

Never before in his life had Ron voluntarily entered a place of worship without his parents at his side. Outside the familiar context of Sunday service, Ron felt lost and awkward, unsure of what to do. He seated himself on a pew and stared at the beautiful arched windows decorated with carefully shaped ashlar limestone.

What to do?

Ron bowed his head and tried to will himself into the presence of God. His heart was full of turmoil, and his mind raced down a thousand paths at once. Before he could even form the words for prayer, he would have to calm the storm in his soul.

Be still. The familiar passage from scripture floated into his mind like a distant voice. *Be still, and know I am here.* Ron breathed deeply, closed his eyes, and slowly, methodically, poured forth his anguish in silent prayer.

He was then that he realized—*there was at least one stone he had left unturned.*

The night had grown sullen and quiet when Ron made his way from the chapel to Fort Benning's library. He let himself into the stucco walled room, flicked on a few overhead lights, and helped himself to a yellow legal pad and pencil from the deserted reception desk. He scanned the titles on the reference shelf, and after a few minute's search, flopped down at the desk with a heavy black leather-bound tome with *The Uniform Code of Military Justice* stamped in yellow letters on its spine. He flipped to a section titled "Conscientious Objectors: Procedures."

A slip of paper was tucked inside. It read:

> *General, man is very useful.*
> *He can fly, and he can kill.*
> *But he has one defect: He can think.*
> *Bertolt Brecht*

Ron had heard rumors of an on-base riot over the war at Fort Benning in March 1968. The military had suppressed all reports of it, and there was no official record of its existence. He wondered if one of those soldiers had left the quote.

Ron began scribbling down notes. The military could ignore a volunteer's request, but they wouldn't dare ignore their own rules.

―

When Captain Wayne Bartlett arrived at his office the next morning, Ron had already been waiting for him for half an hour, document in hand.

Bartlett deemed this a closed issue. Simpson had twice requested assignment to fly medevac, and twice he had been denied. But Bartlett ushered Simpson into his office anyway, took the document to his desk, and reviewed it as the young soldier stood braced at attention.

After a weighty pause, the officer looked up sharply. "I'm to understand that you're now requesting a discharge as a conscientious objector?"

"Sir, yes, sir. I followed the procedures as outlined in DoD Directive 1300.6, dated May 10, 1968."

Bartlett rose and walked out from behind his desk. He towered over Ron. "Have your religious feelings changed since you joined the Army?" he inquired testily.

"What do you mean, sir?" Ron asked, sensing a trap.

"Have your religious beliefs changed as a result of your military experience, or were you a CO when you volunteered?"

"I guess I've always believed killing was wrong," Ron answered honestly.

"You're stating you were a CO before you joined, then?"

Ron considered for a moment, then answered, "If being a CO means that you think killing is wrong, sir. But my feelings matured after I joined. I understand my beliefs better now."

"Your record states you're a volunteer. If you were a CO," Bartlett thumped the form, "why volunteer?"

"I didn't consider myself a CO when I joined. I wanted to help my country, sir. I come from a tradition of service. I just hoped I could do it without killing people. That's why I requested to fly medevac."

Bartlett turned to the shelf of books behind him and removed his copy of *The Uniform Code of Military Justice*. He leafed through the pages, then stopped and read carefully. Then he snapped the book closed with finality and set down at his desk.

"I'll send your request up the chain for review," he said curtly as he scribbled notes. "You'll report for an interview with a chaplain and for a mental hygiene consultation. It's all a waste of time and good paper."

"Sir?"

"You state you held CO-qualifying beliefs before entering the military. Therefore, according to regulations, you can't qualify to become one now."

"But sir, that doesn't make any sense!" Ron blurted, his voice tight with anger.

"Enough!" Bartlett barked, "Another remark like that soldier, and I'll flag your jacket with a reprimand."

"I request to be reassigned to medevac, sir!" Ron tried again.

"For the third time, request denied!" Bartlett shot back. "You'll fly what you were ordered to fly."

"I won't fly a gunship, sir."

Bartlett moved far more swiftly than seemed possible for a man of his size. His face was now inches away.

"You'll fly a goddam gunship, or you'll do hard time in Leavenworth for the next five years. Now step back, or by God I'll put you in shackles and ass-kick you to Indian country myself."

Ron seethed in the captain's face for a long, heavy moment, then stepped back. Ramrod straight. Jaw locked tight.

"Dismissed," Bartlett said, with unconcealed fury. He turned away.

Ron saluted his commanding officer's rigid back, spun on his heel, and left.

Chapter 40

The Kennesaw Line
Pentecost Sunday
June 26, 1864

BAYLIS ENJOYED THE FEELING of settling into a Georgia summer night. The sunset's rich red hues seemed to catch the woods on fire, and now, as the last embers of light drained away, a soft darkness spread along with the rhythmic call of the peepers. A cool breeze rustled the leaves of the hardwoods and brought scents of grassy pastures from the South, driving the starker odors from the trenches.

It was like an oasis, heaven in the midst of hell.

The men built a small campfire and brewed chicory while they chewed on sowbelly and cornbread.

"Wish we could get some real coffee," Private Sanders said, sipping the chicory-flavored water. "Next time we get us a ceasefire, I'll see about trading tobacco to the Yanks for some."

As always, the talk turned to the war.

"Think we'll have a fight soon?" Colquitt asked.

"Johnston surely thinks so," Ulysses said. "He had the surgeons sharpening their saws today."

"A good sign their services will be needed come the morrow."

"Sherman knows if he attacks us here, his bluecoats will be slaughtered," Tedford pushed out his words between bites.

"I don't expect he cares," Ulysses spit. "The Yankees never care how many of their own die. They got plenty more of 'em."

"I hear tell they enlist 'em right off the docks when the immigrant ships make port in New York," a gruff, older private named Thomas said.

"The way the Yanks been cannonading us for days, Sherman will attack, all rightie," Tedford assured them.

"Last time he left the railroad, his tatter line collapsed. His army came damn near close to having to eat their boots. Our artillery on this mountain can hit the rail line below Big Shanty. He's got to knock us off this here anthill or go around and risk getting his army cut off again."

"Yessirree bob, one way or another Sherman's got to get us off this mountain," Colquitt said. "And ol' Joe Johnston knows that this here's our last stand 'fore Atlanta, so he sure as hell ain't leaving without a go-to. He knows if Atlanta falls . . ."

There was no need to finish that sentence. Every one of them knew what Colquitt meant. Atlanta was the center of the south. You kill it, and the south would die as surely as if you'd cut its heart out. No more jumping or spinning, just a body on the floor.

Listening to the men talk about Atlanta, Baylis thought it odd so many were about to die for something so pitiful as that God-forsaken town. He wouldn't pay a thin half-dime to live there. For one thing, its size had nearly doubled in the last ten years. With several thousand people now crammed together like hogs in a pen, the city had grown too large for his tastes. For another, it was a town built around railroads, a place where barkeeps outnumbered policemen, and slave traders, gamblers, and prostitutes outnumbered clergy.

It hadn't always been like that. When Baylis first set eyes on the land as a boy, it was little more than a network of Indian trails that threaded along clear streams and rivers, cut through a lush tapestry of red oaks and the loblolly pines, which the Creek called "pitch trees." In the spring, when the forests were laced with dogwood blooms, wild roses, and red honeysuckle, it was a pretty sight indeed.

Sanders coughed harshly, snapping Baylis back to the present. After listening to the older soldiers, the private said, "I got a letter from my maw. She said ol' *Ape* Lincoln needs himself a victory 'fore the election."

"They're callin' Big Kennesaw Mountain 'The Gibraltar of Georgia.' I reckon it'd make a flashy thing, capturing Gibraltar," Tedford observed with a grim smile.

"Only problem is they ain't gonna do it," Ulysses said.

"True enough," Tedford said, "but I fear they'll try."

"Seeing the fight up at Kolb's farm a few days back, Sherman probably thinks the south part of our line is the weakest," Colquitt said. "He expects Ol' Joe to fall back to Atlanta. But it tain't gonna happen."

"My wager is Jackass Billy will send a bunch of Yanks right at us," Tedford said. "The way this here part of the line juts out, he'll attack us from two sides and try to bite it right off."

"I almost feel sorry for 'em," Sanders said, scratching his red hair.

"Not me," Colquitt said. "I'd like to send all of 'em to hell."

"I can't divine the future," Baylis said. "But if we do fight tomorrow, I'd like a large ration of sleep first."

"Don't worry about missing it," Colquitt said. "Yankee artillery will tell you they're coming."

Baylis took his wool blanket and found a spot of recently turned earth. He picked through the area and tossed the small rocks aside before settling into the soft ground. It felt almost like a bed and smelled of rich soil.

He was exhausted, but he feared his dreams. His nights were as horrifying as his days, for there was no difference between the worst he could imagine and what he did to survive. There was no refuge in sleep or waking. His only solace would be in death.

Chapter 41

March 1970

THE ARMY, IN ITS infinite generosity, granted Ron a few weeks leave. By that time, Ron's mood had so blackened that even the thought of home held little comfort. The mere idea of explaining his quarrel with the military to his father, whose soul and right arm were indelibly tattooed with *Semper Fidelis,* left Ron feeling exhausted, depleted. Ron feared that what he was about to become, through no choice of his own, would taint the whole notion of home and family. His lightless future gaped before him like a chasm.

Ron arrived home in a taxicab on a cool March afternoon as bruise-colored storm clouds gathered on its eastern horizon. Alex's two well-read letters crinkled inside his breast pocket. During the ride from Fort Benning, Ron had puzzled over how he would explain his dilemma to his father. But as his cab rounded the last corner and his boyhood home drew into view, he gave up. There was no acceptable way to announce the unacceptable.

Ron paid the cab driver, shouldered his duffel, and let himself in the front door. His father was talking on the phone in the kitchen. Ron's head was so full of misery that it took him a moment to register the surprise staggering across his father's face. He waved the receiver toward his oldest son.

"It's Alex . . ."

Alex calling from Vietnam? How odd. Ron's mind skidded to a stop at the thought. And then he realized.

~

Alex came home from Vietnam three weeks later. That night, Ron stood waiting in a dour, steady downpour on the platform at Jonesboro's train depot. He was there alone, lost in thought, when Michael moved onto the concrete landing and silently stood beside him.

"I guess the folks called you," Ron said in a grainy voice, not bothering to glance over at his brother.

"Drove in from Athens when I heard he was coming."

"You shouldn't have."

"He's my friend, too."

"It's just that you didn't have to," Ron said. "Alex would understand."

When the Dixie Flyer shrieked a few miles out, Ron and Michael gave no outward sign of acknowledging the train's approach.

"The folks weren't sure where you were, but I knew you'd be here," Michael said.

Ron fixed his brother with a ghost of a smile. "Too superstitious not to be—not when I heard he was arriving on the train."

On the train.

The thought of Alex coming home on the train seemed weird, almost macabre. Their friend wouldn't have traveled that way if he'd had any choice. But, of course, he didn't. He traveled the way the Army sent him.

The Dixie Flyer approached and, with a long, steamy hiss, braked to a halt. Ron and Michael moved listlessly to a freight car where two dripping station attendants were unlatching a heavy door.

The attendants rolled back the solid gate. Inside, lit only by the platform light, was Alex. Their friend was home.

He was inside a metal shipping casket draped with an American flag.

It was the sight they both had dreaded since first hearing news of Alex's death. But the harsh reality was no easier to accept.

Instinctively, Ron braced to attention and saluted. Michael placed his right hand over his heart as his eyes filled with tears. As the attendants moved to the solitary coffin and loaded it onto a wheeled cart, the brothers exchanged a wordless, knowing glance. The irony was not lost on either of them.

Just as Alex had always predicted, the Dixie Flyer had brought his death.

Somehow the church had passed through the war years without a casualty among its own, but Alex's death had brought the ghastly goings-on half a world away to their own doorsteps. It seemed like First Baptist's whole congregation, and then some, turned out for his funeral. Among them were a military honor guard and an army chaplain that had come to lend support at Ginger's request.

Most of the young people present had never attended a funeral for someone their own age before. The experience was nothing like, say, laying to rest some seasoned old codger. A funeral like that was often a celebration of the loved one's long life. Mourners here found nothing whatsoever to celebrate. For them, Alex's death was shocking, obscene, unacceptable.

It was not until the preparations for the funeral that Ron discovered what Alex talked to his father about the night before leaving for Vietnam. Alex had asked Harold that if he was killed to bury him in the Simpson family cemetery, where their kin had been buried since the days of Baylis. Alex had conveyed his wishes to his mother, and she agreed to honor them. Ginger knew that was where Alex belonged, to wait for the boys he called brothers and the man who had been like a father to him.

Ron stood in front beside his father, brother, and mother, surrounded among the birch and oak trees by his family's history. Just a short distance away, near the rusted iron-gate entrance, Baylis Simpson's weathered tombstone held silent vigil. Ron wondered what Baylis would have thought now that six generations after the War Between the States, American soldiers were fighting and dying in another country's civil war.

Ginger leaned weakly against Carlotta, as though the loss of her only child had leached the calcium from her bones. Carlotta's tears flowed freely, and Michael sniffled miserably into the sleeve of his Sunday suit, having failed to bring a handkerchief or tissue.

Mona stood off to one side, dabbing at her eyes. She seemed to be holding up better than Ron had expected. Her inner strength was part of what attracted Alex to her, and it was being tested now in a way neither of them could have imagined.

Outside of Ginger, who was now completely alone in a world seemingly devoid of justice, Ron was most concerned about Harold. Growing up, Ron had mistaken his father's stoicism for a lack of caring. As years passed, Ron came to understand that just because his dad didn't show it didn't mean he wasn't feeling it. In fact, the stonier his father's face, the likelier it was that his soul was overflowing. Today, Harold's face was as unassailable as the polished granite slabs that dotted the Simpson family cemetery.

Since losing his own father, Alex had looked to Harold as a surrogate dad, and Harold had answered the call with valor. He had coached Alex in little league baseball and cheered him in varsity football. His quiet strength had buoyed Alex through many dark times. At Ginger's request, it was Harold who had broken the news to Alex about his father's passing. And at Alex's death, Harold had borne the sad tidings to his own sons.

Harold had also informed Mona. Alex had given Harold a message for her, which he had dutifully repeated. No one knew what he had said, but she clearly had found strength in it.

At a nod from Reverend Fletcher, Ron approached the podium and addressed the gathering.

"Alex was a brother to me," Ron said without preamble, "not by blood, but by choice." Ron pulled a piece of folded notepaper from his pocket and nodded to the Army chaplain. "The chaplain here gave me something I'd like to share with you. This was written by Major Michael Davis O'Donnell, a helo pilot assigned to the 52nd in Dak To, Vietnam. He's now MIA." Ron unfolded the paper and read:

"If you are able, save for them a place inside of you, and save one backward glance when you are leaving for the places they can no longer go. Be not ashamed to say you loved them, though you may or may not have always. Take what they have left and what they have taught you with their dying, and keep it with your own. And in that time when men feel safe to call the war insane, take one moment to embrace those gentle heroes you left behind."

Ron folded the paper and replaced it in his pocket. He locked eyes, gently, briefly, with the kindred souls in the group who had also loved Alex. Then, with no more words needed, he returned to his seat.

"Present arms," the officer of the honor guard said. "Fire!"

The military honor guard fired, sending shudders through many of those present. The ritual was repeated three times.

The guard gathered the spent casings and tucked them inside the corner of a folded American flag, then, with white-gloved hands, the officer carefully presented the flag to Ginger "on behalf of the President of the United States and a grateful nation."

When it was over, the mourners dispersed quickly. It was too painful for many to bear any longer than decorum required, and there was an unspoken sense that Ginger preferred to be alone at her son's grave. Alex's casket made its lurching descent into a freshly dug hole, and the soft red Georgia soil was shoveled over it.

Ginger had not uttered a word since she had arrived. Now, with only the Simpsons to hear, she spoke in a thin, hollow voice. "I keep thinking about what it's gonna be like to go home knowing my boy'll never come through that door again."

Carlotta enveloped her in a hug. "Bless your heart. Come stay with us a while. It's no good to be alone."

Ginger returned the hug, then pulled away. "No mama should have to watch her baby lowered in the ground," Ginger's voice quavered. A hardness crept into her grief-swollen features. "You might as well know," she said bitterly, "I'm not coming to church anymore." The tears began flowing again.

Ron wanted to turn away, so that he would not have to witness a mother's heart breaking before his eyes.

"What would the Lord do something like this?" Ginger sobbed. "He takes my husband . . . and now my only child? I swear I don't rightly know if there is a God . . ."

Carlotta moved to embrace her again, but Ginger waved her away. Abruptly, she turned and stepped to her car. As she drove away Carlotta and her family were left standing frozen and numb.

Ron quietly observed the pain on his mother's face. He knew what she must be thinking. *Her own son might face the same fate.*

Ron watched as, in an unconscious gesture, his mother wrapped herself tightly in her coat and leaned against her husband. She watched Ginger's car disappear from sight through tear-filled eyes.

Chapter 42

March 1970

AFTER THE FUNERAL, THE Simpsons hung listlessly about the kitchen. Funerals are meant to place a mark of finality, a waxen seal on the story of a loved one's departure, so that those who remain behind can resume the messy task of living. But no one in the Simpson household felt like getting on with anything. The energy required simply to move was more than they could muster.

All four Simpsons chose to vegetate in the kitchen, perhaps because it was a place of comfort. A pot of fresh-perked coffee sat, untasted, on the counter, its cozy, nutty aroma as superfluous as the early yellow riot of daffodils blooming outside the kitchen windows.

Carlotta stood blankly at the sink, swishing a dishrag around the inside of the same pan she'd washed ten minutes ago. "Poor Ginger, I don't know what she'll do," she whispered softly.

Harold and Michael leaned against opposite corners of the kitchen counter, hands in pockets, eyes on the floor. In a different mood, Ron might have cracked a grin at how closely they resembled each other. But now Ron sat at the kitchen table, studying a pattern in the tabletop. Flecks of avocado and goldenrod. He'd never really noticed them before.

Harold's low voice broke the silence. "Son, for what it's worth, I talked to that Army captain before the service. He'd seen Alex's KIA report. He said Alex ... he stepped on an antitank mine. He died instantly. It would have been painless."

Ron choked back a wave of emotion. He looked out the window to the back yard, and tried to slam shut the floodgates. He heard his mother ask softly, "Son, can I fix you a cup of coffee?" But he dared not look away from the window. He could not allow himself to cave in front of his parents.

Ron found a momentary pocket of calm in the storm that threatened to sweep him away. He turned to face his father. "I need to clear my head. Think I'll take a walk."

Ron rose and made a beeline for the kitchen door.

The coming evening kicked up a light, cooling breeze. Another ripe, lush Georgia spring was coming, but Ron didn't notice as he strode blindly down the street. He was barely conscious of anything until he found himself on the edge of town. So much the better, he thought. He did not want to meet anyone. The walking, pure and directionless as it was, helped unclog something lodged deep in his soul. It restored the flow of energy he needed to get on with thoughts, with actions, with living. It did not make the loss of Alex one iota less painful, though. There wasn't a thing in the world that could be done about that.

Ron was nearing the railroad tracks when he became dimly aware of a familiar sound. The hair on the back of his neck prickled as he recognized the growl of a street rod's engine. Specifically, the engine of a shiny black 1969 Dodge Charger RT.

The car pulled alongside him. Chuck Leach leaned out the driver's window, gunning the engine along in time to Ron's footsteps.

"Hey, pussy boy, thought you was off popping gooks for Uncle Sam."

Ron kept walking, head down.

"I'm talkin' to you, dipshit. You owe me for my new fender and grill, you butt-reamin' asshole."

Ron stopped walking and turned a baleful eye to Chuck. "I don't wanna fight," he said solemnly. "Not now. Not tomorrow. Not ever."

His words only made Chuck madder. Ron surrendered then to what he knew was coming. He simply let it happen.

Chuck bolted from the car and folded Ron in half with one iron-fisted punch to the gut. While Ron was bent halfway to his knees, clutching his stomach, Chuck linked his hands and brought both fists straight up into Ron's nose.

The roadside gravel slammed Ron in the side of the head before he knew he was falling. Then Chuck was working him all over, landing vicious kicks anywhere he could put them, pouring all his hatred into his fallen rival.

Some time later, Ron became dimly aware that the beating had stopped. Then he heard a voice, close to his ear. It was Chuck's friend Ira.

"Sorry about this, man. I dunno what got into Chuck. He had a real shitty day, got chewed out by the coach and all . . . and then he got this stupid-ass speeding ticket on the way home from Athens. It just totally fucked his mood. It's nothin' personal, understand?"

Two car doors slammed, then the Dodge Charger burned rubber. Then silence.

Ron studied his swollen face in the bathroom mirror. He dabbed at the crusted blood around his nose, squeezed pinkish water from the wadded toilet paper in his hand, and dropped it into the wastebasket beside a growing pile of soggy pink lumps.

After the beating, Ron had limped painfully home and miraculously made it into the bathroom without anyone seeing the swollen mass of raw hamburger that Chuck had made of his face. His mother was growing suspicious. Ron knew he needed to make an appearance at the dinner table, especially since tonight was his last dinner at home for quite a while, if not forever.

When it came to violence, Chuck was a maestro, no question about it. The crowning glory of his work was the nose. The bridge of Ron's nose had become a swollen, shapeless mass, and the ruptured blood vessels were rapidly leaking purple-black fluid into the tissues around his eye sockets. Ron looked like a raccoon.

The nose was by far the worst, but the rest of Ron's face bore testimony to Chuck's handiwork as well. His left eye was swollen to a bulbous slit, a perpetual, damaged wink. Above it, from the corner of his eyebrow, a purplish-blue goose egg continued to balloon. His lower lip was split and puffy in two places; his mother might insist on stitches.

Ron felt on the inside the way his face looked on the outside: raw, throbbing, and ready to explode. His fruitless quarrel with the Army, the senseless loss of his best friend, and now the shameful drubbing from Chuck—the rage kept building within him, until his movements became jerky. He stuck his head under the shower and ran cold water over his mashed features for as long as he could stand, gasping and choking down his fury until he'd beaten it into submission, at least for the moment. Then, solemnly, resolutely, he marched out to join his family at the dinner table.

"Oh, my Lord!" Carlotta shrieked, rushing to Ron, "What happened?"

"You get in a fight, son?" Harold stared at his face.

"It's nothing. I'm fine," Ron sighed.

"It was Chuck, wasn't it?" Michael asked.

His family pressed him for details, but Ron refused to offer any explanation. He simply wanted the incident forgotten. Surprisingly, his parents and brother conceded to his unspoken wish and let the matter drop. Concerned as they were, they sensed that they could not help him.

There was nothing left to do but eat.

Carlotta Simpson had outdone herself again. She had a Southern woman's instinct for recognizing those times when her family's troubles were beyond her control. Even when she could not solve their problems, she could still soothe them, as she had always done, with copious quantities of comfort food.

Carlotta placed the platters of food on the table, smoothed her apron and sat, then reached a hand to her husband and a hand to Ron. Ron took her hand and likewise reached for his brother's, a ritual they had observed since Ron was old enough to sit at the table on a pile of phone books, and Michael was an infant in his high chair.

Ron bowed his head and waited for his father to speak the long-practiced words: "Bless us, oh Lord, and these, thy gifts, for which we are eternally grateful. In Jesus' name we pray, Amen."

In the silence that followed, Ron became aware for the first time of his mother's labored breathing. The air moving in and out of Carlotta's lungs sounded like silk being pulled through barbed wire.

"You all right, Mom?"

Carlotta waved the question away with her hand, "I used my inhaler late, that's all. I'll be fine." But when she answered his question, she didn't meet his eyes.

Ron made a valiant effort to eat the magnificent dinner his mother had prepared. But even the peas choked him. He pushed his food around on his plate, hoping that no one would notice.

But Harold noticed.

"I know this is hard, son," Harold said gently. "Alex's death has come at a damn poor time."

"When'd be a good time for Alex to die?" Ron replied testily.

"I'm just saying, what with your orders to ship out," Harold replied. "I know you're all tore up inside, son. But you need to do what's right."

"*Right?* For who?"

"Our country."

Ron felt his rage rising to the surface again. Every time he had tried to explain to his dad his conflicted feelings about serving as a gunship pilot in Vietnam, Ron had hit the wall that separated their beliefs. *You volunteered. You gave your word. You have an obligation his father would say.* So Ron had always stopped. Before he could think of a way to head it off again, he and his father were in the middle of the argument Ron had promised himself would never happen.

"What about what's right for me?" Ron knew what was coming next.

"Your country comes first," Harold insisted.

"I don't want to murder people!" Ron roared in frustration.

"Harold, Ron, please just—" Carlotta protested weakly.

"What do you think the military does, son? You signed up, and that's that. You need to accept—"

Ron cut his father off, "Seeing how we're all so touched by Alex's death, maybe I should . . . you know what, I will. I'll share with you the last words I got from Alex."

Ron fished out Alex's letter, stabbed a finger at the page. "The important part is here at the very bottom, where it says . . . 'Fuck you, John Wayne.'" He shoved the letter in Harold's face.

Ron folded Alex's letter and crammed it back into his pocket. Carlotta's hand flew to her throat. Her face grew pale. Harold was livid.

"Don't you dare speak that way in front of your mother. You're—"

"Stop! Both of you!" Carlotta pleaded.

Ron abruptly tossed his napkin down and pushed away from the table. He tromped to the sliding glass door in the den and let himself out. He lay on his back on the picnic table in the backyard, staring up at a fuzzy canopy of stars winking through the lattice of hickory branches. Harold had taught both his boys to call many of those stars by name. Tonight, Ron was grateful that his father possessed the decency and good sense to leave him alone with those familiar stars.

For the first hour, Ron stared up at the stars in lonesome silence. The calm darkness worked a healing magic. The vast, endless solitude of the stars placed his own problems in perspective, made them seem more manageable. The cool night air worked like a poultice on his throbbing face, which felt noticeably better when he lay on his back.

Not long into his second hour of stargazing, an aching loneliness took Ron by surprise. Slowly, gradually, he realized that he was outside, alone, cut off. And it was his last night home.

As if on cue, the sliding glass door opened softly. Ron knew without looking that Michael was coming to check on him. His brother padded up soundlessly and took a seat on the picnic table beside him.

"Hey, little bro," Ron said softly, without looking over. A long moment of silence passed. "Thanks for comin' out."

"You don't have to talk or nothin', if you don't feel like it."

"It *was* Chuck Leach, if you're wondering."

"I wasn't wondering who did it. I was wondering why you didn't fight back."

Ron sat up and looked at his little brother.

"How do you know I didn't?"

"'Cause you're two inches taller and about a hundred IQ points smarter than him. Plus you're in the best shape of your life. You'da made roadkill out of that asshole."

Ron absentmindedly fingered the gold cross he wore about his neck with his dog tags. "I just didn't feel like . . . I didn't wanna fight."

"Yeah, but look what happens when you don't fight back. It totally sucks."

Ron managed a slim smile. "I gotta say it more than sucks. It hurts like hell."

The two brothers sat in silence for a moment.

"I still don't understand this thing with the Army," Michael said. "If they won't let you fly medevac, why not just refuse to go to 'Nam?"

"Then I'm looking at a maximum-security military prison. Probably five years in Leavenworth. I got a little taste of life behind bars that one night. It's not something I'd wanna experience again."

"Prison? That's not fair!"

"It's war. Fair ain't got nothin' to do with it, bro."

Ron knew that Michael had been trying to make sense of the war for quite some time. Michael thought about things more than most, delved deep, tried to puzzle them out. It irked him when things didn't make sense. They'd both heard the lame explanations politicians loved to offer, the catchphrases and statistics, the Domino Effect and the Balance of Power. None of it added up to anything a bright young man could get his mind around.

A sudden memory caused Ron to smile. "Remember when we were kids? We dug a hole over there in the yard, put leaves over it, and made a trap?"

Michael grimaced, remembering. "We thought we'd catch a rabbit. And when Mom came out that night to take the dry clothes off the line, she stepped in the hole, twisted her ankle. Boy howdy, was Dad p.o.'d."

"We'd never even thought about Mom stepping in the thing." Ron thought for a long moment, then added, "See, that's sorta what's happening now. Joining the Army . . . it's having consequences I never thought of. I never knew my country was capable of something like . . ."

Ron's voice trailed off.

Ron didn't need to finish the sentence. The unspoken words "My Lai" hung in the stillness. The crickets and cicadas, tuning up for their nightly chorus, filled in the silence.

Ron eased himself to a stand. "I'd best go pack. My flight's early next morning."

He fumbled in his pocket and pulled out his car keys. "I want you to take care of the Mustang while I'm gone."

"You sure you trust me, after what happened to it before? I can't even pay the deductible if something happens again."

"Don't worry about it. Any problems, I'll handle it."

Ron tossed Michael the keys, then playfully messed up his hair. "Just don't go shagging in it and mess up my car seats, understand?"

"I'll take real good care of it. I promise."

Ron held his brother's eyes. "No matter what happens to me . . . you've gotta be strong for the folks. They're gonna need you. Understand?"

Michael returned his gaze, unafraid. Ron felt a surge of pride. His little brother was becoming someone strong, dependable. Ron enveloped Michael in a powerful hug, then quietly moved off toward the house.

Ron awoke the next morning to pitch-blackness. He showered quietly, so as not to awaken his family—partly because of the ungodly hour, but also because he didn't wish to make a scene. So many combustible emotions were running through all of them, and he didn't want to risk stirring anything up again.

Ron donned his uniform, slung his duffel over his shoulder, and let himself out of the house to meet his waiting cab. He climbed in and took one long, last look at the house he'd grown up in. Hell, before long he might very well be making his way home as Alex had, arriving on the Dixie Flyer some bone-cold midnight in a metal container. As the cab moved away, Ron caught a glimpse of Michael peeking blearily out from his bedroom window.

At Hartsfield Airport, Ron ordered a large black coffee and a plate of biscuits and gravy from a twenty-four hour food counter, then made his way to the boarding gate. He joined several other military personnel in the line. A pair of boyish young soldiers glanced curiously at his swollen face. The jetway yawned before him. These were his last few minutes of free will. Once he stepped through that door, he would have no choices left.

A DC10 pulled into the gate next to Ron's, and a stream of passengers disembarked. Ron stared as a flight attendant wheeled a legless young veteran down the concourse. He had seen so many disabled vets recently, but it still gave him pause. A mother with a small baby brushed briskly past. Ron turned to follow her with his eyes, and noticed the pink and white peace sign sewed to her jacket. He had seen a lot of peace signs lately, also.

The line moved forward, and suddenly he was at the entrance gate.

"Ticket, sir," the perky female boarding agent said.

Ron took one more glance backward at the peace sign. He looked at the smiling ticket agent, her hand outstretched to receive his boarding pass and seal his fate.

Then all at once, he stepped out of the line.

It was the biggest decision he'd ever made in his young life, and he made it with hardly any forethought. Just two shuffling steps to the right was all it took to go from an U.S. Army warrant officer in good standing to AWOL, a man on the run.

Chapter 43

March 1970

THE MORNING RON left, Michael wandered the house restlessly. He still had several days left before spring break ended and he would return to the University of Georgia. With no studies to pursue and Diane out of town visiting relatives, he felt lost. He ambled out to the carport to tinker with his motorcycle, but quickly lost interest. Nothing seemed worth doing.

Late in the morning, he found himself standing in the doorway of Ron's room, stared at his brother's weight bench, now worn and frayed from the hours Ron had spent using it. Michael felt like an amputee. Something that had always been part of him had been taken away. It hurt to look at Ron's things. It wasn't the same as when Ron had been in training at one base or another. This time he wasn't just away; he was *gone*.

"House seems lonely, doesn't it?" Michael felt a sympathetic hand rest on his shoulder.

"I didn't know you were home."

"I was having a helluva time getting any work done at the shop. Decided to take the rest of the day off. Thought I'd take the dogs out for some exercise."

Michael spied a heavy leather photo album tucked under his father's arm. He couldn't recall seeing it before.

"Pictures of Ron?" he asked.

Harold cleared his throat uncomfortably. "No. Me in the South Pacific."

Harold fell silent. He cleared his throat again and murmured softly, "Haven't looked at these old pictures for ages. For some reason, I just had to see 'em today."

Michael nodded. His father turned and padded down the hallway.

When the endless afternoon was finally dying, the phone rang. It was Kenny, wanting to know if he'd like to catch a movie. Michael hadn't seen him since Christmas but had heard his friend had grown his hair long and started smoking pot. Kenny wanted to see *Zabriskie Point* because someone had told him there was a hot sex scene in it.

When Michael turned the Mustang onto his street just past midnight, he was astonished to see the lights still on in his parents' house. Harold and Carlotta were habitual early risers; they normally turned in at a sensible hour. As Michael stepped in the door, the tableau that greeted his eyes stopped him in his tracks. His father stood rigid, clutching the phone to his ear. Now and again, he passed a stiff hand through his hair. A vein throbbed in his neck.

Carlotta stood nearby, her arms crossed over her chest. Something in her posture made her look withered, defeated.

Michael's blood ran cold. Had something happened to Ron? He couldn't even have left the States yet.

Carlotta took her youngest son gently by the shoulder and led him into the hall.

"Your father's on the phone with the Army," she said softly. "Ron didn't report in San Diego for deployment with his unit."

At his mother's words, a wave of relief washed through him. *Ron was alive.* But the strangeness of this news was almost as difficult to metabolize.

Harold Simpson's eldest son, the pride of his Marine heart, was AWOL.

Chapter 44

March 1970

RON'S HEART HAMMERED IN his chest all the way to Albany, New York. When he stepped off the plane some three thousand miles from where he was supposed to be, the outrageousness of what he had just done shot through him like an injection of battery acid into his veins. He swallowed hard and swung in behind a group of uniformed young men, following them casually out of the airport.

He checked the time for the next bus departure and paid for the fare in cash. Only after buying his ticket did he learn he was going to Syracuse. Not that it mattered. A stop or two before Syracuse, he stepped off the bus, tired of riding. He hefted his duffle and tramped along the roadside until the afternoon shadows grew long.

After working the kinks out of his legs, he ambled up to a battered Ford pickup parked alongside the road, its longhaired owner lounging in the shade of a poplar tree. The middle-aged driver smiled and waved Ron over. He introduced himself as Cool Breeze, offered a canteen of lukewarm water, which Ron accepted, and a joint, which he declined. Then Cool Breeze invited Ron to share the road with him a while. His energy drained, Ron soon fell asleep to the guttering of the pickup's exhaust and the crunch of tire on gravel.

Ron awoke to the winking of the setting sun through the trees. The truck was ambling along a narrow country road, tall grass swishing on either side. He sat up, knuckled his eyes, and squinted at a blur of colors on a hillside off to the left. Closer up, Ron could make out a swarm of brightly clad young people, wandering, lounging, and dancing.

When the Ford came alongside the throng, Cool Breeze pulled over. "This is where I turn off to go to my farm." He jerked a finger toward the dusty road leading into the heart of the gathering. "There's free music and easy women up that way. I imagine a young man such as yourself might find something to enjoy."

As Ron surveyed the undulating crowd, a wave of doubt washed through him. In his buzz cut and military uniform, he'd be as out of place here as a fifth of bourbon at a Baptist tent revival. But what the hell. He opened the door, slid out of the truck, and grabbed his duffle bag. He nodded his thanks to Cool Breeze, then watched until the Ford's taillights disappeared and the dust settled around his feet.

Ron wandered through the crowd into a large field, eyes a-goggle. The scene was as foreign as an alien landscape. The meadow, lit here and there with bonfires, was draped with bodies, some partially nude, others wrapped in a swirl of wild tie-dyes, beads, and feathers. There was enough hair in those few square acres to clog all the drains in Forest Park. Impromptu musical groups added their voices to the cacophony. Ron's eyes watered from the heavy perfumes of incense and marijuana.

Ron sat down beneath a low-hanging maple tree to catch his breath. He rubbed at his eyes to clear the haze. When he opened them, there was a hand in front of his face, proffering a lit joint.

"No, thanks," he muttered.

"Suit yourself," came a throaty, feminine voice.

The hand withdrew the joint and brought it up to its owner's lips. The brief orange glow revealed the face of a young woman with a pointed chin, a pretty face framed with short-cut hair, and long eyelashes. She leaned against the tree trunk beside him.

Ron hoped the joint had at least one more pull left, so he could get another glimpse of her face. But she stubbed it out against the sole of her moccasin, exhaled slowly, and studied him.

Growing uncomfortable under her gaze, Ron stood up with a nervous laugh. "I guess I'm out of place here."

"It's cool," the young woman replied, placing a hand on his arm. "Just be mellow, eh?"

"I've never heard an accent like that before."

"Canadian," the woman replied, offering her hand, "I'm Vicki."

Ron offered her his hand and his first name, deciding that the less information he gave, the better.

"And your accent would be?" Vicki asked.

"Southern," Ron replied with a ghost of a smile, "I'm from Georgia."

A pair of hippies drifted close to the maple tree. The first, a young man of prime draft-age, sported a tie-dyed headband, a black eye, and an irritable look. The second, a Joni Mitchell disciple, her braless breasts a-jangle, waved a stick of burning incense in the air. The man slowed down to squint at Ron's uniform.

"Who let the baby killer in?" he mumbled through his stupor. "It's harshin' my vibe, man."

Ron glanced away, hoping to let the comment pass. The young man kept glaring until the Joni Mitchell lookalike tugged him away with soothing words.

Ron was happy to let them go, but Vicki shouted after them, "What happened to peace and love, eh?"

"The uniform does make me stick out here," Ron remarked.

"Is it glued on?"

"It's all I brought with me."

"You on leave?" Vicki studied him in the weak light.

"I'm AWOL," he heard himself say. "I deserted." Ron exhaled deeply. It was the first time he'd put words to what he'd done. In an odd way, saying it was worse than doing it.

"You might not want to tell that to everyone you meet." Vicki sounded neither shocked nor offended. "So, where are you heading?"

Ron winced. Sooner or later he'd need an answer for that question. "I'm not sure," he admitted.

"Maybe I can help you."

Ron almost laughed. "Really? How? My life's pretty much in the ditch."

"I work with Amnesty International in Ottawa. We help deserters," Vicki replied, surprising Ron yet again. "We can sneak you across the border so you don't go through U.S. Customs."

"Why shouldn't I cross at Customs?" Ron asked

"If you get caught on the U.S. side, you'll be arrested."

"Oh." Ron wasn't used to thinking like an outlaw. "You don't know me from Adam's housecat. Why would you stick your neck out for me?"

"You don't want my help, soldier boy?"

It took Ron a moment to register the hurt in her voice. He brought his face closer to hers.

"That's not it," he said gently. "I'm still just trying to sort all this out."

"With all those bruises on your face, it looks like you've been beating yourself up pretty well about it."

Ron couldn't help but smile, even though it made his jaw hurt.

"You hungry?" Vicki's tone brightened. "I have food stashed in my van."

She slipped a cool hand inside his palm and led him through the gyrating, cloying darkness, to a blue and white VW Microbus parked by a blackberry thicket. An hour later, Ron still hadn't finished stuffing his face or flapping his jaw. Ron babbled his story through mouthfuls of sauerkraut, which tasted to his Southern palate like salted string. Vicki listened patiently, letting him talk out his anguish.

"What's the big deal, anyway? Killin' strangers. It's legal. Hell, they're *tellin'* us to do it! My father did it. My fathers for generations have done it . . ."

"A lot of brave men did it," Vicki interjected. "And some very foolish ones."

The pain in her words put the brakes on Ron's rambling. There was a history behind her remark. Whatever it was, it had left a trace of bitterness in her voice, and a baleful shadow in her eye. Her sadness took all the wind out of his false bravado.

"Who am I kiddin'? What if I'm just running 'cause I'm scared? Maybe I'm just a coward."

"Believe me, going to Canada is no easy way out. You cross that border, your life here is over." She brought her face close to his, and looked deeply into his eyes. "Tell me, you have a good life, eh?"

Ron stared back, uncomprehending.

"You have family, friends, people who love you here in America?" she added. "Because you're gonna lose all that."

Ron felt the weight of her words. His mother's face swam before his eyes, and his father's. Then Ron's thoughts lingered on Michael: *How would he get by without his big bro? But how much help am I gonna be to him in Leavenworth?* Ron thought grimly. *Or in a body bag?*

Vicki gave him a moment to himself. Then she tossed him a sleeping bag. "Sleep on it. Maybe things will look different in the morning."

Ron needed sleep that night, but it refused to come to him. He tossed and fidgeted, playing every possibility through his mind again and again. None of it added up to something he could accept. Then, too, there was the sweet distraction of Vicki's warm body in the sleeping bag next to his. She smelled of patchouli, fresh-cut hay, and Indian cotton. Her deep, rhythmic breathing filled him with ideas that were a lot nicer to ponder than the decision he'd have to make in the morning.

An hour after the first pink hues of sunrise crept into the meadow, Vicki opened her eyes. She gazed at Ron for a long moment. "It's not too late to change your mind."

"No, I know what I gotta do."

While Ron dashed off a hasty, apologetic letter to his parents, a hopeless attempt to explain things that he couldn't even explain to himself, Vicki made a phone call outside a convenience store. Then she pointed the microbus north. Thirty-six hours later, Ron and Vicki were driving along an ill-used dirt road that took them deep into the coniferous woodlands that flanked the St. Lawrence River. Georgia woods never seemed this dark, Ron thought.

Vicki pulled the microbus behind a clump of fallen hemlocks and killed the engine. With the murk and quiet pressing in on them, Vicki took Ron's hand and led him deep into the forest he could smell and hear, but couldn't see. They stopped at a clearing that Ron could only barely make out.

They waited. An owl hooted. A tree branch snapped.

Vicki patted his shoulder and turned him toward a black patch of woods where a dim light winked on and off, on and off. She pulled a flashlight from her knapsack and blinked back.

A man approached them. Ron could not see his face, only a vague silhouette.

"Evening," the faceless man said in a harsh whisper. "Are you ready?"

Ron nodded, his throat tight.

"In Canada, we have this Prime Minister. Name's Trudeau. He's allowing draft resisters to immigrate. So the Mounties mostly leave the dodgers alone these days unless they get on the wrong side of the law," the man explained. "Just so you know, it's a different story with deserters. Your FBI works with the RCMP to arrest and deport deserters like yourself."

"Then why would I be any better off in Canada than here in the United States?"

"Canada's neutral in the war. Most folks will leave you alone. Stay out of trouble, and you should be safe."

"So what you're saying is, if I do cross over, I'll probably be okay if I stay out of jail, but I can never come back home." Ron said as calmly as he could.

"Not without going to prison," Vicki said.

"Are you ready to accept that?" the man asked.

"I guess it's the best of a bunch of bad choices," Ron sighed.

"This is as far as I go," Vicki said. "I need to go back through customs." She surprised Ron by rolling up on her tiptoes to plant a kiss on his cheek. Then she was gone.

The man with the flashlight moved off into the woods, and Ron found himself scrambling to keep up. Half an hour later, Ron sat shivering in a tiny rowboat without lights in the middle of the St. Lawrence River. The nameless, faceless man handed him over to another nameless, faceless man, who had rowed in like an apparition out of the fog. Now he was being rowed toward a shore he couldn't see, to a land he didn't know.

Ron glanced into the mist behind him, but everything that looked like home had already been lost to sight.

Chapter 45

The Kennesaw Line
June 26, 1864

BAYLIS WOKE TO THE sound of a man crying. In the flickering amber firelight, he could see Sanders, the young red-haired private, slumped on the ground, rocking himself. Tears streaked his cherub face.

"Son, are you all right?" Baylis asked softly.

"I can't see. I've gone moon blind."

Sergeant Tedford stirred awake. With eyes at half lid from lack of sleep, he moved to Sanders.

"Now, now. You'll be better come sun up when there's more light. Let's get you closer to the fire. That'll help you see some."

Tedford guided Sanders over to sit down next to the flames that crackled and sparked. The young man waved his hand out in front of himself.

"I'm too blind to even see my own shadow by the firelight," he lamented.

Tedford pulled a wool blanket over the young soldier's shoulders, then turned to Baylis.

"The boy's had scurvy and weakness for months. It done gave him night blindness. He ain't been gettin' enough fresh vegetables and such. None of us have."

Baylis remembered the onion that Milton had given him. He pulled it out of his haversack. "Maybe this'll help."

"That's a kindness." Tedford took the onion and bent down beside Sanders. "Here son, eat this."

Sanders thanked Baylis, smelled the onion and took a bite. "This here's a sweet one," the boy said as he chewed.

"You eat that and rest up," Tedford said. "Sun will be up 'fore you know it."

The sergeant moved back to Baylis.

"That boy looks too young to be in the fight," Baylis said quietly.

"He made seventeen last month. He said he hadn't even been outside the valley where he was born 'fore the war started. Now, he's seen enough death for a lifetime. Can't rightly blame him for going blind. I sometimes wish we all could."

"Hell of a misery," Baylis replied.

Tedford nodded, then moved back to his blanket and curled up on the ground.

Is that what the war had caused, Baylis wondered? *Were they all going blind?*

In the last few days, Baylis had seen and done things that he didn't believe possible. He'd watched executions, had dinner in a charnel house, and rode with a wagon full of the dead. He had found his daughter raped and had a grandchild die in his arms. He had killed without remorse.

Was it necessary to become blind to it all and do whatever he must to survive? Was that truly the only way left for him?

Baylis knew what they were fighting for, what thousands upon thousands were dying for. This great war would be remembered long after they all turned to dust. So how did he want to be remembered? For what did he stand?

That was the troubling question the old man had asked himself since the first angry shots were fired at Fort Sumter. And he wasn't alone.

Unlike the mostly pro-war lands below Marietta, stamped with vast plantations and wealthy slave owners, many of the poor who survived hardscrabble lives on small farms in Georgia's isolated northern counties had been against secession. Those sharp animosities had turned families against neighbors, fathers against sons, brothers against brothers. Blood against blood.

The war had caused deep divisions within the Simpson clan. Baylis's brothers split over the issue: Reuben served, while Elon wanted no part of the conflict. Larkin, a veteran of the War of 1812, now too old to fight, had sided with Reuben in his support of the war.

When the conflict began, Baylis's older sons had traveled to Virginia to take up arms. Like many on both sides, Silas, Merdit, and Pleasant Marion thought the struggle would be over in a few months, joining quickly for fear of missing out on the fight. They had now been serving more than three years. When the war didn't end quickly, their younger brother Ulysses had joined the Army of Tennessee in 1862. While recuperating at home after his injury, he had argued several times with Virgil, who at ten was already voicing opposition to the war, words he had learned from visits with his Uncle Elon. Ulysses's feelings had only hardened in recent days. It was as though his son now held all Yankees personally responsible for his sister's debasement. And the old man knew there were no words in his own bitter heart that would soften his son.

From the beginning, he had allowed his sons to make their own decisions about the war. But he did so only with regret. Baylis had never been a "fire-eater," as folks called those who were outspoken in their defense of the secession. Truth be told, his heart had never been in supporting the struggle. "That flea's on the other dog's leg" was the way he would explain it. *Why fight a war over something you didn't believe in?* Like most people in the south, neither Baylis nor any of his kin had ever owned a slave. He found the practice shameful.

As a young sharecropper, Baylis had worked in the fields beside slaves. Seeing the horrors of that "peculiar institution" up close only strengthened his moral opposition to the ownership of human beings. Some in the county who supported "the war and its great cause" ostracized Baylis, but he didn't mind. As near as he could tell, it was a poor man's war anyway.

Conscription in Georgia and other Confederate states was not universal. Any man who owned enough slaves was exempt from service, and anyone wealthy enough could buy his way out of it. So most sons of wealthy "paper collar men" had avoided a soldier's life and the dangers of war. The ones who owned the most slaves were the most disinclined to fight. Instead, the wealthy were content to send poor men to do their work. That left the Confederate Army full of soldiers with the least to gain from the war. Men like Baylis and his sons.

So here the old man sat, staring into the darkness and waiting for the sun to come up so he could kill men he didn't know for something he didn't believe in. *If these were his final hours, was that how he wanted to be remembered?*

Maybe both armies would be smitten with blindness before sunrise. He could only pray.

Chapter 46

April 1970

A FEW DAYS AFTER the phone call from the Army, a letter arrived from Ron. His words, full of pain and apology, brought forth a fresh river of tears from Carlotta, but they did little to mollify Harold.

"There's not even a return address," Carlotta said sadly. "No phone number. Nothin'."

"Criminals don't have addresses," Harold barked.

Michael huddled on the living room couch, listening to his parents.

"Ron's up in Canada all alone." Carlotta's voice rang with hurt and anger.

Abruptly, Harold threw up his hands in defeat. "I'll tell you one thing. This is the saddest damn day of my life." He trudged heavily from the room.

Michael found his father in the front yard late that afternoon. Harold stood before the elm tree with a long handle axe in his hands, angry and grim, sweat pouring from his face. When Harold swung a vicious blow at the tree, Michael winced in anguish.

Pale blonde chunks of wood flew up as the axe bit into the elm's trunk. Harold jerked the blade out of the wound, pulled it back, and swung again, throwing every ounce of his battle-hardened muscle into the motion.

Michael would have slunk back into the house if his father hadn't spotted him. Harold gave a nod and set down the axe to catch his breath.

"What are you doing?" Michael asked warily.

"Tree's gone bad. It's diseased."

"What are we gonna do about Ron?"

Harold's face darkened. "Your brother made this mess. It's up to him to clean it up."

Harold hefted the axe and swung it at the elm again. The slender tree shuddered. With a deep groan, it toppled onto the lawn, bounced twice, and lay still.

~~~

By an unspoken consensus, Michael and his parents chose not to mention Ron's desertion to their neighbors. But Forest Park possessed a sixth sense for scandal. The Simpsons knew the news was out when, locking up the print shop one evening later that week, Carlotta spotted Ginger coming up the sidewalk. Dressed all in black, her complexion wan, Ginger glanced up and locked eyes with her friend. Pain flashed in her eyes. Then abruptly, tearfully, she changed direction and hurried away.

"Ginger, please wait." Carlotta called out, starting after her. But Ginger quickened her step and didn't look back.

From inside the print shop's doorway, Michael observed Bobbie Mae Turner, the church gossip, watching the exchange with keen eyes. As Carlotta returned up the sidewalk, Bobbie Mae followed Ginger's lead and changed course to avoid speaking to her.

Carlotta's eyes filled with pain. Her wheezing breath was labored. Harold quickly moved to place a protective arm around his wife's shoulders when she stepped back inside the shop.

"Maybe Ginger just couldn't think of what to say," Carlotta offered generously.

"Poor woman loses her only boy while ours runs off to Canada. What else can we expect?"

"I don't know *what* to expect," Carlotta replied with a shuddering sigh. "I don't suppose I know much of anything anymore." Carlotta fished her inhaler out of her pocketbook and took a deep pull.

Michael snapped to attention. His mother had never needed to use her inhaler this often before.

Chapter 47

April 1970

WHEN THE NAMELESS BOATMAN dropped Ron off on the Canadian side of the river, he'd tossed him a woolen army surplus blanket, a partly mashed Snickers bar, and a slip of paper with the address of the War Resisters' Office in Ottawa. Then he'd muttered, "Good luck, man," and vanished into the fog.

Ron wandered on the bank for what must have been several hours. Then he crawled inside a metal culvert, pulled the blanket over himself, and slept.

He awoke to the sensation of freezing cold water seeping into his shirt collar. The culvert was filling with rainwater. He banged his head on the roof of the pipe, and shimmied his way out into a lightless morning full of drizzle. Rubbing his head and wringing out his clothes, Ron took in the landscape. Even the trees looked alien to him.

He followed the distant rumble of a highway, his unfed guts protesting all the way. It took him most of the day to thumb his way into Ottawa. He might have enjoyed visiting this town of tall spires and European elegance with his folks, but now he only felt all the more a stranger. Ron paid for a cot and a shower at the YMCA on Argyle Avenue, just south of the Ottawa River that curved through the city. After a meal, he slept.

The next morning Ron made his way to the War Resisters' Office. In an open atrium filled with Gothic splendor, Ron waited on a hard wooden bench for his appointment with a counselor. He filled the time by studying the antiwar posters that dotted the walls, bathed in the warm, dusty light that traced the filigree. All about Ron, volunteers scurried, answered telephones, and talked in comforting tones to skittish, solemn-eyed young men, some of whom looked as lost and bedraggled as he did.

When his name was called, Ron was ushered to a seat across a dinged-up metal desk from a pony-tailed counselor in a hand-knitted sweater. He listened patiently to Ron's story. The counselor's eyes narrowed slightly when he learned that Ron was a deserter who had crossed the border illegally.

"You know any place I can find a room?" Ron asked.

"There's a hostel for U.S. draft dodgers and deserters. You need to stay away from it, though. The place was raided ten times in the last year. The RCMP is working with the FBI to return deserters to the U.S."

"The RCMP—that's the Canadian Police?"

"That's right, mate. We call them Mounties."

"I need a job," Ron said. "I'm not looking for a handout, just honest work."

"With no green card, it's damn hard. There is one place. They hire off book. A loonie an hour. Roofing houses."

"A loonie?"

"A loon's a Canadian dollar."

"A dollar a hour? You're jokin', right?"

The counselor shrugged. "Here, nobody cares a good shit about your IQ or your SATs. All they know is you have no green card."

"Okay," Ron sighed. "If that's what it takes."

The counselor penciled a number on a slip of paper and slid it across the desk. "Try to find something else if you can. This'll be okay for a few months, maybe through early fall, but Ottawa winters are brutal." The counselor rose from his chair, signifying that the interview was over. But Ron hazarded one last request.

"You don't happen to know a girl named Vicki? Short hair, thin. She said she works with Amnesty International?" At the counselor's skeptical glance, he added, "She helped me get here. I just want to say thanks. I don't know her last name."

The counselor hesitated for a moment, and then replied, "Try the Rainbow Café on Rue Flora."

Ron spent the remainder of the day wrestling with himself. He despised feeling like an outcast with few prospects; it was a humiliating way to approach an attractive, warm, wonderful young woman. Yet he needed to see her again, and to thank her. And she was his only friend in Canada. He thumbed through a battered Ottawa phone book and found the address for the café. He sat on a park bench across from the building for a half hour before finally working up the nerve to peer in the window.

He saw her as soon as he glanced through the glass. She wore jeans and a blouse, and was carrying an overflowing ashtray and a half-eaten grilled cheese sandwich on a tray. She looked tired, harried, and busy. She has a job and a life, Ron thought bitterly. She doesn't need a fugitive hanging around like a dog begging for scraps.

Ron knew in a heartbeat he couldn't approach her. But at that moment, she glanced out the window and saw him, and bloomed into a warm smile. She pointed to her wristwatch and held up five fingers. Ron nodded.

Five minutes later, she stepped out of the café's front door and all but jumped into his arms. Ron hoped the grease-and-cigarette aroma of the restaurant had dulled her sense of smell. The shower at the Y had been a cold one, with only a discarded nubbin of soap. And the bag of clothes the boatman gave him smelled like they'd been soaked in motor oil. But Vicki didn't appear to notice.

She felt wonderful in his arms.

"Have you talked to your family?" she asked as they strolled along the street, their shoulders nearly touching.

"Just that letter I sent them back in New York. But I can tell you, my Dad's not gonna have anything more to do with me. What else can I expect from a man who's got 'death before dishonor' tattooed on his arm?"

Vicki gazed at him kindly, sympathy playing across her elfish features. It was against everything Southern and male in Ron to receive a woman's pity. It made him irritable.

"Screw him," he said gruffly. "I don't need him anyway."

In the midst of his bravado, Ron froze. Half a block ahead of them, a Royal Canadian Mountie in a brown service uniform stood watching the passersby from atop a sable-black horse.

Vicki grabbed Ron's hand and tugged gently.

"It's okay," she said under her breath. "He won't bother you. Just act like you're *oot* and *aboot*."

Ron would have smiled at her accent had he not been so paranoid. He was sure his rigid posture and nervous eyes would give him away. But it was too late to change direction—that would tip the Mountie off for sure.

Ron felt the man's eyes linger on him. As they moved on down the street, Ron waited for the uniformed man to shout, "Halt!" But they made it to the end of the block and turned the corner. Finally, Ron could draw a full breath.

Vicki just smiled. "You need to relax, eh? Nobody's gonna bother you unless you bother them." She wrinkled her nose when Ron told her of his only job lead.

"At least it's a start," Ron replied, "I can always trade up to something better."

"Don't count on it," Vicki answered. "Where are you staying?"

"Don't know yet," Ron replied honestly.

"I'd bring you to my place," Vicki fumbled, "I mean, I *would* let you stay—as a friend. It's just, I've got . . . *responsibilities*."

"Boyfriend?"

"No, no, nothing like that," Vicki said uncomfortably. "Sorry. I shouldn't have mentioned it." With that, she dropped the subject and teased him back into a better mood.

Vicki led him to an ill-used section of town, where Ron put down half of his remaining cash for rent. It was little more than a broom closet with a hot plate, a threadbare shelter for a well-worn soul.

"Smells like cat shit," Ron said, not daring to look in the corners of the tiny place.

"Could use a feminine touch, maybe," Vicki said as she opened a miniature closet and sent a family of roaches into frenzies. "But it's better than sleeping on the street."

Ron tapped a geriatric baseboard heater, "I hope this works. I'll need it come winter. And look," he said, pointing to a lone can of turnip greens on a lopsided shelf, "a fully stocked kitchen!"

"C'mon," Vicki nodded, "Next stop is the grocery store."

Ron hesitated to leave his duffel bag and his few possessions in the squalid place, but decided he'd better get used to it. The room was the closest thing he had to a home.

Inside a tiny, flea-bitten grocery store, Vicki guided the purchases for Ron's modest budget. "Best nutrition for the money," she said, scooping up a jar of peanut butter and a box of oatmeal. She laughed at Ron's despairing look and dropped the staples into the cart. "*Bon appetit.*"

Chatting with Vicki along Ottawa's sidewalks lifted Ron's spirits. She was the only bright spot in his newly gray world. Once they reached Ron's flophouse, he was nowhere near ready to say goodnight. When Vicki went home, he would be alone again in a strange country. And she was just standing there, gazing up at him with a smile full of promise.

"Wanna come up?" he said on an impulse. "We could have some peanut butter oatmeal."

She laughed and followed him upstairs. The single light bulb in the hall on Ron's floor was out. The door leading to his room was open. Ron was certain he'd locked it before they left.

Cautiously, he moved inside. For half a second, he breathed a sigh of relief: there was his duffle, on the floor where he'd left it. Then he saw that its contents had been strewn about the room. He riffled through the deflated bag.

"My cash . . . jacket . . . gloves. They stole everything worth stealing." He dug deeper into the bag and pulled out his Army uniform—the one possession he would have been glad to get rid of. "A lot of good that's gonna do me."

He tossed the uniform down and slumped into the single sagging chair. Not until this moment had he truly known defeat.

"You shouldn't be around me," he said. "I'm bad luck."

Vicki placed comforting hands on his shoulders. But he shrugged her away. She stood silently behind him, waiting for some acknowledgment. But he was too ashamed to give it.

"Please, just go. Leave me alone."

Moments later, he realized she had gone.

Chapter 48

April 1970

MICHAEL FELT SLIGHTLY RIDICULOUS taking Diane to the Cyclorama at Grant Park, but that's what she wanted to do. It wasn't exactly his idea of how to spend spring break. Both of them had seen the enormous three-dimensional diorama of the Battle of Atlanta many times growing up, but at least it was an excuse to get out of Forest Park for a few hours.

Diane had been withdrawn and sullen lately. Michael suspected her mood had something to do with his brother's desertion, although she had barely mentioned it. She seemed to avoid the subject whenever she could. He was thankful that she had.

The park, nestled on the southeast edge of downtown Atlanta, was named for Colonel Lemuel Pratt Grant, the Confederate engineer who had designed Atlanta's defenses during the Civil War. The area inside Grant Park still contained remnants of the defensive fortifications that had been created to hold back the Union forces during Sherman's siege. More than a hundred years later, the blemishes of the war could be found everywhere around the city if you knew where to look. Michael didn't need to search any farther than his own family to see the wounds left by that conflict.

In the lobby of the broad granite edifice, Michael and Diane wandered beneath a dusty velvet banner that read, "Commemorating the Battle of Atlanta," and stopped at the Texas, one of the steam engines used in the Great Locomotive Chase through North Georgia. As they admired the uniforms and artifacts on display, Michael silently imagined the grim fate of their owners.

Michael stopped in front of one of General Sherman's carefully preserved military maps. He traced his finger over the glass of the case, following the rail line that led south out of Atlanta. He could see Rough & Ready, the rail stop that became Mountain View, and Quick Stop, which later became Forest Park. The town's original name seemed appropriate, since havens for cheap gasoline and processed food were springing up like wild onions.

Michael's finger stopped at Jonesboro, just south of Forest Park. He knew the battle for control of the railroad had been savage there. Thousands of rebels had died trying to stop Sherman from cutting the last supply line into Atlanta. When the Yankees finally broke through, the city quickly fell. And as he had learned as a child, the restless rebel souls of those slain in battle could still be seen and heard around the rail tracks when the night was late and the moon was full. No one would ever convince Michael otherwise.

His eyes drifted up to Kennesaw Mountain, just north of Atlanta. He always felt close to Baylis Simpson when he thought about that mountain. So much of the family's history was etched in blood in that clay soil. For a moment, it felt like the old man was looking over his shoulder.

"What are you looking at?" Diane had moved over to him.

Michael pointed to a spot on the map that Grandpa Melvin had first shown him more than ten years before. "Kennesaw Mountain," he explained in his grandfather's words. "No Simpson has ever forgotten the battle there."

"How come?"

"When Sherman invaded north Georgia, what happened to the Simpsons living in Cherokee County . . . it changed their lives. It changed everything."

"Your family lived in Georgia during the Civil War?"

"Yep. The Simpsons came to Georgia in the early 1820s. We were one of the first hundred families in the Atlanta area."

"I never had a chance to ask my dad anything about our family." Melancholy hung in Diane's voice. "I know so little about our history."

"Sometimes I think I know too much about mine."

The doors swung open. Michael and Diane shuffled with the crowd down a passageway and emerged into the center of the cylindrical diorama. The Battle of Atlanta encircled them in vivid three-dimensional detail: an enormous tableau of life-sized plaster dummies in full Civil War regalia, frozen in the heat of conflict, set against the backdrop of a century-old oil painting that was said to be the largest in the world.

A crisply uniformed hostess took up a wall microphone and began her presentation: "The Cyclorama is a tribute to those who died during the Battle of Atlanta in 1864. There were more than 30,000 casualties in six weeks of fighting. This is their story."

The lights dimmed. Dramatic music swelled from hidden speakers. Rifle fire, cannonading, and the cries of battle, the same recording Michael remembered from elementary school, filled the room. The voice of Victor Jory, the actor who had played the overseer Jonas Wilkerson in *Gone With The Wind*, began to narrate the battle in his somber baritone.

Michael snuck a look at Diane. Her eyes were brimming with tears as she drank in the scene before her, allowing the immense tragedy of it all to sweep her away. Impulsively, Michael reached for her hand. His touch broke her trance. She pulled her hand away.

By the time they climbed back into the Mustang, the evening's mood had completely soured. Michael had no idea what he could have done to upset her. They drove most of the way home in silence.

"Do you wanna come in?" Diane asked reluctantly when Michael eased the Mustang into her parents' driveway.

To Michael's relief, Diane's mother and stepfather weren't home. While Diane went to the kitchen and filled two glasses with iced tea, Michael wandered the impeccably furnished living room, gazing at the photos that hung on the wall. Front and center on the mantel, in a place of honor, stood a black-and-white portrait of a strikingly handsome young man in an army uniform. The soldier was Diane's deceased father.

Michael couldn't tear his eyes away from the photo. His imagination layered another twenty years of age onto the young man's face, rendering him as he might appear today, had a North Korean grenade at the Battle of Chosin Reservoir not snatched away his opportunity to raise his only daughter.

The tinkle of ice against glass made Michael aware that Diane had reentered the room. She stepped up softly and joined him. Heavy tears coursed down her beautiful face.

"Are you okay?" he asked gently, stifling an urge to reach for her.

"Just being silly," she replied, smashing her tears with the back of her hand. "The Cyclorama always gets to me. I've been that way since I first saw it. Mrs. Sharpton's third grade class trip."

Michael's desire to comfort her got the better of his fear of rejection. He stepped closer, thumbed a tear from her cheek, and teased softly, "Just a bunch of mannequins, right?"

Diane backed away. She turned from him, her head bowed.

"I don't know how to say this."

Michael felt a cold flopping sensation in the pit of his stomach. Diane's jaw was working, fighting back more tears.

"I think we should date other people," she blurted.

"Other people?" Michael stammered. "Why?"

"UGA's a big school. Now that we're there, I wanna be able to date around." Diane waved a casual hand in the air, as though the decision were just a whim.

"You knew Georgia was a big school before we started dating," Michael mumbled in bewilderment.

Diane hunched her shoulders, choking back sobs.

"I really thought you liked being with me," Michael said in a small voice.

"Please don't make this hard."

"Did you meet another guy?"

Diane wheeled to face him. Michael read in her eyes that it was worse than that.

"Then what's going on?" he pressed. "Tell me."

Diane took a deep breath. "It's your brother. I know your family's having a hard time, what with Ron in Canada and all."

"What's that got to do with me and you?"

"My daddy gave his life serving our country. I can't—" She stopped herself, took a heavy breath and started again. "I won't dishonor his memory by dating you. Not when your brother ran away."

Michael's blood ran hot, then cold. Where moments ago there'd been a hollow ache, he now felt a white-hot stab of anger.

"You wanna break up, I can't stop you. But don't use my brother as an excuse."

"I'm sorry." Diane cast her eyes to the floor. "Please understand."

Michael straightened up stiffly and looked her in the eyes. "I understand. You think you can make me ashamed of Ron."

He strode for the front door and opened it. "Well, you can't," he said in a voice full of hurt and anger. He slammed the door behind him.

Chapter 49

The Dead Angle
June 17, 1864

AT FIRST LIGHT, THE rebels on the hill began to scuffle awake. Despite the heavy cannonading and musketry of the last several days, bobwhite quail and meadowlarks had survived to greet another sunrise with their songs. That nature found a way to overcome man's violence was remarkable, Baylis thought. The immense sadness was that it was forced to.

Baylis glanced cautiously over the head logs stacked on top of the excavated dirt packed in front of the trench. In the valley below the breastworks, the meadow and woods at the edge of the Union line were illuminated by the soft glow of dawn. To have such beauty surround these two mobs intent on destroying each other seemed like blasphemy to the old man.

Baylis knew that their part of the rebel line, anchored on a steep hill, jutted out like a spear point. This was the most vulnerable part of the defense since it could be assaulted from both sides of the V. It made sense that this would be where the Yankees would attack.

They made no secret of their intentions.

With the sun marching into the cloudless sky, dozens of Federal batteries opened up with thunderous booms. The defenders leaped against the trench walls and hunkered down as canister and chain shot rained along the salient, smashing into the breastworks like a mighty hammer. More shells screamed overhead, pounding trees to the rear of the line.

Concussion shocks pummeled the rebels as the ground erupted around them, throwing a maelstrom of dirt and debris into the air. Soldiers hemorrhaged from their noses and eyes. Eardrums burst, and bladders emptied. Some men prayed, others cursed and screamed, but no one left the line.

Terror-filled minutes passed, and still the shells came. Hundreds now, round after round, wave after wave. Baylis hugged the earth in the long rifle trench and waited for the shell that would call him to eternity. He felt moisture dripping onto his lip and realized his nose was bleeding. A few feet away, he caught the eye of his son. Ulysses offered him a bleak smile before the old man lost sight of him in the smoke and chaos. Private Nicholson crawled over to lean against the trench wall next to Baylis. Unconcerned by the purgatorial violence around them, Nicholson cuddled his revolver and wiped the dirt off it.

After an agonizing hour, the cannonading finally ceased. The soldiers staggered up as they regained their senses, their faces smudged from the dust curling around them. An unnatural stillness hung in the air. The dead calm seemed odd, Baylis thought, almost eerie. He could see that several men in the company had been wounded during the barrage, but, remarkably, few had been killed. A nod from Ulysses told his father that he was unhurt.

Baylis peered over the ramparts, straining to see any movement. He expected the Union army would now assault the line. But nothing was happening.

What were they waiting for?

Hundreds of insurgents scampered up onto the firing line, muskets at the ready, and peered toward the Union trenches. Just beyond rifle range, a young Union officer on horseback paced up and down the Federal line, rousing his regiment to the bloodlust of battle.

The Yankee's voice reverberated across the silent landscape. *"Out spoke bold Horatius, the captain of the gate, to every man upon this earth, death cometh soon or late . . ."*

"If that don't beat all," Private Colquitt whispered in awe as he watched the spectacle below them. "That blue boy is reciting 'Horatius at the Bridge.'"

"And how can man die better," the Union officer proclaimed in a booming voice, *"than facing fearful odds, for the ashes of his fathers and the temples of his gods?"*

A wild, sustained cheer went up in the ranks of the Yankees as the officer's oration reached its crescendo. Then came the sound of a single cannon bellowing in the valley below. The clarion call of bugles filled the air.

In the distance, Baylis saw Union sharpshooters firing from the tree line, several hundred yards across the large meadow where a creek meandered near its edge. Bullets buzzed, tumbling at the edge of their accurate range. They struck the tree trunks and rails before Baylis like an angry rain. Muskets crackled in response from the Confederate gopher holes and rifle pits in front of the trenches. Seconds later, rebel skirmishers and pickets scampered over the breastworks.

Thousands of Union infantry surged out of the woods and across the open field at double-quick step. In the now blistering sun, wave after wave of soldiers moved toward the rebel hill, bayonets glistening at the ready, their regimental colors unfurled with the Stars and Stripes cresting in the center.

The rebel yell that greeted them sounded like the hinges had come off the gates of hell. Its shrieking, savage spirit overpowered even the sounds of guns as the Confederate rifle line opened fire on the Yankees now within range. Dense white smoke bellowed from the Confederate musketry along the breastworks. In the field below them, hundreds of Union soldiers fell in the first blizzard of fire. Thousands more emerged from the woods to take their place as the Yankee line pressed onward, trampling the fallen under boot.

On the firing line, Private Nicholson stared blankly at the blue sea. Snapping out of his stupor, he gathered himself, righting his uniform and brushing the dirt from his shoulders. Then he pulled his well-polished Cash & Wesson revolver and checked the load.

Sergeant Tedford cheered Nicholson on: "Show them blue boys!"

Nicholson glanced at Tedford. "Yes. Show 'em," he said, with no trace of emotion. Nicholson cocked the trigger, stood high on the breastworks, placed the steel barrel against his head, and pulled the trigger. His brains splattered all over the sergeant as his body tumbled backwards into the trench.

When it appeared that the huge meadow was as packed with Yankees as sardines in a can, the Confederate cannon batteries finally opened up. Enfilading fire of canister and grapeshot fell upon the Yankee line, turning what had been a battleground to an abattoir. Still the Union Army came. Stepping over more than a thousand corpses, the Yankee line pushed forward, its leading edge now up the hill and closing on the Confederates.

As the blue line grew closer, Baylis could see the faces of the enemy. He aimed, fired and saw them fall, screaming for God's mercy. His hands sweated, and salty moisture dripped from his brow, stinging his eyes. He had no sense of time, only a blurry awareness of men dying in front of him, beside him, behind. Down below, it looked like half the Union Army was moving across that meadow and up the hill.

And they just keep coming.

The Union soldiers were now so densely packed that the rebels no longer took the time to aim, just loading and firing, loading and firing, until the barrels grew so hot the powder flashed before the ball could be rammed in. The only thing the rebels could do was pick up the musket of a dead man and keep firing. The day had reached more than a hundred degrees. In this inferno, some would kneel, vomit from fatigue and heat, and stagger up to fight again. Others collapsed from sunstroke.

The Union line had reached the rifle pits halfway up the hill, a blur of blue now sweeping up toward the rails and berm protecting the main Confederate trench. The first Union regiment was beginning to breach the breastworks. The fighting was brutal and close on now, the Yankees near enough to touch. With their rifles too hot to fire, both sides were hurtling rocks, beating heads in with muskets, and carving flesh with bayonets.

A wounded soldier emerged directly in front of Baylis, bayonet at the ready. Baylis could see his eyes, full of fear. The Union soldier froze, uncertain. The young man, who had come so far against such terrible odds, now stood face to face with his enemy. Baylis could not bring himself to kill the young man, who could barely stand. The soldier understood the look in the old man's eyes. They both had had enough of the killing. A flicker of relief crossed the soldier's face.

Baylis reached out to wave him down into the trench as his prisoner. In that instance, a bullet ripped through the jaw of the bluecoat. He staggered forward and managed to right himself, only in time for a second, mortal round to tear through his heart. He collapsed, tumbling down in front of the breastworks. The boy coughed, blood gurgling from his mouth, then died, his eyes frozen into some dim distance beyond life.

Suddenly, the Union survivors began to retreat back down the hill, passing over a carpet of the moaning wounded and the mangled dead—their blood soaking the soil.

After two hours, the fighting had ebbed.

Chapter 50

April 1970

AT CHURCH ON A cool Sunday morning, Michael could feel hostile eyes on him, steely glances that abruptly shifted away whenever he caught their look. It was a small town where everyone was always in everyone else's business. After Alex's death and Ron's desertion, his family had become a target. It was one thing if they rejected *him*. Once spring break ended, he would leave for college and wouldn't have to deal with any of them anymore. But they were snubbing his parents.

When the family entered the church, some people on either side of the aisle turned away to avoid speaking to them. Carlotta, bewildered by their behavior, greeted several in the congregation who gazed past her, as though she were merely air.

During the service, Michael watched his mother in the choir, her face awash with hurt and sadness. Nellie Eubanks, who had sat beside Carlotta for twenty years, sharing colds and cooking recipes, had moved over one seat, leaving the one next to her conspicuously empty. The entire congregation could see this. The message was clear: *the Simpsons were to be shunned*.

Michael had never heard his mother's singing so tentative and subdued. It was as though the pain had drawn the life force out of her. He fumed his way through the service. When it was over and the Simpsons were walking to their car, Michael was surprised to see Mona approaching. They hadn't spoken since Alex's funeral. She had drifted away from church attendance and stopped hanging around any of the usual spots in town.

"You probably don't wanna talk to me," Michael said meekly. "It could hurt your reputation."

Mona flashed an amused smile. "How could it be any worse?"

Michael managed a weak grin in return.

Mona leaned in and met his eyes. "I just wanna say I know Ron must've had a good reason for doing what he did. People got no right to treat your family this way."

"Thanks," Michael said sincerely.

"Things just aren't the same, are they? Everything's changed." Her eyes brimmed with tears. "I miss 'em both."

Michael knew what she meant. It was like both Alex *and* Ron had died. "The whole world feels upside down," was all he could manage.

"You take care of yourself," Mona said. Then she slipped away.

Michael was about to leave when he heard a familiar, whiskey-worn voice behind him.

"Everyone should've known. Your brother's just like you. You boys are quitters. Always running away." It was Mr. Andrews, making one of his rare church appearances.

Michael turned and shot him a stony gaze. That was it. Some line inside him had been crossed. He'd had enough.

"Your brother Ron—" Shaky started again when Michael cut him off abruptly.

"You may be just a foolish old drunk, but you say another word about my brother and I swear I'll kick your ass across this parking lot or die trying. I don't care one iota whether we're at church or not. My brother's name better not pass your lips again."

The force of Michael's words surprised even himself, but his clinched fists told Andrews that he meant what he said. The man stood back in silent anger as Michael moved away to join his parents.

The Simpsons made their way along the sidewalk past groups of churchgoers who gave them a wide berth. Carlotta pulled her sweater tightly around her, as if it could comfort her from the coldness of some in the congregation. She wouldn't let them see how badly they had hurt her, but Michael could hear her breath coming in faint wheezes. She always needed her inhaler when something upset her.

It was too much for Michael. "How can you stand to have people treat you like that?"

"Our friends won't judge," Carlotta said weakly. "They're all good people. In time they'll understand."

Michael's anger gathered steam. "I don't give a damn what any of 'em think."

"Show some respect, son," Harold said, "I swear it's hard to know what you kids believe these days."

"What's to believe?" Michael shot back. "If those people are Christians, and this is their God," he waved his Bible angrily, "They can have Him." Michael threw his Bible down and stormed toward the family car in bitter silence.

Chapter 51

April 1970

THE PHONE WAS RINGING when the Simpsons stepped into their house filled with the smells of pot roast, carrots, and potatoes cooking in the oven. No one had spoken for the short ride home. No one had the heart to even try. Michael picked up, hoping against hope that his brother was on the other end of the line.

"Hello."

"Michael? It's Loraine," the warm voice floated through the receiver. The reference was so alien to his world at home that it took him a moment to realize: *it was Loraine from the lake.*

"Hi!" His surprise rippled through the word. He hadn't heard from her since the day he quit working at Pinerock.

His parents passed through the kitchen. Carlotta softly placed Michael's discarded Bible on the counter by the phone and moved down the hall with Harold toward their bedroom.

"I thought you might be home on spring break," Loraine said. "How's school?"

"Fine, I guess." Michael tried to not let his funk seep into his voice, but failed miserably. "Everything else pretty much sucks, though. Diane and I broke up."

"What happened?"

"Well, you probably know about my brother."

"Yeah, I did hear about that." To his relief, her voice held comfort, not ridicule.

"Diane wasn't crazy about dating the brother of a deserter, so that was the end of that."

"I'm sorry, sweetie."

"How have you been?"

"Oh . . ." She started, then her voice sputtered out. He could hear her sadness in the silence. She was so depressed the last time he had seen her at the lake. What was causing it?

"Maybe I can cheer us both up," she started again after a moment. "Would you like to come see me Monday morning?"

"Tomorrow?"

"Yes. That'd be the best time for me."

Michael had no idea why Loraine was suddenly so interested in seeing him after all these months, but it didn't take him long to make up his mind.

"What time?"

"Early would be good. Anytime after nine in the morning."

"Okay." His voice danced and cracked. "Around nine then."

She gave him her address, then hung up.

※

Michael arrived, tingling, on Loraine's doorstep the next morning. The thought of what he might have been summoned here to do had kept him awake most of the night.

He rang the bell and stood waiting, eyes half-closed in heady anticipation. Fuzzy honeybees droned in the spring flowers along the walkway. The morning air was swollen and fragrant with heat and wetness.

Loraine answered the door clad in tight jeans, a soft sweater, and a secret smile. All her curtains were drawn. She stepped aside to let Michael in, then closed the door behind him and locked it. In the delicious half-darkness, Michael felt her slip a warm hand around his fingers. She guided him toward a back bedroom with silk pillows and rose-scented sheets, where a warm, sweet breeze lifted the curtains.

No words were spoken. None were really needed. Loraine took both Michael's hands and slipped them underneath her sweater, guiding them up to her breasts. She wasn't wearing a bra. A rush of adrenaline hit Michael so hard that his knees buckled. She was right. Being with her *had* lifted his spirits. And certain parts of his anatomy, too. He clumsily groped her erect nipples.

"Do it like this," she whispered. She took one of his fingertips and gently caressed it over her smooth skin. "That's how to do it, sweetie."

She lifted her sweater over her head. Though Michael had seen Loraine's bikini-clad body many times, seeing it up close and ready to be touched excited him beyond all thought. She pulled him down onto the bed, then eased out of her jeans. She took his hand and placed it on her Venus mound. Michael could feel the wetness.

"Rub me there. Softly."

He did. She took his fingers and gently slowed him down. With a shuddering breath, she moaned and held him tightly.

The emotions he had felt for weeks—the loss and hurt, the anger and rejection, the sense of failure, the loneliness—all were cast away. What he was doing was forbidden, but he didn't care. At that moment all he cared about were Loraine's caressing fingertips and the mysteries of her quivering body.

Although that morning's journey into manhood would linger in his mind for weeks, Michael heard little from Loraine until she called his dorm almost three weeks later, her voice filled with the same urgency and need. She wanted to see him again the following Thursday. When he asked if it could wait until the weekend, she was empathic: *it had to be Thursday*. In a sensuous haze, Michael agreed to return to her at the prescribed time.

Driving to Forest Park that Thursday morning, Michael prepared to lay himself at the feet of a teacher, someone who would instruct him on the art of touching a woman's body. Loraine's mature lines and curves, her confident moves, dwelt in a different world from Diane's shy, coltish awkwardness. Being with Loraine was a supremely adult act. It had bestowed upon Michael a vigorous new maturity that soon made its presence known in every other part of his life. He was carrying himself differently, thinking of himself differently.

Michael was so caught up in the thrall of his goddess that he failed to observe certain nuances about their relationship. Loraine's appetite for him would turn ravenous, insatiable, for days at a time. Then her ardor would cool, the nameless sadness she revealed at the lake would return, and she'd all but lose interest in him. Two or three passionless weeks would pass, and then she'd call, urgently needing to see him, to devour him again.

Then, too, she'd only permit them to talk about certain subjects once they'd finished their lovemaking and lay in each other's arms. She listened sympathetically whenever he spoke of Diane; she nodded and cried knowing tears when he tried to describe the pain he felt. Loraine never volunteered any details, but Michael sensed that some lover must have left her with a similar wound. Yet when he spoke of Ron, or his family, or anything having to do with college, her eyes drifted away to some private place. He could tell that she was only listening politely. Her mind and her heart were somewhere else.

And so it continued for three months, until Michael returned home to Forest Park at the end of spring quarter. In late June, one sentence from Loraine abruptly changed everything.

"This is the last time I'll be seeing you."

They were lying intertwined in the warm embers of another fiery afternoon. It took a moment for Loraine's words to sink in. When they finally did, it felt like ice water.

"Why?" Michael managed, his heart thudding.

"I'm pregnant," she said simply, softly.

"Pregnant?" Michael could hardly push the word out of his lips. He felt dazed. "Are you sure?"

"Yes, sweetie, I am."

Michael laid on his back for a moment and studied the ceiling, thunderstruck, a queasiness churning in the pit of his stomach. She pushed his dark hair out of his face with her fingers.

"I don't want you to worry. Everything's gonna be okay."

"How could it be okay?"

She opened a drawer on the nightstand and slipped out a photograph of a handsome young man in a pewter frame. He had red hair and a light, ruddy complexion.

"Who's that?"

"My husband," she replied in a small, sad voice.

"Is he . . . deceased?"

Loraine shook her head. No.

"Then why's the photograph put away? Are you divorced?"

Loraine shook her head again. A tear rolled from the corner of her eye.

"I didn't want you to know I was married." She sighed deeply.

"You're married? *Now?*" Michael bolted up, turned his back to her and sat on the edge of the bed. He tried to make sense of what she was saying. They had never discussed her personal life. He had never asked her if she was married. He assumed she wasn't, or that's what he had convinced himself, anyway.

There had been clear signs that she was hiding *something* from him, but he chose to ignore them. She never allowed him to visit her at night or weekends, only during the day. She never allowed him to call her. He didn't even have her telephone number—she always called him. They never went out in public together. He had assumed it was because of the difference in their ages. And there didn't seem much point in suggesting they do something else anyway. She never appeared interested in anything other than lovemaking. And that had certainly been enough for him.

"Why didn't you tell me?" he asked finally.

"I needed you . . . to see me. I was afraid you wouldn't if you knew."

In that instant, Michael realized that he was so drunk on the nectar of her attention that he would've wanted her even if she had told him the truth from the beginning. He needed her too much to care whether she was married or not. But what was done was done. It was too late to avoid "the occasion of sin," as they called it at church. He'd already crossed the line. And he would willingly linger there still, if only she would let him.

But something didn't make sense. Something was missing. He turned back to her and stared. *Why had she needed to see him?*

Loraine could see the question in his eyes.

"Patrick, that's my husband. For some time, we haven't been getting along. We've had problems—bad ones." She paused to compose herself. "This is so hard, sweetie."

"You wanted to see me 'cause you're having problems in your marriage?"

"Patrick wants a baby. We both do. We've tried for years, but I haven't been able to get pregnant. He blames it on me. It's been tearing us apart. He's even been talking about a divorce. I didn't want to lose him, so I needed to see, I had to know, if I was the problem."

She reached out and tried to touch his arm, but he pulled away.

"I don't want you to take responsibility for the baby, sweetie. Patrick thinks it's his, and I want to keep it that way. I don't want to lose my husband over this. I did it to save my marriage." She turned her back to him and curled into a fleshy ball, refusing to say more. She didn't have to. She had used him. She wanted to get pregnant, and now she was. *With his child.*

Speechless, he eased off the bed and started dressing. He could hear her crying on the bed. But he didn't care. He didn't care about anything but leaving.

Chapter 52

October 1970

IN RON'S OPINION, YOU'D have to stack ten of Ottawa's autumns together to make even one of Georgia's. To his dismay, the leaves of the northern city's trees had no sooner flushed golden than a sharp frost nipped them brown, and a razor-blade wind sheared them away.

The biting chill of Ottawa in October was already miserable, and Ron knew it was going to get much worse. Working on rooftops ten hours a day, he hoped that sooner or later he'd harden to the cold. But without a proper coat, hat, or gloves, it wasn't going to happen. He'd taken to tying strips of old bandanas, discarded by his better-dressed coworkers, around his hands in a futile attempt to keep them from growing too numb as he poured tar and pounded shingle nails.

At first, he'd conjured up memories of Vicki to warm him. This worked well because it also made him mad, which raised his body temperature a little. He was angry at a world that made it impossible for him to court her with dignity and left him poor in a country without family or friends. He was angry with himself for the ragged hard-luck case he was becoming. Vicki still knocked on his door from time to time, but his pride wouldn't let him answer. He felt a little more like a loser every time she gave up and left him to himself.

As he worked on the rooftop with his back to the wind, the leaden sky started down dropping snowflakes. Ron stared at the light frozen moisture. To a boy from Georgia, who had seen snow five or six times in his life, it was a foreboding sight.

"Shit," Ron mumbled.

Two of the other carpenters' assistants glanced in his direction but didn't reply. From his first day on the job, they'd kept a suspicious distance, perhaps smelling something illegal about him. One of the workers carried a tinny transistor radio slung from his tool bucket. As the last song set ended, Ron picked up the sound of an announcer's voice: *"In music news for October 4, 1970, blues queen Janis Joplin, twenty-seven, was found dead in Hollywood today of an apparent drug overdose."*

Ron's hammer froze in mid-swing.

"This comes less than a month after the death of famed singer and guitarist Jimi Hendrix. He was also twenty-seven."

As the announcer concluded, the raunchy strains of "Me and Bobby McGee" faded in: *"Freedom's just another word for nothin' left to lose . . ."*

Ron felt the hairs on the back of his neck rise. Even from the grave, Janis had a way of driving it home.

As the cold, damp autumn weeks rolled onward, Ron's loneliness grew like a deadly cancer. While his frugal diet was taking a harsh toll on his body, his bitter isolation was taking a worse one on his mind. Depressed and paranoid, he seldom spoke to coworkers beyond what was necessary to get the job done. He had met few people in Ottawa and considered none of them friends. He had called home a few times, but the conversations were brief, awkward, and full of strong, bitter emotions. In recent weeks, he had given up on even trying. *What was the use?*

In November, Ron fell behind in his rent after becoming too sick to work. By late December, the landlord was threatening to evict him if he didn't catch up. Now, to top it all off, he was getting sick *again*. Over the past couple of days he'd developed a niggling tickle in the back of his throat, which now had grown into a phlegmy cough.

Car tires crunching on the worksite's gravel entrance jarred Ron to attention. He glanced over the roof's edge to see two dark-suited men step out of a government car that bore the insignia of the federal immigration agency. The two men stepped briskly up to speak to a construction worker digging a trench for pipe. The man fished for his wallet and handed the agents his green card.

Ron's heart pounded in his throat. He willed himself to move slowly. If he bolted, they'd be on him. He eased up and over the roof gable and down the far side.

Shit. No ladder on this side.

Running out of time, Ron hooked his fingers around a downspout and shimmied down the corner of the house. He glanced around and spotted a small, ragged gap in the fence just as one of the officers spotted him. Ron squeezed through, vanished down an alleyway, and sprinted away.

When he'd put a few blocks between himself and the immigration agents, he slowed to catch his breath. The effort had made his lungs burn. He coughed weakly.

"There goes my plush paycheck," Ron sighed to himself. By the time he made it back to his roach-and-rat infested room, he was shaking with violent chills. He crawled into bed, tucked his single threadbare blanket around his legs, and lulled himself to sleep with visions of Vicki's smile.

Ron awoke with a raging fever. His head was so hot it frightened him. Knowing that his body needed liquid, he steeled himself to rise and walk to the sink in the shared bathroom down the hall. But his head spun so wildly that he had to fling himself back down on his bed to keep from throwing up. Exhausted, he drifted again into a dreamless sleep.

He woke in pitch darkness hours later, his tongue stuck to the roof of his mouth.

If I was like this at home, Mom would have me off to the hospital, Ron thought. But since Carlotta was a thousand miles away, he would have to doctor himself.

This time he forced himself to make it to the bathroom, hugging the walls and one-eying it all the way. When he returned to his bed, he had to will himself to finish the water. To take his mind off his pounding head, he pulled Alex's letter from his pocket and read: *"I don't know what to tell you, Ronnie boy. Nothing could prepare you for what you see and do here. I'm always looking over my shoulder. I'm always afraid. The paranoia is unbelievable . . ."*

A loud sob escaped him. Then, all at once, his shoulders were shaking as he wept in anguish. Through it all, his eyes remained dry: the fever had burned up all his tears. As weak as he'd become, the sobbing took the last of his strength, and he collapsed heavily on his side. He had hoped, and expected, to pass out again.

Instead, he lay staring through the open closet door at his military uniform, which hung on a solitary wire hanger inside. Illuminated by the room's single dingy bulb, dangling from a greasy chain above him, the uniform held a silent, mocking vigil.

He had never felt so alone. *Or so ashamed.*

Ron guessed that days had passed, but he couldn't be sure how many. He'd drifted in and out of consciousness, but now his brain felt clear, and his head was cool and dry. Some time during his illness, an unknown benefactor had refilled his water bottle, spread an extra blanket on top of him, and left him with a can of pineapple juice and some chicken bullion cubes. He suspected the visiting angel was probably Vicki. But there was no note, and he was too embarrassed to contact her and ask. Ron devoured the anonymous gifts and felt his appetite coming back. He checked his jeans pocket and found a loon and three quarters: enough to buy a decent meal, if he was careful.

Feeling a hundred years old, Ron left his room and eased himself slowly down the stairs. The street outside was blanketed in snow; the air was so cold it made his breath freeze on his scratchy, days-old beard. When he caught a reflection of himself in a storefront window, he understood why the other pedestrians looked away from him as they passed down the street. Ron Simpson didn't even recognize himself anymore.

His jeans, sneakers, and hooded sweatshirt, the only clothes he still possessed, had been reduced to near rags. Strips of a torn red bandana served as his gloves. The bulging muscles he'd built over years of sports and months of military training had withered away. His bony face had taken on the dry pallor of crusty oatmeal. The dull emptiness he observed in his own eyes unnerved him.

Christ, if I met me on the street right now, I'd look away too. Ron stifled a giggle, then choked on a sob.

It took him nearly an hour to wobble down to the convenience store on the corner and return with a tiny sack of groceries. He made his way painstakingly up the stairs to his room and was fumbling with his key when he discovered the fat steel padlock that had been slapped over the knob. Dimly, he looked up to find an eviction notice pasted on the door.

His head reeled. How long had it been since he'd paid his rent? *How long had it been since he'd had the money to pay his rent?* He sat down on the stairs, nibbled on his meager meal and tried to think of what to do next, until the landlord ordered him out onto the street.

Ron pulled his hooded sweatshirt as tightly around himself as he could. When a newspaper blew up against his leg, he grabbed it, crumpled it, and stuffed it inside his shirt for extra warmth. Holes in his worn-out sneakers let in the biting-cold air. The wind stung his face raw. He had to get someplace inside—*fast*.

But where? He feared going to the hostel and didn't have enough money even for one night's stay. The only place for him was skid row. He knew it was full of draft evaders and deserters who had come to Ottawa and been unable to find their way to a better life. Maybe that was his fate, too.

Framed by tall buildings, nightfall crept upward from the bustling streets. This far north, the light went to its rest at the end of day with all the glory of a fallen hero. It painted the sky in crystal hues of indigo and turquoise that brought the spires of the town into razor focus.

Damn, this is a pretty city, Ron mused silently. If only he had the luxury to enjoy its beauty.

As night fell around him, a wicked wind whipped up, dashing spiky little flurries of ice against Ron's face. He wandered several blocks before the cheery lights of a department store beckoned to him. Maybe he would warm himself inside for a moment. He crossed the street and started toward it. In his weakened state, it took a focused effort to keep his feet moving forward.

The store was covered with Christmas decorations. A mechanical Santa turned and waved and *ho ho ho'd* in the display window. As the last customers stepped outside, a clerk closed and locked the doors behind them. The lights went out. The store was closing early, and Ron finally understood why: *it was Christmas Eve.* He stood shivering on the sidewalk, staring bleakly into darkness, trying to decide what to do.

Hours later, he was still plodding along darkening streets, searching for a place to get in out of the cold. Almost without thinking, he'd reached inside his shirt to finger the gold cross that hung there. He prayed silently for guidance. He had not finished his prayer when it came to him: *the Catholic Church three blocks away ran a cold-weather shelter.* If he could make it there, they'd take him in. It would cost him the last of his strength, but he loped toward the church. He could see its white spire, rising misty and floodlit through the flurry of snow. He was almost there.

"You there! Hold up!" a voice called behind him.

Ron wheeled around to find a policeman ambling up the sidewalk toward him.

"You been drinkin'? You're walking funny."

"I'm sick, sir," Ron replied honestly.

The officer sniffed his breath suspiciously. "*Lemmesee* some identification."

"I don't have it," Ron admitted, and then added hastily, "I left it at the shelter."

"If you're stayin' at the shelter, what are you doin' out this time of night? Shelter locks up for the night at ten o'clock, and it's already five of."

"Yessir, that's why I need to hurry," Ron tried.

But the officer had spied his gold cross. "Where'd you get this? It looks expensive. You steal it?"

"No sir. I was a gift on my baptism."

"Somethin's funny about you. I probably oughta run you in." The officer seemed to consider it for a moment but relented, "Aw, what the hell. It's Christmas Eve. Get on back to the shelter."

"Yes sir."

The shelter was straight ahead. Ron started down the church's basement steps, and then froze. Inside, a police officer wearing a Santa hat was giving out presents. Ron had cheated fate once that night. He knew he couldn't risk it again.

Ron turned away, and limped weakly into the night to wander the snow-dusted streets. There was little sensation in his toes and hands. He'd had nothing to eat but bullion soup for days, and his legs were spongy from lack of food.

His mind began to fade. Snippets of street conversation mingled in his ears with the voices of his family. He heard his mother singing softly in the kitchen as she pulled a batch of biscuits from the oven. He could almost smell them. Then a taxicab would roar by, and he'd find himself alone.

Ron found himself wandering along Rideau Canal. This time of year, the canal was a smooth plate of ice, a popular spot for skaters. On Christmas Eve, it was nearly deserted.

Stumbling past the United States Embassy and the Canadian War Museum, Ron's feet came to rest on the edge of the massive Pont Alexandra Bridge. He dimly realized that this was where he'd been heading all night. A car passed him, the driver's window inched down to let the cigarette smoke inside escape. Music seeped into the frozen night air.

"It's no good you getting angry," a male was singing, *"We must try to act our age. You're pursuing your convictions, like some hermit in a cage . . ."*

Ron had never heard the song before. It sounded like Elton John.

"You're the son of your father, try a little bit harder . . ."

What happens when you're tired of trying? Ron thought dully. He had lost his family, his hometown, his best friend, and his country. He had lost his dignity and his pride. He felt like he'd even lost his God. *What was left to lose?*

As he made his way onto the dour steel structure, a piercing chill rose from the half-frozen river spilling past in the darkness below. The snow was falling heavily now. The silver glow of the city illuminated the white flakes that flew past and vanished. Ron ran a hand along the rough, rusted bridge rail, barely feeling the knobby lumps of each rivet as they slid beneath his frigid fingers. A third of the way across the steel truss, Ron stopped and looked down into the frigid, dark abyss of the icy river below.

Just a few more seconds, and it's done. Just one short hop. After that, I won't feel a thing.

Ron's exertions caused the letter he carried in his breast pocket to crinkle. The last letter he'd received from Alex. He paused, remembering the searing final sentence. *Fuck you, John Wayne*, Alex had scrawled.

"Fuck you back," Ron shouted loudly. "Turns out you're the lucky one." He threw one leg up over the bridge rail.

"This ain't one of your better ideas, Ronnie boy," Alex's voice boomed in Ron's ear, as clearly as if he were standing there beside him. From somewhere over Ron's shoulder, a smoldering cigarette butt flew over the railing and vanished into the darkness below. Ron glanced to his left.

As a matter of fact, Alex was standing there, right beside him. Alex should have been the last person Ron expected to see. But in his current state of mind, nothing could surprise him.

Alex looked just the way he did the day Ron watched him vanish through the jetway door. He was clean-shaven and crisply dressed in a brand-new uniform. He was in perfect health. Though Alex had never been plump, next to Ron's withered form, he appeared almost hefty. His cheeks still glowed pink from a recent infusion of Pabst Blue Ribbon. It was as if 'Nam had never touched him.

"Leave me alone. I know what I'm doing," Ron growled.

Alex snagged a fresh cigarette from behind one ear, pinched it between his lips, and cupped his hand around a match.

"I'm speaking from experience here, Ronnie boy. Once you're down there," Alex indicated the black river below with a jerk of his head, "It ain't like you can take it back."

"I got no choice."

"Sure you do, Hoss."

"I'm not going to prison!"

"Who are you fuckin' kiddin'?" Alex countered, "You're already in prison. There's nothin' the military could do to you that you haven't already done to yourself."

Ron's pain poured out like a boil being lanced. "I don't deserve to live. I destroyed my family. I've hurt everyone who tried to help me. I even let you down . . . I should've been there to help you."

"Don't put this shit on me. You can't save everybody, Hoss. Haven't you learned that yet? Sometimes you can only save yourself."

"I'm not worth saving," Ron muttered grimly, pulling himself up on the rail.

Alex reached out a hand, but stopped short of touching him.

"Think of your brother. What kind of example are you giving the squirt? What happens if Michael gets drafted? You're tellin' him his only choice is to go jump off a bridge somewhere."

"Damn you! What am I suppose to do?"

"Fuck, do anything," Alex snapped," Just don't do this!"

"There's no place else for me to go."

"Jesus H. Frog, I don't believe this shit," Alex shook his head, exhaling a jet of cigarette smoke. "You really think this is your only goddam choice?"

Ron paused at that and gazed down into the swirling abyss. He was fully prepared to let himself fall. He would have made quick work of the job, too, if Alex weren't being such an asshole. *Why couldn't he understand that it was the only reasonable thing left to do?*

Alex was wearing him out, wasting the precious energy that he needed to pull himself over the railing. "Go fuck yourself," Ron snarled, then steeled himself for the plunge.

As he was swinging his other leg over, his fading mind registered another presence on the bridge. Not Alex, but his father.

"Let me help you, son," Harold said kindly.

Ron turned to see his father extending a hand. He stared, dumbfounded. He blinked his eyes hard, squinted again through the driving snow. The image changed. Not Harold, but a middle-aged stranger with dark eyes and a face full of concern.

"Why don't you come down from there?" the man said gently, "Lemme buy you a cup of coffee."

Ron's sense of southern decency overruled his impulse to push off from the bridge. The man was offering a kindness—it would have been bad manners to perform such an ugly act in front of him.

What the hell. A cup of coffee, let the old guy feel good about himself for a few minutes, then I'll be back out here in half an hour to finish what I started.

∼

The man's name was Hugh, and he worked in a paper factory a couple of towns away. He'd served in the Korean War, where he had lost close friends, and his wife had died of breast cancer last year, leaving him alone at fifty-three. Over a hot meal, coffee and pie, Ron found himself babbling at the man with the sympathetic eyes. He even told him about seeing Alex beside him on the bridge. Hugh didn't bat an eye; instead, he nodded sagely, as if it was to be expected, given the circumstances.

"After my wife died, I crawled into the bottom of a bottle and stayed there. I lost my job—truth be told, I pretty much lost everything. I got as low as a man can go. And then one day, I realized God had a plan for my life. There was a reason He took my wife and left me here."

The man nodded at the cross around Ron's neck. "Son, I can't pretend to know what you're going through. But I believe you're a man of faith. And where there's faith, there's hope. You want your answers, look to the cross."

With food in his stomach and warmth creeping back into his fingers and toes, Ron could entertain the idea that the man—and Alex—might have a point. He thanked the man for his concern and wished him a Merry Christmas. Then he pushed through the door of the diner to face the frigid night.

Maybe, just maybe, there was an answer out there somewhere. Maybe there was hope. He knew it would take a miracle. But, after all, *it was Christmas Eve.*

Chapter 53

The Dead Angle
June 27, 1864

BLINKING INTO THE SOMBER light of the late afternoon sun, Baylis could see human flesh littered across the battlefield, torn and ripped in grotesque and unimaginable ways. Across the steep hillside in front of the breastworks, sporadic rifle fire punctuated the chorus of the wounded and dying. Moans and wails announced their suffering with such intensity that the ground itself seemed to weep.

In the trenches around Baylis, so many rebels lay dead that there was no place to move the bodies. There was no man among the living who didn't have wounds or rips in his clothes.

Had any man ever seen such slaughter?

"Pa, you all right?"

Baylis looked up to see Ulysses. His son's face and clothes were splattered with blood. He had a strip of cloth wrapped around his forearm that was stained bright red.

"Fine, I reckon," the old man said numbly. "My head feels like I got kicked by a mule. You?"

"Took the bad end of a bayonet in my arm. Nothing that a stitch or two won't settle."

Baylis realized his son was staring at him oddly.

"Pa, you got a bullet hole in your hat."

Ulysses eased the cap off his father's head. A nasty gash above Baylis's left ear was bleeding. Ulysses sat him down on a camp chest and gingerly felt along the edge of his hair. "Looks like you were grazed by a bullet. You just missed gettin' your ear shot off or worse."

Ulysses poured water from his canteen onto a piece of cloth and dabbed at the wound. "That will sure enough get you a day or two off the line."

Baylis realized that the corpse of young Private Sanders was on the ground next to him. It appeared the red-haired boy had been shot in the jaw and chest. His dead green eyes stared up at Baylis as though waiting for the answer to some important question. Baylis reached down and gently closed the boy's eyes.

"We damn near lost our whole company," Ulysses said grimly.

Colquitt slumped down in the trench next to them, shaking with fatigue. "I need to find Sergeant Tedford," he said, then promptly vomited. He wiped his mouth with his sleeve.

Ulysses saw the sergeant and motioned to him. Tedford approached.

"What is it?"

Colquitt coughed out his words. "I think those Yankee sumsabitches are tryin' to tunnel under our line."

The sergeant considered it a moment, then turned to Private Thomas, who was nursing a hand wound. "Where's the company field drum?"

Thomas began rummaging around, turning over bodies and debris until he found the drum under a collapsed tent.

Tedford scratched around in the dirt, picking up pea-size stones. "Everyone stop moving!" Tedford yelled.

Dozens of men around them froze. The sergeant sat the drum on the ground and placed the gravel on its head. The small stones bounced and danced on the tight skin.

"*Got tam* it to hell. I'd say those blue boys are tunneling like field mice."

The soldiers scuttled up to the firing line and peered carefully through the headlogs.

Yankee survivors had sought shelter behind the dead bodies of their fallen comrades and against the trees and rocks that dotted the bloody hillside. They were now feverishly entrenching, using bayonets, cups, spoons, forks, and their bare hands. In some places, the lines of the two armies were no more than thirty yards apart.

"I can't see where they're tunneling," Ulysses said.

"It would have to be close," Baylis said.

"I think it's under the lip of the hill yonder, right behind that trench," Colquitt said, nodding toward a point where Union soldiers were constructing a parapet.

Tedford eased up to take a better look. A Union sharpshooter thumped a round right beside his head. The sergeant quickly ducked back down.

"We're too far back on the hilltop to see. But they're sure doing something down there they don't want us to know about."

The men dropped off the line and rested against the berm.

"What can we do?" Ulysses asked.

"I'll report to the lieutenant and see," Tedford said, moving off.

"Someone said Ol' Joe is sending extra rations of whiskey and tobacco tonight." It was Private Thomas, who had returned to the ditches with his hand wound dressed.

"Sounds like he's afraid we won't hold the line," Colquitt said.

"We'll hold the line as long as Johnston wants us to," Ulysses said quietly. "He can rest easy on that point."

"I wouldn't give the Yankees the satisfaction of forcing us out," Colquitt said.

Baylis looked at the dead men stacked around them. His brow dropped low, weighted by the sight. "Let's help move these poor souls to a better resting place."

As twilight gathered around them, the old man and his son stood and solemnly began picking up bodies out of the trenches and placing them onto the sparse ground behind the line. Baylis thought it seemed like some horrible factory Billy Sherman had shipped down from the industrial north, processing healthy young men into mutilated corpses.

As dusk faded at last into gloomy night, the cries of the injured and dying Union soldiers by the breastworks began to dwindle. The worst of the wounded had bled out and died, while those able to crawl used the cover of darkness to pull themselves down the hill toward their brothers-in-arms.

The rebel soldiers left on the line passed their time drinking their extra ration of whiskey and smoking. There was little talk, just faraway stares filled with the sullen hope that the sting of liquor would dull the horrors of their godless day.

A sudden commotion rolled the men out of their dark thoughts. Sergeant Tedford came down toward his company.

"Every man to the line!" he shouted. "The lieutenant got word the Yankees are getting ready for a sneak attack."

"That's why they're tunneling," Colquitt said. "The blue boys plan to blow a hole in the line right under us, sure as spit."

The soldiers grabbed their rifles from the stacks and scrambled up along the breastworks. They peered out into the darkness, straining to see any movement.

"How could anyone know what they're planning? It's darker than Jonah's stomach out there," Baylis said.

"I know one way to see what they're doing." Colquitt took a large cotton ball, soaked it in turpentine, and lit it. He pitched it over the headlogs, briefly illuminating the hillside in front of them.

Soon rebels up and down the line began doing the same thing. The lighted balls looked like primitive fireworks as they arched in the sky, then fell to earth and rolled down the hill.

By the time the rebels were satisfied that the bluecoats had no fight in them that night, several of the fiery orbs had landed on dead Union soldiers between the lines. The burning corpses added to the already ghastly smell, a stench that would only get worse with the rising sun.

Chapter 54

December 1970

MICHAEL LET HIMSELF IN the back door of the Simpson home, stopping on the way to his room for a swig of tea from his glass in the refrigerator. On holiday break from the university, he had spent Christmas Eve at a department store, lifelessly roaming the aisles making last-minute purchases while shoppers bubbled around him with festive cheer. It had been an altogether miserable experience, a sadly fitting end to a miserable year.

Only months earlier, everything in his life had seemed perfect, or as perfect as it could be for a young man entering college and staring at an incandescent future. Then his whole world had burned down around him. *Alex's death. Ron's desertion. Diane dumping him. And then Loraine.*

He'd heard nothing from Loraine for months. He had struggled to honor her wishes, but the guilt over the affair and her pregnancy had eaten away at him, twisting his insides into a tight coil of raw emotion.

The final, crushing loss had been the death of his beloved Grandpa Melvin Simpson that fall. Through the ordeal of Ron's desertion, Papa Simp had been a solid rock, offering his quiet understanding and sympathy. He and the rest of the Simpson clan had never wavered nor judged. As Grandpa had said: *Family is family. It's that simple.*

And now he was gone.

After spending the morning stripping and varnishing furniture in his poorly ventilated wood shop, Melvin Simpson was finishing lunch at his kitchen table. He set down his fork, told his wife what a fine lunch she had fixed, then calmly asked her to phone Doctor Harvey—the same family doctor who had delivered Michael eighteen years before. When his wife Lara reacted with alarm, Melvin told her gently that he loved her, and that everything would be all right.

Lara hurried into the living room to make the call. She returned to find Melvin sprawled on the kitchen floor. Doc Harvey said later that Melvin's heart attack was so massive that he had probably died before he hit the linoleum.

Papa Simp's death marked the first time that Michael had ever seen his father's eyes tear up. But Harold handled his grief like a Marine: he turned away to do his crying in private, got it done, and went on with the business at hand.

Papa Simp was memorialized at a service in the chapel of the Atco Baptist Church, where mourners read the verses of his hard life etched across his wrinkled face. He was attended by friends and a horde of relatives—more than fifty children, grandchildren, great-grandchildren and "outlaws" as he lovingly called those who had married into the Simpson clan—all bearing somber faces and loving memories of the family patriarch. With sincere prayers and tributes, Melvin was laid to rest in the family cemetery, joining the line of his fathers dating back to Baylis.

After the funeral service, Michael overheard an uncle proclaim that Melvin's father, Mallie Simpson, had met a similarly abrupt fate at the breakfast table. Harold joked that he, in turn, expected to die at the dinner table. Michael wondered idly if this meant that his own demise would come during some far distant midnight snack.

After the final sledgehammer blow of his grandpa's death, nothing much could hold Michael's attention. He buried himself in school and playing music with friends from his drama class.

Four fun loving, rock 'n' roll pirates—Ralph, Willi, Butcho, and "Smooth Touch" Brown—had recruited him to front them as a singer in a band. Ravenstone—the group took its name from a field in 15th-century

Germany where they executed people convicted of being witches—quickly began to attract crowds while performing in local Athens nightclubs.

Beyond the band, little else in Michael's life was easy that autumn. Most days it was like a Dixieland jazz funeral was sashaying through his head; he felt empty and lost, yet full of a jangly, jittery energy that he funneled into the ravesters' music and his increasing interest in politics. Michael knew he had it easier than his parents. In Athens, a world away from Forest Park, his new friends had never heard of Ron Simpson's desertion. But sooner or later Michael had to come home, where the gloom and tension were waiting. Although he could ignore it, he couldn't escape it.

Even at college he couldn't be rid of it entirely. In early December, at a club where Ravenstone was playing, Michael spotted Diane amid a cluster of girls in front of the stage, gazing sadly at him as he performed. She held his eyes for half a moment. In that instant he saw something in those soft blue orbs, what he had first seen on that moonlit beach so long ago. Then she looked away and disappeared into the crowd.

Michael stared after her, bewildered. He fought off the urge to jump off the stage and follow her. Ralph, the rhythm guitarist and the only married guy in the band, caught his look.

"Was that somebody you know?" Ralph asked after the song ended as he tuned his guitar and slipped behind the keyboards for the next song.

"Not anymore," Michael replied distantly.

Although the music and partying raged on all around him, Michael had lost the spirit. After they finished playing that night, he excused himself and headed back to the ramshackle, antebellum-style house the band rented on Prince Avenue. He spent most of the night staring at the ceiling, thinking about Diane and everything he had lost when she left his world.

Despite the time and distance, Michael still had not gotten over her. He wished for some way to bridge their differences, to bring her back into his life. But there was nothing that could be done. The wall between them was too high to climb.

∽

Carols drifting wistfully from a radio broke Michael from his jumbled thoughts. Through the living-room door, he caught a glimpse of his mother reaching up to drape tinsel on the Christmas tree. The family had a long tradition of putting the finishing touches on the family tree on Christmas Eve. Carlotta's eyes were rimmed red, and she paused every few seconds to catch her breath. She didn't expect him back until later; had she known he was watching, she would never have allowed her illness to show.

After a moment, Michael's father walked in the front door, dressed in his hunting jacket, his Browning "sweet sixteen" 16-gauge in hand, a shotgun that Harold had often noted was "good for quail hunting and not much else." He had spent the day tracking a covey of bobwhites with Sport and Ramus, his German shorthaired pointers. He didn't spot Michael in the kitchen.

"What did the doc say?" he asked his wife gently, setting the shotgun down.

"That I must be allergic to everything in the world," Carlotta replied with a weak smile. "He was kind enough to see me before he closed up for the holiday."

Harold took her into his arms. "It doesn't help that you've been so upset lately."

By the time Michael realized he was eavesdropping on a private moment, it was too late to creep away unnoticed. He edged back into the shadows of the kitchen and stood quietly.

Together Harold and Carlotta began to decorate the long-suffering artificial tree. Carlotta reached into a box and came up with a tiny pewter ornament in the shape of a cradle. Michael recognized it at once. He'd received one just like it on his first Christmas. Ron's ornament read, in spidery engraving: *Ronald Simpson-First Christmas!*

"It just doesn't seem right without my boy here," Carlotta sighed. "I don't expect I've been this sad at Christmas since the big war, when most everyone was away."

Bing Crosby's "White Christmas" began to play softly on the radio. The light of a long-ago memory drifted into Harold's eyes. "1944 . . . that was the worst Christmas of the war for me."

Carlotta smiled wistfully. "That was when you first heard this song, wasn't it?"

Harold nodded somberly. "I was stationed in the Marshalls. We'd taken Majuro from the Japs earlier that year after defeating them at Kwajalein.

We were using the island as a staging area for air strikes."

Harold stopped, lost in his thoughts as Crosby crooned. Then his voice sparked again. "When that song came on Armed Forces Radio, the whole mess hall went quiet. There were these big green lizards running around, and I swear they stopped and listened, too. We all just sat there in the coral sand and heat while Bing dreamed about a white Christmas." Muffling his emotions, he added, "I saw a lot of Marines weep that day."

Carlotta gauged her husband's mood carefully, then said in a gentle voice, "I expect Ron is missing home long 'bout now."

"I'm sure he is," Harold shook his head sadly and sighed. "And I wish to God that he was here. Maybe I could talk some sense into him."

Carlotta polished Ron's candle ornament with a tissue. "What would you say if he was here?"

"I'd tell him a man's word means something. It's the most valuable thing you can ever own. And I'd tell him he gave his word to his country."

"Country," Carlotta insisted quietly. "That's not you personally."

"What would you have me do?" Harold voice was rough with emotion. "Side with my son against my country?"

"I don't know." She carefully placed the pewter candle on the tree. "But he's our blood. We can't just deny him."

"I haven't denied my son anything," he said. "I gave Ron a good home. A family. Everything I possibly could. And he threw it all away."

Carlotta's eyes dropped, weighed down by the heartbreak of it all. "I don't rightly see how I can just turn my back on him, not while breath is in my body."

Harold looked for a moment as though he were about to say something. Then he wobbled his head in defeat. "I've got quail to dress."

Carlotta listened to her husband's retreating footsteps, and then broke into rhythmic, wheezing sobs.

Michael waited for his father to push out the front door, and then he slipped silently out the kitchen. He knew the only way to make things worse would be to let his parents find out they'd been overheard.

Chapter 55

December 1970

BY SIX O'CLOCK ON Christmas morning, Vicki was already up and dressed and headed out the door. She'd been out late the night before, combing the streets for Ron. She had come to his room with a brightly wrapped new wool scarf, hoping that the gift, and some Christmas cheer, would lift his spirits. When she saw the padlock, she feared for his life. She knew he wouldn't last long on Ottawa's winter streets.

Vicki spent her Christmas morning checking doorways and peering down stairwells. Her heart leaped when she found Ron sleeping on top of a steaming grate outside the Canadian Parliament, huddled under a piece of cardboard. His skin was blue and felt cold to her touch. She pressed an ear against his chest. She made out a faint thread of a heartbeat and breathed a sigh of relief.

~

When Ron Simpson's eyes fluttered open, he was in a dark bedroom. He had no idea how he'd gotten there. But he was warm and indoors, and that was all that mattered for the moment. Vicki opened the door and tiptoed in, carrying a tray.

"I must be dreaming," he smiled weakly.

"You almost bought it out there, soldier boy, do you know that? If I'd found you a few hours later, it would've been too late. You've got one helluva guardian angel, eh?" She switched on the lights, then sat beside him and began feeding him hot chicken soup from a bowl on her tray.

Ron eyed the room between spoonfuls of broth. Not fancy, but comfortable, full of Vicki's offbeat essence. She'd tacked a colorful tie-dyed scarf across the single overhead light, and draped others over the two bedside lamps. The muted, rose-colored light gave the room the aura of a tarot-card reader's parlor. The makeshift bookshelves, of scavenged boards and bricks, held stacks of paperback novels with cracked spines, handmade candles, rescued houseplants, and beaded macramé projects in various stages of completion. Ron glanced at the stack of books on her bedside table.

"*Green Eggs and Ham?*" he asked.

At that moment, the bedroom door opened, and a dark-haired little girl scampered in. Her brown eyes sparkled with excitement as she held up a new doll in a crisp white nurse's uniform.

"Mommy! Look what Santa brought me!" The young girl spotted Ron and was overcome with shyness.

Ron stared at the child, stunned speechless.

Vicki scooped up the little imp. "Kimmy, this is Mommy's friend, Ron."

"Did Santa bring you a friend?"

Vicki couldn't help but smile. "Well, I guess Santa did, baby. He's having some soup. Would you like some?"

Kimberly shook her head no. Vicki gave her a squeeze, and then set her down.

"Your Trix are on the table," Vicki told her.

"I want *Froot* Loops," she protested, the way little kids do.

"We're out of Fruit Loops, baby. Maybe next time," Vicki combed her dark, curly locks with her fingers. "Besides, silly rabbit," she said, "Trix are for kids. Now run along. We're going to see Grandpapa later."

Kimberly scampered out of the room.

"Now I get what you meant by 'responsibilities'—unless you have another surprise in store."

"No, she's it," Vicki said quietly.

"Where's her dad?" Ron had to ask.

Vicki raised an eyebrow. "Being fed chicken soup in my bed doesn't mean you get to ask personal questions." She picked up the tray and smoothed Ron's covers. "Now rest."

She rose, switched off the light, and closed the door behind her, leaving Ron alone in the comfortable darkness, full of thought.

~

Ron had fallen in love with Kimberly at first sight. The adorable five-year-old was slow to warm to the new stranger, but in a few days she adored him right back.

Vicki would let Ron read to the little girl for half an hour each afternoon, the highlight of his day. He attributed his rapid recovery to the pleasure he took in making Kimmy laugh and smile. Then, too, there was the delicious comfort of snuggling up with Vicki each night.

But Ron harbored no illusions. He was a dead weight in their lives, and he hated himself for it. As soon as he was well again, he knew he'd wear out his welcome. His frustration at his helplessness often left him irritable, distant.

On sunny Saturday afternoons, Vicki took Kimberly skating on the Rideau Canal. When Ron had recovered enough to venture outdoors, Vicki invited him to come along and watch. Kimberly was in her element on the ice. She took her mother's hand and skimmed across the canal at breakneck speeds. When they reached the edge where Ron was sitting, Kimmy reached for her mother's other hand and pulled her to spin in a dizzying circle. Then they tumbled onto the ice, laughing and hugging. Ron caught them both glancing over at him to make sure he'd witnessed their antics. He smiled, in spite of the black mood that clutched him tight.

It made something ache inside Ron to watch them. He longed for his own family and cursed his inability to become part of a new one. But he still felt Vicki's eyes lingering on him. She'd sent Kimberly off to skate with a gaggle of little girls her own age, and now looked at him with concern.

"You want java?" she asked, pulling off her skates. She led him to a nearby coffee stand, and soon they were walking side by side along the canal, sipping from steaming cups and watching Kimberly frolic on the ice.

"You have a beautiful child."

Vicki held his eyes somberly. "You asked the other day about her father—"

"It was stupid to ask," Ron cut in. "It's none of my business."

"He's dead," Vicki said matter-of-factly. "He was Canadian, but he went to America to volunteer for the war."

A pang of sympathy jolted through him. "I'm sorry," he answered with downcast eyes. "I know what it's like to lose people you love."

"You just have to start all over again." Vicki took his hand and squeezed it warmly. "Find new people to love."

Ron's heart should have soared at the promise in what she'd said. If only it had come under other circumstances. He pulled his hand away.

"Don't. I don't deserve this."

"I just wanna help you, that's all."

Ron saw the pain in her eyes. "Can't you see? I hate myself. I hate everything about my life."

"Do you hate me? I'm part of your life. Or I'm trying to be."

"You got Kimmy to think about. You don't need a loser like me hanging around."

Ron studied her face a moment. He contemplated giving her a goodbye kiss on the forehead, but then thought better of it. Instead, he simply turned his back and began walking.

If she thinks I'm a calloused shit, she'll be too mad to miss me as much.

"You can't just keep running away," she called after him.

He turned and gave her his saddest smile. "Why not? It's what I do best."

"When are you going to quit feeling sorry for yourself, *eh*?"

He dropped his head in shame. She was right. He did feel sorry for himself. "Why do you care what I feel?"

"'Cause I'm trying to stop the fight. The war you're waging on yourself."

"I just . . . I feel like such a coward."

She moved to him and tilted his head up until his eyes met hers. "You had convictions. You gave up everything for them. That's not the act of a coward."

Her words hung heavily between them.

"You have a choice to make, soldier boy. You can make a life here, a good life, with people who care about you. Or you can keep filling yourself with self-hate until it crowds out everything good and decent in you."

"Why do you even bother? I've got no job, no future. I've got nothing."

"You have a heart, and it's as big as all outdoors. I knew that the first night I met you. That's a precious gift." She held out her hand. "You can't change the past, Ron Simpson. But you can change your future."

He could see the deep currents of affection in her eyes. Maybe she was right. There was only one way he would ever know. He reached for her hand. She folded herself up close to him. They held each other tightly for a long moment. Then they turned and faced the future together.

Chapter 56

January 1971

MICHAEL WOULDN'T REMEMBER MUCH about that winter, other than a heavy sadness. On Ron's birthday that January, it snowed: a diamond dusting that sparkled on top of the dormant, brown grass.

While Harold was busy cleaning the slush off the driveway, Michael and his mother scurried about the kitchen, preparing a few surprises for Ron. Michael wrapped a new pair of gloves while Carlotta stirred up batter for a cake that would travel across the Canadian border in a sealed cookie tin.

In the midst of their preparations, Harold strolled in. He dipped a finger into the batter and tasted it. "Mmm. That would be . . . carrot cake?" he pretended to guess.

"It's January 1," Carlotta said.

"Ron's birthday. I know."

She followed her husband's eyes to the wrapped present on the table. "I'm sending him a pair of gloves. I know we agreed not to send him money but—"

"I wouldn't have my son freeze to death."

Harold's gentleness surprised Michael.

"You're so mad sometimes, I do wonder." Carlotta said softly.

The phone rang. The Simpsons exchanged glances; instinctively, they knew who was calling. Carlotta moved to pick up the phone.

"Hello? Yes, we'll accept the charges." Carlotta said, her eyes brightening. "Happy birthday, honey. I'm so glad you called."

Harold watched his wife as she spoke into the receiver, cupping it protectively. He worked his jaw, narrowed his eyes, turned and left the room.

After wishing his brother a happy birthday, Michael followed his father outside. He found Harold at the woodpile, where he had dragged the stump and the larger branches of the elm he'd chopped down the spring before. Months ago, he had zipped the trunk into smaller pieces with a chainsaw. Now, he was splitting the remaining pieces into firewood—with a vengeance. He plopped a large chunk of elm onto the stump, then hefted his axe and dealt the wood a fierce blow. He attacked the wood again and again, his face going beet red from the effort. He barely paused in his chopping to acknowledge his youngest son.

Michael steeled himself for the encounter. "Why won't you at least talk to Ron? It's his birthday."

"I don't care what day it is, son. I already told you. I have nothing to say to him 'til he comes home and does what's right." Harold swung at the wood again.

"Don't you think Ron is suffering enough?"

"What about the rest of the family, Michael? You know how some folks around town treat us. This sorry mess is affecting your mother's health."

Harold set down his axe and breathed heavily. "It's my own damn fault for not teaching you boys that there are things in life worth fighting for, things worth protecting."

Like your own children? Michael fumed silently. He'd never in his life wanted so badly to shout at his father. Instead, he said in an icy tone, "Maybe so, Dad, but Vietnam is not one of them." He began to walk away.

"Don't turn your back on me when I'm talking to you." Harold grabbed Michael's shoulder.

"Take your hand off me," Michael said with quiet rage.

Harold moved to spin his son around to face him. But Michael ducked and shoved his father's hand away. Harold tipped backward, lost his balance, and fell heavily against a protruding branch on the stacked wood. Michael froze, watching in horror the grimace of pain on his father's face. The son's eyes filled with tears as Harold heaved himself upright and, clutching his back, gingerly made his way toward the house.

Michael made a beeline for Ron's room, the only place that promised to bring him any comfort. Behind the closed door, he wandered, examining Ron's high school pennants, trophies, and graduation tassel. On one wall was a photo of Ron with Cindy, the girl he'd dated for most of his senior year. Beside it, a photo of Ron and Alex in their Army uniforms. Michael couldn't look at it for long. He turned away, swiping at his eyes with his sleeve, and seated himself at Ron's weight bench. He fingered the cold round metal, then lay down and pressed his palms against the barbell. The weights wouldn't budge. He pressed harder. Nothing.

Michael sighed, defeated. This was the weight Ron used to *warm up*, and Michael couldn't even move it off the stand. Michael felt eyes lingering on him. He turned to find his mother standing in the doorway.

"Michael *Alan* Simpson." She never called him by his full name unless she was upset. "What's wrong with your father?" Carlotta's voice broke in mid-sentence, and she coughed weakly. "He locked the door to take his bath. He hasn't done that once in twenty years of marriage."

Michael couldn't meet his mother's eyes, which was enough to confirm her suspicions.

"If something happened between you two, it would break my heart."

A sob fought its way up Michael's throat, and he choked it back down stubbornly. Anger and embarrassment mingled together to force hot tears out of his eyes. "Dad treats Ron like he's a criminal!" he blurted.

"A lot of people think he *is* a criminal."

"Ron only did what his conscience told him to. Isn't that what you always taught us?"

Carlotta sighed. "Yes, it is. And in time your father will understand that. Your dad comes from a different time. He was taught not to question whether your country was right. That's a hard notion to turn loose of."

"But Ron didn't start this lousy war. Why does Dad have such a chip on his shoulder?"

"Lord knows your father has reason enough. I think he brought more scars home from the war than just the ones on his back." She ran a hand through Michael's hair, then placed a gentle hand to his face. "You look so much like your father when he was young. Guess I got what I wanted."

Michael glanced up, confused. Carlotta smiled at his puzzlement.

"You know your brother favors my side of the family. I love Ron, but, truth is, I wanted another baby after he was born. One that'd look like your father." She smiled wistfully. "At first he didn't warm to the idea. He'd just gotten drafted back into service. That was Korea. He didn't think we could afford another mouth." Her eyes twinkled. "But he came around." She smiled at the memory. "I told Harold it'd be a boy that would look just like him."

"How could you know something like that?"

"Women know things that men don't. Someday, when the right girl comes along, you'll understand."

Michael gazed at his mother. She'd borne the brunt of Ron's desertion, losing friends and her church community. Recently, her failing health had taken away another of her greatest joys in life: her singing.

Carlotta had always enjoyed performing solos and duets with the Minister of Music at church. After news spread about Ron, she was no longer asked to sing. But Carlotta had kept her dignity and continued to lend her angelic voice to Sunday worship. But slowly, as her condition deteriorated, her lilting notes began to quaver.

When her voice gave out, Carlotta had moved from her usual seat in the choir to a pew among the congregation. She sang as best she could, but her voice was reduced to a wheezing whisper. Michael recalled the heartbreaking Sunday when his mother had stopped singing. Carlotta stood, opened the hymnal, and simply looked at the words, her eyes filling with tears. It was as though a light had gone out. Now, standing before her, Michael could see how waxen her complexion had become, how her eyes had begun to sink into their sockets.

Carlotta took his hand and gazed into his eyes. "This family is all we've got left. Our only hope is to hold together. If we don't, we're gonna lose everything. There's not strength in my body to do it alone. Will you help me?"

Michael took a deep breath and let it out slowly. His mother's body may have been failing, but the strength of her heart was still amazing.

"I'll try," he said at last.

Carlotta pulled him to her in a hug. "That's all a mother can ask."

Late that night, Michael was slumped at his desk in his room, textbooks spread in a heap before him, when a knock came on his bedroom door. Harold slipped inside, holding a bottle of rubbing liniment.

"Would you put this on my back? I don't want your mother to see this."

Harold lifted his tee shirt to reveal a broad, plum-colored bruise on the small of his back. In awkward silence, Michael warmed a dollop of lotion between his palms and spread it onto his father's skin.

As he rubbed, Michael's fingertips passed over the knobby edges of scars that crisscrossed his father's back. Michael's hand froze at the unfamiliar texture. Harold stiffened.

"Dad, these scars . . ."

Harold turned abruptly, jerking his shirt down. "What about 'em?"

"You never talk about them, that's all."

Harold stood up as if to make a quick exit.

"Who's turning his back now?" Michael called testily.

Harold paused and turned slowly. He eyed his son. Then, with an almost imperceptible nod, he began to speak.

"When I was an air gunner, our bomber crashed on the far side of an island we were invading. The pilot was killed. The Nips took me prisoner . . ."

Harold moved to the window and stared out into the empty darkness. After a moment, he spoke slowly but firmly.

"They took me to where they were holding other POWs. The Japs had been starving them so they couldn't escape. They told me that if I tried to run, they'd send two guards after me. If the guards came back without my severed head, they'd be killed. I knew I'd never be stronger; if I was gonna escape, it had to be right then. First chance I got, I did. I ran for hours. I collapsed about sundown. I'd lost the guards. I learned later that the Japs executed the other POWs before retreating off the island."

Michael couldn't find his voice for several moments. The idea of anyone doing such a thing to the ironclad Harold Simpson sent chills through him.

Finally, the son choked out, "You never said anything."

"War's not something you dwell on. Wondering why one man lives and another dies—it'll make you crazy."

"How'd you find the courage to run?"

Harold sighed heavily. "It was either run, or submit. I wasn't willing to give them that kind of power over my life. So I ran."

"Doesn't that sound familiar?"

The words hit Harold so hard that Michael almost wished he could have taken them back. His father's eyes registered the blow.

"I'm tired, son," Harold said in a gravelly voice, "I'm going to bed."

As Michael was climbing into Ron's Mustang on his way back to Athens the next morning, his father came outside with a weary look on his face. Neither of them had slept much the night before.

"I'm going hunting next Saturday. I was wondering if you want to come along?"

If not for the talk he'd had with his mother, Michael would have made an excuse—any excuse. Instead, he reluctantly agreed.

When the day of the hunt arrived, much to his surprise, Michael enjoyed himself. Tromping around with his father in the millet fields of rural Georgia, away from the disapproving eyes of the church congregation and their neighbors, Michael felt that, maybe, not quite *all* of his life had fallen apart.

They had been traipsing after Sport and Ramus, the two pointers, since sunrise. His father kept silent for most of the time. Close to noon, the dogs scented their quarry and tracked a covey of quail, which Harold flushed. The birds broke from the undergrowth, flying low and fast. Harold hoisted his 16-gauge shotgun and got off a quick shot, dropping one of the birds out of the air. Once Sport retrieved it, Michael took the bird and handed it to his father. The men seated themselves under a pine tree to rest.

Michael patted the dogs. "Sport and Ramus are looking good."

"They're real healthy. The winter's been so cold that their coats are nice and thick."

A thought sparked in Michael. "You ever notice how Mom wraps herself up in her coat?"

"When she was a young girl, this was during the Depression, her parents bought her a coat for six dollars from Sears." He paused, waiting for his son's full attention. "They got behind on the payments, something like fifty cents a month, and they had to return it." Harold's voice broke off with emotion. "Your mother's a woman who appreciates a coat."

Michael stared at his father. He'd never seen such unguarded tenderness on the Marine's leathery face.

Harold laughed at Michael's expression. "I guess you think I'm just some old slab of granite." He heaved a weighty sigh and gathered his thoughts.

"My country made me a promise once. Back when I volunteered for the Big One. The military said I was fightin' to make sure my sons wouldn't have to." Harold stared off across the field. "I've been thinkin' 'bout that promise a lot lately. It's made me realize nobody has all the right answers. Not my country and not me."

They both stood up and walked along in silence across the field back toward the dirt road.

"I told Ron before he joined that he didn't have to die in Vietnam to be my son," Harold said in a measured tone when they reach the pickup truck. "I meant it."

Harold carefully unloaded his shotgun. "Like I've said from the get-go, Ron's gotta come back and do what's right." He placed the red shells in his vest pocket. "But if he'll do that . . . if he'll come home . . . I'll stand with him, shoulder to shoulder. Father and son. And I'll do everything I can to help him. That's my promise."

For the first time in months, Michael was able to ride beside his father without feeling like tension had squeezed all the air out of his lungs.

When they pulled in the driveway, Michael volunteered to feed the dogs.

"I'll go see what your mother's got planned for supper, then clean the quail," his dad said before disappearing into the house.

Michael was leading Sport and Ramus out to the pen behind the house, thinking of how he'd break the good news to Ron the next time he called, when he heard the back door slam.

"Michael, get in here quick!" his father cried in a strangled voice.

～

An hour later, Harold and Michael, still in hunting clothes, sat waiting in gloomy silence outside the emergency room at the county hospital. Michael couldn't shake away the image that had met his eyes when he'd raced inside the house: *his mother passed out on the rug, her outstretched arm fallen inches short of the phone she'd tried to reach.*

She had barely stirred through the frantic journey to the hospital. Michael had sat in the car's backseat with his mother, cradling her head in his lap. Most of that time, he hadn't been sure she was even breathing. At the emergency room, the staff had immediately taken her away, leaving them to wait, wonder, and worry.

After what seemed like hours, Carlotta's physician, Dr. Edwards, approached the Simpsons, his eyes full of concern.

"We've done all we can do. For now, it's just wait and see. Why don't you go on home and get some rest? There's nothing you can do here."

"I'm not leaving my wife," Harold said. Then he turned to Michael. "I could use a change of clothes, though."

"I'll take care of it," Michael volunteered. "Mom needs her things anyway."

"Bring her light blue housecoat. That's her favorite."

～

Michael was at home, packing his mother's things and trying vainly to iron her favorite pair of pajamas, when the phone rang.

"How's my bro?" came Ron's voice, surprisingly strong. Michael couldn't remember his brother sounding this good. It was the first time Ron hadn't called collect since he arrived in Canada. Something must have changed.

"Ron, oh man. I'm glad you phoned."

Before Michael could explain, Ron's news gushed out like water flooding over a riverbank. He had gotten a job washing dishes—not a great job but at least it was indoors—and he had a woman in his life, someone who loved him. And her young daughter had become the light in his eyes. Ron had even managed to save a little money. He felt at peace for the first time in a very long while.

"You gotta come home," Michael managed to wedge in as Ron paused to catch his breath.

"Aren't you listening?" Ron said, so lost in his own good feelings that he didn't understand the sadness in his brother's voice. "I finally have a life here, little bro. I thought you'd be happy for me."

"Mom's in a real bad way."

The line went silent. "What do you mean?"

"She hasn't been well since you left."

"Why didn't you tell me this before?"

"Mom didn't want you to worry. But now she's in the hospital."

There was a long silence.

"If I come back, I'm going to prison. For years. And it's not county lockup. It's a maximum-security military prison."

"If you wanna see Mom alive, you need to come home," Michael persisted, his voice rimmed with panic.

"Do you understand what you're asking, bro?"

"I'm asking you to help our mother."

"I finally have a chance for a life here in Canada." Ron's voice seethed with emotion. "And you want me to throw that all away?"

"You've gotta come home. If you don't—"

"I gotta go," Ron said, cutting him off. "Take care of yourself."

The phone line went dead. To the empty receiver, Michael said softly, "Mama might die."

Chapter 57

The Truce
June 29, 1864

TWO DAYS AFTER THE battle, the human carnage was putrefying. On the hillside between the entrenched armies, the corpses of hundreds of Union soldiers were now bloated and rancid. Many of the bodies still leaned against the rebel breastworks where they had fallen, frozen in fearful death poses that seemed to mock the living. In the searing sun, the odor of human decay was so nauseating that the Confederates in the trenches were unable to eat.

Through the constant threat of sharpshooters, the ragged army in gray had stubbornly refused to yield. Brute force and repeated cannon bombardments had not dislodged them. But none of them knew how much longer they could withstand this profane assault on their senses and spirits. The stench of death was slowly beating the rebels.

Fighting through the throbbing pain and dizziness caused by his head wound, Baylis wondered if he had descended into purgatory. Staring bleakly through the slits between the headlogs, he could see the young Union soldier that had died on the breastworks in front of him, his corpse now as dark as a Negro. Maggots were swarming out of his mouth.

Perhaps I've died, and this is my punishment, Baylis thought. *I'll spend eternity staring at that corpse.*

In the few days since joining this war, Baylis had seen senseless death of such a magnitude that he had gone morally numb.

Finally, he had enough.

He stood and ripped a large white cloth and held it in his hand. He began to climb over the breastworks.

Ulysses was slow to realize what his father was doing. And by the time he did, it was already too late. Baylis had climbed over the breastworks, waving the white flag as he went. Ulysses started after him, but was forcefully restrained by Colquitt and Thomas. As he struggled against them, Colquitt tried to reason with him.

"You can't save your Pa. You'll just get yourself killed."

"What the hell is that soldier doing?" a rebel officer shouted, seeing Baylis outside the defensive berm.

"Shoot the deserter," a private down the line yelled.

It seemed for a moment that the Union sharpshooters would do the job for them. *Thump. Thump. Thump.* Bullets thudded into the breastworks around Baylis, but he would not be dissuaded from his task.

He carefully pulled the young soldier's body off the front of the breastworks and laid the corpse gently on the ground.

Then he began to dig.

Reverential silence fell on both sides of the line as it became clear Baylis wasn't deserting or insane. The old man was simply doing the only right thing he knew to do. He was trying to give a fallen soldier his dignity. After a moment, a flag of truce went up on the Yankee side. A Union officer appeared and stepped gingerly through the corpses toward the middle ground. A Confederate officer crawled over the breastworks and met him there. After a brief conversation, a truce was arranged to allow for the interment of the dead.

It was agreed that the burial parties would be unarmed. The corpses were too bloated and decomposed to be moved from the field of battle, so they would be buried where they lay on the field and marked with each man's name and regiment. Weapons of the Union soldiers were to remain on the field or be buried with them.

To begin the ceasefire, a line of armed Federals walked toward the Confederate entrenchments, then turned and sat down facing the Union line. The rebels mirrored the Yankees, sending out guards with rifles to sit facing their own men with their backs to the bluecoats. Then the two armies sent out burial parties to deal with the dead.

As Baylis struggled to pull the body of the Union soldier into the shallow grave he had dug, a gaunt Yankee came and silently helped to lift the dead man's shoulders. After they had placed the body in the ground, the soldier in blue paused, staring down with mournful eyes.

"That's my younger brother," he said barely above a whisper. "I promised Mama I would watch out for him. I seen him when he fell."

"If you want to say words, I'll listen," Baylis said quietly.

"I'm not good with words, but I reckon I should say something," the soldier said. He stared down at the blackened face of his brother. "Damn you, Earl, you had to go and get your fool self killed. Now who's going to help milk the cows and feed the chickens and help with the harvest? Who's going to . . ." His eyes filled with tears.

The Yankee picked up a handful of soil and tossed it onto his brother's body. The two men began to push dirt over the body.

"We're from Illinois," the Yankee said as they moved the earth. "Me and Earl, we got ourselves a farm. I sure miss home. I rightly do. Where you from?"

"You're standing on it," Baylis answered simply. "And I sure miss home, too."

The Yankee's eyes said he understood. Having finished, the Yankee offered his hand. Baylis shook it.

"Thank you for doing what you did. I wish you luck, mister." The Yankee turned away.

Ulysses stepped over to Baylis. "You almost got yourself shot. For a moment there, I wasn't sure which side was going to do it, though. You're a lucky man, Pa."

"Or a damn fool."

Around them, the two armies were now mixing freely. Whiskey and newspapers were being swapped, and Union coffee traded for rebel tobacco.

They were drinking from each other's canteens and laughing at each other's jokes. Two sturdy soldiers, one from each army, had started a good-natured wrestling match as men from both sides playfully urged them on. Baylis could see many of the grey and blue soldiers were talking as though they were the best of friends. And he knew they probably would have been under saner circumstances.

After several hours, the burying was finished. The soldiers said their good-byes to those on the other side and retreated to their trenches. Then the grey and blue guards stood and moved back to their respective lines without looking over their shoulders. Soon rifles were seized from the stacks, and the two lines begin to fire furiously at each other, trying once again to maim, kill, and cripple the enemy.

What an odd thing war is, Baylis thought, as he loaded his rifle, sighted down the barrel, and fired.

Very odd, indeed.

Chapter 58

February 1971

RON SIMPSON VIVIDLY REMEMBERED the night he and Alex had spent in the Jonesboro jail. The idea of spending the next several years of his life in such circumstances—or worse—sent a chill through the deepest part of his soul. He had heard stories about "Leavenworth Max." The military's only maximum-security prison housed rapists and murderers who also happened to be professionally trained killers. It was known as one of the most dangerous prisons in the world.

Ron had only one choice: *He could not, and would not, permit his mother to die if his presence might help her. If it meant sacrificing his new life with Vicki and Kimmy, or even going to military prison, it was the only choice he could live with.*

But if he was going home, he was determined to do it the right way. He wouldn't sneak back into his country the way he had left it. He would do it looking people in the eye, standing straight with his warrant officer's uniform on. He was through running, and he was through being afraid. He'd looked over his shoulder enough.

The landlord was still holding his uniform and his few meager processions against the back rent he owed. He hadn't gone back to the flophouse since he was evicted. He had assumed he would never need the uniform again, and the place held nothing else but bad memories.

How to pay the back rent? The money he had saved was barely enough to cover a bus ticket home. The only other thing of value he had left was hanging around his neck. The gold cross and chain he had been given by his parents, the symbol of faith that had helped him though many dark nights.

But if that was what had to be done . . .

Arriving at the flophouse an hour later, Ron offered his cross and chain to the landlord in exchange for his Army uniform and duffel bag. The portly man obliged and dug Ron's belongings out of a storage locker in the basement. The uniform was dusty and the brass was tarnished, but otherwise it was in fine shape. Ron spent the afternoon carefully cleaning his uniform by hand, then had his hair cut to military regulations. Then a showered and shaven Ron Simpson, dressed in his Army uniform that no longer fit, knocked at the back door of the Rainbow Café. At the sight, Vicki fell into his arms, sobbing.

He spent the evening with her and read *Green Eggs and Ham* to Kimmy one last time before they left for the bus station.

"I wish you two would come with me," Ron said to Vicki as they waited.

"I can't," her eyes brimmed with tears. "My life's here. And your country, I could never live down there. It's already taken one man I love away . . ."

Ron understood. He kissed Kimberly on the forehead, then pulled Vicki close. He owed her so much. She had helped him regain his health, his life, his dignity. He knew he might never see her again. He closed his eyes and tried to hold the moment, her scent, the feel of her body close to his, to etch it in his memory.

"I love you," he said to her.

She kissed him a kiss to last a lifetime. "Good-bye soldier boy." She turned, took her daughter's hand, and pushed through the bus station.

Early-blooming yellow crocuses were breaking through a crust of snow when Ron Simpson presented himself to U.S. Customs at the Canadian border. The befuddled customs officer glanced at Ron, squinted hard at his Army ID, and looked back at his ill-fitting uniform. Something wasn't adding up.

"Your Army ID's expired. This is the only identification you have?"

"Yes sir." Ron could tell that the officer suspected that he was a deserter.

"No driver's license or passport?"

"No sir."

"You say you're going home?"

"Yes sir, to Georgia."

The customs officer studied Ron, scratching his chin as he weighed a hard decision. "I have a boy of my own about your age," he said, handing back the ID. "I hope you're coming back home to do the right thing, son."

"Yes, sir. I am."

Chapter 59

The Kennesaw Line
July 1, 1864

THICK CLOUDS SHROUDED THE moon and stars as the Confederate Army quietly began its withdrawal from the mountain. After five days, the Battle of Kennesaw was finally over.

Under the mantle of darkness, rebel cavalry slipped into position along the line, making noise and tending fires to distract the enemy as the last regiments pulled off the salient that survivors were already calling the "devil's elbow" and "the dead angle." Baylis looked one last time across the hill, sanctified by the blood sacrifice of so many ordinary heroes. He knew no man who had endured it would ever forget what had happened when "hell came to Georgia," as one soldier put it.

"They're pulling our company out of the ditches," said Ulysses, his voice full of weariness. "Sergeant Tedford wants you to join with the wounded that can walk. They're forming up in the rear."

Baylis didn't want to worry his son further, but he was still grievously ill from the head wound. His vision was blurry, his balance unsteady, and he could barely hold his rations down.

"You go on ahead," Baylis said. "There's something I need to do first."

"Don't be long." Ulysses placed his hand on his father's shoulder, then turned away.

Baylis felt in his coat pocket and pulled out the letter that his daughter Sarah had written to her husband before William's death. The old man had carried it with him for months, uncertain what he should do with it.

Now, at last, he knew.

He could think of no better final resting place for these words than this dying ground. Baylis knelt and began to dig in the earth. He placed the letter in the hole, said a silent prayer, and covered it with dirt.

Moving down the hillside trail in the darkness, Baylis could only see a few stragglers in front of him. The walking wounded had set a quicker pace than he expected. Perhaps if he cut down the hill's slope, he would be able to catch up.

Suddenly, his legs gave way, and he was rolling down the knoll. A large tree rose before him. It was the last thing he remembered before he was enveloped in a nauseous darkness.

Baylis wasn't sure how long he had been unconscious, but as he eased himself up, he could see the first light of dawn low in the east. He must have been out for hours. The gash in his head was bleeding again. Somewhere in his tumble, he had lost his rifle. He was unarmed.

Baylis tried to make sense of where he was. He could tell from the sun that he was at the bottom of the hill behind the Kennesaw line. But which way had the rebel army retreated? He quickly discovered he wouldn't need the answer to that question.

"Don't move," came the loud command.

Baylis did as he was told.

"Put your hands up where I can see them, and turn around slowly."

Baylis shuffled around to come face-to-face with two Federal soldiers holding repeater rifles. They herded him out of the field at bayonet point onto a dirt road where a company of mounted Union Cavalry was waiting. Behind them, a motley group of grey-clad prisoners was tied together under guard.

"Found another straggler," one of the soldiers shouted, pushing Baylis forward with the butt of his rifle.

"Put him with the other crackers, and mount up," a Yankee lieutenant with a nasty scar on his cheek said.

The soldiers tied Baylis into the prisoner line. The officer pulled on the reins and turned his horse to face the captured rebels.

"Any man who tries to escape will be shot," the lieutenant barked loudly. "And any man who helps him will be shot." He nodded to a burly sergeant beside him.

"Move 'em out," the sergeant commanded.

The prisoners were pulled forward. As the rebels began to move, Baylis tried to steady himself enough to walk. The men around him stared bleakly ahead or at the ground. Several were injured or sick. They all looked spent and defeated.

After walking for what seemed like hours, Baylis saw that they were approaching the outskirts of Marietta. He could hear the sounds of people singing "Amazing Grace" from inside a wooden church just ahead.

The prisoners were ordered to stop. The lieutenant motioned, and dozens of Union cavalry dismounted and stormed into the house of worship. The hymn came to an abrupt halt. Baylis heard screams and shouting from inside the building, then the sounds of scuffling.

Moments later, the soldiers began forcing the congregation outside, dragging and beating those unwilling to go or slow to respond. Nearly all the people herded out the door were women, children, and the elderly. The young boys and old men were separated from the others, who were freed.

Baylis saw a well-dressed man ride up in a buggy and approach the scar-faced Yankee lieutenant. They spoke briefly, then the civilian turned and began pointing out certain men from the captured congregation. Baylis could see the man's face: *it was Henry Cole.*

Cole stopped in front of a man whom Baylis recognized. It was Milton Milton. The teacher was talking to the union officer and shaking his head in protest. A Federal soldier jerked Milton's knapsack away from him, turned it upside down, and dumped the contents out. Two Confederate uniforms and officer braids tumbled onto the ground. It was the garb Baylis and Ulysses had returned to him.

The soldier struck Milton a savage blow in the face with his rifle butt, knocking him to the ground, dazed and bleeding. The men and boys that Cole had selected were tied to the rope line. Baylis was able to catch Milton's eye before the professor was shoved to the end of the line. The cavalry turned their prisoners over to a Union guard detail, and soon the line was moving again.

By the time the prisoners arrived at the Georgia Military Institute, the grounds were already overflowing with incarcerated rebel soldiers. Baylis and the other captured men were untied and herded into a stockade that had been built in the center of the grounds. It looked as if more than a thousand prisoners were being held there.

Baylis worked his way over to Milton, who was standing in the shade under a large oak. The teacher's face was badly bruised from the beating, and his lip was split.

"I fear that your kindness in providing me and my son clean clothes has caused you great misfortune."

"I would not say such a thing," Milton managed through his busted lip.

"Surely you were taken captive because of the uniforms," Baylis insisted. "I'm sorry."

"They would have taken me anyway, kind sir. Henry Cole accused me of helping the rebels." Milton smiled weakly. "I told them if notifying the next of kin of a loved one's death is assisting the Confederate Army, then I am guilty."

Milton looked at Baylis more closely. "You don't look well yourself. You've been wounded."

Baylis nodded. "On the Kennesaw Line."

"I heard that the fighting was most fierce."

"That'd be God's truth."

A sudden commotion in the stockade caught their attention. Prisoners were jostling each other, trying to see something outside the compound. Baylis and Milton pushed their way toward the fence, where they found Captain Jeffers, who had also been captured. Jeffers quickly greeted them, and then turned his attention back to an ambulance stopped near the gate.

Baylis saw a young Union soldier on a stretcher beside the wagon. He had been shot and his throat slashed. There was a crude, handwritten sign hung around the neck of the corpse.

"Can you read that sign?" Jeffers asked. "My eyes are no longer sharp in the distance."

Baylis tried to make out the sign but failed. "My vision ain't been clear since I was wounded."

Milton squinted. "Oh, dear. 'Death to foragers,' it reads."

"He must be a bummer caught stealing from some farm," Baylis said.

"Serves him right," Jeffers snapped. "The Union Army pilfers without regard to the misery it causes. They leave our widows and orphans to starve."

A group of Yankee soldiers rode up on horseback to where the ambulance was stopped. A thin-framed officer with disheveled red hair and piercing eyes looked at the body of the Yankee soldier.

"I do believe that to be Sherman," Milton said. "I have seen a photograph of him."

As Baylis watched, General Sherman turned to a heavyset Union major and spoke briskly. The major gestured, and Yankee soldiers quickly placed the body inside the canvas-covered wagon. Sherman peered over to the stockade, then made another brief comment, his craggy, bearded face animated with harsh emotion. There was another heated exchange between the two officers. Then Sherman spurred his horse away at a gallop, with his staff in pursuit.

The Union major and a detail of guards stepped over to the compound where the prisoners were being held.

"I'm Major Dilworth. I'm in command of this stockade," the officer said loudly. "You are to be sent north by train to prison, where you will be held until war's end. Before we transfer you, for the death of a Union soldier at the hands of rebel partisans, General Sherman has ordered that one man among you be executed."

Strident discontent rippled through the prisoners.

"What justice is that?" one Confederate shouted loudly over the den.

"You would take the life of an innocent for the crime of another?" another yelled.

"Sherman is a coward who commands thieves," a man hollered from the back.

Dilworth motioned, and the guards fired their rifles into the air above the prisoners. The commotion quickly dissipated.

"Any more talk like that, and the next volley won't be over your heads," Dilworth said forcefully.

A bluecoat soldier holding a hat moved to stand beside the major.

"This soldier will pass among you. Any man who tries to harm him will be shot without warning. He will choose one hundred prisoners to take a lot from his hat. The man who draws the mark will be executed."

A line of armed guards moved to the fence, rifles at the ready. The gate was opened, and the Yankee soldier stepped inside the corral. He held the hat up high, so that no one could see inside it, and began to randomly select prisoners. Each man designated took his chance, some reluctantly, others with only misery in their eyes. A few stepped forward, defiantly and without hesitation, and reached into the hat. One by one, relief passed over the men's faces. No one had yet chosen the cursed paper.

When the guard came to Baylis, the old man looked the soldier square in the eyes and chose his fate. He looked at this paper. It was blank.

Captain Jeffers followed. He glanced at his lot, which was also blank. He crumpled the paper, threw it on the ground, then spat defiantly at the Yankee soldier's boots.

The soldier chose Milton next. The teacher, taking silent succor from his comrades, slid his hand into the soldier's cap and pulled out a slip. He stared at it without emotion before quietly handing the paper to the soldier. The Yankee glanced at it, then gazed at Milton as if looking at a dead man. He was: Milton's scrap had a large black X marked on it.

"I've never been a man to make a wager," Milton said with a gallows smile. "Never was very lucky when it came to games of chance."

The soldier took Milton by the arm and began to move him away. Baylis reached out to stop him.

"Sir, I wish to volunteer in his stead," Baylis said.

The guard stopped. "You're asking to take the place of a man who will be executed?"

"Yes sir, I am. This gentleman was brought here through no fault of his own other than kindness of spirit. He was arrested because he had

Confederate uniforms that belonged to me and my son."

Captain Jeffers stepped forward and looked at the guard.

"Sir, I am a captain in the Army of Tennessee. I have Yankee blood on my hands and am proud of it. I would kill you now if given the chance. Would it not be better to take my life than that of a man whose only sin is compassion for others?"

"Kind sirs," Milton said, "I can't allow either of you to make such a sacrifice."

"The man isn't even American," Jeffers protested. "He's an Englishman."

The guard thought about it. "The three of you follow me. I'll let the major sort this out."

The Federal soldier held Milton's arm firmly and pushed through the prisoners toward the gate. Baylis and Jeffers trailed in their wake. Once outside the stockade, the three men were brought before Major Dilworth.

"I will accept one of your lives in substitution for this man's, but only with his consent," Dilworth said after each man made his case.

Baylis turned to Milton. "Sir, I ask you again to allow me to stand for you."

"I cannot. You have a family and children."

"As do you," Jeffers said to Milton. "But I am nothing more than a one-armed widower who has lost his only son. I'm dying of consumption. I humbly beseech you—allow me to take your place."

Milton sighed deeply, his eyes moist.

"I am touched by your friendship and courage. But my life, as it has always been, is in God's hands. I accept what He offers me. I must ask that both of you do also."

Baylis knew then he could not change Milton's mind. He nodded reluctantly and stepped aside.

Jeffers turned to Major Dilworth. "What manner of coward are you to execute an innocent man? Have you no shame?"

The major's face filled with rage. "You sir, know nothing about me. But I know that you are a one-armed buffoon. And if you call me a coward again, I shall pistol-whip you, then personally relieve you of the continued use of your remaining arm."

Dilworth's eyes narrowed, and his voice dropped. "When General Sherman gave me this order, I refused to carry it out until threatened with court-martial. I consider it unlawful and unjust. But if I do not obey, another officer will finish the job in my place."

"And so, sir, like Pilate, you choose to wash your hands." Jeffers's voice spilled over with anger. "If you aren't a coward, then, pray tell, what might you be?"

"An officer of the United States Army doing my duty to God and country." Major Dilworth turned to a master sergeant. "Escort the prisoner to the firing line."

As Baylis and Jeffers watched helplessly, Milton was taken over to a tree, where a firing squad stood at attention.

Dilworth approached Milton. "Sir, if you have any last words, you may speak them now."

Milton cleared his throat, and then spoke evenly so that all could hear him. "I'm a God-fearing Christian, a devoted husband, and a doting father of five lovely daughters. I have never fired a weapon in anger." His voice faltered, and he paused to gather his words. "I came to your country for the opportunity to teach. I have watched with sadness over these last years as your great nation has torn itself apart. I wish only peace for your people."

Milton looked kindly at the firing squad, then at Dilworth. "I hold no anger in my heart toward you or your men."

The soldiers in the firing squad were now blinking back tears. Many looked away, full of humiliation.

"Order in the ranks," the master sergeant commanded.

"Do you wish a blindfold?" Dilworth asked.

"Thank you, but I do not. I willingly accept the fate my Lord gives me, kind sir."

Dilworth took a handkerchief out of his pocket and handed it to Milton. "Hold this, and when you are ready, drop it." He stepped back to the firing line beside the master sergeant. "Instruct the men to aim sharply. Do not let this poor soul suffer."

The master sergeant nodded and moved to the squad, spoke in hushed tones, then stepped back. "Present arms," the sergeant commanded briskly. "Aim."

Silence fell across the stockade. Prisoners and Yankee soldiers watched, transfixed by the white cloth the teacher held. Milton stared toward the heavens, let out a deep breath and relaxed his hand, gently releasing the handkerchief. Instantly, a flurry of bullets pierced his body. He slumped to the ground, dead before he hit. Blood flowed from the multiple wounds, staining the ground around his body pasty red.

In the stillness that followed, every man looked to his soul and found only shame.

Chapter 60

February 1971

HAROLD HAD HARDLY LEFT his wife's side since she'd been admitted to the hospital. He'd spent three fretful nights on the cot the nurses had kindly arranged for him in the corner of Carlotta's intensive care station. It exhausted Michael to think of the round-the-clock vigil his father had kept. Carlotta, who had drifted in and out of a coma, showed no signs that she even knew her husband was with her, or that relatives and a smattering of family friends had come by to offer solace and emotional support.

At Harold's insistence, Michael had driven each day to classes in Athens. But the son always joined his father again in the late afternoons, when the doctors made their rounds. Each day, Harold and Michael were gently shooed from the intensive care unit by the nurses. Father and son would sit with thousand-yard stares on hard vinyl seats in the adjoining waiting room, where they could still observe Carlotta through the plate glass. After a few minutes, the doctor would bring them the report, shaking his head. Every time, the news grew more grim.

Tonight, when Dr. Edwards walked in, a second doctor accompanied him. From their expressions, Harold and Michael immediately knew that it was time to prepare themselves for the worst.

"Harold, this here's Dr. O'Brien. He's a specialist in internal medicine."

"Mr. Simpson, your wife's not responding to treatment," O'Brien said bleakly. "Her condition has worsened. Her lungs are filling with fluid. The prognosis is not good."

Harold put his head in his hands. Dr. Edwards placed a hand on the marine's powerful shoulder. "Harold, if you and your boy want to say your goodbyes . . . she probably won't be able to respond, but she'll know you're there."

Harold gestured to Michael to go first. Numbly, Michael rose. *Was he really about to speak to his mother for the last time?* He entered Carlotta's curtained station and knelt beside her bed. The oxygen mask gave her face an odd, pinched look. Her eyes were closed.

He took her hand and squeezed it. Her eyes flickered open, and rested on him momentarily. She tried to squeeze back, but the effort was too much. Michael could not bring himself to tell her goodbye. It was too much like giving her permission to leave. He fought to hold back his tears, and lost.

After a moment, Harold stepped in the curtained cubicle and placed a gentle hand on his son's shoulders. Michael moved outside to give his father some privacy, but he continued to stare through the plate glass. He saw his father bend over her to touch her face, speaking to her softly.

Then Michael sat up, blinked, and rubbed his eyes. Beside his father, there appeared a ghostly, translucent image of Ron. It took Michael a befuddled moment to realize that he was seeing Ron's reflection in the glass. He turned to find his brother, in the flesh, standing just outside the door of the waiting room.

Ron let himself in, and Michael enveloped him in a hug. He was startled at Ron's emaciated form, the bony angles he could feel protruding sharply from his uniform. But there was no time to comment. Michael solemnly led his brother into the intensive care unit.

The moment he laid eyes on his eldest son, Harold Simpson stood up stiffly, staring in disbelief. They exchanged a long look, somehow saying more than they could have managed with mere words. Then Harold spoke in an awkward, croaking voice, "Welcome home, son."

"Dad, I—" Ron began.

"There'll be time enough for speaking our regrets," Harold said quietly. "You need to be with your mother right now."

Harold put a hand on Michael's shoulder and led him from the room while Ron knelt before his mother's motionless form, kissed her forehead, and took her hand.

As he sat on the vinyl seat outside the unit, Michael could hear Ron weeping softly at his mother's bedside: "Mom, I'm home. Can you hear me? I'm home..."

~~~

Ron's presence didn't make it any easier to sit at the hospital hour after hour on Carlotta Simpson's deathwatch, but at least her family was together again. And as they sat in the stiff, tender silence of grief, they talked out their differences, delicately, courteously. The rift in the Simpson family slowly began to knit itself back together. But there could be no talk of moving on, no thoughts of what came next; not while the woman they all loved lay dying before them. For now, the future was a forbidden subject.

Dr. O'Brien and Dr. Edwards came on rounds again in the morning to find the three Simpsons still on watch outside the unit, slumped and half asleep. Carlotta still clung to life, but her vital signs had deteriorated further.

Michael rose and listened in on what the doctors had to say about his mother.

Dr. O'Brien was shaking his head in bewilderment. "A battery of tests, every possible drug therapy. Nothing works. I'm stumped."

Dr. Edwards looked up abruptly from his chart. "There's one thing we haven't tried: taking her off all medication."

"We do that, she'll die." Dr. O'Brien whispered hoarsely.

"She *is* dying." Edwards insisted. "We've pumped so many chemicals in her it's like a voodoo cocktail. It's impossible to know what's doing what. I say we take her off everything. We have nothing to lose."

The two doctors looked at each other, weighing the risks. Then Dr. Edwards called to the ICU station nurse, "Take this woman off all medication."

The Simpsons received the decision helplessly. *If they were losing her anyway . . .*

The three men sat in tense silence as the I.V. was unhooked from Carlotta's arm and wheeled away. They braced themselves for the worst. An hour went by, then another. The next thing Michael knew, Ron was shaking him awake. Michael shot upright. "Mom gone?"

"She's still with us, little bro. The doctors say she's doing some better."

By evening, Carlotta's vital signs had stabilized. "It's amazing," Dr. Edwards told the relieved family. "Our best guess is that she's allergic to antihistamines. The very thing we gave her to help her breathe almost killed her. If there's no further complications, she should be able to go home in a day or two."

Harold Simpson was making a disaster of Carlotta's kitchen, although what he was trying to make was breakfast. Michael watched in amusement as the oatmeal bubbled over, the toast burned, and the scrambled eggs turned green in the overheated pan.

Ron entered from his mother's bedroom, bearing a mostly empty meal tray. "Mom sure looks a lot better. She wants to go to church tomorrow. You believe that?"

Michael shook his head sadly. "Church is the last place you'll wanna go."

"Why's that?"

"Some people there treat us like lepers. I mean, not our real friends but others do."

"I think some folks at church just didn't know what to say to us," Harold reasoned.

Ron sighed. "I'm going anyway. I wanna see Mrs. Granger."

Harold's eyes dimmed. "Ginger doesn't go to church anymore, son. Not since Alex . . ."

With the mention of his best friend's name, Ron glanced away, the pain coming back to him full-force.

"You need to lay low anyhow," Harold added. "You can't afford to draw attention until you turn yourself in."

Ron shook his head. "No. I'm tired of living that way. All I've been doing is running and hiding. I made a decision when I came back. That's over."

~

On Sunday morning, Ron Simpson slid behind the wheel of his Mustang for the first time in what seemed like years. He passed his hands over the leather steering-wheel cover and inhaled the mechanic's favorite perfume of oil, vinyl, rubber, and grease.

He drove to the Granger's house, marveling at how oddly unfamiliar the streets he'd known all his life now seemed.

When Ron pulled up in front of Alex's house, the sight that met his eyes caused him to swear softly under his breath. The house he'd considered a second home now stood shuttered and blind to the street. The grass that Alex once mowed—as seldom as possible—had been choked out by tall, spiky weeds. Alex's Plymouth Fury still stood on blocks in the garage, gray with dust. The place was quiet, eerie.

Ron knocked on the front door. No one answered. He knocked again, and stood waiting with a sinking sensation in his heart. Finally, as the church's bells began to ring, calling the faithful to service, Ron gave up and turned back to the Mustang.

But as he drove away, he thought he saw a curtain flutter behind one of the darkened windows. He almost imagined that he saw Ginger, unkempt and in her housecoat, peering wistfully after him.

~

When Harold, Carlotta, Ron, and Michael stepped into the church, they were greeted by looks of surprise and stony glares. In what had become habit, Carlotta and Michael bowed their heads and refused to meet anyone's eyes. Harold simply ignored the congregation's coldness as he helped his still-weak wife to a pew. But Ron returned their gazes directly, one by one, until they all looked away.

As Reverend Fletcher entered, the choir and congregation began to sing, *"Have you been to Jesus with the cleansing power? Are you washed in the blood of the Lamb?"*

Ron, glancing about, did a double take: *Ginger Granger had just entered at the back of the church.*

As she made her way up the aisle toward the front, the congregation turned to stare. First, just a few noticed her. Then more people did, until finally most everyone in the worship service was watching, riveted by the sight. The singing faltered as Ginger shambled quietly toward the Simpsons. The woman who had not been to church since her son's death had picked the day the deserter showed up to return. It couldn't be mere coincidence.

Ginger slipped into the pew beside Carlotta and her family, nodded a gentle smile, then took up one side of Carlotta's hymnal. The women exchanged a dewy look, and began singing together, *"Lay aside the garments stained with sin, and be washed in the blood of the Lamb . . ."*

Ginger's heartfelt act was not lost on anyone in the chapel. With one gracious gesture, she had challenged the congregation to again accept the Simpsons into the fellowship of Christ and His church.

When Reverend Fletcher stepped to the pulpit after the song had ended, his gaze rested on Ron. The pastor glanced down at the sermon he'd prepared, then pushed it aside. Other words were stirring in him. The worshipers waited in silence as the preacher opened his Bible, thumbing through it until he found what he was searching for.

"God carries my heart this morning to Luke, chapter fifteen: *'A certain man had two sons . . .'"*

With that, Reverend Fletcher began to recount the tale of the Prodigal Son who journeyed "into a far country." The congregation grew listless and agitated: some dropped their eyes in contemplative shame, while others cleared their throats nervously, casting furtive glances.

Reverend Fletcher continued, *"When he came to his senses, he said 'I will go back to my father,' so he returned home. The son said to him, 'Father, I have sinned against heaven and against you. I am no longer worthy to be called your son.' But the father said to his servants, 'Quick! Bring the best robe and put it on him. Put a ring on his finger and sandals on his feet . . . Let us have a feast and celebrate. For this son of mine was dead and is alive again; he was lost and is found.'"*

Reverend Fletcher closed the Bible quietly, let his eyes linger on the silent congregation, and said, "Let us pray..."

～

When the service ended and the congregation rose to leave, Ginger took both of Ron's hands and held them warmly.

"I'm glad you're home," she said, giving him in a hug.

Bobbie Mae Turner paused at the end of the pew. "Ginger, I'm so glad to see you back in the Lord's house," she said, pointedly ignoring the Simpsons.

"It's good to be back," Ginger replied.

The woman started to turn away, but Ginger placed a hand on her arm. "Bobbie Mae, I believe you know Carlotta."

Bobbie Mae went stiff. "Oh, yes, of course," she said, with a honeycomb smile full of sting. "How are you, Carlotta?"

"Fine, thank you, Bobbie Mae."

"... And their son, Ron." Ginger directed, "He's home. Won't you say hello?"

With a hangdog look, Bobbie Mae said, "Ron. Hi." She offered her hand coolly, and then made a quick exit.

Ginger took Carlotta's arm and led the family outside to where the rest of the congregation mingled. Slowly, hesitantly, church members approached them. In fumbled words and tremulous smiles, the ice began to break.

Chapter 61

February 1971

THE QUAKERS WAR RESISTERS Office across from Atlanta's Piedmont Park was nearly the same as the one in Ottawa, but instead of Gothic architecture, this stateside branch operated out of a modest two-story converted Colonial. The same antiwar posters were hung on the walls, the same hushed, furtive murmurs of desperate work being accomplished.

The two men across the desk from Harold and Ron looked as though they'd come straight from a comedy sketch. The first, a lanky youth, exchanged suspicious glances with Harold, who couldn't take his eyes off the young man's ponytail. The second, a doughy man in a secondhand business suit, talked animatedly with his hands while mashing a cigar between his teeth.

"You were right to contact us first," said the ponytailed man, who struck Ron as the kind of person who would paint stripes on a horse and call it a zebra.

"We checked around, and as near as we can determine, you're the first volunteer warrant officer to desert during Vietnam as a conscientious objector," the man in the ill-fitting suit said, wagging one emphatic finger in the air. "We figure we can generate a lot of publicity on this. Get the media there when you turn yourself in."

"It'll be like drawing bees to honeysuckle," the younger man affirmed. "Media from all over the world are in Georgia covering the Calley trial. It should be easy to get their attention."

"We'll get you a high-profile ACLU lawyer," said the older man, reaching for a telephone.

Harold shot a look to Ron.

"Me and my son need to talk this over," he said curtly, sending a signal that the meeting was over.

"If you call that much attention to yourself, you'll back the military in a corner," Harold said as they headed down the steps toward their car. "I know how they think. They'll just come down on you harder."

Ron looked away despondently, wondering if his fate had already slipped from his hands. "Maybe I should just turn myself in quietly and take what's coming to me."

Harold slid behind the wheel of the forest green Ford and thumped the dash lightly with a fist to help himself think. Then an idea came to him. "Reverend Fletcher once offered to help. I'd say now's the time to take him up on the offer."

The man Reverend Fletcher had in mind wasn't the kind of old boy you'd want to take along on a fishing trip. His florid face carried an edgy tension that quickly infected his clients. After a few moments in his presence, even the most placid individuals found themselves chewing on an eraser or obsessively checking their watch. But Jack Redwald's record as a defense lawyer was almost unparalleled.

The next morning, Harold and Ron sat before his enormous mahogany desk. The lawyer penned indecipherable notes on a yellow legal pad as Ron finished his story. "Normally, I wouldn't touch a case like this," Redwald said flatly. "Most men who claim to be COs would kill their own mamas for milk money."

The attorney eyed Ron critically, then cocked his head toward Harold.

"But your father's a veteran of two wars. I deeply respect that. And I've known Reverend Fletcher since before he went off to seminary. He vouched for you. So if these two men believe you're the genuine article, that's good enough for me."

"I'm not a rich man, but I own a small business," Harold said evenly. "I'm willing to mortgage it and my house to help pay you."

"That's not necessary, Mr. Simpson. We'll work something out. This case interests me because I believe there's an important constitutional question here."

He turned to Ron and began to speak rapidly.

"I figure this case'll be hotter than pan-fried grits. Because of the Calley case and the mood of the country, the military will play hardball. They'll want to make an example of you. We got ourselves one chance to keep you out of Leavenworth. It's a legal Hail Mary pass."

"What do you have in mind?" Ron asked.

"Simply put, to set up the play, first I need to bring the military into civilian court."

Ron looked stunned. "On what grounds?"

"For illegally detaining you."

Ron and Harold looked at each other.

"I'm afraid you've lost me," Harold spoke up. "Doesn't the military have the right to try him for desertion?"

"Not necessarily." Redwald sketched an invisible diagram of their legal strategy on the desk with a finger. "It plays like this: Rather than serve in Vietnam, Ron filed for discharge as a conscientious objector. The Pentagon arbitrarily refused his lawful and correct application. Therefore, his contract with the military is null and void."

Redwald look to Ron. "Once you turn yourself in, I'll immediately petition the U.S. District Court in Atlanta for a writ of *Habeas Corpus ad subjiciendum*."

"That sounds like Latin," Harold said.

"You familiar with the dead language, Mr. Simpson?"

"Just two words—*Semper Fidelis*."

"A damn fine phrase that is," Redwald smiled. "I used to have a law professor who said anything spoken in Latin sounds profound."

"What's this writ of *Habeas Corpus*?" Ron asked.

"It's an order that a prisoner be brought before the court that issues it.

The purpose is so that the court can determine whether they are being held lawfully or serving a lawful sentence."

"You really think you can make the military bring me into a civilian court?" Ron asked nervously. It did sound like a long shot.

"If we can show that there was an arbitrary application of the Army's regulations in your case, then we have a precedent for civilian courts to review." Redwald gave a hard smile. "First, we'll get a temporary restraining order to prevent the Army from transferring or deploying you before we get our day in court. That'll keep them from sending you off to Timbuktu."

"Why would they do that?" Ron asked.

"They'll want to move you far away from friends and family, to psychologically break you. Then they'll court-martial you."

"So, you bring me into a civilian court," Ron said. "Then what?"

Redwald leaned forward and held each man's eyes for a measured moment. "Then we throw our Hail Mary."

"It's your call, son," Harold said when they were again alone in the car.

"I don't know what to do," Ron confessed. "I stood against my country once by deserting. Doing it again, trying to stand up to the military like this . . . I mean, who am I? I'm nobody." Ron dropped his head despondently.

Harold felt his son's anguish. "Ron, are you up for a little drive?"

An hour later, Harold and Ron were trudging through the battlefield at Kennesaw Mountain National Park, the same ground that had drunk the blood of two great armies more than a hundred years before. A century had rolled over since the last soldier fell, yet a reverent silence still hung over the consecrated ground. In the misty twilight, a spotted brown doe and her fawn slipped across the edges of the field that pushed up to Cheatham's Hill and the Dead Angle. Harold led his son across the meadow and up the slope to its crest, now marked with an obelisk-shaped monument erected to the Federal dead.

"More than a hundred of our kin fought during the Civil War. A fair number of them struggled here at the Battle of Kennesaw Mountain." Harold looked out across the land, soaked in the moment, then turned to his son.

"You said you're nobody." Harold reached down and took a handful of red clay. "I want you to tell that to Baylis Simpson." He pressed the rich soil into Ron's hand.

"The blood that flows in you once spilled on this hallowed ground. Here your name means something. Here you are somebody. For two hundred years, the sons of your fathers have served on battlefields from Trenton, New Jersey, to the Marshall Islands in the South Pacific. Every one of us fought for your right to stand up and be heard. Draw strength from that, son. You'll find your answers."

Harold turned and started down the mountain, leaving Ron alone.

Chapter 62

July 1864

BAYLIS STEADIED HIMSELF AGAINST the wall of the unventilated freight car and struggled to breathe. Having no place to relieve themselves, the rebel prisoners packed inside were urinating and defecating in their britches where they stood. The fetid smell was so thick he could taste it. The odors of war were worse than the fear of death, he thought. After all, fear eventually surrenders to exhaustion and apathy.

The timber rails on the Western & Atlantic line were in terrible condition. As the boxcar rocked, rumbled, and jerked, the inmates knocked against each other like billiard balls. With the sun baking the inside of the wooden box like an oven, many of the captives already had swollen tongues and split lips from the heat and lack of water. Soon the sickest and frailest would begin to die.

Also with them were civilian captives, mostly younger boys and tottering elderly men. None had been allowed to write their families before being shipped out to the northern prison. Baylis knew that even if they survived the journey, many would die while incarcerated. Their loved ones would never know what had happened to them. That sad and lonely end could well be his own. There would be no way for Permelia to know his misfortune. The bleak thought crawled into Baylis's gut and stayed there.

Next to Baylis, Captain Jeffers silently stared out between the wooden planks at the passing countryside. Jeffers had spoken little since Milton's execution. Neither had Baylis.

As the wood-burning engine slowly chugged toward Chattanooga, Baylis lost himself in the rhythmic clank of the train's cast-iron wheels and tried to clear his mind. Like always, his thoughts turned to his family.

Baylis wondered if he would ever see his Irish rose again. It would be the greatest gift God could bestow on his miserable soul. It seemed like an eternity since he'd heard Permelia's soft voice and felt her alabaster skin. He needed to kill the caring, or else he would die of grief. It was his only hope. He swore that he would sand away his emotions and harden his heart.

Suddenly, the whistle bellowed. The wheels screeched in protest as they locked against the iron rails. The abrupt braking threw the men inside the car forward, squeezing them together like an accordion box and unleashing the discordant music of men screaming with pain and anger.

Baylis recovered his balance and peered outside through a slit. The train appeared to have pulled onto a spur just south of Allatoona Pass. Baylis knew the area well. As a young man, he and his brothers had often hunted in the forests and meadows just to the east. He could hear the Federal guards on the roof above him climbing down to the ground. There was shouting outside the boxcar, then the door slid open. Fresh air wafted inside.

"Everyone out," a Yankee soldier shouted, waving his rifle at the prisoners. It was an invitation that did not have to be offered twice. The men stumbled out. Baylis sat at the door and carefully pushed himself off the car, and Captain Jeffers climbed down after him. The two men turned to help the wounded disembark.

Up ahead, the commander of a company of Union cavalry was talking to Major Dilworth and the train's engineer. Baylis could see that Dilworth and the cavalry officer were having a heated exchange. They looked like a pair of prized pigs snorting at each other and flinging mud.

"I wonder what that's about?" one prisoner asked, a rebel private with a slight limp and the body odor of pork. The man had smeared his skin with bacon rinds, a common practice to stave off chiggers.

"Perhaps they felt mercy and decided to let us have some fresh air," Baylis replied, maneuvering himself upwind.

"Unlikely," Jeffers said. "The Yankees don't give a paper penny for our well-being." The one-armed captain studied the terrain around them. There was a hill just ahead and off to the right. A tree line was within fifty yards of the tracks across a meadow that ran the length of the train.

"It is the act of a fool for the Yankees to stop here," Jeffers continued. "They risk an ambush. There have been attacks by partisans all along this line in the last month."

"I'd wager there's some problem with the engine," the private offered.

Major Dilworth and a guard detail approached a cluster of prisoners that had disembarked from the boxcar behind Baylis, which was the last in the convoy. Those captives were mingling with the men from Baylis's car. Something was deeply troubling Dilworth. There was a haunted look in the major's dark eyes.

"You men, uncouple that car and push it back," a pug-faced sergeant growled, motioning toward the train's rear container.

"Let's give the boys a hand," Jeffers said.

Dilworth caught Baylis's eye. The major's gave a slight nod of his head, perhaps warning him of some danger. Baylis reached out and stopped Jeffers from moving off with the other prisoners of war.

The guards herded the rebel captives forward. Two men unclasped the link and pin coupler. Groaning from the strain, the group slowly nudged the boxcar back down the spur line and onto the main track. The work detail was then moved to the opposite end of the car. The men pushed the freight car up the rail line until it was past the cutoff for the spur.

With a blast of its whistle, the steam engine reversed itself and began pushing the remaining cars still coupled to it down the spur and onto the main rail line. What had been the last car of the train was now in front of the iron horse.

As Baylis and the remaining captives looked on, the prisoners that had pushed the car forward were forced inside it.

"Why would they put a boxcar in front of the engine and fill it with prisoners?" Baylis asked Jeffers.

"I know not. But no good will come of it, I'd wager."

Jeffers examined the ground around them. An odd look tussled across this face. He elbowed Baylis discreetly and nodded toward the uneven horseshoe marks stamped on the ground. "Yankee horses have keg shoes," he said under his breath.

Baylis, who had once worked as a blacksmith, understood: *Keg shoe prints were uniform. These tracks were irregular. Slipshod horses had made them.*

"Rebel cavalry?"

Jeffers shook his head. *No.* "The tracks are too fresh. Our boys wouldn't be operating up here now. More likely partisans."

The Federal cavalry captain watched as Union guards locked the wooden door of the boxcar in front of the engine. Then he rode his horse to where Major Dilworth and his guards were holding the other captives.

"I am Captain McCook with the provost guard of the Military District of Etowah," the Yankee cavalryman announced loudly. "A land torpedo planted by partisans has been discovered on the tracks just ahead. The planting of these explosives is a crime. By special field order of General Sherman, any torpedo found on a rail line will be tested with a car of prisoners."

Major Dilworth looked away, unable to witness what was about to happen. Captain Jeffers stepped forward. "As the ranking Confederate officer present, I protest this outrage. Some of those held captive in that boxcar are innocent civilians."

"No Confederate, civilian or soldier, is innocent," McCook responded curtly. "I have my orders."

"Even your own Yankee newspapers call Sherman a madman," Jeffers said. "If those are his orders, then Lincoln has given a lunatic control of your army."

"Would you like to join the prisoners in the front car?"

Jeffers bit his lip and stared ahead.

"I accept by your silence that you decline the invitation," McCook said. He turned and signaled the train's engineer with an abrupt wave.

As the rebel captives grimly looked on, the strap-iron cowcatcher anchored on the front of the engine pushed the freight car up the tracks.

Jeffers turned to Baylis.

"This makes no sense," Jeffers said bitterly. "Our partisans have only made attacks against the 'down' trains coming from Chattanooga carrying supplies to Sherman. Why plant a land torpedo in the path of an 'up' train and risk killing civilians and rebel prisoners?"

Reaching the mine planted on the tracks, the boxcar rolled over it with a loud clang. For a taut moment, everyone expected a hellish explosion. But nothing happened.

"It's a decoy," Jeffers realized. "They planted an unarmed torpedo to get the train to stop."

McCook rode forward to inspect the torpedo.

Baylis watched a nearby Union cavalry mount. The animal was twitching its ears skittishly.

"That horse," Baylis indicated. "I think it hears the guerillas coming."

"We must create a diversion to help their attack. Are you willing?"

"I have never ridden on a train before today. I have no wish to do so again."

"If we fail, we'll both be as dead as flies in winter. The Yankees will kill any prisoner who stands against them."

"I accept the risk if it means a chance to return home to my family."

"Then it is agreed."

"Any idea how to arm ourselves?"

Jeffers quickly glanced around.

"Distract that Yank." He indicated the mounted cavalryman closest to them.

Baylis approached the Union soldier from the rider's left side. "Would you spare a thirsty man a drink from your canteen?"

"Get back with the other prisoners," the Yankee said sternly.

While the Federal was distracted, Jeffers quietly moved toward him from the right.

"Just a sip, sir," Baylis persisted. "My throat is parched."

"If you don't move back, I will shoot you."

Too late, the soldier turned to find Jeffers drawing the Yankee's Colt pistol from its leather holster. Before he could react, Jeffers fired, scattering his brains out the other side of his head.

Jeffers spun and gunned down the two guards closest to him. At the same time, Baylis pulled the Union soldier's repeater rifle off the saddle and began firing. Some prisoners quickly grabbed weapons off the wounded and dead guards, while others attacked the blue-clad soldiers with rocks and tree limbs.

The Union force returned fire, cutting down the captives like wheat at harvest. Prisoners scattered, diving for cover behind rocks and trees and under the train.

Just then, breaking over the top of the hill, mounted Confederate partisans charged toward the train. They began strafing the Federal soldiers with fire.

Jeffers calmly stepped through the melee, shooting two guards as he walked toward McCook. The captain turned in the saddle just in time for Jeffers to put a bullet through his eye and out the back of his skull, killing him instantly. McCook collapsed like an empty sack and fell from the horse, his right foot tangled in the stirrup. The horse panicked and dragged him along the grass, kicking at his corpse to get free.

Jeffers dropped to the ground to grab bullets from a dead soldier's cartridge pouch. Before he could reload, a round tore through his chest.

Under withering fire, Baylis crawled to Jeffers and dragged him by his arm behind a tree. Bullets zipped through the air all around the men and thudded against the tree trunk like a message in Morse code.

"Grab a horse and go," Jeffers managed, his voice gurgling from the blood pouring out of his mouth. The captain's chest wound had dyed his shirt red.

"We'll ride together." Baylis tried to ease Jeffers up, but the man winced in agonizing pain.

"I'm done, sir. You have a chance. But you must take it, now."

Baylis knew he was right.

"Load the pistol for me, and I'll cover you," Jeffers said weakly.

Baylis quickly chambered the Colt, then ripped a piece of cloth from his shirt and wrapped it around Jeffers's hand and the pistol, tying it in place.

"Prop me up and turn me to face those Billy boys," Jeffers said. "I'll be damned if I'll die with my back to a Yankee."

Baylis eased the captain against the tree.

"We will meet again in a better world," Jeffers said. "Now go!"

Baylis gauged the distance to the Yankee horse, checked the load of his rifle, then glanced around the edge of the tree. A savage battle stormed around them. Prisoners were in fierce fights with guards, beating them with rocks and choking them with their bare hands. Foes slashed and gouged each other with swords and bayonets, firing pistols at point-blank range. Many captives raced into the nearby woods trying to escape.

Baylis dashed toward a riderless horse. As he tried to mount, the animal spooked and bolted, throwing him hard to the ground. Scrambling up, he fired his rifle until it was empty, then turned to find a cavalryman charging him with saber drawn.

As the rider bore down on Baylis, a shot ripped through the Yankee's chest, killing him instantly. It was Jeffers. Baylis owed him his life.

A Yankee guard came out of nowhere, lunging at Baylis with his bayoneted rifle. Baylis deflected his thrust, then swung his rifle like a club, bashing the soldier to the ground. Baylis grabbed the reigns of the horse and pulled himself up into the saddle. He turned the horse in time to witness two Union soldiers driving bayonets into Jeffers's heart.

Baylis boot-heeled the horse into a gallop toward the woods. Almost to the tree line, a bullet ripped through his shoulder. In the next instant, another round tore through the horse's sinews. The animal reared and collapsed on its side, pinning Baylis underneath. He tried to pull his leg out from under the animal, but it was no use. The horse was too heavy, and his injured arm was of no use. There was little he could do but wait to be killed or bleed to death.

The wild-eyed horse snorted and tried to raise its head, only to crash its weight back down on Baylis's leg, sending a sharp jolt of fire through him. The animal was in horrible misery. Baylis didn't know which of them was in worse shape. He reached up with his good arm and tried to calm it.

"Easy now," Baylis managed through his own pain. "Looks like we're both at the end of it."

Baylis heard a rustle and shifted his head to see Major Dilworth hovering above him, his revolver drawn. Baylis hoped that he would make the shot true and his death painless. Dilworth cocked the Colt with his thumb and fired. The bullet tore through the brain of the horse, killing it instantly.

"I hate to see a horse suffer." Dilworth holstered his pistol, then reached down and pulled Baylis out from under the animal. He sat down on the ground beside the old man.

"Your name is Baylis Simpson, isn't it?"

"Yes sir, it is. We spoke at Marietta."

Dilworth winced and nodded at the memory of Milton's death. "You strike me as a brave man, Private. I saw what you did to try to save your captain." The major pulled out his pocket flask, took a sip, then passed it to Baylis. The old man thanked him with a nod, drank deep, and handed the container back to him.

"You warned me not to help move the car. Why?"

"You and Captain Jeffers offered your life for the man we executed in Marietta. I repaid your valor."

Dilworth examined Baylis's wound.

"The ball missed your bone. This will sting." The major poured whiskey from his flask on the wound. "Some think that repeater rifles or cannon do the most damage, but the humble Minié ball and the simple musket do all that is needed."

The two men sat in silence and looked out across the meadow. The partisan raiders had retreated over the hill in the distance, and the last of the prisoners were putting down their arms. Guards and cavalry were rounding up the escapees. Dilworth took another swallow of whiskey, then twisted the cap back on his flask and slipped it into the breast pocket of his uniform jacket.

"Can you walk?"

"I reckon." Baylis stretched his leg slowly and moved his foot. "But if you plan to take me back to that train and have me shot, I'd just as soon as you do it here and now yourself."

"I believe you mean that." Dilworth looked at him for a moment, then stood. "Sorry I can't oblige you."

He offered Baylis a hand and pulled him up. "For three years, I've fought from Shiloh to the Shenandoah. I've killed more men than I can count. I've got enough blood on my hands."

Dilworth pulled his hat off and dusted it with the sleeve of his jacket. "This is what I will do, sir. I will stare at this pretty meadow for a few minutes, and when I turn around, I hope to discover that you gave me the slip."

Baylis studied him, unsure what to make of the offer. The major's even look told Baylis that he was telling him the truth.

"Major, I'd shake your hand. But if I did and someone saw me, we'd probably both be shot."

"The provost guards will beat around in the bushes searching for escapees for the next hour or so. Then most likely, they will give up. If you run hard, I'm pretty sure we won't catch you."

Dilworth turned his back to Baylis and stared out into the field. The old man limped into the forest.

At last, Baylis Simpson was going home.

Chapter 63

March 1971

RON WAS ON HIS knees. He wasn't sure how long he'd been there listening to the whispers of ghosts, echoing from more a hundred years before. But at that moment he realized what he needed to do. What must be done. Baylis had given him the answer: *to find your peace, sometimes you had to turn loose of the past.*

Ron began to dig in the earth with his hands. The rich soil was moist from the mulch that covered it and easy to scoop out. After several handfuls were removed, he stopped and rubbed his hands together, wiping the dirt from them. He reached into his coat pocket and carefully took out the last words Alex had written him before his death, the letter that had been his constant companion. He held the paper like a precious thing, pressed it against his lips, then placed it into the ground.

"Good-bye friend," Ron said softly. "Go in peace."

He slowly pushed the soil back into the hole, smoothing the earth gently. He stood, bowed his head in silence, then turned and started down the hill. Harold was leaning against the car when Ron approached, his son's eyes now as clear as a mountain stream.

After they had climbed into the Ford and started home, Ron said, "Turning myself in quietly after all that's happened would be like performing card tricks on the radio. It doesn't make a whole lot of sense."

"What do you want to do?"

"It's time I fought for what I believe in. The military can have a CO, or they can have a convict. But I will not go quietly."

Ron could not remember a single time in his life when he had heard his parents pray for themselves. Their prayers were always for others: a sick neighbor or a church member suffering a personal hardship, never their own needs. But that morning at the breakfast table, as he held his family's hands, he heard his mother ask, "Dear Father in Heaven, if it's Your will that my boy be taken away from us again, if he's got to spend the rest of his youth behind bars, I ask only that You grant us the strength to accept it. Amen."

After breakfast, Ron drove to Fort McPherson in the Mustang, with Harold riding shotgun and Jack Redwald fiddling with his briefcase in the backseat. The MPs let Ron shake Jack's hand and hug his father. They waited until Harold had driven the Mustang out of sight before they snapped the cuffs around Ron's wrists and the shackles onto his feet.

For better or for worse, it was done. When Ron turned to let the MPs escort him to his cell, he felt a sudden lightness in his soul.

Chapter 64

February 1971

MICHAEL HADN'T BEEN TO the Varsity in almost a year. When Ron was in Canada, it felt like a betrayal to enjoy any of their old haunts without him. It was also the first time he'd hung out with Kenny in months. The wholesome all-American kid Michael had once pitched baseball with now smoked pot and wore his hair down to his shoulders. Kenny, who had been working as a carpenter's assistant, favored provocative tee shirts. Tonight's tee had a smiley face with a joint dangling out of its lips.

Michael felt as though he were trying to squeeze into an old set of clothes that no longer fit. He wasn't the same kid as before, tagging along in Ron and Alex's shadow. He'd outgrown this place. He wondered if he hadn't also outgrown Kenny.

Michael was seriously considering cutting the evening short when two young women walked in. The first, a slender brunette Michael knew vaguely from college, kept an arm around her companion, who walked with hunched shoulders and nervous glances, and kept a scarf pulled tightly over her head.

Michael did a double take. *The girl under the scarf was Diane.*

Gone was the lilt in her step. The disarming smile that Michael loved had withered into a tight-lipped grimace. Her golden hair was chopped into a short pixie cut that curled around her ears, and she kept her heavy-rimmed sunglasses on inside the restaurant.

Kenny elbowed him out of his trance. "Are you gonna stand here staring like a dorkwad, or go over and talk to her?"

Diane's friend, whose name Michael now remembered was Judy Ann, steered her to a booth and went to order food. Diane kept her eyes lowered. Underneath the table, her foot tapped nervously.

When Diane saw Michael approaching, she looked like she wanted to shrink away and vanish inside her oversized jacket. Michael couldn't think of a graceful way to begin the conversation, so he simply stated the truth: "I just wanted to say hi."

"How are you?" Diane asked reluctantly.

Something seemed wrong with her face. Michael couldn't place it, but whatever had transformed her gorgeous Nordic features was even more disturbing than her vanished smile.

"My brother's back," Michael replied, conscious of the newfound confidence in his voice.

"I heard," Diane replied. "His story was on the local news tonight."

Under the garish fluorescent lights, Michael realized what else was different about Diane's face: *she was wearing makeup. Lots of it.*

"I can't really talk right now," Diane said. She turned to stare out the window.

As she pivoted her face, Michael caught a glimpse of a dark shadow under her makeup: a purple-brown bruise ringing the bottom of her left eye like a shadowy crescent moon. Below the black eye, the side of her face was dark and distended. Michael was horrified.

"Are you all right?" he asked stupidly and immediately regretted it.

"I need to go—" her voice cracked as she fought back tears. She rose from the booth and shoved past him.

"Wait, Diane please."

She threw herself out the Varsity's side entrance, her face contorting with emotion.

Michael waylaid Judy as she returned to the table with baskets of food. "What happened to Diane?"

Judy considered it for a moment, weighing what to say. "I don't feel comfortable talking about it, but—look, I know she really cared about you. Just please don't tell anyone I told you this." She pulled him aside and whispered, "Chuck raped her."

Chuck raped her.

The words hit Michael so hard that the air, the very life, seemed to drain out of him. He opened his mouth and tried to speak, but couldn't.

"She didn't date anyone for a long time after you two broke up. She loved you so much. She was too torn up. It's all she ever talked about. Then, after that night when we saw your band playing at the club . . ." Judy's voice sputtered. "Chuck had been asking her out all year. She was so lonely she finally said yes. As soon as he got her alone . . . When she tried to resist he beat her senseless."

As Michael stood reeling, he heard Judy say in a rush of words, "The pig got away with it. It's just horrible. She dropped out of school 'cause of what he did."

Judy excused herself and hurried outside to attend to Diane, leaving Michael clenching and unclenching his fists, paralyzed with rage.

~~~

For the next several days, Michael was a ticking time bomb. He knew he had to do something, or at least talk to somebody. If he didn't do it soon, he feared that he might explode.

In a bygone era, he would have gone straight to Ron. But his brother was now sitting in the brig at Fort McPherson, waiting to do battle with the U.S. Army in a court of law. He could *not* talk about it with his mother; just the thought of bringing the subject up with her went against the grain of his upbringing. He didn't feel that he could approach his father, either. Although it showed signs of healing, their relationship was still hot to the touch.

He couldn't imagine bringing it up with his old high school friends from Forest Park. And none of his new college friends, not even the guys in the band, were close enough to trust with such a delicate issue.

Michael decided that if he couldn't talk out his frustration, he'd *sweat* it out. He spent hours in the gym on campus, and each Friday after classes, if Ravenstone wasn't performing, he would drive back from Athens and spend the weekend working out. He moved Ron's weight bench out of the bedroom and onto the lawn, under the shade of the trees in the backyard. He pumped away at the barbell, hissing out his rage. His young body responded readily, and his wiry muscles quickly burgeoned under his tee shirt. Before long, he was even managing a few reps at Ron's training weight. Rage made a potent fuel.

Weeks into his obsession with the weights, Harold approached him. Michael had just added another ten pounds to the bar and was blowing hard under the weight, his muscles quivering.

"Son, is there something you want to talk about?"

Michael set the bar into its brackets and blinked. Normally, Carlotta was the mind reader. He mopped his face with a tee shirt.

"You ever wanted to hurt somebody? I mean *really* hurt 'em?"

Harold considered it briefly. "What's this about?"

"Chuck Leach. He did something . . ."

"To you?"

"No, sir. To someone who wasn't able to stop him. Someone who couldn't defend herself. He did something bad. *Really bad.*" Michael looked down. The word was too much for him to say out loud.

"And you want to hurt him because of what he did to this young woman?"

Michael nodded. "I would if I was strong enough."

"Son, you have to know when to fight and when to walk away."

"It doesn't help to walk away from Chuck," Michael insisted. "He just shows back up. He's like a disease that you can't beat. That just keeps eating away at you."

Michael expected a lecture on handling his aggression. Instead, his father said matter-of-factly, "If you feel like you have to stand up to him, you need to use your speed and smaller size to your advantage."

"How?"

"I've watched Chuck play enough ball to know that he may be a mountain, but he's slow. He's great at smashing into lineman, but he's got no agility. He's not light on his feet. So you need to stay away from his fists, let him wear himself down." Harold motioned his son off the bench. "Put your hands up like you're fighting."

Michael was surprised that his father had accepted his decision to fight. Michael himself hadn't yet come to the conclusion that a showdown with Chuck was inevitable. But as he put his fists up and prepared to spar with his father, he realized that the decision was already behind him. All that remained was to prepare for the confrontation as well as he could.

"Never fight a man on his own terms. You make him fight on yours. Closer together," Harold coached, dancing lightly on the balls of his feet. "Now deflect the blows, push them away, you've got it. Now come in close. Let the blows hit on your back, that's it. Now back up. Make him extend his arm fully, and when he does . . ." Instead of deflecting the blow, Harold grabbed Michael's hand and pulled him forward, off-balance. Michael went sprawling across his father's outstretched leg. From there, Harold deftly flipped him onto the ground.

"If you use that, a large man has less advantage," Harold explained, extending an arm to help his son up.

"Dad, I didn't know you could do that!"

"I did some boxing in the corps." Harold clapped his son on the shoulder. "I guess old Marines are good for something other than war stories." He turned and strode toward the house.

Michael marveled at the way the last several months had transformed his father. But it wasn't really Harold that had changed, only his perception of him.

Michael was seeing his father for the first time through the eyes of a man.

Chapter 65

July 1864

BAYLIS HAD NO IDEA how long he had been stumbling through the darkness. The past few hours had been a blur. He had started out in a faltering run through the woods, making the best of it for as long as he could. Then his mind began to spin. He wretched until it felt like his belly button touched his backbone, and then collapsed on the moldy forest floor. He remembered the stream, the feel of the water on his parched lips and the liquid washing over his swollen tongue and down his throat, cooling his feverish face and his chest.

He was long past running now and hardly able to walk. His legs felt like iron shackles were weighing them down. His wound and the blood loss had given him a fever that dulled his senses. His shirt was drenching wet, and sweat ran down from his scalp to burn and cloud his eyes.

There was nothing much left in him except for one thought. *Home.* He would find his way back to his family, or he would die midstride. As long as he could, he would keep walking, one step at a time. And then he would crawl.

He had found a blackberry bush earlier, but the fruit gave only scant relief, and the pangs of hunger made him light-headed. In the gathering twilight, he looked at his fingers, stained from the fruit. The color reminded him of Melissa's tongue. He could almost hear her giggle.

A sudden noise.

Something was up ahead in the shadows. He thought he saw a child running through the woods in front of him. He could hear the sound of a young girl laughing. *Was it Melissa?* It would be nice to see his granddaughter again. He sorely missed the twinkling light in her eyes. He lost sight of the child in the tangle of darkness and foliage.

Maybe it was all in his mind. He knew a man's wits could turn on him, making him for a fool. No, it couldn't be Melissa. She wouldn't skip away. She would be running to her grandpa. She would have a warm hug for him.

He fell, and the earth slapped him hard. Dazed, he tried to push himself forward with his legs, but they were having none of it. He dug his hand into the earth and clawed forward with his good arm. A foot maybe. And then again. Another six inches. It was no use. His old body had given him all it could. There was nothing left in him.

He rolled over and looked at the sky filled with stars and a gorgeous moon. Is this all that was left in his life, the earth under him and the heavens above? Maybe that was enough, more than any man needed really, just somewhere to lay your head and something beautiful to look at.

This was as far as he was going. Perhaps he should close his eyes. Maybe it was time. If he closed his eyes, it would all be over soon.

Forgive me, Father, for I have sinned. Forgive me Permelia. I wanted to come home. I really did.

He was going to a better place. He would see Melissa again.

He could already hear her laughter.

Chapter 66

March 1971

RON SPENT THE DAYS leading up to his court-martial confined to the brig at Fort McPherson. He knew little about what was going on in the outside world. His attorney, Jack Redwald, the only visitor the Army would allow him, had not checked in for days. Ron hoped that this was a good sign, that perhaps Redwald was busy securing his hearing in federal court. But as the date of his court-martial loomed larger, Ron began to lose hope. Just as Redwald had predicted, the Army ordered him shipped out of state.

When it was time to make the trip, Ron obediently held out his wrists for the handcuffs, and stood patiently while the MPs shackled his ankles and passed the chains around his waist.

Do they really think I turned myself in just so I could try to run off again? Ron thought, but said nothing.

The MPs led him to a military transport waiting out on the tarmac. Ron was boarding the plane when he saw Redwald pop out of a military sedan with a young lieutenant, an attorney from the Judge Advocate General's Corps. The JAG officer spoke briefly to the officer in charge of the guard detail, who then called off the flight with a sweeping gesture.

The JAG officer folded a document into Ron's cuffed hands. Phrases popped off the page: *"We command you that the body of Ronald H. Simpson, in your custody detained, you safely have before Honorable . . . U.S. District Court for the Northern District of Georgia . . . and have you then and there this writ . . . pending final disposition of this petition, the respondent is hereby enjoined from removing the petitioner from the Northern District of Georgia."*

The U.S. Army had been ordered to bring him into a federal court in Atlanta. Redwald caught Ron's eye. He pretended to throw him a football, then crossed himself and gave a thumbs-up. Ron understood: *Redwald was throwing the Hail Mary Pass.*

Ron was delivered to the U.S. District Court in Atlanta in shackles and chains, but it didn't matter. He knew that when he entered the arena, he'd have loved ones in his corner. However the trial turned out, their support would make it bearable.

As Ron stepped into the courtroom, he was overtaken with a wave of stage fright. The court was packed; all eyes lingered on him. On the Army's side of the room stood a small platoon of JAG lawyers, starched and battle-ready. Redwald had told Ron that the man who headed the team was Captain James Seldon. Ron guessed that the fierce-looking man with the merciless eyes, standing nearest to the judge, must be him.

Ron scanned the crowd for friendly faces. Jack Redwald sat alone at the defense's table, and the Simpsons were seated behind him. Harold met his son's eyes with a solemn nod. His mother managed a faint smile. Michael strained to keep his eyes off Ron's chains.

Judge Dyer, a broad, muscular man with silver temples and a tendency to squint, addressed the court. "The matter before this court is the petition for a writ of *habeas corpus* brought by Warrant Officer Ronald H. Simpson of the United States Army, naming his commanding officer, the U.S. Secretary of the Army, and the U.S. Secretary of Defense as respondents. If Warrant Officer Simpson is present, please identify yourself to the court."

Ron rose slowly and lifted his shackled hands. "Your honor, I am Warrant Officer Ronald Harold Simpson."

Redwald jumped to his feet. "Your honor, I object!"

Judge Dyer turned his gaze to the solitary lawyer. "Object to what, sir? This gentleman being Ronald Simpson?"

Seldon and the other military lawyers snickered.

"You're out of order," the judge said impatiently. "The court has not recognized counsel."

"Your honor, I apologize," Redwald said quickly. "I'm Jack Redwald. I represent Warrant Officer Ronald Simpson. There's an immediate prejudicial bias against my client when the Army parades him into court in chains."

"Plaintiff's arguments will come in due course, Mr. Redwald. For now your objection is noted. Mr. Redwald and Mr. Simpson, please be seated." Judge Dyer narrowed his eyes. "Would counsel for the military identify itself to the court?"

The man with the unforgiving eyes stood. "I'm Colonel John Seldon with the Judge Advocate General's Corps. I represent the U.S. Army in these proceedings."

"And what are the military's charges against Warrant Officer Simpson?"

"Warrant Officer Simpson has been charged with desertion with the intent to avoid hazardous duty under Article 85 of the Uniformed Code of Military Justice."

"Mr. Redwald?" the judge said. "You filed this petition for a writ of *habeas corpus* for Warrant Officer Simpson?"

"Yes, your honor."

"Why do you believe that this matter is under the purview of this federal court?"

"Courts have held that members of the military may bring *habeas* petitions when they are being held in the military in violation of law."

"Did Warrant Officer Simpson exhaust administrative remedies afforded by the military before seeking *habeas* relief, counsel?"

"Yes, your honor, he did."

The judge scratched his jaw, then looked to Colonel Sheldon. "Once the petitioner demonstrates a *prima facie* claim, the burden shifts to the respondent to demonstrate basis in fact in the record to support the military's reason for denial."

Judge Dyer examined the documents in front of him. "Regarding the plaintiff's temporary restraining order. It will remain in place pending the outcome of these proceedings. We'll reconvene Monday morning at nine a.m. to hear oral arguments." He then raised an eyebrow at Seldon, "Warrant Officer Simpson will be unshackled when he's in my court. Adjourned."

Outside, a small crowd of media had gathered. From behind him, Ron heard Redwald mutter, "Damn. The last thing we need is press. This is going to only make things worse."

Chapter 67

March 1971

LIKE A DOG GNAWING on a hard bone, Michael had chewed over what to do about Chuck Leach. No matter how hard he worked out, no matter how much he ducked, sidestepped, and rolled with the punches, there was little chance he would ever be able to physically punish Chuck for what he'd done. During his freshman season at the University of Georgia, sportswriters had nicknamed Chuck "The Locomotive" for the way he terrorized opposing teams. He was a brute without mercy on the football field, and a sadist without conscience off of it.

And there seemed to be no legal recourse. Michael had heard that Chuck's father, a powerful attorney, threatened to financially destroy Diane's family if they pressed charges. To add insult to injury, he had sent Diane's family three tickets for the Bulldogs season opener, as though an afternoon of football would expunge the horror of what his son had done. Enraged, Diane's stepfather had torn them up and mailed them back to him.

As the weeks passed, the question kept eating at Michael—*where was the justice?*

He knew what Baylis Simpson would have done: his wrath would have been Biblical. The ancient Simpson Bible was marked at

Deuteronomy Chapter 22, 25–28. Family folklore was that Elon Simpson had given Baylis the verses to read for consolation after avenging the rape of his daughter Terissa:

"*But if in the field the man finds the girl . . . and the man forces her and lies with her, then only the man who lies with her shall die. But you shall do nothing to the girl; there is no sin in the girl . . .*"

And Michael was certain that Alex would have taken a Louisville slugger and made sure Chuck never raped another woman—or played football—ever again.

But neither answer felt right. Even if Michael somehow managed to injure him, he would pay for the crime. There had to be another answer.

What would Ron do?

Michael remembered his brother's words the night of his last race to Blue Lights. *"It's the smartest,"* not the fastest or strongest, *who wins. Why resort to flying fists if he could figure out a way to get the bully to make an ass of himself?*

Back in Forest Park from the university for the weekend, Michael lay on his bed staring at the ceiling, trying to come up with a plan. Nothing made sense until his eyes flicked over to his patron saint, Steve McQueen, saddled on his customized Triumph motorcycle. Michael thought about taking his *Great Escape* poster down. It had been on his wall for years now.

Then Steve spoke to him like an avenging angel. Or at least McQueen's character Virgil Hilts did, forever frozen in the photograph as he was making his immortal motorcycle jump over the concertina wire fence.

The idea McQueen inspired was brilliant in its simplicity, and the punishment would suit the crime. The trigger would be Chuck's unfailing ego. But exacting the revenge would mean that Michael would have to risk everything—even his life.

~

Michael waited until the time was right. Chuck was home Sunday afternoon doing what he did best: drinking beer with his buddy Ira in the Leach family's front yard. Toward sunset Michael knew the two jocks would be plowed and as easy to stir up as a hornet's nest.

Michael drove up to the Leaches's in Ron's Mustang and rolled down the window. "Chuck, we've got unfinished business. How about we settle it with a race to Blue Lights?"

Chuck laughed drunkenly. "Get lost," he said.

"What's the matter? Chickenshit?" Michael asked. It was all the taunting Chuck needed.

"I'm gonna smash in your fuckin' pie hole face," Chuck growled like a junkyard dog, "just like I did to that sissy boy brother of yours."

"So smash in my face," Michael replied with all the calmness he would muster. "You'd still be a chickenshit who's afraid to race me to Blue Lights."

Michael knew that he was risking the worst ass whipping of his life, but Chuck had to get mad for the plan to work.

Chuck and Ira exchanged looks that said: *What the fuck, it's been a boring afternoon anyway.*

"Meet me at the lights at dark thirty." Chuck leaned into the window of the Mustang with eyes full of venom. "I'm gonna beat your ass racing, then I'm gonna fuck you up real bad. I want you to think about that while you're waiting for me to show up."

An hour later, just after the sun had set, Michael pulled into Blue Lights on his Triumph 650 motorcycle after stopping at home to drop off Ron's Mustang. He glanced around him. He was in luck. The entire stretch was deserted.

Except for Kenny.

His friend ambled out of the woods and into the beam of Michael's headlight, breathing hard, saw and hammer in hand.

"All set," Kenny called, a marijuana joint dangling out of his mouth. He hid the tools behind a bush at the side of the road. "Look for the small white stripe I painted in the road. Align your bike to it. You'll have just a few seconds."

"I sure hope you know what you're doing," Michael said.

"Bubba, I've been driving nails for my ol' man's construction company for months." Kenny's eyes glistened under their heavy lids. "I can do this sorta shit in my sleep."

"I just wanna make sure you can do it stoned," Michael said with a nervous smile.

"You think Chucky Poo will show?"

"I called him a chickenshit. What do you think?"

Kenny sucked on the herb and choked out a laugh. "I think you better pray this works. Otherwise you're a dead man."

The growl of a massive engine split the night. A shiny black 1970 Chevelle SS454 crested the hill. Chuck had *another* new car.

Michael knew what a car like that was capable of: it would rocket through a quarter mile in under thirteen seconds. But he knew that from a standing start his bike could easily beat Chuck to the turn. The trick would be to keep the race interesting and the brute mad.

"Where does that monkey get the skin for all these new cars?" Kenny's eyes were full of wonder.

"Daddy Warbucks. Where else?"

Chuck gunned the Chevelle toward him, swerving to a halt at the last moment. Michael stood his ground as Chuck and Ira spilled out of the car, laughing like jackasses.

"I figured you'd be in the 'stang," Chuck sneered. "You expect me to race you on your little tricycle?"

Michael mounted the Triumph and revved its engine. "I expect you to eat my dust, Chuckles," he said.

"By the way, I learned your brother's little e-brake trick. So guess what, tonight I'm gonna use it."

That was bad news that Michael didn't need. He tried to not let it shake his fragile façade of confidence.

Michael looked at Ira. "You sure you wanna ride with dick-for-brains?"

"Worry 'bout yourself, asshole," Ira smirked. "You really are begging for a beatdown."

"Your funeral." Michael edged a look over to Chuck. "Are we doing this, or what?"

Michael tightened his helmet, zipped up his leather jacket and swung his motorcycle around to line up at the starting point. Chuck and Ira piled into their car and followed. Kenny took up his position as flagman between them, arms raised.

Chuck hammered the accelerator in staccato bursts, the engine rumbling hard. Michael responded in turn, building up the RPMs.

Kenny bellowed over the roar of horsepower, "Three, two, one . . ."

A half-second before Kenny gave the signal Chuck peeled away. But Michael was expecting this: he popped his clutch and catapulted off the line *ahead* of him. The motorcycle ate up the asphalt as Michael leaned over the handlebars and opened the throttle. The motorcycle raged forward.

They both gunned down the asphalt, Michael careful to make sure that he was pacing Chuck and not pulling too far ahead. The dogleg curve and the dark tangle of woods beyond it loomed up fast.

The wind stung Michael's face. Out of the corner of one eye, Michael could see Chuck watching him, waiting for Michael to brake and downshift. That would give the brute his opening to beat him.

The pavement was already starting to arc to the left when Michael spotted the white strip. He centered his bike and held his course, straight ahead. So did Chuck, still waiting for Michael to ease back. The brute's eyes widened as he realized too late: *Michael wasn't going to slow down. And he wasn't going to turn.*

In an instant, Michael shot off the pavement, riding an inconspicuous, narrow ramp Kenny had built over the elevated cement curb to sail into the warm night air. He landed hard, careened down the bank along the tight path Kenny had cleared. The motorcycle skittered out from under him. Michael pitched headlong off the bike and somersaulted through the darkness into the bushes.

The Triumph's engine died just in time for Michael to hear a thundering crash as Chuck's car collided with the trees that braided the slope beside the road. Then silence.

Kenny was beside Michael in a flash, easing his helmet off. "You were Steve McQueen, man!"

Michael, still dazed, took a moment to wiggle his fingers and toes. Then he slowly moved his arms and legs. Cuts and bruises, but nothing seemed broken. His left ankle was throbbing though, probably sprained. He cocked an ear toward the wreck of Chuck's car. The only sound coming from it now was the hiss of a cracked radiator, and the erratic ticking of a mortally wounded engine. Chuck and Ira were silent.

"Fuck, maybe they're dead!" Kenny breathed.

Kenny eased Michael up. They crept toward the Chevelle. The rich-boy car had been impaled in several places by oak saplings. A head-on impact with a large hickory trunk had caved in the front fender. The rear axle hung askew at a crazed angle.

A faint whimper sputtered from inside.

Kenny whipped out a pocket flashlight and slowly passed its beam over the interior of the car. Chuck and Ira were slumped together in the front seat like spent lovers, dazed and moaning. Gigantic purple goose eggs were swelling rapidly on their foreheads where they'd smacked them against the windshield.

Chuck stirred and grimaced sharply. "My legs. I can't move my fuckin' legs!"

Kenny took his flashlight and tapped at them through the door window. "Tell me, which one hurts the worst?"

Chuck screamed in pain. He glowered at Michael.

"You cheated," was all Chuck could manage. "You didn't turn."

"And you're a rapist with busted knees," Michael spit back. "Good luck with football."

Ira stirred beside Chuck, nursing his arm. From the way it was hanging, it appeared broken.

Kenny helped Michael right the motorcycle. Kenny started to push it back toward the pavement.

"You did this to me," Chuck screamed.

"You did it to yourself. For once in your life, take some damn responsibility." Michael turned away.

"You can't just leave me here," Chuck was almost crying now.

"I'll call an ambulance when I get to a phone." Michael slowly limped up the bank toward the pavement. He was certainly in no hurry.

Chapter 68

March 1971

WHEN RON ARRIVED, UNSHACKLED, at the courthouse Monday morning, the crowd of unruly media waiting on the granite steps had swelled. Redwald had to push them away as they made their way inside, a pissed-off, jowly Moses parting a nattering sea of arms, legs, flashbulbs, and microphones.

The courtroom was even more tightly packed than before, the spectators already growing sticky and aromatic in the overstuffed benches. Anticipation hung in the room, like the scent of magnolia blossoms on a hot summer afternoon.

As Colonel Seldon and his legion of Army lawyers strolled in and took their seats, Redwald murmured to Ron, "I tried to negotiate you out with a dishonorable discharge. The military wouldn't buy it." He slipped a folded newspaper from his briefcase, snapped it open, and slapped it down on the table. Ron's own face stared back at him the front page, alongside a prominent article with the headline: *Soldier Of Conscience Takes On U.S. Army*

"Once they saw this, they went ballistic."

Colonel Seldon offered a stack of legal papers to the bailiff and motioned for him to take them to the judge.

"Your Honor, here is a copy of the original contract between Mr. Simpson and the United States Army. There's also a copy of Warrant Officer Simpson's military record, demonstrating that his request for dismissal from the U.S. Army on grounds of conscientious objection was given sufficient administration review within chain of command."

"Mr. Redwald?"

"I would like to call Mr. Simpson."

Ron moved to the witness stand in front of the courtroom and was sworn in.

"Mr. Simpson, while serving in the U.S. Army as a warrant officer, did you volunteer to fly medevac helicopters, to transport wounded soldiers out of fire zones?"

"Yes sir, I did. I volunteered twice."

"Medevac helicopters are unarmed. Is that correct?

"Yes sir."

"When you volunteered to fly medevac helicopters, were you aware that medevac pilots had the highest mortality rate of any U.S. military pilots in Vietnam?"

"Yes sir, I did. Dustoff pilots have three times the fatality rate of other chopper jocks."

"Are you aware of the term '*the walking dead*'?"

"Yes sir. That's what our flight school instructors called medevac pilots."

"Knowing the increased risk, why did you volunteer to pilot medevac?"

"I believed it would allow me to serve my country without killing."

"Were you a conscientious objector when you joined the Army?"

"No sir. I didn't consider myself one."

"When did you become a conscientious objector?"

"My religious feelings matured while I was in the military. The turning point was the My Lai massacre."

"Is that when you requested to be discharged as a conscientious objector?"

"Yes sir. After my request for transfer to fly medevac was denied."

"And your conscientious objector request was denied?"

"Yes sir."

"No further questions, your honor."

Colonel Seldon paced up to Ron and eyed him contemptuously. "Were you aware when you deserted that you could face military prison for your act of cowardice?"

"Your honor! I object to counsel's prejudicial name-calling."

"An apple, your honor, is an apple."

"Let's pull the reins back to a gallop, Colonel. Answer the question, Mr. Simpson."

"I was told that I'd face five years in Leavenworth if I refused the order to be shipped to Vietnam as a gunship pilot."

"You say you're a conscientious objector. Are you a conscientious objector to all war, or just Vietnam?"

"Vietnam is all war for me. It's the only war I've ever known."

"Unresponsive, your honor," Seldon snapped.

"Answer the question, Mr. Simpson." Judge Dyer sighed.

Ron gathered his thoughts and charged ahead. "I can't say that there'd never be a war I could support."

Redwald was on his feet again. "Objection, your honor. The court held in *Gillette v. United States* that an applicant's unwillingness to state that he would not change his mind about some hypothetical future war is not a reason to deny his request to be discharged as a conscientious objector."

"I withdraw the question," Colonel Seldon said curtly.

Harold, seated in the front row, leaned across to Redwald. "I don't understand. Why's that important?"

"The military doesn't recognize selective conscientious objection," Redwald replied in a whisper. Beads of sweat popped from the attorney's upper lip. "If they convince the judge that Ron is selective in his beliefs, it blows us out of the water."

Seldon looked out across the courtroom. His eyes settled on Carlotta. "Warrant Officer, your mother is in the courtroom this morning, is she not?"

"Yes sir."

"Would you please point her out to the court?"

Redwald rocketed up. "Relevance, your honor."

"It goes to the question of conscientious objection, your honor."

"I'll allow. Warrant Officer, please point out your mother to the court."

Ron glanced out across the courtroom to his mother, who met his eyes evenly. He raised his hand and pointed.

"Warrant Officer, if you were home alone with your mother and someone broke in the house intent on killing her, would you defend her?"

"Yes, sir."

"Would you defend her if it meant killing the intruder?"

"I object!" Redwald interjected, dueling again with Sheldon. "Willingness to use force outside of war is not grounds to deny conscientious objector status. In *United States v. Purvis*, the court held that willingness to use force to restrain wrongdoing as a last resort is not a selective objection to war."

"Objection noted. I'll allow the question," Dyer replied.

"Warrant Officer Simpson, answer the question," Sheldon's voice rose for emphasis, "would you be willing to kill if your mother's life was threatened?"

Had he somehow backed himself into a corner? Ron knew that there was only one honest answer: "Yes sir. I would."

"So you're not against killing when it suits you?" Seldon shot back. "According to your military record, you told your commanding officer that you held CO-qualifying beliefs before entering the Army. Is that correct?"

Ron took a long moment to consider his answer. "No sir, that is not correct. I said that I had been morally opposed to killing when I entered the military. My commanding officer described that as a CO-qualifying belief."

"Did your commanding officer say that if you held conscientious objector beliefs before you joined the military that you were not qualified to be dismissed as a CO while in service?"

"Yes sir, he did."

Seldon beamed a reptilian smile. "No further questions."

It was Redwald's turn to redirect. He took a sip of water from a glass on the table and bought himself a moment of time by shuffling a stack of papers.

As Redwald rose and made his approach, Ron read something he didn't like at all in his lawyer's eyes: *anxiety.*

"Warrant Officer, when you submitted your request for discharge as a conscientious objector you were ordered to submit to a mental hygiene consultation by an Army psychiatrist."

"Yes sir. I was."

"What were his findings?"

"He found no contradictions to my claims to be a conscientious objector."

"And you were also ordered to be interviewed by an Army Chaplin who stated you were sincere in your conscientious objector beliefs. Is that correct?"

"Yes sir."

"Would you tell the court why you voluntarily came back to the United States from Canada?"

"My mother was very ill. She was in intensive care in the hospital. My brother was afraid she might die."

"You came back to the U.S., knowing you faced imprisonment in a maximum-security military prison, because of your concern for your mother?"

"Yes, sir."

"Doesn't sound like the act of a coward."

Redwald went back to the defense table, checked his notes. "Warrant Officer, you told the court that, for you, Vietnam was all war."

"Yes sir."

"In your own words," Redwald said, "Can you tell the court how you feel about the Vietnam War?"

Ron closed his eyes, focused inward. Then he opened them and spoke simply, from the heart.

"The Vietnamese are in a civil war, and we're in the middle of it. That's a horrible mistake. We're destroying thousands of lives. For what? Victor Charley can't hurt our country. They can't bomb us. They can't invade us. I'm certainly not worried about them breaking into my home and attacking my family." He paused, letting the thought ripen. "So why are we there?"

Ron surveyed the room, gathering strength from the many supportive gazes he found, before continuing. "It's funny, but when you ask that question, some people want to talk about dominos, like it's a game or something. The Vietnamese aren't our enemy. We're the ones bombing and invading somebody else's land. *We're* the enemy. Near as I can tell, most Vietnamese just want us to get out of their country and go home."

Ron felt a sure, quiet power surge through him. He addressed the people on the benches. "You can justify this war anyway you like. You can call it duty or honor. But what it comes down to is murder. Senseless murder. The only way to stop this insanity is for people of conscience to stand up and say 'no more,' regardless of what the personal consequences may be." Then he turned, looked directly at Seldon and his acolytes, and said, "If you want to put me in prison for doing that . . . then do it."

Ron kept his eyes on Seldon, who abruptly looked away. The assembled spectators sat in silence.

Redwald said softly, "No further questions."

Ron returned to his seat.

"Colonel Seldon, your summation," Judge Dyer said.

Seldon rose and addressed the room. "War's not pretty. It's not meant to be. If we let soldiers decide when and how they want to fight, it will undermine our ability to protect our nation. Conscientious objectors in the military have no constitutional right to be discharged on that basis. And volunteers who hold such beliefs prior to entering the service cannot later be dismissed from service on the basis of those beliefs. Military regulations were consistently and fairly applied in Warrant Officer Simpson's case." He narrowed his eyes at Ron. "What we have here is a deserter and a coward. Nothing more. The military should be allowed to deal with him that way."

Seldon sat down.

Redwald rose, his eyes lingering on Ron. "When I look at Ron Simpson, I don't see a coward. I see a young man who loved his country and volunteered to serve it. A man who asked only that he be allowed to save other young Americans by flying unarmed into harm's way. How many of us would be willing to do that?"

Redwald looked at the audience, then back to Ron. "And when I look at Ron Simpson, I see a young man whose maturing religious beliefs wouldn't allow him to kill."

Redwald glanced to Colonel Seldon and shook his head. "The military seems to want it both ways. First, they attempt to discredit Ronald Simpson's conscientious objections. They do this even though an

Army chaplain found his beliefs to be sincere and recommended that he be given a discharge. And then the military argues that because the plaintiff held those beliefs before he volunteered, he should be prohibited from being discharged as a conscientious objector."

Redwald paused to let his words linger. "The question the military has failed to answer is this: if Ronald Simpson was a conscientious objector before he joined the military, why would he volunteer to serve his country? There is no basis in fact to rebut Ronald Simpson's *prima facia* claim that his professed religious views developed and matured after his entry into military service."

Redwald looked at Judge Dryer.

"Your honor, the facts in this case come down to a simple fact: Ron Simpson is a conscientious objector. He asked for discharge as a conscientious objector. He should've been granted one. He wasn't. That's wrong."

Redwald turned to the spectators. "Our country rightly places great emphasis on warriors. They are our heroes. We build statues to them. We even elect them President. We are proud of, and humbled by, their brave and noble sacrifices."

Redwald opened his palms to his audience. "But what about those warriors for peace, those who serve what President Lincoln called the 'better angels of our nature'? President Kennedy, a decorated veteran of World War Two, believed that 'war will exist until that distant day when conscientious objectors enjoy the same reputation and prestige that the warrior does today.' I pray for the time when we hold these gentle heroes in such high regard."

Redwald quietly returned to his seat.

"This court will reconvene at nine a.m. tomorrow morning, at which time I'll render my decision," Judge Dyer said, gaveling the proceedings to a close. "We stand adjourned."

Chapter 69

July 1864

TU-WHEET-TUDU. The sound echoed in the stillness, calling to Baylis. *Tu-wheet-tudu.*

The melodic clatter pulled the old man out of unconsciousness and toward an overwhelming radiance. He blinked and focused slowly. Where was he? He shielded the light from his eyes with his hand and tried to make sense of it.

Tu-wheet-tudu.

He was in woods on the edge of a millet field. From the angle of the sun, it appeared to be late morning. His body ached, but his fever had broken.

Tu-wheet-tudu. The rich warble cut through the woods. Baylis eased his head around and saw a bluebird on a high tree branch.

He gathered himself up and stood shakily, weak from hunger. He could hear water gurgling. A steam must be nearby. He shuffled toward the babbling sound until he came to a rivulet on the far side of the meadow. He knelt down and drank deeply, felt the cool air touch his face, then carefully washed his wound. It ached like a railroad spike had been driven in his shoulder.

Huckleberries were growing along the creek bank. He scooped up the purplish black orbs and devoured them, but he needed greater sustenance. He knew where to find it: the stream held a bountiful feast for any woodsman.

Baylis followed the wide tributary until he found a bend. A large tree lay on the bank's edge with its roots exposed in the water like large, gnarled fingers. Baylis stripped off his clothes and eased down in the creek. He cautiously felt into a dark hole between the roots. He knew he was as likely to find a water moccasin as a slow-moving fish, but fortune favored him. In a single swift motion, he cupped his hand over the gills and pectoral fins of a catfish, grappled it out of the water, and threw it high up on the bank.

After gathering dried twigs and flint rocks, he started a fire. He cleaned the fish, spiked it on a stick, then cooked it until its flesh began to flake. As he ate, he began to feel almost like a whole man.

He rested after eating and watched the sun slowly parade across the sky. He could tell from the sun's direction and the landscape around him that he was at the edge of the foothills just west of his farm.

He found a walking stick and began to make his way into the hills. He was going to be home by nightfall. The thought focused his mind and gave him succor.

~

As the day spent itself into twilight, Baylis took the final steps up the steep trail toward his farm. Although it had only been days, he felt like he hadn't been there for a long time. So much had changed in him and in his life.

The first thing he saw was Permelia under a tree. Vigil was sitting on a stool in front of her with a bowl on his head. She was cutting his hair. Elon was hammering clapboards onto the frame of the house. Terissa was helping him.

Permelia was the first to spot the backlit figure trudging up the hill. She studied him for a moment, then staggered and dropped the scissors. Her mind skidded to a stop as her face went blank. She was afraid to trust her eyes. Virgil realized that his mother had stopped cutting his hair. His eyes followed hers to the path.

"Pa!" Virgil hollered.

Her son's shout kicked Permelia out of her frozen astonishment. She raced down the dirt path to Baylis. Breathless, she held his face in her quivering hands.

"Blessed Lord and savior, you're home." Tears pooled in her beautiful Irish eyes.

Baylis buried his face in her long raven hair. He wanted to spend eternity there.

He felt a tug on his arm. It was Virgil. He took his young son and scooped him close. Elon and Terissa were soon beside them.

"I feel a sermon a-coming on!" His brother shouted loud enough to put the squirrels to running. "I'll preach the resurrection."

Terissa's still-bruised face was streaked with tears. Baylis noticed her short hair and the men's garments she wore, but said nothing. He was thankful just to see her.

"You're hurt, Pa," she said. She hugged her father around his neck.

"I had a go of it," was all he could manage.

Enveloped in the warmth of his family's embrace, Baylis forgot the fear and anguish and pain. He was home.

Chapter 70

March 29, 1971

RON SPENT A LONG, restless night staring at the moon through the tiny window of his cell at Fort McPherson wondering whether this would be his only view of the night sky for the remainder of his youth. At precisely 8:30am sharp, Warrant Officer Simpson padded down the Federal building's sparkling marble floor escorted by MPs and entered the courtroom of the Eleventh U.S. Circuit Court to learn his fate.

At the defense table, someone had placed a copy of the city's morning newspaper with a bold headline reading, "Calley Convicted of Murder, Gets Life Sentence." In what was already being called "the trial of the century" military jurors had found Lt. William Calley guilty of killing at least twenty-two unarmed, docile South Vietnamese civilians—old men, women, children—under Article 118 of the Uniform Code of Military Justice. After the longest deliberation by a court-martial jury in U.S. military history, Calley was sentenced to spend the rest of his life in prison, at hard labor. The paper reported that when Calley heard the verdict, he saluted, swiveled precisely, and left the courtroom.

Ron bowed his head. Harold approached quietly and laid a hand on his son's shoulder. Ron looked up into his father's face, smiled, and stood.

"I just want to say, no matter what happens today, I'm proud of you, son." Harold hesitated awkwardly, then threw his arms around his son and embraced him.

Redwald took his seat at Ron's side, clapping him reassuringly on the back with a sweaty palm. He could not meet his client's eyes.

Everyone rose for Judge Dyer as he entered the court, then took their seats again. Ron closed his eyes and took a deep breath as Dyer addressed the court.

"As has been noted by counsel, conscientious objectors in the military have no constitutional right to be discharged on that basis."

As the words hit Ron's ears, his emotions sank. It didn't sound good. He opened his eyes and stared at the judge.

"However," Dyer continued, "moral objections to war have challenged the conscience of our nation since the founding fathers. Our country has a historic respect for valid conscientious objection to military service. As the Defense Department itself has recognized, Congress has deemed it more essential to respect a man's religious beliefs than to force him to serve in the armed forces."

The judge studied his written decision, took off his reading glasses then looked up.

"By any reasonable standard, Ronald Simpson is a conscientious objector. Therefore, I find that there was an arbitrary application of Army regulations in the plaintiff's case. It follows that the petition for a writ of *habeas corpus* must be granted. Having granted the petition, judgment is hereby entered in favor of the petitioner and against the respondents. This court hereby orders the U.S. Army to grant Ronald Simpson a honorable discharge from military service forthwith, or show cause by timely notice of appeal."

The courtroom was now abuzz. Judge Dyer had to raise his voice to be heard. "I further order that Warrant Officer Simpson be awarded a full and complete G.I. Bill of Rights and all back pay from the time he was AWOL until the date of discharge. With no further business before this court, we stand adjourned."

The courtroom erupted in cheers. It took Ron several long moments to absorb what had just happened. He was still sitting, his back to the spectators, when Carlotta, Harold, and Michael enveloped him.

Unnoticed by anyone, Redwald and Seldon were exchanging harsh words. Seldon turned away, wearing a sour look of defeat. Redwald then approached the family.

"The military won't be appealing," the attorney said. "They're taking so much heat from the Calley verdict they don't want more bad publicity."

"You mean, it's over, then?" Ron could hardly comprehend the sudden change in his fortunes.

"You'll be processed out within forty-eight hours."

"I don't know how to thank you, sir," Ron choked.

Redwald patted his shoulder. "Make us proud." Then he turned away.

∼

Stepping out of the courthouse as a free man, Ron was bombarded by reporters.

"How does it feel to be a hero in the eyes of people who oppose the war?" one journalist yelled.

"I'm not a hero," Ron replied. "If you're looking for heroes, they're the men and women who fight and die for our country."

Harold tugged his son away from the chaos and down the street. Ron breathed in the spring afternoon. He glanced self-consciously at the departing crowd. So many familiar faces.

"Hey, bro. I think I see Diane," he said.

Michael followed Ron's gaze. Diane was there on the edge of the crowd, watching them go. Michael and Diane's eyes connected and lingered, and she offered a soft smile. She mouthed the words "thank you," then vanished into the throng. At that moment, in his heart Michael knew he would never see her again.

As the Simpson family made its way to the car, an unnerving sight met Ron's eyes: a young homeless vet with a sign, panhandling for change. He wore a stained khaki windbreaker with a busted zipper, a medal earned during service pinned over his left breast. His clothes hung limply on his emaciated frame. His disheveled manner rang all too familiar to Ron, who dropped his gaze.

Harold stopped before the man with the premature gray hair and grizzled chin stubble. "You really a vet, son?"

The young man fumbled in his pockets and retrieved a tattered, out-of-date military ID. "Lance Corporal, Company B, 3rd Recon, 3rd Marine," he recited in a bullet-train mumble. "My lieutenant Pappy Schlack once said he was gonna open a saloon for the survivors of Khe Sanh, and if it ever got more than two deep at the bar, he'd know somebody was lying." A phlegmic smoker's laugh rolled out from his gap-toothed grin. He shuffled nervously, his eyes darting about, no doubt the legacy of wartime trauma.

Harold Simpson rolled up his sleeve, revealing his *Semper Fidelis* tattoo under his shirt. "Marines take care of our own," he said, offering the young man a dollar.

With wordless gratitude, the man pulled a cobweb-thin wad of Kleenex out of his pocket and accepted the money, never touching it directly.

Harold turned to Ron and put a hand on his shoulder. "Let's go home, son."

Chapter 71

August 1865

IT HAD BEEN ALMOST a year since the Battle of Kennesaw Mountain and what was now called the Dead Angle. Most of the slain had been buried, but in remote woods or among the ruins of war, you could still find forgotten corpses, reduced to bones and rotted clothing.

With the end of the war in April 1865, reconstruction had come to Georgia, but it felt more like occupation than rebuilding. Still, it was better than the hungry winter that had just passed, when a shriveled Irish tater was a feast. The countryside had been burnt and looted bare, and the whole state's larder held nothing but hungry rats. No one had ever seen so many rodents, driven out of their hidey-holes by starvation, like everybody else. They were acting crazy. People were eating them too, but to make it go down better, they called it squirrel stew.

The wagon ruts of two armies were still cut deep in the dirt roads, but the shattered landscape was softened by new spring growth. Luckily, the military government had expressed no interest in the fate of deserters and outlaws.

The war had mercifully spared all the Simpson sons. Silas Milton, Merdit, Ulysses, and Pleasant Marion returned to Cherokee County and helped Baylis rebuild the family home. Ulysses married Ann Tate the following spring. Baylis was his best man.

Baylis chiseled the headstone for his granddaughter Melissa himself and planted blueberries around her grave. Every year on her birthday, Permelia would bake a pie and place it next to her granddaughter's tombstone.

Terissa never fully recovered from her ordeal. Like many veterans, when the wind rustled the trees and brush, her eyes darted nervously, suspecting some unseen danger. She showed no interest in men and stayed close to Permelia. Baylis suspected she would never marry.

For the men who had fought in the Confederate Army, a loyalty oath administered at the county seat was the price of regaining citizenship rights. When Baylis announced at supper that he wanted his sons to walk to Canton with him to take the oath, it set off a family mutiny. The four brothers who had fought were still bitter over the loss of the war, the death of family and friends, and their own wounds.

"I don't think I can do that," Merdit said.

"I'd still be fighting if we hadn't been short of places to run and food to eat," Silas said.

"If the politicians and generals made their peace, don't you think this family can?" Baylis asked.

"From where I sit, the politicians and generals didn't get the worst of it," Pleasant Marion said. "They seem to have done a good job of landing right side up."

The temperature in the room rose with the passion. Permelia patted her forehead with her cloth napkin.

"Except the ones who are dead," Ulysses said.

"Most of them are right side up, too. They're just lying down," Merdit said.

"Hush. I won't hear talk like that at my table," Permelia said.

"Sorry, Ma." Merdit smiled. The war had given him a strange sense of humor.

"I agree with Pa," Ulysses said.

"I can't believe I'm hearing that," Merdit said.

"I got wounded, and spent time as close to hellfire as I ever want to be," Ulysses said. "But I'm married now. Me and Anne plan to start a family. I'm not going to do that with one hand tied behind my back. I got to make peace and let the past be the past."

"Even if it means signing some Yankee paper?" Merdit asked.

"Paper's only paper," Ulysses said.

"It's not just a paper. It's an oath," Baylis said.

"I'm with Merdit on this. I can't do it," Silas said.

Unnoticed, Terissa had balled her hands into tight fists. She pounded on the heavy table until the plates began to hop.

Permelia touched her shoulder, and she winced but stopped.

"What is it, darling?" Permelia asked.

Terissa spoke with a voice full of tangled emotion. "I just want it all to be over. Why do we have to go on and on about it?"

No one could find anything to say after that, or if they could, they hadn't the heart to say it. Terissa had as much reason to hate the Federals as anyone at the table, perhaps even more.

Baylis spoke calmly. "You boys listen to your sister. Ain't nothing going to heal if you keep picking at the wound. Our family lost a lot. Too much. Now, we need to stand up and move forward. I'm getting sick of starving. It don't suit me."

They continued eating in silence. When the meal was over and Baylis rose to take his leave, he said, "We're walking to Canton tomorrow morning."

Everyone kept his own council at breakfast. It was a glum assembly that began the journey to Canton. Young Virgil was desperate to find chores so he could avoid the undertaking.

It was a pleasant day. But you couldn't find one of them willing to admit it. The five men made no sound beyond the occasional scuffing of a foot until Baylis broke the silence.

"I remember when I was a child, me and my brothers found this black snake in the corn crib and killed it. Well, my papa, John, he raised Cain. He said that the black snake lived for a reason. It ate rats and kept them away from the feed. There just wasn't no point in what we had done. We all felt real bad about it."

The sons all looked at each other. *Where was Pa going with this?*

"So Elon dug this long skinny hole and buried the snake, and he gave it a funeral. It was his first one. He prayed for the snake, and he prayed we would be forgiven for killing one of God's creatures, who was only trying to do us a favor by eating rats before they got our corn."

"You figure you might follow in Elon's footsteps and start sermonizing?" Merdit asked, trying to make light of his father's story.

"I don't have the words for it," Baylis said. "But I figure if you need a lesson in pride and folly, this war was a good one."

Ulysses understood. "We got to bury the snake."

"That's right." Baylis was proud of the man Ulysses had become. "You carry a burden too long, it twists you into being disfigured. It's not a virtue any longer. You cultivate hate, that's a bitter fruit."

When they reached the outskirts of Canton, the talking stopped again. At the small wooden courthouse, Baylis and Ulysses made ready to go in while the other three held back. From the size of the crowd waiting, it appeared to Baylis that most everyone in the county had showed up.

"I just can't do it, Pa," Merdit said.

"Me neither," Silas said.

Baylis looked at his sons and spoke calmly. "We all lost more than a war or a cause. Our family lost blood. We need to respect that, and never forget it. But we must move on. To do that, you need to break loose of the past."

Merdit, Silas, and Pleasant Marion studied the ground.

"Look at me boys. All of you."

They did.

"If you can't find it in your heart to step inside and take their oath, then I want you to take one for me. Raise your hands."

This was unexpected. With some hesitation, the four brothers flipped their arms into the air.

"You will never stand against your country again. Can you promise me that?"

"I'll promise that," Ulysses said.

Merdit, Silas, and Pleasant Marion nodded in reluctant agreement. "I promise," they said as one.

"And promise me that you will remember that your country, right or wrong, is still your country. And if your country calls, you go and you serve. And I want you to teach that to your sons and tell them to teach it to theirs. What happened to our country these last sorry years can never happen again. We got to stand together always. As a family and a country."

Baylis looked each of them in his eyes. "Now, repeat after me. 'For now and forever, so help me God.'"

The sons repeated the words, but were still confused about the practical meaning of the promise they had made. Baylis and Ulysses then walked up the courthouse steps, leaving the other three unrepentant rebels behind.

"He's our pa," Merdit said after their father had disappeared inside. "We come this far; we might as well go the rest of the way for him."

Silas shook his head angrily, unable to believe what was happening. "The Yankees can go to hell," he said. "Damn 'em all." He spit on the ground.

"Merdit's right. We need to do it for Pa," Pleasant Marion said.

"If Merdit's right, it'd be the first damn time." Silas almost smiled.

"If you don't do this, then you're just letting the Yankees pull us apart," Marion said pleasantly. "Like Pa said, we got to stick together. That's what family is about."

"Can't be much worse than walking into rifle fire," Merdit cajoled his older brother. "I reckon you did that a few times."

Pleasant Marion and Merdit started up the steps, but Silas remained. Pleasant Marion walked back to Silas and spoke quietly. "What do you think Terissa would want you to do?"

The boys seldom spoke of what had happened to their sister, but they knew her grief had crushed her heart and broken her spirit.

It was a logic that Silas couldn't avoid. He kicked at the dirt. "What the tarnation. I might as well go in. Knowing you two, you boys would probably get lost in there without me."

The three made their way into the courthouse, following their father and brother. Each silently tried to make peace with their actions, just as they were about to make peace with the Federal government. Moments later, the ceremony began. Spoken by a chorus of voices, the oath spilled down the courthouse steps and overflowed into the dirt street.

"I do solemnly swear, in the presence of Almighty God, that I will henceforth and forever faithfully support, protect, and defend the Constitution of the United States, and the Union of the States thereunder..."

Once the words were said, the boys felt a weight pass. They felt the bitterness and resentment leaving their young bodies.

Walking home, the warmth of the sun lay on their shoulders like a loose garment. They thought of the beautiful women of the county who smiled at them as they passed. They had guarded against hope, but this war, this damned war that had taken so much, was finally over.

~~~

And so it came to pass that Baylis and his sons swore an oath to their country and regained their citizenship. And none of them ever forgot the personal oath they had also given their father that day.

When the time was right for the telling, each of Baylis's sons taught the oath to his own sons, who in turn passed the oath down to the next generation and the next. Over time, the when and where and why of the oath was lost, but the beliefs remained.

Never stand against your country. Your country, right or wrong, is still your country. When your country calls you serve. We stand together always, as a family and a nation.

Ulysses passed this oath on to his son Mallie, who gave it to his own son Melvin, who passed it on to Harold, who taught the beliefs to his sons Ron and Michael.

The oath lasted for five generations.

Epilogue

SEVERAL MONTHS AFTER RON'S return, Loraine called Michael and asked him to visit her. She showed him a beautiful baby boy, with dark hair and eyes like his own, and let him hold the infant for a while. The next time Michael drove past her house, Loraine had moved. Michael realized that he had no way of tracking her down—he didn't even know her last name. He never heard from her again.

Michael never saw Diane again either. He heard years later that she was married with three children. He was happy for her.

Michael performed with Ravenstone for several years. The band, with its stripped-down roots rock, rowdy stage antics, and passionate political activism, became known as one of the "Godfathers of Athens rock," the internationally renowned Athens, Georgia music scene that gave birth to the B-52s, REM, Widespread Panic and many other groups.

The Military Selective Service Act was amended in 1971 as a result of the decision in Ron's federal court case and other similar cases that produced important decisions on conscientious objection from the U.S. Supreme Court that still stand decades later.

In 1971, the Department of Defense issued a Directive that all claims made by conscientious objectors would be judged by the same standards, whether made before induction or after entering military service. A DoD Directive, published on August 20, 1971, authorized military personnel who develop conscientious objections to military service to apply for discharge or noncombatant duty. Another DoD Directive in 1971 charged each service branch with implementing regulations providing for conscientious objectors to be reassigned or discharged.

Shortly after Ron's decisive court case and honorable discharge, the 26th Amendment of the United States Constitution was ratified. Finally, if you were old enough to die for your country, you were old enough to vote. The Simpson brothers knew Alex would have toasted the occasion with a beer and a cigarette, so they did so on his behalf.

In the end, the horror that had forced Ron to examine his own convictions about the Vietnam War stirred his country's soul. Two weeks after the Calley verdict was announced, a Harris Poll reported for the first time that a majority of Americans opposed the conflict.

On April 30, 1975, Saigon fell as the North defeated the South and the conflict ended. Ironically, Harold Simpson's beloved holiday song marked the war's final moments. As the North Vietnamese choked off Saigon, the evacuation code was given: a radio DJ announced that the temperature in Saigon was "105 degrees and rising," which was followed by Bing Crosby crooning "White Christmas." His baritone warble cued a mad scramble for the U.S. Embassy, where helicopters took the remaining Americans on their flight to safety and into the mists of history.

Later that year, Lt. William Calley was paroled after serving only three and a half years of house arrest. He found work in a jewelry store outside the gates of Fort Benning and refused to speak of the Mai Lai massacre.

The Vietnam War cost 58,220 American lives and, by some estimates, more than two million Vietnamese causalities. American draftees produced 172,000 conscientious objector applications, and 17,000 of those came from active-duty soldiers.

On January 21, 1977, President Jimmy Carter granted an official pardon to all Vietnam-era draft evaders. Of the estimated 150,000 American resisters living in Canada, fewer than 10 percent chose to return. U.S. military personnel who deserted as conscientious objectors during the Vietnam conflict were never pardoned as a group.

After the war ended, most young Americans simply wanted to forget about the tragic conflict that had scarred and divided their generation. By the time John Travolta's Tony Manero strutted down the sidewalk carrying a gallon can of paint, the bouncy rhythms and driving beats of *Saturday Night Fever* had already drowned out the memories of *Good Morning, Vietnam*. The war resided quickly in the country's rearview mirror.

As a generation's music tastes migrated to FM, WQXI, the Top 40 AM radio station that Alex, Ron and Michael had grown up listening to, gradually lost market share. But the fabled Atlanta station lived on, at least in Hollywood.

When Hugh Wilson, who had worked at "Quixie in Dixie," created *WKRP in Cincinnati* in 1978, it was reported that WQXI was the inspiration for the television series. Many people believed that the show's character Johnny Thunder was based on WQXI's legendary DJ Skinny Bobby Harper.

The town of Forest Park was never the same after the war. Its close-knit sense of community had been shattered. The all-American small town that had once turned out *en masse* to cheer its Little League teams as they paraded down Main Street on Opening Day became a suburban sleeper town of distant strangers. By the late 1980s, Atlanta's Hartsfield International Airport killed much of the town north of the railroad tracks. The southern end sprouted new subdivisions, shopping malls, and freeways like so many weeds, until it bore little resemblance to the place the Simpson family remembered.

With one exception.

The Dixie Flyer, unbowed by the passage of time, continued its nocturnal journeys through the town, rousing young boys from sleep as it had Ron, Alex, and Michael a generation before.

Ron never saw Vicki again, although he spoke with her over the years. She never remarried.

Ron always held a place inside himself for his lost childhood friend. When he married, he had a son. He named him Alex.

For many years, the young boy didn't understand why his Uncle Michael insisted on calling him "Junior." Then one day, about the time that the Buggles were announcing to the MTV generation that video had killed the radio star, his dad and uncle decided to tell him. It was young Alex's tenth birthday, the same age as when Michael had his first great adventure in life.

The two brothers took the sandy-haired boy to the cemetery where generations of the family were buried. The spring day was full of sun and a soft breeze, and the trees were just beginning to bud. It was a time of renewal and promise, and it seemed a perfect moment for the Simpson brothers to bring young Alex there.

"These are the sons of your fathers," Michael explained to the child as they stepped through the rusty iron gate. "Grandpa Melvin always said we came from good stock. And he was right."

The three Simpsons strolled down the ancient tombstones, an unbroken line, father to son, through six generations.

"That's a really old grave," Alex said, pointing.

"Baylis Simpson," Ron said. "He's the patriarch of our family here in Georgia. He lived during the time of the American Civil War."

"He lived until 1901," Michael added. "Baylis saw the dawn of a new century." Michael pointed to another grave. "That's Permelia, his wife. When she died, Baylis carved her headstone himself."

"Wow." The boy's eyes filled with wonder.

"That's Ulysses, another of your fathers," Ron said. "He was Baylis's son. He married Anne Calley Tate. They had five children. Ulysses became the manager of a mill in Canton. He died of typhoid fever in 1875."

"Who's that?" The young boy stopped in front of a gravestone close to Baylis's.

"That's Terissa. She was the youngest daughter of Baylis and Permelia," Michael said. "She never married."

"Why?"

Michael and Ron exchanged a glance.

"That's a story for another day," Michael said gently. "Today, we want to introduce you to someone down here." He motioned toward the more recent graves at the far end.

"Son, I'd like you to meet Alex," Ron said simply when they reached his friend's grave. The boy looked at the tombstone.

"Alex's the reason your uncle calls you Junior," Ron said. "Of course, Alex never called Michael by his right name, either. Isn't that right, *Mikey?*"

"Hey now," Michael laughed.

"You're named after Alex Granger," Ron told his son. "He's your godfather."

"Like Uncle Mike?"

"Yes, like Uncle Mike."

The young boy studied the tombstone in silence. He ran his small fingers across the chiseled letters of the name. *His name.* Then he looked at the dates.

"He died young, Daddy," Alex said.

"Yes, he did, son. Too young."

"Why did he die?"

"That's a very good question," Michael said to his nephew.

"To understand that," Ron said, "I guess you'd have to go back to the beginning. Don't you think, bro?"

"Yes, back to the very beginning." Michael nodded toward a towering oak. "Why don't we rest under this tree while we talk? Pops planted it after Alex died." The sapling had grown large and strong over the years, providing plenty of shade.

As the Simpsons settled down onto the red clay earth, Michael thought about the story of a quiet town of hard work and modest dreams deep in Margaret Mitchell Country, of a time of hoop-skirted ladies who thought about things tomorrow and men who frankly didn't give a damn, of Sherman's neckties, Confederate ghosts, and the Dixie Flyer, of a mother's warm lullabies and a father who was forever *semper fi.*

And then, sitting in front of Alex's headstone, Michael began to scatter his childhood memories like seeds. "This story starts like all good stories do, with 'once upon a time,'" he said. "Once upon a time, there were three little boys. One of them, the youngest, was just about your age."

"Was that you, Uncle Mike?"

"Yes. And your dad was also one of the boys. And then there was Alex," Michael said with a warm smile. "Alex, well, he was cool beyond cool. And Alex knew how to talk the other two boys into doing things they'd never do otherwise. And so it happened one night . . ."

~THE END~

Cherokee co July the 21 1862

My dear and loving Husband I one time more take my pen to drop you a few lines to let you no that we are all well at this time and I hope these few lines will reach you and find you alive and well I haint much news to write you at this time Brother Milton got home last tuesday he is as well as could be expected his arm looks very bad he got a furlow for [ ] days but I dont think it will get well by then you dont no how glad I was to see him come home a brother of ours near but they aint to be compared to the love of a companion O William you dont no how lonesome I am one week seems as long as a month use to I want to see you so bad I cant sleep of a night I want you to come home if Mary is away or no if tho I reals abed one [ ] suppose captin Granthom has got has got home I wish you could all get pudin for you captins think then you would all get furlows home I do hope and pray to our heavenly father that the time is not far off that you all will have to stay thare

The report is know that France and ingland has landed at New orleans and she runch with 90 vessels and 90 fulthings and nine to guard those too places the people is beginning to fix their cotton for market I hope peace will be made shortly and I hope the Lord will spare your lives that you all may be permited to return to your dear-selves sometimes to enjoy a few more days of pease in this [ ] [ ] I wrote the [ ] to the capitol my a word I belive as concerning you they said if they would not send those home that was with out the request of their wives I wrote to him to send you home if you this to do thus it is my [ ] wish if it is yourn for you to be sent home if you this to [ ] off there I want you to remember me in your prairs and pray to our father who liveth in secret to spair our lives to see each other in this one I ware if it is not his will that its shoul meet in this low [ ] that the may meet at his rite home whare we may sing prases to him for ever so farwell for this time you loving wife [ ]

Transcript of the letter

Georgia Cherokee Co.
July 21, 1862
My dear and loving husband,

I one time more seat myself to drop you a few lines to let you know that we are all well at this time and I hope these few lines will reach you and find you alive and well. I haven't much news to write you at this time. Brother Milton got home last Tuesday. He is as well as could be expected. His arm looks very bad. He got a furlough for ____ days but I don't think it will yet heal by then. You don't know how glad I was to see him come home, a brother held dear, but that can't be compared to the love of a companion.

William, you don't know how lonesome I am. One week seems as long as one month use to. I want to see you so bad I can't sleep at night. I want you to come home if there is any chance of it, though I know it's a bad one. I suppose Captain Grantham has got home. I wish you could all get passes from your captains, think then you would get furloughs home.

I do hope and pray to Our Heavenly Father that the time is not far off that you will be here to stay. _____ the report is now that France and England have landed at New Orleans and Savannah with 30 vessels and 30 thousand men to guard those two places. People are beginning to fix their cotton for market.

I hope peace will be made shortly and I hope the Lord will spare your lives, that you all may be permitted to return to your absent families to enjoy a few more days of peace in this world.

William, I wrote a letter to the captain _____ awhile ago concerning you. They said they would not send you home without the request of their wives. I wrote him to send you home if you was to die there. It is my wish if it is yours for you to be sent home if you was to die off.

I want you to remember me in your prayers and pray to our Father who hears in secret to spare our lives to see each other in this _____, if it is not His will that we should meet in this world that we may meet at His right hand where we may sing praises to Him forever.

So farewell for this time, your loving Sarah E. Fowler

Orange County
This March 23 1862

Dear Father & Mother
I Sead my self to drop you a few lines to let you know that I am well and hope thies few lines will find you all well. I received your letter by Mr Johnson and also one from George and was glad to hear that you was all well. we have had some rite stiring times since I rote last we have left Mannassas and are some 40 or 50 mills this side we was frome the 9th until the 20th getting to this place. though we lay over on the way a few days ther was great distruction when we left mannassas for I supose that every thing was burnt that they could not get away and thir was a goodeal for there was the barrels broke open and the left such as they wanted barels of molases poured out on the ground and we had a very fategueing time while on the march for we had a very good load to tate our knapsac & Cartarag box thower and canteen and it was ver hard on us and how long we will stay hear I can not tell the wagons after ouls for I know that the old ones was burnt up

Camp Jaurico Wednesday Sept 21 1863

for we sent them to this Depot
hant last in all of our best clothes &
we sent them also & I Received they
are all distroyed.
William Johnson landed they and
we had to start the 9 Martin
Fowler & Seanes Stads it finely
though it was lite times for
the first to brake recruits
the nelves was that the yankeys
was folbing on after as all the
time and was said to be in
five miles of us one night
but they have not come yet
it is suposed that we will make
as stands at gordanville about
30 or 35 miles from this place
There is Three Brigades here and
suposed to be about 12 thousand men
I want you to tell William
that when he gets off he must
write to me and let me know
where he is tell George I will
anser his letter soon if for god
I got a letter from William
by Johnson and will anser it
too I want you to write to me
So I will close for this time
Direct your letter to Orange C H
Va in cal of Capt Garison 28 Reg Ga Vol
I will write more the nice time
So I Remain yours untill
S. M. S.
To B W Simpson.

Letter written by Sgt. Silas Milton Simpson to his parents Baylis and Permelia Simpson. It was written by Silas after spending the winter of 1861-1862 in garrison duty with the 28th Regiment, Georgia Volunteer Infantry, at Manassas Junction following the First Battle of Manassas (Bull Run). At the time of the writing, the Federals had attacked Manassas Junction. The rebel army was pulling back to Gordonsville, VA.

Transcript of the letter

Orange County, VA
This March 23, 1862

Dear Father & Mother,

 I seat my self to drop you a few lines to let you know that I am well. I hope these lines find you all well... We have had some right tiring times since I wrote last. We have left Manassas and are some 40 or 50 miles this side. We were from the 9th to the 20th getting to this place though we (had) a lay over on the way for a few days.
 There was great destruction when we left Manassas. I suppose everything was burned that could not be taken and that was a good deal for there were boxes of clothing broke open and the men took such as they wanted. Barrels of molasses (were) poured out the ground.
 We had a very fatiguing time while on the march for we had a very good load to tote, our knapsack & gun, cartridge box, haversack, canteen, and it was very hard on us. How long we will stay here I cannot tell. The wagons were sent after tents. I know that the old ones were burnt up. We sent them to the depot & packed up all our bedclothes but one and sent them also. I reckon they were all destroyed . . .
 It was a tight time to break (new) recruits. The news was the Yanks were following after us all the time and was said to be in ten miles of us one night but they have not come yet. It is supposed that we will make a stand at Gordonville about 30 or 35 miles from this place. There are three brigades here and supposed to be about 12 thousand men . . .
 I want you to write to me often. I will close for this time. Direct your letter to Orange County, Virginia in care of Captain Garrison, 28th Regular Georgia Volunteers.
 I will write more the next time. I remain yours until

S. M. Simpson
To B. W. Simpson

R. M. Simpson, Baylis Simpson's nephew, fought for the CSA. Dozens of Simpson kin served during the Civil War.

My father, Harold Simpson (second from right) with U.S. Marines attached to the Fourth Marine Air Wing in the Marshall Islands. The Marines are preparing thousand pound bombs.

Permelia Simpson's grave, who died September 15, 1886. Grave marker is made of soap stone, letters cut with a chisel and is believed to have been carved by her husband Baylis Simpson. It reads: "In memory of Permelia Simpson Age 71 11 m" (months). Located in the Simpson family cemetery in Smyrna, GA at the site of the old Bethel Baptist Church. An estimated 50-75 Simpson graves, including Baylis and his father John, are in the cemetery that dates back to the mid-1800s.

My dad, Harold Simpson, age 18, while serving as a U.S. Marine.

U.S.S. Enterprise aircraft carrier (on horizon, far left in photo) off the coast of Majuro. Dad was transported to the Pacific Theater of Operations on this carrier during WWII while serving as a "Flying Leatherneck" in the 4th Marine Air Wing. From Kwajalein and Majuro the 4th Marine Air Wing pounded the Japanese fortresses of Mille, Maloelap, Wotje, and Jaluit, making it unnecessary for ground forces to assault and occupy those heavily held atolls. The 4th Marine Division's casualties for the operation were 313 killed in action or died of wounds, and 502 wounded in action.

Harold Simpson next to a two-crew Douglas SBD Dauntless, the type of aircraft that he flew in as an aerial gunner during WWII. The legendary Dauntless, a carrier-based dive-bomber, reversed the course of World War II in the Pacific at the Battle of Midway in June 1942. In a single sortie, the SBDs sunk four aircraft carriers of the Imperial Japanese Navy in a matter of minutes, ending Japan's hopes of victory in the war.

My brother, Ron Simpson, during basic training at Fort Polk, Louisiana.

Ron Simpson, left, after graduation from Advanced Flight Training, Fort Rucker, Alabama.

Warrant Officer Ron Simpson piloting a helicopter during maneuvers.

UNITED STATES DISTRICT COURT
NORTHERN DISTRICT OF GEORGIA
ATLANTA DIVISION

RONALD H. SIMPSON)
)   CIVIL ACTION
          vs.   )
)
COMMANDING OFFICER,)   NUMBER 14749
FT. McPHERSON, ATLANTA,)
GEORGIA; THE SECRETARY)
OF THE ARMY; and THE)
SECRETARY OF DEFENSE)

        The order of April 16, 1971, is hereby amended by deletion of the last full paragraph and insertion of the following:

             It follows that the petition for a writ of habeas corpus must be granted. <u>See</u> Helwick v. Laird, _____ F.2d _____ (5th Cir., No. 30059, filed February 16, 1971). Accordingly, unless a timely notice of appeal is filed, the respondents shall grant the petitioner discharge as a conscientious objector forthwith.

        IT IS SO ORDERED.

        This the 22nd day of April, 1971.

                                        _____
                                        Sidney O. Smith, Jr.
                                        United States District Judge

---

The summary page of the decision of the U.S. District Court in Ronald H. Simpson vs Commanding Officer Ft. McPherson, Atlanta, Georgia; The Secretary of the Army; and the Secretary of Defense. The Federal Court ordered Ron's discharge as a conscientious objector.

Mom and Dad share a honeymoon kiss.

My dad with my brother Ron (right) and me.

My love affair with motorcycles began early. I'm riding one in Panama City, FL in 1967.

My parents 50th Wedding Anniversary with my wife Judy Cairo. My parents were married for more than 65 years until mother's death in 2013.

Riding up the California coast.

My dad, his grandson Alex (Ron's son) and great grandson Caden, on Caden's first day.

About the Author

Michael A. Simpson is a writer, director and producer of award-winning documentaries and feature films, including "Crazy Heart," "Hysteria," and "Kidnapping Mr. Heineken". He continues his brother Ron's tradition of questioning authority and speaking out against social and political injustice, as his friends, both real and virtual, will attest. He's a connoisseur of raisin oatmeal cookies, a walking storehouse of music knowledge and trivia, finds reasons to get his passport inked whenever possible, and remains a "rebel without a pause." This is his first book.

Author's Note

My guiding principle in writing this book can be summed up by two quotes: "Drama is life with the dull bits cut out," which is attributed to Alfred Hitchcock, and "when the legend becomes fact, print the legend," which I first heard in 1962 while watching *The Man Who Shot Liberty Valance* at Mr. Butler's cinema. Or as my brother Ron said after reading the book: "It's not all true, but it's all true enough."

Although the dramatic license first granted by Aristotle was amply taken in several instances, the essential details in this book concerning my family during the Vietnam War era are true, including my brother's experiences as a U.S. Army Warrant Officer and helicopter pilot, his time in Canada, and his decisive U.S. Federal court case—*Ronald H. Simpson vs. Commanding Officer, Ft. McPherson, The Secretary of the Army and The Secretary of Defense*. Events described concerning my two summers as a lifeguard, including the death of the young swimmer and the woman named Lorraine in the book, are also factually based.

Characters other than my immediate family, including Alex Granger, are composites of real people, or are based on individuals and altered to obscure their identity. The chapter involving my witnessing a train wreck as a young boy was significantly embellished for dramatic effect.

Though many details concerning the family of Baylis and Permelia Simpson are beyond the scope of surviving historical documents, their story is based on information provided by Nona Williams and her Simpson Clan genealogy website; Georgia court and national census records; Confederate States of America (CSA) military records; the Baylis Simpson family Bible; letters written by Baylis and Permelia's children, Sarah Elizabeth and Silas Milton; the "Simpson Letter of 1874," written by a cousin of Baylis Simpson; the written histories of North Georgia and Cherokee County during the American Civil War, including *The History of Cherokee County* by Lloyd G. Marlin; family folklore and oral history, as well as my own conjecture.

Four of Baylis' sons—Ulysses Melvin, Silas Milton, Merdit and Pleasant Marion–served the Confederacy during that great conflict, as did Baylis. His youngest son, Virgil, was too young to enlist. That his daughter Terissa never married is also historic fact.

The description of the Battle of Kennesaw Mountain and the Dead Angle contained in this book, although not intended to be historically accurate, is based on historical documents, public records and numerous books including the *Historical Sketch and Roster GA 1st Battalion Sharpshooters*, *The Battle of Kennesaw Mountain* by Daniel J. Vermilya, *Sherman's 1864 Trail of Battle to Atlanta* by Philip L. Secrist, and *Kennesaw Mountain: Sherman, Johnston and the Atlanta Campaign* by Earl J. Hess.

Members of the Simpson clan fought at the Battle of Kennesaw Mountain, including Sergeant R. M. Simpson, who engaged near the Dead Angle with the Georgia 1st Battalion Sharpshooters, Army of Tennessee, CSA; and C.V. Simpson who engaged at the Dead Angle with the 63rd Regiment Georgia Infantry, Army of Tennessee, CSA.

Dear Reader,

I'm deeply grateful for allowing me to share my family saga with you. You, the reader, complete me as a writer. As John Cheever noted: "It's precisely like a kiss—you can't do it alone." Would you please take a moment to review the book on Amazon and let me know what you think? Hearing from you would be much appreciated.

Sincerely,
Michael A. Simpson

Printed by Libri Plureos GmbH in Hamburg, Germany